Wings of the Wicked

Also by Courtney Allison Moulton

Angelfire

Courtney Allison Moulton

Wings of the Wicked

AN *Angelfire* NOVEL

KATHERINE TEGEN BOOKS
An Imprint of HarperCollins Publishers

Katherine Tegen Books is an imprint of HarperCollins Publishers.

Wings of the Wicked

Copyright © 2012 by Courtney Allison Moulton

All rights reserved. Printed in the United States of America.

No part of this book may be used or reproduced in any manner
whatsoever without written permission except in the case of brief
quotations embodied in critical articles and reviews. For information
address HarperCollins Children's Books, a division of HarperCollins
Publishers, 10 East 53rd Street, New York, NY 10022.

www.epicreads.com

Library of Congress Cataloging-in-Publication Data is available.
Moulton, Courtney Allison, date

Wings of the wicked : an Angelfire novel / Courtney Allison Moulton.
— 1st ed.

    p.   cm.

Summary: Seventeen-year-old Ellie, who has the reincarnated soul of
an ancient reaper-slayer, falls in love with her immortal guardian angel,
Will, while fighting monstrous creatures who devour humans and send
their souls to Hell.

ISBN 978-0-06-200236-5 (trade bdg.)

[1. Reincarnation—Fiction.   2. Soul—Fiction.   3. Angels—
Fiction.   4. Monsters—Fiction.   5. Horror stories]   I. Title.

PZ7.M85899Win 2012   2011009151

[Fic]—dc22   CIP

                                                          AC

Typography by Joel Tippie

11 12 13 14 15   LP/RRDH   10 9 8 7 6 5 4 3 2 1

First Edition

For Kari, who helped me survive this book

Wings of the Wicked

PART ONE

The Hammer of Gabriel

1

I HIT THE FREEZING PAVEMENT ON MY BACK, AND
the air rushed from my lungs. I lay there for only moments,
but long enough for a few snowflakes to settle on my face.
The pain in my back shot in waves down to my toes and ricocheted through my skull. That thick, musty smell of reaper
fur and brimstone smothered me as the ursid reaper's throaty
growl shook the ground and rattled my ears. I wondered why
she hadn't tried to bite my face off already—she was certainly close enough to do it. I opened one eye to see that she
had stopped to watch my Guardian, Will, who was battling
her companion a few yards down the alley.

Dragging myself to my feet, I looked up to see the
reaper turn back toward me, hate spilling over her ugly face.
I tightened my grip on both my sickle-shaped Khopesh
swords, and they burst into angelfire, the bright white flames

licking up the blades. The light danced across the reaper's features, the sharp highlights and shadows making her appear even more like the Hellspawn that she was.

"It's going to hurt so bad when I pay you back for that," I promised, my voice ragged with pain.

"I think not." Her black lips pulled back, revealing saber canines as long as my forearm. She snapped her jaws and laughed, grinding her talons into the pavement. "I'm shocked you're back on your feet after that one, Preliator," she sneered.

I didn't know how the reapers made that purring growl sound whenever they said my title aloud, but it never failed to make the hair on the back of my neck stand up. I took a deep breath, shaking off the malice in her voice. "Don't get too excited. I've been hit harder than that by things a lot worse than you."

The reaper's lips curved into a grotesque smile, baring as much of her giant teeth as possible. She rolled her shoulders like a cat, crouching on her haunches, ready to spring. I stepped back on my heel, my gaze locked on her empty black shark eyes.

She launched herself into the air, claws spread wide. I dropped to the ground, spun on the slick pavement, and swung my sickle-shaped blades with precision through the air—and through flesh. The reaper's body turned into a fireball before it hit the ground, and her burning head helicoptered through the air over me. In moments, nothing was left of her but ashes.

I took a deep breath and rose just in time to see Will plunge his sword into the side of the second reaper's chest. He pulled his blade back out and the reaper fell dead, its skin hardening to stone instead of bursting into flames, which was something only my angelfire caused.

Will came to me, trying to catch his breath, and he thumbed my cheek and lifted my chin. I'd gotten used to him inspecting me for injuries. His touch was businesslike at first, but when he was satisfied that I hadn't been hurt too badly, his hands became softer. "Are you okay?"

I nodded and let my angelfire die. "Yeah. She hit me with just about everything she had and I landed pretty hard, but nothing broke. Doesn't it seem like more and more of them are traveling in packs these days?"

His lips tightened for a moment, hardness crossing over his handsome features. "It does. You shouldn't have let her get such a good hit."

I rolled my eyes. "Yeah, sure thing there, Batman. I'll bring a bazooka next time. Screw these swords. Can we call it a night?" My entire body ached like I'd been hit by a van—a van-sized reaper, to be exact.

Before he could answer, something landed just behind him, shaking the earth beneath us. Will spun around and stood over me like a shield. A creature—a reaper even bigger than an ursid, covered in dark leathery skin—had landed in the street. The skin of its face stretched tight over jutting bone, and its long, gnarled snout was filled with jagged, yellowed teeth. Its eyes were sickly, pale, glazed-over orbs staring unfocused right through us, and wide ears topped its skull. Instead of true arms, bones were stretched into gigantic, membranous wings like a bat's, with foot-long, hooked claws that gouged the pavement for support. Its hind legs were thick with muscle, and it had a long, lizardlike spiked tail that swayed back and forth like that of a cat whose eyes had spied a bird within reach—only this reaper's eyes saw nothing.

My lips quivered and I took a frightened step back. "What the hell is that?"

"Nycterid" was all Will said as his hand tightened around his sword. "That's Orek, one of the oldest and strongest of them."

And then two more landed behind the first. My stomach leaped into my throat as I gaped in horror up at the towering monsters. There was no way we could fight all three of them at once. I wasn't even sure I could fight *one* of them.

"Step aside, Guardian," Orek rumbled in a deep voice, his long jaws snapping, forked tongue flicking as he spoke human words. His glossy pale eyes stared unseeingly and made what felt like worms crawl through my stomach.

Will straightened and said nothing.

"So be it." Orek craned his long neck toward one of his companions. "Take her, Jabur."

In a flash, Orek lurched forward and slammed a wing

into Will, sending him soaring through the air. The nycterid chugged toward Will and snapped his jaws like a crocodile. Will pounded his fists into Orek's head as the jaws crunched air, questing for soft flesh. Orek's tail swung around and smashed into Will's body, sending him flying again across the alley and into the wall of the nearest building, crushing brick. He hit the ground with a low groan, and Orek descended on him.

I bolted forward to help Will, but something massive slammed into me before I could react, knocking my swords out of my hands and to the ground. The second nycterid, Jabur, grabbed me with the talons of his hind limbs. His gigantic wings spread, and he took off with me in his clutches.

"*Will!*" I screamed, wildly reaching for him. I beat and clawed at the reaper's leathery skin, but he ignored me as we flew up and away. Panic sent shock waves through my body as I twisted and flailed, desperate to get away. The alley was disappearing far below me.

Will broke free from Orek, tearing away from claws and gnashing teeth, and he dived beneath beating wings.

"Ellie!" He ran down the street, his ivory wings spreading from his back, and he jumped into the air after me, sword in hand. He was lighter and faster than the nycterid, and when he reached us, he swung his sword, but Jabur's other foot collided with Will's chest, sending him careening downward. The wind rushed violently into my face like an arctic hurricane, and I struggled to see where Will had fallen, my heart pounding in my ears. I cried his name again, but I couldn't catch sight of him. Jabur lurched suddenly, dropping several feet in the air, and my stomach jerked into my throat before we steadied again. I twisted my head to see Will's wings stretched out above Jabur. The nycterid swung his body left and right, trying to shake Will off. Jabur's long snout crunched his crooked teeth together, and he made a dragonlike hiss.

The nycterid jerked into a barrel roll, and Will slid free. He dropped through the air until he was beneath us. His wings beat hard and he flew up ahead of Jabur. He slashed his sword down with a furious cry, slicing the blade through Jabur's neck. The reaper's head fell away and vanished. The rest of his body slowed its flight as it hardened into rock.

And then I fell, still trapped in the clutches of the stone reaper. I plummeted much faster than we'd risen, the immense weight of the giant reaper's stone body hurling us both toward the ground. I screamed until I was nearly deaf from the sound of my own voice and the wind rushing into my face. I beat at the rock leg, trying to break free, and I saw Will diving past me like a falcon. He swung his body, and then he was in front of me, his sword gone and his hands freed.

"Get me out of here!" I shrieked, tugging my trapped body uselessly.

Will pounded his fist over and over again on the stone limb. I stared past him at the rapidly approaching street below. The limb cracked at last, and Will threw it into the air and kicked the body away from me. His arms wrapped around me, but we didn't stop falling. He swore as he beat his wings, futilely trying to catch us in the air, but we were falling too fast. I held back a scream of terror as we plunged toward the earth. At the last moment, Will flipped us in mid-air so that he was below me and I stared into the blinding green blaze of his eyes.

Then we hit—Will's back cracked pavement beneath us as I buried my face in his chest. We lay frozen, clinging to each other, his arms still tight around me as if he thought I'd keep falling if he let me go. At last I lifted my head and looked into his face, my body shaking violently. His eyes were closed and he was breathing raggedly, his chest rising and falling dramatically under my body. His wings were splayed flat out on the ground, but they looked unharmed. The falling sensation still sickened my gut as I looked around in disbelief and found the smashed remains of the nycterid littering the area around us.

"Are you okay?" Will asked up at me, his warm breath on my cheek.

I nodded, taking long, slow breaths to put myself back together, my hands still clutching him. I needed my head in the game, but I didn't want to let go of Will.

I climbed off him weakly, my legs trembling on solid ground, and looked around for my fallen swords. I picked them up, and the angelfire sparked once again. The two remaining nycterids loomed over us. My body screamed at me, begging me to run, but I had to stay and fight.

Orek took a step toward me, dipping his head and curling his lips back into a freakish smile. The talons on his wings grabbed at the pavement, hooking into cracks. "We were not supposed to lose one of our own."

"Sorry, but I always leave a body count," I said, tightening my grip on my swords.

Orek laughed, sending splinters of ice through me.

A form dropped between us and I stepped back on my heel. It was one of the humanlike vir reapers, like Will. This one's back was to me, and his sparrow-brown wings folded behind him. Another reaper descended—a girl—and she landed facing me. Her wings, the feathers dark silver like pencil lead, spread wide and gave a shudder. Blue-black hair fell around her shoulders, and she stared at me with a hardened gaze. I didn't think I'd ever seen anyone so terrifyingly beautiful. She looked from Will to me and back again.

For a moment, I felt like I was still plunging through the air. *More* of them? Had half of the demonic reapers in Detroit been sent to kill me tonight?

The girl's eyes brightened to an iridescent blue-violet, and she held out her hands. I sucked in a sickened gasp as her fingernails all lengthened into horrible foot-long talons made of pale bone. If I had to fight her, I'd have to chop off her hands before things got too serious.

"What is this?" Orek hissed, backing away. "You called for reinforcements?"

Weren't the new reapers demonic? I took a step toward Will, just to feel his comforting presence.

"We didn't anticipate this," Orek's remaining companion growled in a strangely feminine voice.

Orek snarled. "Come, Eki. We'll return when we have a greater advantage."

The two nycterids spread their massive wings and took to the air like a pair of misplaced dinosaurs. But I couldn't breathe a sigh of relief that they were gone. I raised my swords to the mysterious newcomers, prepared to keep fighting.

2

THE GIRL SAID NOTHING, AND HER NAILS SLIPPED back into her skin as the boy turned to face Will and me. He had sharp, handsome, tanned features, and his dark hair was shorter than Will's. I studied his face and noticed that covering the right side of his neck and creeping up his jaw was a vicious line of tangled, marbled scars. It looked as if the scars might continue down his shoulder, but they were covered by his shirt and leather jacket. His wings folded and vanished.

"That was about to get a little too serious," he said, and a lazy smile spread on his lips. Something about his face was so uncannily familiar.

"About to?" Will's shoulders relaxed, and he let out a long breath. "It's good to see you, Marcus. Surprising, but good. I've never been happier to see you."

Marcus? Where had I heard that name before? Memories suddenly flooded back to me, memories of a smiling face, happy times, and of . . . *fire*. Why fire? I thought back to the scar on his neck.

Marcus laughed. "We were in the neighborhood."

"We have been tracking Orek for some time now," the girl said, folding her wings. She paused and smiled at Will in a knowing way that made something dark swell in my throat. "Hello, William."

"Ava." Will acknowledged her politely.

I was very sure that if she took a step toward him, I would smash her nose into her brain.

Will put a hand to the small of my back. "Ava, this is Ellie. You've never met each other before. She is the Preliator."

Marcus stepped forward and gave me a friendly smile. "I, on the contrary, know you very well. It is wonderful to see you again."

It was strange how things came back to me the way they did. Memories washed through me, warm like hot chocolate and just as sweet. Marcus was my friend. We'd fought side by side for over a century, gotten ourselves in and out of trouble, laughed at each other's jokes. . . . Looking into his face gave me a sense of familiarity like when Nathaniel smiled at me in that silly way of his. There was no threat here, and I let my swords disappear. "Hi, Marcus."

"We saw the nycterid grab the Preliator and take off with her," Ava said. Interesting that she avoided my name and referred to me by my title. "Why didn't he just kill her?"

"I wondered that myself," Will agreed.

"He probably just wanted to get me away from you," I offered. "Maybe he figured it'd be easier to fight me if you weren't around. A lot of them think that."

"Or maybe they wanted you alive."

My jaw locked. What if he was right, and why? Did the why even matter? I just had to make sure they didn't get me. Alive or dead. The uncertainty left an ill feeling spreading through me, and my weariness was suddenly overwhelming. Will seemed to sense this, as he always seemed to know when something wasn't right.

"Are you ready to go home?" he asked, his voice soft.

I nodded.

"Are you hunting tomorrow night?" Ava asked.

"Yes." Will's wings and sword disappeared, folding back into him.

"We'll join you," Ava said. "Call me."

"See you then," Marcus said with a smile.

Their wings grew again, and the two reapers leaped into the air, cloaking their presence by entering the Grim. As they flew they were hidden from human sight, except mine, since I could travel in and out of the Grim just as easily as the reapers, and that of powerful psychics. I assumed Will used the Grim when he was flying, though a part of me would have loved to see the reaction of a human who saw Will airborne with his white wings. He looked like an angel. But the ironic thing was that he wasn't really an angel, and I was. I was the archangel Gabriel, reincarnated into the body of a human girl. The idea would take some getting used to still, since I never felt anything near angelic.

"Want me to drive?" Will asked, interrupting my thoughts.

"Please." I gave him a faint, grateful smile.

We walked back to my car, which was parked a few streets down. The white Audi was dubbed Marshmallow II after the original Marshmallow was demolished by a particularly violent ursid reaper. I avenged Marshmallow in the end, though.

We left the city to return to my hometown of Bloomfield Hills, and on these drives I tend to get interesting information out of Will.

"How come I've never met Ava?" I asked.

He paused before answering. "She isn't very social. She keeps to herself for the most part, and she takes killing the demonic very seriously."

"How do you know her then? If she keeps to herself?"

"I met her on a hunt a long time ago. She's become very, very good at what she does."

"Killing?"

"Yes."

I was glad that was what she was good at—and not something else. My jealousy surprised me. I spent so much time with Will that I'd forget he was his own person and there were nearly two decades when he was by himself between my reincarnations and my awakenings. I didn't like thinking about my dying, which was probably why I forgot about Will's loneliness while I was . . . wherever I was. Heaven, or so I'm told. I was glad he had Nathaniel, and up until tonight, I hadn't met any of his other friends, at least not in *this* lifetime. I loved Will—was *in* love with him—and there was no reason for me to get jealous over his friends. It wasn't fair to him. He didn't get to spend a lot of time with anyone but me, because of his duty as my Guardian, so I was always eager about going to see Nathaniel. I wished I could have said the same thing about Ava, but I guessed it was the jealous non-girlfriend in me who wondered if Ava had ulterior motives.

"Well, she was . . . nice." I winced at that last word, trying not to sound nasty, but it was hard. I wanted to slap myself out of this funk. Maybe I was cranky because I was tired and a little hungry.

"Liar."

I blinked in surprise. Either my disdain was painfully obvious or he just knew me that well. "She didn't seem to like me."

"She's not the friendliest," he admitted. "But I think you'll at least respect her once you get to know her. I think tomorrow night will be good for you. You haven't met many angelic reapers."

"And it'll be nice to spend time with Marcus again."

He smiled. Anything that proved my amnesia was waning made him happy, and that made me try harder to remember things. "I agree," he said. "It's been a few years since I've seen him myself. We might end up needing his help. His and Ava's."

"Are they . . . together?" I asked.

"What?" He looked genuinely confused.

"I mean, are they dating?"

"What? No."

"Did you ever date her?" There. I said it. I held my breath.

"What are you talking about?"

I regretted asking, but I had to know. "It's just a question."

"Why would you ask me that?"

"Curiosity." He was six hundred years old. I shouldn't have had to spell out my concern to him. He should be able to read girls by now, especially me.

"Well, it's not what you think," he said at last, his gaze lingering on me until he had to look back to the road. "We never . . . dated."

My stomach turned over. His response was so dodgy that, no matter how desperately I wanted to believe his every word, something deep inside of me wasn't so unquestioning. It was clear he didn't want to talk about it anymore, and in truth, I didn't either. I chewed on my lip, thinking about the nyc-terid who'd tried to fly off with me. I tried *not* to think about falling a thousand feet through the air, very nearly to my death. "Do you really think the reapers wanted to take me somewhere alive?"

"It's a possibility," he said. "But we don't know enough to make serious assumptions. We'll just carry on as usual. If we see the nycterids again, we'll destroy the rest of them."

A terrible thought clawed its way to the surface of my mind, and I shivered. "Do you think it has something to do with the Enshi?"

"It's gone," Will said with a sternness that made me flinch.

"But Michael said—"

"Michael was wrong. There's no way Bastian could've dragged that sarcophagus up from the bottom of the ocean. The Enshi was destroyed."

I exhaled, doubt pulsing through me. We'd managed to drop the sarcophagus containing the creature called the Enshi off a boat only miles from the deepest part of the Atlantic Ocean, but the archangel Michael had appeared to me and warned me that Bastian would retrieve it and I was to prevent that.

Bastian was a demonic reaper of unimaginable strength, so powerful that even I couldn't get anywhere near him. His power brushed me off as if I were a fly. I wouldn't be excited to have to face him again, and I'd be even less excited if Michael ended up being right and Bastian managed to get the Enshi out of the ocean.

"Everything will be okay," Will said in that way of his

that turned my insides to jelly.

I forced a smile and paused to study his face. He was gorgeous, undoubtedly so, and as soon I acknowledged that, the memory of his lips on my skin made heat rush into my cheeks and spin through my insides. I zipped my head around to look out the passenger window because, thanks to my light complexion, my cheeks turned into tomatoes whenever I was embarrassed, and nothing was more certain to make me blush than thinking about being kissed by Will.

My heart sank as quickly as it had fluttered. It wasn't like he'd ever kiss me again. Since he'd learned that I was an angel, a divine thing, he'd been distant in every way imaginable. He was still my infallible Guardian, but he wasn't allowed to touch me *that way* because I was Gabriel, the archangel.

Centuries ago, my brother, the archangel Michael, gave Will his sword and the duty of being my Guardian. With that enormous responsibility, he was forbidden to be any more than that, and Will was not one to disobey. He could be my friend, but Michael believed it would be improper and dangerous for Will to become romantically involved with me. To angels, the reapers were nothing but instruments to be used up so Heaven's forces wouldn't have to get their wings bloody. If Michael thought Will wasn't good enough for me, then he couldn't be more wrong.

As much as I hated to admit it, it had been easier to be around him before he'd kissed me that first time. I was a seventeen-year-old girl. I wanted to be loved by a great boy, and I *was*, but I couldn't have him. And it broke my heart.

"You're very quiet." His voice startled me.

"I'm just tired." I rested my head against the cold window and closed my eyes, relaxed by the gentle hum of the moving car. I'd come so close to dying tonight, so, *so* close. More than anything, I wanted to curl into his arms and just be held. We were confronted by our mortality so often that it gave us an intimacy that few shared, even those in love. It was heart wrenching to have something so amazing just out of reach. It would be simpler if he was just there to protect me because it was his duty, and not because he was in love with me.

"How are you feeling?"

I shrugged. "Just another night on the job. I'll live."

"You had quite a fall."

"Well, you caught me, didn't you?"

He was silent after that. When he pulled into my driveway, I knew that in a moment he'd slip into the Grim and be gone. He was my secret, but he wasn't *mine*.

It was the last week of January, and I was finally off the hook after my mom had grounded me for almost two months when she'd discovered I'd lied to her. I was forced to confess to her that instead of going up north with Kate for Thanksgiving weekend, I'd been with Will the whole time, though I left out the "flying to Puerto Rico with a fake I.D." thing. As far as she knew, Will was my boyfriend, but since he'd tried to distance himself emotionally from me after our trip, she thought we were broken up. It was best to leave it at that.

"See you tomorrow?" I asked him. "We can train after my homework is done and hunt at dusk."

"Perfect. I'll meet you at Nathaniel's, then."

After I'd destroyed the old warehouse where we used to train (incidentally, in the process of avenging Marshmallow), Nathaniel had set up a full workout room in the basement of his house for us. If we wanted to spar and take it up a notch, he made us go outside. We didn't need what happened to that warehouse to be repeated in Nathaniel's house.

I sneaked into my house through the back door by traveling invisibly through the Grim. Will returned to his post on my roof, where he always stayed until dawn, keeping a lookout. Demonic reapers tended to come out only at night. They were sensitive to daylight, and while they didn't burst into flames from anything but my angelfire, they smoked like chimneys under the bright sun, and direct sunlight was extremely painful. Will spent his days hanging out at Nathaniel's so he could eat and shower and relax while I was in school. It was good for him, and school was good for me too. I needed my friends, and while school threatened to eat me alive, it helped to feel like a normal high school senior on occasion.

Except on exam days. I'd rather face Bastian than an econ test any day.

3

THE NEXT DAY, MY BODY WAS STILL SORE AND I WAS still shaken up. I never thought I'd have a fear of heights, but I guess falling a thousand feet was enough to ignite that fear. At one point after homeroom this morning, I stood up too fast and had a swirling bout of vertigo and nearly fell to my knees. My class right after lunch was psychology, and it was my favorite. There were only thirteen students in the class, including my friends Kate and Chris. Landon had tried to get into the class with us, but enrollment was closed before he signed up. Served him right for sitting on his ass about scheduling. Today we were working in groups of mostly three on a learning-and-conditioning project. Instead of focusing, I flipped through my book absently as Kate and Chris argued about what to do our project on.

"We could just stick Ellie in a Skinner box," Chris offered.

That got my attention. I glared at him from over the top of my textbook. "Or not."

"Just think, Ell," Kate chimed. "Solve a puzzle, get a cookie? Easy A for sure. Plus, you get cookies."

"Or *not*."

They laughed, but I knew they were serious about locking me inside a box. I'd like to see them try to overpower me, since I could throw them both through a wall with a flick of my wrist. My powers were scary, but at least I didn't have to worry about anyone hurting me—unless they were winged reapers who ate people and dragged their souls to Hell. Yeah, they were a lot scarier than any human killers I'd ever heard of. Jeffrey Dahmer was a buttercup compared to some of the things I'd faced and defeated.

I needed to use the restroom, so I stood up from our table and asked for permission from the teacher. With the hall pass in hand, I walked toward the classroom door.

"Okay, everybody who's not cool, leave the room."

I'd already walked out the door when Chris's words sank in, and I spun on my heels. Poking my head back in the door, I flipped him off, and pretty much the entire class laughed their asses off. "You are such a jerk," I growled, and continued on my way.

My friends considered teasing me an Olympic sport, but

when it really came down to it, I knew they had my back. Especially Kate. She was my best friend and had defended me on countless occasions.

The hallways were empty. As I passed by the windows on my way to the restroom, a figure standing out in the courtyard made my heart stop dead.

A demonic reaper stood in the sunlight, steaming like dry ice in a bucket of water. I didn't stop to stare, but I registered that it was a he and a vir reaper. Gray feathered wings sprouted high from his shoulders, as if he'd landed just a moment ago. And then he was gone, disappearing into the Grim before anyone else noticed him. He wanted me to see him. Fear shuddered through me and I bolted. I wasn't ready to face a vir reaper on my own. Their human guises were clever, but I knew they were the most powerful of all reapers.

"Ellie," called a careful voice.

The reaper suddenly appeared right in front of me, wings folding and disappearing, and I couldn't help the cry that escaped my lips. Adrenaline pounded through me, and I could barely hear anything above my own wild pulse. I swung a fist without a thought, but he grabbed my wrist and held my arm tight, away from his face.

"I'm not here to fight," he said.

"Yeah, right." I yanked my arm down and shot a knee into his gut. He let out a *whoosh* of air, and I slammed a palm into his chest, shoving his back into the wall. Tiles cracked and he doubled over.

"Wait," he pleaded as I curled my hand around his throat and pressed him harder into the wall.

My eyes went wide when I recognized him. My spiked adrenaline hadn't allowed me to think straight right away, but I'd know that ethereally beautiful face and pale-gold hair anywhere. It was Cadan. He was like the real-life version of an ancient Greek statue—except not totally naked. Thank God . . . or maybe not. I grimaced and shook my head, trying to banish the thought.

"What are you doing here?" I demanded.

"Nice to see you, too," he said with a grin, as if reading my mind.

My heart slowed down, but I didn't release him. "What *are* you doing here? Isn't this a little early for you to be up, seeing as how the sun's out and all? Pretty gutsy of you, if you ask me."

"I needed to catch you without your Guardian," he said. "He'd never let me speak to you otherwise."

"Can you blame him?"

His grin widened, and something dark flickered there. "Not in the slightest."

"If you came here to speak, then speak," I said, my voice ice cold.

His smile vanished. "I've come here to warn you."

I almost laughed. "About what?"

"Bastian has the Enshi."

My blood ran cold and my lips went numb. I stared into

his opal eyes, watching the flames flicker there, searching for any sign that told me he was lying.

Footsteps echoed down the hall. I quickly released his throat in exchange for his arm and dragged him into the girls' restroom for some privacy. Humans couldn't be allowed to overhear our conversation, and while the Grim could conceal us from sight, we could still be heard.

"How?" I barked, and let go of him a little too roughly.

"I have no idea," he said, rubbing his arm. "A submarine, maybe a leviathan, who knows. But he has it. I've seen the sarcophagus with my own eyes."

I studied his face, perplexed. "Why are you telling me this?"

"I like things the way they are," he confessed. "This Enshi, whatever it is, scares me, and I'm not ashamed to admit it. It could be more dangerous than anyone ever imagined."

"That's strange for one of the demonic to say. I thought you guys loved chaos, death, and destruction."

"Chaos is a treasured pastime, but I'm not really interested in destroying the world."

"I thought Bastian just wanted to destroy my soul."

"You're only a stepping-stone, angel girl. Bastian wants a war. Like in the old days. Hell on Earth, if you catch my drift."

"The Second War," I concluded. "The Apocalypse."

Something flickered in my senses, and I shoved Cadan

into one of the stalls. The door opened suddenly. I spun around, my heart pounding, as Kate emerged.

"Dude, where have you been?" she pressed, her annoyance obvious.

"Just in here," I said with a smile. If I'd gone into the Grim and no one could find me, I would've created a lot more problems for myself.

"You're going to get into trouble if you don't come back soon."

"I'm just fixing my hair," I lied. "Another minute and I'll be back."

She narrowed her eyes, frowning. "Your hair looks fine."

"Whatever. I'll be back in a minute. I promise."

"'Kay. See you." She disappeared out of the restroom, her long blond hair swinging behind her.

I turned back and pushed open the door to the stall I'd shoved Cadan into. His grin made me want to punch him. Again.

"Imagine what would have happened if you hadn't heard her coming."

"Screw you," I growled, and grabbed his collar to drag him out of the stall.

"In a public restroom, Ellie? Really? Didn't think you were that kind of girl."

My jaw ground tight. "I don't have all day and neither do you. Finish what you came here to say and get lost."

"I'm here to warn you that you're being hunted," he

said, suddenly serious, his words edged with something frightening.

"I'm always being hunted."

"They want you alive, and Bastian's sent his nastiest to snatch you up. The nycterids are only the beginning. If they fail, Bastian has worse things lined up. Worse than me, worse than Ragnuk, worse than Ivar. Things that know what they're doing. They've lived a long time, even by my standards, and they calculate every move they make. They aren't fueled by rage or madness like those you've fought before. Killing is their occupation, and they are very likely to succeed in capturing you if Orek and his ilk don't get you first."

I leaned back against the sink and crossed my arms over my chest. Pressure built in the front of my skull as I weighed his words. This was not what I wanted to hear the day I had to start a new psych project. Why couldn't evil wait for summer, when I had nothing better to do than fight it and get a tan?

"Are they vir?" I asked.

"Yes."

Oh, great. The humanlike vir reapers were the strongest by far, and I'd only killed two before in this lifetime—and barely. If these could scare a demonic vir like Cadan, then my future was bleak. "Why doesn't Bastian come for me himself?"

"Because he's looking for a key of some kind," Cadan explained. "The Enochian prayer on the sarcophagus is actually a spell. Angelic magic has it locked up tight, but every spell can be broken. Something will unlock it, and I think it has to do with you. That's all I know. I'm no longer in Bastian's private circle, and he doesn't trust me—for good reason."

I nearly laughed. "Is this because you didn't help him stop us from throwing the sarcophagus to the bottom of the ocean?"

"Something like that."

"Will he kill you for telling me all this?"

"If he finds out, then I don't doubt it."

My gaze darkened. "If you think you've just won amnesty from me, you're wrong."

To my surprise, he glared at me in anger. It appeared I'd struck a nerve. "You have trust issues, you know."

"You're a *reaper*. Of course I don't trust you."

"I'm putting myself at risk by coming here, out in the middle of the day, no less. Who knows if your overzealous guard dog will smash my face through a wall any second, or if Bastian will be waiting for me when I get home? In any case, I've told you what I know, and I want you to make use of it before we *all* die."

"Are you finished?" I slid along the wall to the exit so that my back was never to him.

"So eager to get away from me, I see. How disappointing."

"I have to get back to class," I said. "I'm not getting detention because of you, and I don't want to get caught with a boy in here. If I get expelled, then I'll never get into college."

He laughed softly. "College? Really? If only things were still that simple for you."

"Don't talk to me like you know me, vir." I started to turn away from him.

He grabbed my hand and my throat tightened. The touch reminded me of the night of the Halloween party, when we'd first met and he'd taken my hand to dance with me. His grip was gentle in a way that frightened me. I stared at him, frozen like a deer caught in the glare of headlights, until my senses finally returned to me. I yanked free with ease. "And don't touch me, either."

"I'm sorry," Cadan said, and swallowed hard.

His apology startled me. I'd expected a wiseass remark or for him to grab me again, but he just stood there looking conflicted. My gaze wandered unbidden over his shoulder.

"Your wings," I said. "They didn't have feathers before. On the ship when we threw over the sarcophagus, your wings were leathery, like bat wings."

He looked at me inquisitively and shrugged. "Some of us can change more than others. Feathers aren't as waterproof, and flying over the sea was dangerous. I took precautions. Why? Do you like the other wings better? I can change for you." His wings burst free, the feathers replaced by a strong hide. They were so massive, it felt as if the room had closed in around us suddenly. For a moment I could only stare and keep myself from reaching out to feel them.

"You should put them away," I said shakily. "What if someone comes in?"

"Then they'll probably run screaming."

"I have to go and so do you."

"You're no fun, angel girl." His wings vanished.

I could sense the energy from his transformation. When his wings grew, the air crackled with electricity, and now that they were gone, the relief was instant. "I can't leave you here. How will I know you won't decide to snack on some of the students?"

"I have never eaten a human." He said it with such disgust that I almost believed him.

I had a brief flashback to the night on the ship: Geir clutching Jose's body in the darkness, the poor ship captain's blood dribbling past the mad demonic reaper's shark teeth and down his chin and chest. I shuddered, desperate to keep the image of Cadan doing something similar out of my mind. "Sure you haven't."

"What is your problem? I'm trying to help you."

"You're a demonic reaper," I said, almost laughing. "I have no reason to trust you."

A stab of anger darkened his brow. "And I've given you no reason to treat me like an animal. As I recall, you didn't have a problem with me until you found out what I was."

"Good-bye, Cadan," I said, backing out the door.

"If I hear anything new, I'll come to you."

"Be careful," I warned. "My guard dog bites."

He grinned, and that impish gleam returned to his eyes. "And you don't?"

"Wouldn't you like to know."

"Don't get me excited."

I couldn't tell if Cadan was just being an idiot or if he was seriously trying to flirt with me. Disgusted, I said nothing more and left the reaper in the restroom. Some part of me believed him when he said he'd never eaten a human. It was hard to imagine a boy that hot eating people, and eating people was just all kinds of wrong.

But, then again, Cadan wasn't just a boy, and he was all kinds of wrong, too.

4

AFTER SCHOOL, I DID SOME HOMEWORK AND THEN
headed over to Nathaniel's. Instead of buying a swanky mansion with the untold millions he'd earned from the sale of
rare original works of art, Nathaniel lived in a pretty normal
house. I parked in the driveway and let myself in the front
door. The house was older, but big and beautiful, and backed
right up to one of the billions of small lakes in this part of the
state, and its nearest neighbor was probably a quarter mile
down the road. The inside was full of really cool old things,
especially books. Nathaniel was a big nerd, but I loved that
about him. He told lame jokes and always wore a friendly
smile. He was also a flawless shot with large-caliber fire-
arms, but he'd had a few centuries of practice. Nathaniel and
Will both had a careful patience that astounded me.

I set my purse and backpack on the sofa in the living

room and started toward the kitchen. The boys were most often found in there, since they had monstrous appetites, amazing metabolisms, and too much free time.

"Will?" I called. "Nathaniel?"

I paused to listen, and instead of voices, I heard music coming from a guitar. I moved through the kitchen to the doors out to the deck. I had pushed the oak-trimmed glass door open when I saw Will, pick in hand, on a wooden bench. The snow-covered lawn behind him stretched out to the edge of the frozen lake. The deck was swept free of snow and my hoodie barely kept the chill at bay, but Will was sitting out there comfortably in a long-sleeved shirt. Cold and heat never seemed to bother him much, but I figured it was a reaper thing. He may have been comfortable in twenty-degree weather, but I was shaking like a Chihuahua.

One of my favorite things in the world was watching Will play the guitar. It never failed to wash away any bad feelings weighing down my heart. He looked up and smiled at me when I stepped out onto the deck.

"Hey," he said, and stopped playing. "How was your day?"

"A little too exciting." My teeth chattered.

He frowned. "What's up?"

I hugged my hoodie tighter as an icy breeze rolled down my collar and stung my bare flesh. "Can we go inside? It's freezing."

Without a word, he swept up to me and guided me indoors

in that way of his. He set his guitar onto a stand inside and shut the door to keep out the cold. He'd do anything I asked without hesitation, but that also meant I had to be careful with him.

"Better?" he asked.

I nodded. "Where is Nathaniel?"

"Out with Lauren."

I smiled secretly. Lauren was a psychic who helped Nathaniel often, and I had a suspicion that they were more than friends. Lauren and Nathaniel sometimes went on non-dates that Will described as "business." Yeah, right. They adored each other and it was obvious.

"So what happened that was exciting?" Will asked.

I realized that I'd been holding off on telling him about Cadan. I was afraid Will would kill Cadan if he found out that the demonic reaper had come to my school, my only remotely safe place. I didn't want Will to hurt Cadan for nothing, and I didn't want Will to invade my school time, the only time I had where I could forget that I was the Preliator and concentrate on being a normal girl.

"I saw Cadan today." I braced myself for whatever would come next.

"Why didn't you call me?" His jaw clenched and his hands tightened into angry fists. "I'll turn his skin inside out—"

"Okay!" I said, and threw up a hand. "Hulk smash. I get it."

"Did he hurt you?"

"No," I said quickly. *"No."* The second no was more firm, more confident. "Actually, I tossed him around a bit. He came to warn me that Bastian has the Enshi and he's looking for a key that will break the Enochian spell. That's what the Enochian on the sarcophagus is, an angelic spell keeping whatever's inside imprisoned. The nycterids from last night were sent to capture me alive, and if they fail, Bastian has more reapers to send after me. Cadan says that I have something to do with the spell, but he doesn't know what it is."

"He's one of *them*," Will snarled. "He works directly under Bastian. You can't trust anything he says."

"If we don't at least consider what he says, then we'll be making a mistake. You told me once that you didn't like to gamble when it came to my life."

His eyes met mine with a fierceness that made my heart skip a beat. The only thing that gave his emotions away was the color of his eyes. The more emotion he felt, the more beautiful and vibrant the green became, and then there was no denying he wasn't human.

"It's not like we can really do anything about it anyway," I said. "Bastian's sending his worst after me, but at least they want me alive. I think we can use that to our advantage, since they don't want to kill me. That nycterid had every opportunity to kill me, but he didn't. He could have just flown up there to drop me to my death, but he was determined not to let me go. Don't forget that."

"I haven't forgotten. But we can't trust Cadan. You don't know him like I do."

"Stop being so cryptic," I grumbled. "You keep saying how bad he is, yet you've never told me why."

"For one, he's demonic. He's manipulative, deceitful, violent, and cruel. He's just like the rest of them."

I opened my mouth to tell him how prejudiced that was, but I clamped it back shut. My amnesia hadn't totally worn off, but everything I could remember told me that the demonic reapers were evil. Will had fought them for centuries without ever forgetting anything. Demonic reapers constantly tried to kill us. That should have been reason enough to mistrust all of them.

But why did I want to find a reason to redeem them, especially Cadan? He'd never tried to hurt me, and before my current incarnation, I had never met him. In truth, we'd caused him more damage than he'd caused us. Was my humanity making me more forgiving than I should have been? Gabriel wouldn't have given Cadan a second thought before destroying him.

"If he's telling the truth, then I'm kind of scared," I confessed. "He said the things after me are really nasty."

"Then we'll fight them. I won't let them take you."

I forced a smile. I knew how strong he was—and how much stronger *I* was than him—but it was how hard he fought for me that made me feel the safest. He loved me and he did his best to protect me. If Will wouldn't tell me what had happened with Cadan, then he wasn't ready to tell me. It had taken me a while to figure that out about him.

In any case, I had a long night ahead of me. Who knew what the reapers had in store for me—and I wasn't just talking about the demonic. We were supposed to meet with Marcus and Ava.

"I have something for you," Will said suddenly, his face brightening. "Wait here."

He disappeared through the large kitchen for a moment and returned with my present: a chocolate-dipped waffle bowl with a scoop of my favorite ice cream in it. I squealed as I took the ice cream from him, dancing a little with glee. I set the bowl down and threw my arms around his neck. His scent filled my head, and it felt like home to be so close to him. He wrapped his arms around my waist, his hands touching my bare skin as my hoodie and tank top rode up, and warmth fluttered through me.

"I can't believe you went to Cold Stone for me!" One would have thought I'd get sick of their ice cream, but nope. It was impossible to get sick of Cookie Doughn't You Want Some.

"I like when you're happy," he said, smiling at me as I dug through the drawers for a spoon. "You had it kind of rough last night, so I hope this will cheer you up."

"Totally does!" I flashed him a grin and sat down on a stool at the breakfast bar.

He leaned over the counter in front of me, resting his

weight on his forearms. "Is it good?"

"Hell yes," I mumbled through a mouthful. "What a stupid question."

"Someone once told me that there was no such thing as a stupid question."

"That definitely qualifies as a stupid question."

"What if somebody doesn't like cookie dough? Then they wouldn't think that ice cream was very delicious."

"Nobody doesn't like cookie dough," I said with a soft laugh. "Especially not my angelic reaper Guardian and his sweet tooth."

His gaze fell for an instant, and the way he tried to hide his smile made it obvious that I'd embarrassed him a little. "I'm sure there's someone."

"You'll never find a human being alive who doesn't like cookie dough."

"So now you're adding restrictions to this bet?"

"Who said it was a bet?"

"I felt it was implied."

"Well, all right then."

"So it has to be a human?" he asked, visibly struggling not to smile. "And alive?"

"We could always add in that dead humans can be included. Your call. Good luck getting them to answer you, though."

"Let's stick to living humans."

"Fine," I said, staring him down. "It's a bet."

His smile grew wide and gorgeous. To say the very least, Will was beautiful. Handsome was too mortal a word. And he was completely unaware of it. And I really wanted him to kiss me right now.

But he wouldn't. I took a breath and tossed out the thought. I didn't want to be sad right now. Instead I decided to flirt with him and make his self-imposed distance from me even harder for him to stand. It didn't matter if he wasn't human. He was still a guy.

I took another bite, very careful of the way my lips moved around the spoon.

"Want a taste?" I said, arching my mouth into a suggestive smile. I tried hard not to think about how much I sucked at flirting and being sexy. He probably saw right through me.

But as he watched me with a careful gaze, I wondered if I'd succeeded. My nerves lit on fire. He studied every inch of my face, his eyes flickering all over, and my smile faded. "Yeah," he said at last. "I do."

My stomach tied in knots and did a series of backflips. My hand turned to jelly as I scooped a spoonful for him and gave him the bite.

He seemed to contemplate the taste for a moment. "Well, I like cookie dough, but it's still not as good as a melted root beer float."

I laughed a little louder than I should have. My next spoonful wasn't as smooth as I watched his eyes flash brightly, but the distraction didn't totally mess me up. That was, until he laughed and I knew the jig was up.

"What?" I asked, eyeing him suspiciously. Something was apparently hilarious.

He reached for my face and I froze solid, unsure of what he was going to do. He thumbed the tip of my nose and said, "You got ice cream on your face."

My cheeks flushed with heat, and I felt like a five-year-old who needed a sippy cup.

"You eat like a reaper," he said with a grin.

I narrowed my eyes. "Thanks, jerk."

His smile softened, and he brought his thumb to his mouth and licked up what he'd cleaned off my nose. He watched me, and my heart revved like an engine as he reached across the counter again. He tucked my hair behind my ear and drew his fingers around the edge of the ear and traced the line of my jaw.

He started to say something, but then the door to the garage opened and he jerked his hand back. Nathaniel and Lauren appeared, and she was laughing at something he'd just said. I was surprised to see that Nathaniel had attempted to tame his usually untidy, curly copper-brown hair. They looked so happy together, so obviously not just friends, and for a moment I was very jealous of them. I'd never seen them kiss, but I'd bet they did when no one was looking.

"Hey, Lauren," Will called, slipping away from the counter to stand up straight. "Do you like cookie dough?"

I laughed out loud, and both Nathaniel and Lauren

stared at me like I was the village idiot.

"Not really," Lauren said, hanging her coat and purse on the coat rack by the door. "Gives me a stomachache."

Will smirked at me with a flick of his brow and a teasing curve on his lips.

I decided right then that the next time I caught him sleeping, I'd shave his eyebrows off.

"So what?" I grumbled. "We didn't wager anything."

"The satisfaction of proving you wrong is reward enough for me."

"You cheated. You knew that she didn't like cookie dough."

"Maybe I did."

"What are you talking about?" Nathaniel asked, staring at us both.

"Nothing," Will and I said in unison, and I broke off a piece of chocolaty waffle cone and dipped it into my ice cream before I gave anything away.

5

REAPERS GAVE ME A NEW REASON TO HATE THE dead of winter. The sun had completely set by six, so the scary things had longer to play outside. Will and I suited up for the hunt, though not exactly in Matrix style, since I wore jeans, sneakers, and a tweed peacoat over my hoodie.

"There's been a change of plans," Will told me as I pulled a white wool beanie over my hair. "We're not patrolling tonight with Marcus and Ava."

"We're not?" I asked as we climbed into my car. That didn't disappoint me; in fact, I felt quite the opposite. Last night had been rough, and Will was good about letting me take nights off. "So then why are we getting ready to go?"

"We're going to train instead of hunt tonight. They want to see what you're made of before we take on the nycterids again."

My stomach turned. Sometimes facing demonic reapers was easier than sparring with Will. He didn't go much easier on me than they did. And with Marcus and Ava involved—well, I didn't know what to expect. I hated surprises, unless they involved ice cream. "But Marcus has seen me fight."

Will's mouth twitched. "It's mostly Ava. She doesn't think we need you."

My heart sank. What she meant was she thought Will was better off without me. "When did you talk to her?"

"Today. While you were at school."

Fantastic. So Ava was talking shit about me *and* talking to my non-boyfriend. "You hung out with her today?" I tried to keep my voice as even and casual as possible, but I was so transparent when it came to Will.

"I didn't hang out with her. She just stopped by."

"That's not helping."

"Nathaniel was with us. It's not what you think, Ellie. Trust me."

I took a deep breath. "What did you talk about?"

"You," he said. "Bastian and his thugs."

"Why does she think I'm useless?" My chest was tight as I struggled to stay calm.

"She doesn't think you're useless."

"Isn't that what you just said, though?"

His smile was gentle and reassuring. "She's been fighting demonic reapers for a very long time without your help. She doesn't understand how much stronger you are than any of us or what your angelfire can do."

I didn't respond, and my eyes fell as my mind wandered far away from our conversation.

"Ellie." His voice was firm but kind.

Whenever he said my name like that, I knew he was serious.

He watched me with a calm gaze. "Ava underestimates you, and I don't blame you for being defensive. But don't worry. She doesn't know you like I know you."

I smiled then. No matter what happened, Will was on my side. I was as sure of that as I was that Ava was wrong about me. A dark part of me wanted five minutes alone with her. I'd wasted way scarier reapers than Ava. What did she have that Ragnuk didn't have? Killer crazy cat-lady nails?

"Are you ready?" he asked.

"Yeah."

Will directed me to an old factory in a crumbling district of Detroit, much like our old warehouse. As I pulled Marshmallow II into a concealed spot behind the building, a flood of old memories came back to me. Memories of our old warehouse, where I realized I was in love with Will, where he had kissed me for the first time in the middle of its wreckage.

Inside, Marcus and Ava were waiting. They were certainly dressed better for training than I was. Both wore black bodysuits in a material that looked soft and supple, and combat boots that looked like they would hurt if they connected with my face. I felt like a cream puff next to them.

Marcus gave me an easy grin. "Ellie. How are you tonight?"

I pulled the collar of my coat tighter. "Less sore than earlier."

"All right, Will," Ava said, her expression stone hard. "Show me what she's got. Did you even change your clothes after you got out of . . . school?"

It took me a moment to realize she'd directed that question at me. I didn't like the way she said "school." She made it sound like a silly word, like I was a little kid. "I did change. It's cold out there."

She watched me with such disdain that I felt very self-conscious. I took off my coat and laid it by the exit, along with my purse. It was bad enough that she said rude things about me and tried to get Will to abandon me. Why did she have to go knocking my outfit? My coat was really cute.

"I didn't mean anything by it," Ava said. "I just thought that you'd prefer to wear something more durable when you fight."

"Whatever," I said, narrowing my eyes. "Let's do this." I called my swords into my hands, and the blades erupted into angelfire. The flames were bright, swallowing the silver Khopesh blades. Ava studied the swords carefully, the flames shining off her eyes. Angelfire affected only the demonic and burned nothing else. "So what do you want to see?"

She studied my face for a moment, as if I were a science experiment. She gestured to Will. "Fight him."

Before I could respond, a power surged behind me. I spun on my heel and threw my sword over my head, catching Will's blade midair. Anticipating a kick as his next move, my second blade swept through the air just as his foot rose to strike my stomach. I drew my power into my center and let it explode in his face, the force of it sending him rocketing across the factory. He righted himself and landed with one knee on the floor. I was there in an instant, slicing with both swords. His blade clinked off mine, over and over, our strikes fast as lightning, our power rushing all around, colliding with the floor and walls in waves each time his sword struck mine. I swung both swords high and cut down, forcing a blast of my power with the blades, and Will ripped his own up with both hands to meet my strike. Our blades collided and power detonated, crunching the concrete at our feet until Will sat in a crater. His expression was hardened with concentration, but when our eyes met, I caught the faintest glimmer of a smile. I bounced away, and my feet slid across the floor as I landed. Just as I was about to launch forward again, Ava's hard voice made me stop.

"Enough."

Will and I rose, sweeping our energy back into ourselves, and my angelfire died.

Marcus stepped forward, clapping. "Nice job. She was kicking your ass."

I grinned brightly as I caught my breath, happy to have impressed.

"You know each other too well," Ava said. "You're each too predictable to the other."

Will shrugged. "I've been her Guardian for five hundred years. We know each other inside and out."

"Fight me, Preliator," she said.

Nerves bit at my gut. I could beat her. No one was tougher than Will, and I got good hits in on him regularly. Angelfire burst from my blades once more.

"Relinquish the swords," she ordered.

"What?"

"You heard me. Lose them. I want to see what you can do without weapons."

I looked back at Will, who gave me a nod, and I did as she asked. Ava stepped toward me, her power pulsing around her darkly, as if it came from the deadest corner of the universe. If Will hadn't insisted that she was angelic, I would've put my money on her being demonic. She *had* asked me to put away my swords. Was it possible that—?

She shot for me, cutting off my thoughts, and my eyes widened when her talons jutted out from her fingers, outstretched and slashing. I gasped and swung my body to the side, letting her fly past me. I didn't like fighting unarmed. If I didn't have my swords, I usually got tossed around like a rag doll.

Ava came to a sliding stop and spun to slash her talons

at me again. I jerked back, but her nails snagged my sweater and slit through the fabric like butter. I swore and wheeled away as she came at me a third time.

"Ellie, *fight*!" Will's voice was in my ears, giving me strength and courage to face the reaper trying to rip my throat out.

Ava lunged for me again, and I summoned my power. Blinding white light swarmed about me, swirling like a raging blizzard, whipping my hair around, and I slammed it into Ava. She flew high through the air, smashing into the far wall and leaving an Ava-shaped dent in the concrete. Just as she began to fall, her dark silver wings sprang from her back and she landed gracefully. Her gaze snapped up to meet mine, blazing bright blue-violet with anger, and she snarled. She launched, her wings spreading wide, drowning my body in her shadow, but I shot forward to meet her midway. She swiped her talons, and I grabbed both her wrists, shoved my shoe into her chest, and kicked full force, smashing her back into the wall. She crumpled forward, dazed, and the second dent she left in the wall made me pause in awe as the debris settled. The dent was Ava shaped, but her wings had also shattered the concrete this time, and their imprint took my breath away. The impression in the wall was shaped like an angel.

Ava stood straight and shook her head dizzily. She vanished for a moment and reappeared, her hand clamping around my throat as her form materialized. She squeezed until I nearly passed out from pain and suffocation, and she lifted me off the floor.

"I shouldn't have been able to overpower you so easily," she said, her hard gaze dissecting my fear. "I didn't want to be right about you."

I didn't want her to be right about me, either. Power shivered across my skin, making my hands red-hot. I grabbed Ava's wrist and burned her skin. She hissed and swore but didn't let go. I kicked into her stomach and ran up her chest until I flipped all the way over and broke free. She staggered back, and I dropped to the ground and kicked out at her ankles, knocking her off her feet. She hit the ground on her back, and I leaped on top of her, fist raised to punch her in the nose.

She threw up her hands. "Enough! Enough. Get off me."

I hesitated, staring into her eyes as their color dulled, until I felt satisfied. I stood and met Will's gaze. He smiled at me, full of pride.

Ava climbed to her feet. "How did you burn me like that?"

The accusing tone in her voice caught me off guard. "I— it's the angelfire. I can use it to make my power burn. I've done it before on an ursid reaper. He was demonic, though." I remembered that last fight against Ragnuk. I'd used my power to burn up half of his face when he'd been about to bite my head off. It seemed I'd just done it again. Was the mysterious energy really my angelfire, or something else?

"You shouldn't be able to do that," Ava said, fear lacing her words.

I was about to open my mouth when Will spoke. "She is an archangel. Angelfire is hers to control."

Ava scowled. "But it's only in the swords. How is she able to transfer angelfire to her power and make herself stronger? Not that I'm complaining. I'm sure it's very useful against her enemies."

"This is a new ability," Will admitted. "We don't quite know what it is. Her most recent reincarnation took forty years to occur, and we have no idea what has changed in her in that time. At least you know now that you can't underestimate her." The tone in his voice and the look in his eyes made it clear that his last words were a warning to Ava.

I couldn't help wondering why it had even worked. If she was angelic, then the angelfire shouldn't have harmed her. I'd used it as a last-ditch effort. I studied Ava's dark beauty. What if she was truly demonic? A double agent of sorts? Will trusted her. Marcus trusted her. But I didn't. Not a Popsicle's chance in Hell of that ever happening.

Marcus beamed at me. "Well done, Ellie."

"You want a turn?" I teased, desperate to get my mind off Ava's possible betrayal.

"No thanks." He laughed. "You scare me plenty. No need for you to make it worse by beating me to a pulp the way you just beat Ava."

Other than the minuscule frown in one corner of her

mouth, Ava's expression remained stone cold.

"I think we're done here," Will said. "Ava, Marcus. Patrolling tomorrow night?"

"I can't," I interrupted. "Movie Night. Remember? I'm off being grounded, so I get to be social now."

He sighed. "Saturday then."

I thought a moment. "Is Sunday okay? Kate was planning a party Saturday, so we'll see if that falls through. I haven't done anything lately but go to school and kill reapers. I need a break."

Ava stared at me then Will. "Movie Night? Party? Is that wise?"

"It's important that Ellie have a somewhat normal life," Will explained. "It keeps her happy."

"And *sane*," I said with a laugh. "It's fine. Just two nights this week."

"You're being hunted," Marcus said. "Ava has a point."

I shrugged. "We don't know that for sure yet. And it's not like I'll be alone. Will is always with me when I go to these things. I'll be *fine*."

"I could join you," Marcus suggested with an edge to his voice. "Maybe you'd like backup. You know, in case the demonic drop in."

"Oh, no." I laughed. "I'm not sure how my friends will take to your . . . everything. They'd be dangerously curious about you."

"Would you kill me if I crashed?" he asked, grinning.

Something told me he wasn't kidding with that question.

"Please don't do that," I begged. "You wouldn't even enjoy yourself around all those human teenagers. Will always sulks when he goes to these things with me."

Marcus's grin widened even more. "He sulks anyway."

"You should see the way he broods, too. It's very sad," I said with a faux frown.

"I don't brood," Will cut in. "Or sulk."

"I'd love to see this," Marcus insisted. "It sounds very entertaining."

"I don't know," I confessed. "Bringing two reapers would be pushing it." But then again, my friends would love it. Marcus could have an alias similar to Will's. In truth, I didn't think I'd be able to babysit two reapers at one party, and I remembered from my past lives just how rowdy Marcus could get.

"You're certainly no fun," Marcus mused.

"You must have me and Will mixed up."

He laughed, but I wasn't kidding.

6

ON THE DRIVE HOME, WILL WAS IN A GOOD MOOD. He was proud of me. But there were things I needed to know, and I was pretty sure asking him would upset him.

I broke the silence between us with an easy question. "Marcus was born in the eighteenth century, right? I remember he was about two hundred years old when I knew him last."

"Right," Will confirmed. "He's not that old for our kind. It doesn't mean he's weak, though."

"How old is Ava?"

"A few decades older than I am."

I chewed my lip. "Is she demonic?"

"Ellie . . ." At least he didn't laugh.

"No, I'm dead serious."

He glanced at me and frowned. "I'm very sure she's not."

"How sure?"

"Positive."

"Could you be wrong?"

"No," he said firmly. "She's not demonic. Why would you ask?"

I shrugged. "Well, she's not very nice and she didn't want me to use my swords with her. And the way my power burned her? I know I've only ever tried that on Ragnuk, but it made me wonder. Angelfire only burns the demonic, right?"

"Yeah, but it's not completely the same," he said. "You're an angel, an *arch*angel. Your power is virtually limitless, and we don't completely understand it. Whatever it is about your power that is able to burn, it may not even be angelfire at all. You spent decades of mortal years in Heaven, training, before you were reincarnated this time. Maybe this is one of the results of that training. Once your memory returns fully, then perhaps more of your new powers will as well."

I let his words sink in, wanting so much—so, so much—to remember everything that I'd forgotten, and not just bits and pieces. Most of it had come back to me, my past lives and such, but the deeper, darker things still eluded me. It felt like something evil pulsed at the very root of my strength, feeding on it, even though I was supposed to be divine. Human emotion was supposed to make me stronger, but it seemed to just make me crazier. Maybe it was the humanity getting to me, the evil of humanity contaminating my power the way the frailty of humanity made my body weaker than my enemies'. My power may have been greater than theirs, but this body was mortal, and mortality was synonymous with death. Will had never died, because however much he resembled a normal guy, his body was not human. He was a reaper, and they happened to be difficult to kill, for many good reasons.

My lips grew tight as I thought hard. "But how do you know the difference between a demonic reaper and an angelic reaper? Like, *really* know without testing with angelfire. It's not like it's tattooed on their foreheads or anything. Do they feel different to you? A vir reaper is just a vir reaper until it tries to kill me, and then I know it's demonic."

"It's the darkness," he explained. "The evil that fuels them. The brutality they've known since birth and that runs through their veins. Violence is the only thing that makes sense to them. When their power and emotion grow, they begin to feel very different from my own kind. The wickedness of the demonic has a powerful effect on the angelic."

"So you can't tell just by looking at them?"

"Evil is deeper than just what's on the surface. Something can look frightening and be pure and innocent." Then he grinned. "Unlike shoes, evil doesn't have designer labels."

I scowled at the metaphor, completely aware that he was making fun of me. However, I did remember the strange things that'd happened to me since my powers were awakened. The feeling of darkness in my power, the black spidery lines that I'd seen on my own skin—a vision I still to this day didn't understand the meaning of. Was I mistaken in thinking it was evil in me that made me experience those things? How distinct was the line between good and evil, and how much of it all blended together? "I still don't get how a reaper is inherently either good or evil, depending on their genetics."

"That's just the way things are. Ava is an angelic reaper."

"So she won't turn bad?"

"Of course not. She can't become demonic. Or vice versa."

"So she isn't a demonic reaper that turned good?"

"No." The stern finality in his voice signaled to me that this was the end of the conversation.

"All right," I conceded. I needed to trust Will's judgment, no matter how confused I was over Ava . . . and Cadan. He was even more confusing. I wanted to see the best in Cadan—and perhaps the worst in Ava, for stupid reasons—but Will would know, right? He was one of them, after all. And despite who and what I was, I was still an outsider.

But at least I could kick all their asses.

There was one more day of school before the weekend, and this would be my first fun weekend in a few months. My grades were up and I was no longer grounded. Along with my friends, my parents believed Will and I had broken up from our imaginary relationship. If he was my boyfriend, they would expect me to bring him around the house and to do family things together—and by they, I meant just my mom, since my dad preferred to be MIA unless he was yelling at me for something or another.

"So, Movie Night tomorrow?" I asked as we got close to my neighborhood.

"If you wish."

I smiled slyly. "If I wanted to go shopping and asked you to hold my bags, you'd do it, huh?"

He frowned and glanced at me. "I'd dislike that."

"But you'd still do it."

"You wouldn't ask me to."

He was right. I didn't think I had it in me to abuse our relationship. "No, I wouldn't. But don't press me. You don't know what I'm capable of."

That made him laugh a little. "I know exactly what you're capable of. I've see you at your best and at your worst. Nothing you could do would shock me in the least."

"Is that so?" I gave him a challenging look. "That better not be a bet, either."

"You know, for an angel, you sure do gamble a lot."

"You're a bad influence."

"Oh, okay," he said sarcastically.

"Maybe I'm just above the rules."

"Or you're not."

"I'm the Preliator. I do what I want." I stuck my tongue out at him.

"You're exhausting, that's what you are."

"And you're obnoxious."

"And you're childish."

"You think I'm childish?" I looked at him pleadingly, feigning hurt.

He looked crushed. "I didn't mean that."

"Yeah, you did."

"Ellie, I didn't. I'm sorry."

"You're mean," I said through a small laugh disguised as a sob. I couldn't keep a straight face to save my life.

He blinked at me. His lips made a slight curve. "Faker."

"Am not. I'm really devastated. I'm shocked you would say such things."

"You know I'd never say anything to hurt your feelings on purpose."

I sat back and winked. "Of course."

We pulled into my driveway and Will shut off the car.

"Are you making me go to that party Saturday, too?" he asked.

I noticed the change in subject, and my mood took a sudden turn as well. "I want you to be there, and not just keeping a lookout. I want you *really* there. With me." We were supposed to be broken up, according to my friends and family, but we still had to pretend to be just friends, even though we weren't and would never be just friends. Even if the world ended and the reapers took every last mortal soul, I would still be madly in love with him. Nothing would change that.

He turned to look at me again, but his gaze held mine a

little longer than before, and this time with softness. Maybe a little sadness, too. "Okay. I'll go with you."

I tried to hide my frown, but I knew I had failed by the look on his face. "I miss you. I mean, I miss *you*."

His body sagged a little, and he looked away from me to the floor at his feet. His hand tightened on the console and his thumb tapped it, but I wasn't sure if that was from impatience or indecision. His eyes were dark, and his expression turned to stone. I hated when he froze up like that, impenetrable and distant. When he opened up to me, things were their best, like only a minute ago when we'd been laughing and teasing each other. Some things needed to be said, though. We couldn't keep living each day pretending everything was fine. Every day, another tiny shard of my heart broke away. If we kept going on like this, I'd never be able to piece it all together again. Will had my heart, and it would never belong to anyone else, but if he didn't take care of every little piece of it that broke away, then it might be lost to us both forever. I couldn't let him forget that. If I forgot it, if we both did, then my heart would never be whole again.

"I know," he said, and left my car without another word.

My friends noticed how quiet I was the next day. Kate especially. She'd been my best friend since elementary school, so she knew if anything was on my mind. In third-period civics, I felt the vibration of my cell and slipped it out. Kate had sent a text from her desk in the row next to mine.

Why are u moping?

Instinctively I touched the winged pendant around my neck for support. I frowned and stared at the sentence for a moment before I typed one word in response.

Will.

I watched the teacher, Mr. Johansson, until he turned his back to scrawl more definitions on the dry-erase board. The whiny squeaking of his markers was utterly maddening. In my peripheral vision, I watched Kate chew on her lip as she held her cell underneath her desk and texted back to me.

Cant be friends?

Well, that wasn't the problem, of course. What would I write back? What *should* I write? The truth? Maybe a little of it.

Still in love with him.

No chance of getting back together?

This was where I'd have to lie.

Different places in our lives. College keeps him busy and he doesnt think itll work out.

LAME.

I know. Tell u more at lu—

My phone was snatched out of my hand so fast, I bounced in my seat and my heart stopped. I jerked around and saw Mr. Johansson had come out of nowhere and now held my phone in his clammy hand. When had he started doing rounds through the aisles? I should have been paying attention. Getting detention was not going to look good to my mom when I was already on thin ice. My pulse pounded in my head, and I exchanged looks with Kate. Her face was completely calm, as if she had nothing to do with it and feared no consequences.

Mr. Johansson *tsk*ed as his watery eyes and index finger scrolled through my text conversation. He smelled like a moldy old sweater in one of those antique shops my nana dragged me to on rainy Saturdays when I stayed with her. His hands were stained from the dry-erase markers he used all day, and I could just imagine the kind of grubby fingerprints he was leaving on my phone's touch screen. "Sounds scandalous, ladies. Still in love with him, huh, Miss Monroe?"

Mortified, I turned away from him and stared at my notebook in front of me. I heard my classmates' laughter and whispers, and I felt all their eyes on me. I couldn't believe this was happening. I thought teachers only read notes to the whole class in stupid teen movies. This was not happening. *Not* happening.

"Detention, for both of you, after school today," Johansson barked, his voice lilting proudly like he thought he was awesome for catching two girls texting each other. "You'll have plenty of time then to copy down my notes from class instead of sending your own. You can have your phones back after that."

He grabbed Kate's phone from her hand and sauntered

up to the front of the room. I made a deliberate attempt not to hear another word he said for the rest of the hour.

Kate stabbed her salad with her fork like she was trying to kill the cucumbers before she devoured them. She swore loudly enough to make her mother faint. "We should kill him."

"We so should."

"I can't believe he read the texts out loud *and* gave us detention."

"Seriously." Why couldn't a reaper have eaten *him* instead of Mr. Meyer?

"Babes!" Landon greeted us as he slid into the seat beside Kate and blew a raspberry on her cheek. She scowled and swatted at him, and then explained what had happened with Mr. Johansson.

"Don't sweat. Detention is only like an hour. You'll have plenty of time to get ready for tonight." Landon said it with a smile, but he failed to make either of us feel better.

"Yeah, but it's Friday," Kate whined.

"At least it's not Saturday detention," I offered.

"True," she said. "So what did you want to tell me? About Will?"

"Girl talk," Landon mumbled. "That's my cue." He got up and moved to the end of the table where our other friends, Chris and Evan, sat.

"So?" Kate pressed.

I let out a breath and ate a bite of my lunch. "I don't know. It's just so hard, seeing him so much and not being *with* him."

"He's still tutoring you, right?"

"Yeah. He's coming tonight and to your party Saturday."

"Pretending to be friends is impossible when you like someone that much."

"Even if we stopped hanging out, I'd have to see him for our tutoring sessions." If one considered my sparring, patrolling, and fighting evil soul-stealing monsters with Will tutoring.

"Can't you get a different tutor?"

"Not really. We were sort of paired together."

"Has he kissed you since you broke up?"

My stomach considered imploding. "No."

"Well, that makes things easier. I don't know. Keep hanging out with him. If he still loves you, then it's got to be hard for him, too. He'll cave. He's a guy. And it's not like you can stop loving someone just like that. It takes a long time, not overnight. It takes a long time to fall in love and to fall *out* of love. My advice is to remind him of what he's missing as often as possible."

"Like how?"

"Be cute. Be sexy. Just use what you have, lover. I'm sure you know what he likes best about you. Flaunt it. When he misses it—misses *you*—too much, he'll come running back.

You see him so often. It can't be difficult."

I wished it was that easy. But she couldn't know the entire story. I was divine, pure, untouchable in Will's eyes. I was the Left Hand of God. Trying to seduce Will wasn't going to get him to ignore Michael's threat. But I knew that Will loved who I was, and that's what I needed to remind him of.

I smiled. "I might have it figured out. Thanks, Kate."

"You got it. Think I should start my own dating hotline?"

I laughed. "You give everyone the same advice."

"Well, duh. You do know who you're talking to, right?"

"Yeah, well," I started, and shifted uncomfortably in my seat. "I don't think I'm ready for that with Will yet. Even if we *were* together."

"If you're not ready, you're not ready," she said with a shrug. "You don't want to look back on it and think, Oh my God, what was I thinking? Before you take that next step, make sure it's a good idea. It doesn't have to be special. You just don't want to regret it."

I admired Kate for a moment, quietly reflecting on what she said. If Will and I slept together—and thinking about it made my insides flutter—would it be a good idea? Would I regret it later?

She took another bite and winked at me, flashing a secretive smile. "You know it's a good idea."

My cheeks burned and I shook my head, laughing. "Like I'll ever get the chance to find out."

Did I have any regrets? I was afraid Will would become

one. I'd lived countless lives, and I wondered about what had happened in those lives—the big and small things that I couldn't remember. Had I ever been married? Had I ever had any children? Did I have descendants somewhere out in the world? My eyes bugged. That was too much to handle. *Smaller* things, Ell, I told myself. Don't think that hard.

7

AT KATE'S PARTY ON SATURDAY NIGHT, I STOOD BY
the snack table, picking out a plateful of crackers and cheese
slices, with Will at my side. Nobody was in the kitchen
besides us, but the commotion from the thumping music and
crowd of people in the den poured over the half wall and
allowed us no privacy. Kate's basement was like an underground finished house, even complete with spare bedrooms.
Her parents pretty much let her have the run of the place.

Will reached out randomly and pulled on one of the thick
ringlets I'd molded into my ponytail, and then let it bounce
back into place. "You're obnoxious," I noted, and popped a
cheese cube into my mouth.

"Why'd you put your hair up?" he asked. His voice
reminded me of a child pouting over not getting a second
piece of candy.

I shrugged. "I don't know. Because I wanted to do something different with it tonight."

"Your hair is beautiful, and I like it better when it's down," he said wistfully.

I peeked at him out of the corner of my eye, and the longing look in his gaze made my stomach bottom out. He watched me for another moment before leaving the kitchen. What was he getting at? He could not intentionally be a tease. Will never did that stuff on purpose. But if he was going to play this game, I could work it to my advantage.

As soon as he'd gone, I scooted into the bathroom and pulled the hair tie out of my hair and shook it loose. Maybe I shouldn't have taken my ponytail out only because he wanted me to, but I'd do it again just for the chance at stealing a kiss from him. Anyone who'd ever tasted his kisses wouldn't blame me.

When I emerged from the bathroom with my plate, I pushed my way through the pack of gyrating bodies and back over to the sofas, where Kate, Landon, and a handful of other seniors were sitting and laughing. The heavy bass coming from the speakers was beginning to make my left eye twitch.

I sat down in a sofa chair and ate, watching them shout at one another over the loud music. Will appeared next to me and I glanced up at him, catching a triumphant flicker of a smile on his face. He might feel pretty cocky after I'd changed my hair, but by doing it I'd guaranteed that he'd be staring at me for the rest of the night. That smile of his faded when I flipped my hair over my shoulder, exposing my throat, and let my hair cascade down my back.

Will, one point. Ellie, five thousand.

"We have to go to Florida for spring break," Landon said with certainty.

"Any place but PCB," Kate groaned.

It took a moment of decoding for me to realize she meant Panama City Beach.

"God, that place is disgusting," she continued. "The last thing we need on our consciences before college is spending our senior spring break in some cheap seventh-story hotel room with unidentifiable stains on the walls, puking up ten-dollar whiskey."

I grimaced. Kate certainly had a way of making situations very . . . *colorful*.

Landon turned to me. "Ell, are you in?"

"Yeah," I said through a mouthful of crackers. "If I can afford it and my parents actually let me go." I wondered if I'd be able to take Will along. As my Guardian, he'd have to go. The most difficult task concerning that would be explaining to everyone why my non-boyfriend would be joining me on my out-of-state spring break.

Will laid a hand on my shoulder and his fingers tightened. I turned my head to look up at him, but instead he bent over and whispered into my ear, "Don't be angry."

That was random. "What are you—?" And then I saw him.

Marcus.

The reaper stood just inside the doors everyone used to get in and out of the basement without bothering Kate's parents. He hadn't even taken two steps into the party and already he was surrounded by girls. He stood a head taller than most people there, so he wasn't easy to miss. Plus he was hot and he was fully aware of that, which probably made girls flock to him. Even in the low light, I could see that sweeping smile across his face that made him even more attractive.

Of course I wasn't fooled.

I shot to my feet, but Will grabbed my hand before I took a single step.

"He's not going to hurt anyone," Will said with a serious expression.

That wasn't even the point. He was a reaper, and I didn't want my human friends exposed to the supernatural world. Will was more than enough. Despite my annoyance, I couldn't help but admire Marcus for plainly displaying his gnarled burn scar around his collar as if he wore it proudly and felt no shame at all.

When Marcus spotted me, he waved and pushed through the gaggle of girls. Blatant hate twisted their faces when they saw him ease right toward me.

"Ellie, Will, how are—?"

"What are you doing here?" I demanded.

He blinked in surprise. "Well, I—"

"You shouldn't be here," I said, not letting him finish. "I told you not to come."

Will's voice was gentle in my ear, soothing. "He doesn't mean any harm."

I glared at him. "Don't defend him." I turned to the other reaper. "Marcus, you need to leave."

"Oh, I'm not leaving," he said with a soft laugh.

"Who's your friend?"

I practically leaped into the air and spun around to see that Kate had walked up behind me. I slapped the back of my hand against Marcus's chest, hard enough to force him back a step. "This is Marcus. Ignore him. He's a bad seed."

As she checked him out, that growing smile of hers told me she was up to no good. She held out a hand for him to take. "Hi. I'm Kate. I'm a bad seed, too."

Instead of shaking her hand, he swept it up and bowed his head to press his lips against the back of her hand. "A pleasure."

If I were Kate, I would have swooned. But I wasn't Kate and she wasn't me. Instead of doing something apocalyptically uncool, she let two simple words roll off her tongue as if we were all in some classic Hollywood movie: "All mine."

Marcus let go of her hand and she turned to me. "Where did you find this one?"

I thought quickly. "He's a friend of Will's . . . from . . . school."

She glowered at me. "Why do you always get the hot college guys, and why didn't you tell me you were bringing an extra?"

"Oh, I'm even more shocked than you are," I said through my teeth as I smiled bitterly at Marcus. His eyes were glued on Kate. She had that effect.

"So, Marcus," Kate said. "You go to college with Will?"

His smile widened almost imperceptibly. "Foreign exchange."

"Interesting. Where are you from?"

"Spain," he answered smoothly, voice like cream. "While I'm here, I hope to explore every last inch of America."

Her brow arched suggestively. "Oh?"

I looked up at Will pleadingly. Strangely, he didn't feel bothered at all by Marcus's interest in a normal human girl. Was it common for reapers to date humans, or did they just sleep with them? If Will seemed to think it was okay for Marcus to do so, then was he guilty of it himself? The thought of Will with another girl was sickening, but I had to accept the fact that he was a guy, even if he was a reaper. Mortal girls practically threw themselves at him. Not to mention there was Ava and whatever history I suspected they had together.

"Would you like a drink, Marcus?" Kate offered.

"I'd love a drink," Marcus replied.

"Okay then." She beckoned for him to follow her into the kitchen.

I looked at Will. "Stay right here."

He frowned. "I'm not a dog, Ellie."

"Fine," I chirped. "Then no biscuit for you."

When I smiled at him, he grinned and rolled his eyes. "You don't have to throw him out. Just leave him be."

"I'm only going to talk to him," I assured Will, and jogged to catch up with Marcus. I put a firm hand on his arm, stopping him before he went into the kitchen.

"What do you think you're doing?" I demanded.

"As I please." He gazed down at me, his eyes challenging. He had no fear.

"Why would you come here, when I asked you not to, and then shamelessly flirt with my best friend? Who is *human*, no less."

His expression darkened, and he leaned over me so close that I felt his breath on my cheek and no one else could overhear us. "Need I remind you, *Preliator*, that I am not your Guardian? You cannot control me."

The way he said that reminded me of how very dangerous he was, no matter how well I had known him in past lives or the fact that he was an angelic reaper. But I wasn't about to let him walk all over me. "But you serve the angels. I am the archangel Gabriel."

He took a deep breath through his nose, brushing the tip of it across my cheek, very much like an animal. "You smell human to me."

Reapers were very weird. At least Will didn't sniff me like I was dinner. When I tried to speak, I realized I'd been holding my breath. "What are your intentions with her?"

He drew away, and that devil-may-care attitude returned in a heartbeat. "They're entirely chaste, I assure you."

"If you hurt her, *reaper*, I will take both of your balls."

He stared at me for a moment before he huffed and smirked. "You'd try." That momentary hesitation told me he knew I sure as hell *would* try. I'd probably succeed, too.

Marcus knew me just as well as I knew him from decades ago, and he knew what I was capable of. I didn't quite remember his full strength, but his pause after my threat gave me hope that I could handle myself if things really went down.

Marcus walked past me into the kitchen without another word.

I closed my eyes, rubbed the bridge of my nose with my thumb and forefinger, emotionally exhausted. These reapers were going to kill me. Again.

Later I entered the kitchen to find Kate and Marcus laughing and joking. Marcus had on a genuine smile, rich and gracious. It was strange to see him act so normal, like he was just another guy at a party talking to a pretty girl and not an immortal Hellspawn fighter. The other vir I'd known acted aloof, like they thought they were better than humans. Or they were like Will, who felt he just didn't belong around humans. Even Nathaniel didn't attempt to make friends with humans other than Lauren, and in that case they'd met under special circumstances.

"So really," Kate said, touching his shoulder. "Where did you get the scar?"

His grin was playful, but I could tell he was dead serious. "I told you. It's from a fight. The guy had a knife that was practically a sword."

There was puzzled look on her face behind her smile. "But it looks like burn scars, a very clean line of burn scars."

"I'm not lying."

I crossed my arms over my chest when they noticed me. "Well, aren't you two just hitting it off?"

Kate kissed me on the cheek and petted my hair when she saw my frown. "Marcus was just telling me stories of back home in Spain. We should go backpacking through Europe this summer after we graduate. Wouldn't that be amazing?"

It would, but only if I survived to see my diploma. "Definitely, as long as we avoid any hostels. I saw those movies."

Marcus laughed. "That was fiction, Ellie. The hostels are a great place to stay, and you meet incredible people from all over the world."

"*Mmm-hmm,*" I said sarcastically. "I'm sure."

I sensed a body behind me and knew instantly it was Will. I turned to see him.

"So are you and Marcus finally getting along?" he asked.

"She threatened to castrate me," Marcus said.

I nodded. "Sure did."

Will blinked and stiffened uncomfortably. "Oh."

"That's not nice, Ell," Kate scolded. "Boys need those." She turned to Marcus and looped her arm through his. "Let's go enjoy the rest of the party, shall we?"

As they left the kitchen, Kate flashed me a gentle smile, but it didn't make me relax. I just had a bad feeling about the whole thing.

"Hey," Will said. He gave me a reassuring smile and rubbed my shoulders with his hands. "Everything will be fine. Marcus isn't going to hurt anyone, least of all Kate."

I frowned. "What does he want with her?"

"Well, he's just looking for some fun."

"And by fun you don't mean playing pool with the guys, do you?"

He averted his gaze and stared without focus into the crowd. "Marcus likes girls a lot, especially human girls. That's not unusual among our kind. Human girls are different from vir girls."

"He needs to find some different girls to like," I said with a huff. "At the very least not my best friend." I weighed Will's words for a second and hoped he hadn't included himself in that observation about reapers and human girls.

Will's gaze returned to mine. "Ellie, don't worry," he said. "He treats them well, and he doesn't stick around long."

"So he can use them up and break their hearts?"

"No, he knows the kind of girls he's after, the ones who are looking for a little fun too. Kate's a smart girl. She knows how to stay out of trouble."

"Yeah, but Trouble's got his eye on her."

He cupped my chin and lifted my face. "You have to let her make her own decisions, and Marcus too. He can be a little wild, but that's just his nature. He's never had to grow up and face consequences the way a human does. Everything's a game to him. He lives for challenge."

"But you aren't like that," I said. "Are you?"

"Marcus doesn't have the responsibilities that I have. If he had someone like you, then he might become a very different person."

I gave him a suspicious look. "What's that supposed to mean?"

His returning smile was warm and beautiful. "You know what I mean." He leaned forward and kissed me on the cheek, letting his lips linger for an extra heartbeat, but it was long enough to send my pulse racing. He was going to drive me insane.

"Come on," he said, taking my hand. "Let's go make you smile some more. You'll see that Marcus isn't going to hurt

Kate, and you can trust him. You should be spending time with your friends."

"Okay." I followed him out of the kitchen and squeezed his hand just a little tighter as he led me through the crowd.

8

ON SUNDAY NIGHT, WILL AND I WERE PREPARING TO meet Ava and Marcus to hunt the last nycterids. I struggled with what to wear for patrolling gear. Ava's comments about my outfit shouldn't have bothered me, especially since she was a reaper and the freezing February air didn't bother her like it did me. I had to stay warm out there, or I'd be shivering like crazy instead of defending myself. I rummaged through the winter clothes in my closet with the door shut while Will waited. There was a pair of leggings that I went running in that would work. Fighting in stretchy pants would be a lot easier than in jeans. A turtleneck sweater might be enough to keep me warm, since I could just discard my coat if anything attacked.

"Are you ready yet?" Will called.

"Just a sec." I tugged on a black turtleneck and then

realized that my leggings were also black. There was no way I was dressing up like a ninja. I threw off the sweater and picked out a purple one. Huge improvement. I scrounged through my shoes and picked out a pair of cute purple snow boots with fur trim to match. Even bigger improvement.

I emerged from my closet and found Will sitting on my bed. "Have you been staring at my door since I went in there?"

"There wasn't much else for me to do," he said. His gaze dropped to my feet, and his brow flickered. "Nice boots."

I put my hands on my hips and glowered at him. "You're really mean."

He laughed. "I just complimented you!"

"No," I growled. "You're making fun of my boots. I'm not stupid."

He shook his head, grinning. "Are you ready finally?"

I picked up my scarf and coat. "Yeah. Are you?"

"Yeah. I've been waiting."

I laughed and tossed my scarf into his face. He caught it effortlessly.

"You probably shouldn't wear this out hunting, anyway," he said, examining it and frowning.

"Why not? It's pretty and warm."

He held it out. "It's easy for claws to grab. Strangulation is a bad way to go."

I scowled and grabbed it back. "Fine. I won't wear the scarf. I swear, you guys just want me to freeze to death."

"Once you get moving, you'll warm up."

"Not likely. It's like ten degrees outside," I grumbled.

He grabbed my sweater, tugging me closer to where he sat, and gave me a fake serious look. "Stop whining."

I swatted at his hand, forcing him to let me go. "I'm going to kick your ass." I smoothed my sweater back out.

He laughed and rose to his feet. "Really. You look like a cupcake. Are you ready to go? We have to meet them in a half hour and it's already dark out."

I saluted him. "Yes, drill sergeant."

We parked my car in a safe lot downtown and walked quite a ways into a grubbier area. The demonic reapers liked to hunt in the rougher neighborhoods. Fewer people walking around at night meant there were more quiet places to kill and feed without interruption. We found Marcus sitting on the stoop of an abandoned, boarded-up house.

"You aren't still mad at me, are you?" Marcus asked as he came down the steps.

I let out a breath and walked up to him. "No. Just remember what I said."

He grinned playfully. "I remember everything."

Ava landed to my right, making me jump. She must have stepped off the roof. Her long hair was tied into a ponytail, and she matched Marcus in the same sleek black outfit as the other night. "Do you have any preferred method of patrolling?" she asked, her gaze lingering on my leggings. There was just no making her happy, I decided.

I stared at her. "Method?" I looked at Will.

"We're on combat patrol," he explained gently to me.

We'd never discussed terms to describe our hunting habits. We went out, looked for reapers, maybe killed one, and went home. I didn't know there were other ways of doing it. "Which means we go out looking for bad guys, right?"

Will turned to Ava. "We don't practice advanced tactics."

Ava's brow flickered and she said nothing.

"Don't give them such a hard time," Marcus said. "They get the job done, obviously."

"If they were more organized, then the Preliator would have a better track record of staying alive."

That stung. My jaw tightened and I tried to smile. "Well, maybe I'll just leave you to show me how it's done, then. Staying alive, I mean. Best of luck." I turned toward Will and lowered my voice. "I really don't want to be criticized the entire time I'm trying not to die."

"I understand," he said. "But I wouldn't have us work with them if I thought we didn't need it. We don't really know what we're up against, and we can use all the help we can get."

"I just—"

"And I wouldn't do this if I didn't think you could prove her wrong," he said. "I believe in you, and I know what you can do. She doesn't, because she doesn't know you like I do. Teaming up with them will be worth it if we can stop Bastian."

His expression was filled with conviction, and for a moment I believed him. And then I felt like I didn't want to disappoint him. And I wanted to prove Ava wrong. I was useful. I was strong. And I knew what I was doing. My soul was thousands of years old and I was an angel. I was Gabriel. Ava had nothing on me and I'd already proven that. If I had to kick her ass again to make a point, then I would.

I must have been thinking too hard again, because Will grinned at me the way he did when I made funny faces— which was often. "Shut up," I said.

"I didn't say a thing."

I gave him the stink eye. "You were thinking it."

"Are we ready?" Ava asked behind me.

I turned around and marched down the street. "We sure are."

Marcus laughed. "I told you I liked this girl."

A black shadow passed over my head, and the world swelled with the thick odor of brimstone.

"Ellie! Swords!" Will's voice shouted from behind me.

My eyes shot to the sky. The nycterids had arrived.

I threw off my coat and summoned my swords just as one of the nycterids dived at me. My vision filled with the reaper's sunken, bony face, her jaws stretching and jagged teeth gleaming. Angelfire erupted, and I sliced one blade through the air. The nycterid lurched left, but my sword ripped deep through her leg. I spun on my heel and sliced the second sword through her leg again, this time through bone. The limb flung free in a spray of blood, and the reaper let out an earsplitting shriek so shrill that I fell to my knees. I groaned as my skull felt like it was about to implode. Forcing my eyes open, I watched the nycterid spiral through the air and crash through a decrepit apartment building across the street. Her body slammed hard through the steel and concrete and made half the building collapse on top of her in a deafening roar.

I bounced to my feet and shot toward where the nycterid had vanished. Will called my name from somewhere around me, but I kept going. The nycterid was wounded, and I had to finish her off now. I leaped through the rubble and climbed into a hallway. I could hear the beast's cries from deep inside, below me.

The floor exploded in front of me, and the nycterid's horrible face burst through wood and carpet. I slid to a stop in shock, my angelfire dancing off the reaper's skeletal face in a sinister way. Her wings struggled through the hole, hooking her talons every place she could to drag her body up and forward. Her teeth snapped at me in between her shrieks.

In a wave of certainty, I climbed to my feet and let out a cry as I swung my sword at her long neck, but she twisted away. My blade made a fiery, shallow gash and the reaper screamed and thrashed her head, slamming my body through a wall and into one of the apartments. I crashed through the wreckage and hit the floor of a kitchen. My head spun and swam with chaos. My ears felt as if they were underwater; the cries of the nycterid and Will screaming my name were so far away. Both my swords were still in my hands, and I climbed to my feet, reigniting the angelfire. Beyond the hole in the wall my body had made, I could distantly hear the colossal reaper struggling, no doubt breaking more and more of the floor beneath her weight.

My pulse slowed, and time slowed with it, as I waited for the reaper to appear. I exhaled and steadied my blades.

And then her body exploded through the wall, the ceiling crashing down on her head like a waterfall of dust and debris. She fought forward, and I tightened my grip on my helves. Her gnarled snout shot at my face, fangs gnashing, pale orbs for eyes gleaming and staring into mine without seeing me. She chomped and I twisted. She swung her neck back around, and I screamed as I plunged my sword into the side of her skull. Angelfire engulfed the reaper's head, spreading down her long neck to the tip of her tail until the flames swallowed her massive body and wings. She vanished in seconds and left only falling bits of flame and ash behind.

I staggered back breathlessly until I hit a wall. Part of me wanted to drop my weapons and relax against it, but I was afraid of something else bursting through. The building was destroyed. The floor groaned and walls creaked. More stuff fell from the ceiling. Will's voice called my name again. I wasn't sure if it was adrenaline that made me feel like a zombie or if it was shock.

He appeared out of nowhere, grabbing me and pulling

me into him. His hands cupped my face, fingers threading into my hair. "Are you okay? Ellie, are you all right? I couldn't follow you. Are you hurt?"

I shook my head, forcing my gaze away from the empty space the reaper had filled only moments ago, and looked up into Will's emerald eyes. In the failing light and billowing dust, they were like bright jewels guiding me home. He was out of breath, and I realized how much I must have terrified him by following the reaper into the building alone.

"The last—Orek—is outside," he said, his voice rushed. "I think Ava and Marcus will take care of him. You did amazing."

He led me through the rubble and down a steep decline of concrete chunks. My boots slipped, and he caught me before I fell. My body was still shaky, but Will had gotten hold of himself enough to guide me safely from the building. The world slowly became real to me again as I heard the reapers battling outside. Furious voices and roars filled my head, and I felt myself wanting to retreat and run away from the horror. But I had to keep going.

As soon as we emerged from the collapsing apartment building, I saw Ava fall and smack the pavement. Marcus ran to her side and shielded her, staring up past us at something high above. I twisted around and looked up to see Orek perched on the roof, his wings spread as wide as they could, his tail lashing. His long neck arched and his head swiveled toward me. His pallid eyes blinked, and he hissed, snapping his jaws in warning. His tail beat the pediment, tearing up chunks, and they fell. Will yanked me out of their path and they crashed to the ground.

Orek raised his head toward the sky and roared, his voice quaking with rage. The howl was shrill and mournful, sending strips of jagged ice down my spine. *"Eki!"*

I stepped away from the building and lit up my blades. Instead of diving to attack, Orek clamped the talons of his hind legs deeper into the pediment. If he planned on continuing the fight, he'd be an idiot. He was one demonic reaper against three angelic ones and myself. No matter how huge he was, he was at a disadvantage.

Orek beat his wings, roaring as he lifted himself into the air and disappeared into the night.

I let out a long breath of relief and let my angelfire die. I was covered in dust and the dead reaper's blood. My sweater was torn across my collarbone, and I had the dried remains of a gash on my cheek, but the healed wound didn't even ache anymore. Will's hand cupped my chin, and he guided my face around, his touch without fear this time. He inspected quietly, and when he was satisfied, his hand swept along my chin and down my neck.

"I'm in one piece, I promise you," I said.

He forced a little smile. "Just making sure. You scared me. She thrashed you around in there."

"Well, I'm the one who made it out alive," I said. "Not her."

"Preliator," Ava called. "You destroyed the nycterid by yourself. I've never seen anyone take on a nycterid alone. That was very impressive."

She didn't elaborate, but I recognized right away that I'd just been given an extreme compliment. Beside me, Will beamed in his subtle way that only I noticed. Maybe she wasn't as bad as I'd thought. "Thank you, Ava."

"Phenomenal," Marcus bellowed. "Two down, one to go."

"I'm ready for Orek," I said. "And for whatever's lined up after him."

"What happened up there?" Will asked, glancing over his shoulder at the destroyed building.

I shuddered at the fresh, terrifying memory. "She was trapped. Eki. She fought her way through the building, but I don't think she could see me or anything else. They're blind, aren't they? The nycterids."

"Yes. They use echolocation and the supernatural sense that we reapers have to navigate their surroundings and locate prey."

"Like bats," I added.

His expression was distant and hard with thought. "Sort of. This combination in the nycterids is even more effective than eyesight, but Eki was disoriented in the building."

"Yeah, like she couldn't find me and started tearing the building down," I said. "Everything happened so fast."

"Maybe that's what you need to do," Ava suggested. "Stay fast. If and when Orek attacks again, keep moving. He may not be able to sense you, and you can gain an advantage over him."

"That's not a bad idea," Will said.

That was if he didn't come back with reinforcements. I knew that somewhere out there, Orek was pitching a rage over the loss of Eki. I wasn't sure if his kind was capable of love the way humans and the vir were, but I wondered if the two nycterids had been mates. The thought made me feel regret for tearing them apart, but I had to defend myself. I also knew that if Orek cared for Eki, felt any sort of affection for her at all, then his next attack would be personal. It might be more difficult for him to take me alive when he would probably ache to just tear me into pieces.

9

SCOURING THE MALL WITH KATE THE NEXT MORN-
ing, I still felt shell-shocked. These days it wasn't common
for me to feel so exhausted the day after a hunt, but last night
had taken its toll on my body—not to mention my mind. The
nycterid reapers . . . they were just too out of this world, like
some kind of demon dragon. Kate and I roamed far ahead of
our moms, who chitchatted while strolling behind us, taking
their sweet time. Kate and I, on the other hand, were on a
mission. But I was tired of missions, and Kate was tiring me
out even more.

"I'm going to ask Marcus if he'll go to Josie's party with
me," Kate said as she picked through the dresses in Neiman
Marcus.

I frowned at her but kept my eye on a red strapless David
Meister she had passed over. Josie Newport was having a

pre-Valentine's Day party called Hearts Afire, and the dress code was red or black. Organizing my thoughts on potential dresses while playing shrink for Kate was very conflicting. "If you think he'll say yes, go for it."

"Why wouldn't he say yes?"

"I—" I stammered. "Well, he probably wouldn't be into a high school party."

"He came to mine a couple weeks ago," she said, frowning. "And you're bringing Will, right?"

"Maybe, but I haven't even talked to him about it," I said, and pulled the red dress out. My thoughts were far away. Something about Kate potentially dating Marcus didn't sit well with me. He was a reaper, and she was completely human, mortal, and unaware of the supernatural. I couldn't let Kate get involved with reapers, and I had my doubts he'd ever tell her the truth about himself. How could they be together without Marcus keeping such an enormous truth from her?

Kate selected a dress and examined the fabric. I already knew it'd look gorgeous on her.

"Why are you trying on a black one?" I asked. "Get red like me."

She made an ugly noise and held the black dress up to her chest. "Uh, no. Kate is not a matchy-matchy kind of girl. I'm not going to a party wearing the same color as my best friend."

"You always wear black," I noted, picking at the chiffon.

"It's slimming," she grumbled. "Don't you read *Cosmo*? They tell you all this stuff."

I rolled my eyes. "Right. I knew that."

She grinned. "Want to come over tonight?"

"Of course," I said. "I'm meeting Will after the mall, but after that, definitely. I'll bring my homework so we can get both of ours out and not do any of it."

She laughed. "Okay. I could really use some girl time, for sure."

"So I'll call you as soon as we're done?"

"You'd better."

Our moms walked into the dress area with their hands full of shopping bags. Kate's mom eyed the dress in Kate's hands.

"Did you guys find anything you like?" Mrs. Green asked.

Kate handed the dress over. "I'm trying this on."

My mom thumbed the dress I'd chosen. "Are you considering this one?"

"Yeah," I said. "Isn't it gorgeous?"

She eyed it with a tight mouth. "Don't you think it's a little mature for your age?"

On the other side of Mrs. Green, Kate scoffed. "She'll look hot in it, Mrs. M."

"That helps so much, Kate." My mom sighed. "If this is the dress you want, then all right. Go try it on, but it's the last for a while, Ell. You just got a really nice one for your birthday."

"Thanks, Mom," I said with a smile as Kate grabbed my hand and dragged me toward the fitting rooms. Will would have a heart attack when he saw me in this dress.

Nathaniel's house was empty when I arrived. Any chance they got, the boys were outside, which was unfortunate for me because I was the only one who noticed how cold it was. Today I wasn't really there for Will. Instead, Nathaniel had said he had a surprise for me.

I pulled open the sliding door and stepped out. "Hey, guys," I called, and hopped down the porch steps. They were hanging out by the shooting range, and a number of guns were spread out across the table on the platform. Nathaniel wore ear and eye protection and aimed an awfully large handgun at a target board placed at the very far end of the yard. The target was so distant that I could barely make out the lines. Nathaniel fired and, a moment later, frowned.

"Damn," he grumbled. "Just outside."

I squinted and put up a hand to squelch the sunlight gleaming off the snowy yard and into my eyes. If the bullet hit the target, I couldn't even tell. It was yet another advantage reapers had over my human body, I supposed.

"That's because you suck," Will called out in a bored voice.

Nathaniel frowned. "That's one time out of three clips that I didn't hit the bull's-eye. Why don't you get up here and show me how much *you* don't suck?"

He frowned dismissively. "I don't like guns."

"That's because you suck." Nathaniel fired again. He hit the dead center of the target.

"You're a smart-ass, too."

Nathaniel chuckled and removed the clip from his gun and reloaded.

I let out a sigh loud enough for them to notice and turn their heads. "You're both ridiculous. I want my surprise."

Nathaniel beckoned me. "Come here, Ell."

I moved forward cautiously.

"You're going to learn how to use a gun."

A small involuntary noise of glee escaped me. "Really?"

"Oh, yeah."

He removed his goggles and earmuffs for me to put on. He held out the gun and I picked it up. It was heavier than I had imagined it would be.

"First rule," Nathaniel began, "is muzzle direction. Always point it at the ground, and don't touch the trigger until you're ready to shoot a target. Safety's off." His finger flicked a little lever near the trigger. He flicked it back the other way. "And it's on."

"Okay."

He took out the clip and handed it to me. "Unload like this. You try it."

I did as he said.

"Now put them back in. Watch your fingers."

I pinched my fingers on the first five bullets. At last the clip was loaded. I stuck it back into the gun. "Okay."

"Now, aim for the twenty-meter target. Safety off. Finger on the trigger. There's a little nub on the end of the muzzle. Line it up with the target. Fire when you're ready. Try not to shoot Will. He's grumpy enough already."

It was difficult to steady my hands as I laughed, but I forced myself to get it together. Following his directions slowly and carefully, I steadied the gun with my arms out in front of me. I exhaled and fired. The bullet tore through the bull's-eye.

"Well done!" Nathaniel said with a smile. "For you, a target this close should be no trouble. Let's do some more difficult targets."

I surprised myself with how much fun I had as Nathaniel taught me how to shoot, and after emptying a couple of clips, I was getting pretty good.

"So, Will," I said, turning to face him. "What happens if I trade in my Khopesh swords for a shotgun?"

He stared at me, gauging how serious I was. "Then the world ends. Bullets don't come with angelfire, sorry to say."

"That's too bad," I said. "Guns are effective against zombies, but not reapers?"

I was rewarded with a little smile. "Real life is a lot different from movies and video games."

"Hey, now," Nathaniel said. "Guns can be very effective. Just not as effective as Ellie's swords. But imagine what we could do with an angelfire flamethrower."

At that moment, something prickled across my senses and I looked to the sky. Ava pulled out of the Grim midflight, her dark silver wings stretched out gloriously as she landed in the snow. Her hair was tousled from flight, but she still managed to be beautiful. She moved right past Nathaniel and me.

"Will," she said. "I have a lead. I think I know what Bastian is looking for that might break the Enochian spell."

Will snapped to attention and got to his feet, his expression serious. "Is he close to getting it?"

She shook her head. "I don't know. Last night I caught a demonic reaper in Birmingham who I know deals in magical items. He told me, after some persuasion and a lot of his blood on the ground, that Bastian came to him looking for a necklace."

"A necklace?" I asked. "How is a necklace going to break an angelic spell? Unless he just wants to wear it so he can look pretty . . ."

"It's a relic," she said, giving me a very unamused look.

That was a word I recognized. Relics were very powerful magical items that could be used to give the possessor massive power, as a key to unlock something, or to summon an angel or one of the Fallen. The possibilities were many and terrifying.

"He's not looking for *my* necklace, right?" I asked Ava. I touched the pendant below my collarbone, and the carved wings felt warm and gave off an electrical hum against my fingertips. It was a strange piece, and I couldn't remember where it had come from, but I felt naked and empty when I wasn't wearing it—like the necklace was a part of me. There was something more to my winged necklace, but I just didn't know what exactly.

Ava shook her head. "No, this is something different, a well-known relic of great power."

"This could be what Bastian's new vir are searching for," I said. "They sound like your worst nightmare, from what Cadan told me. He said they were after a key of some sort to break the Enochian spell on the sarcophagus. This relic may be powerful enough to do it."

"We have to find this relic before Bastian does," Nathaniel said.

"Do you know where it is?" Will asked.

"I recognized the necklace the demonic reaper described," Ava explained. "And I'm pretty sure I know exactly what he's talking about. It's protected by an angelic reaper I know."

"A relic guardian?" Will asked.

She nodded curtly. "His name is Zane, and he may not be so willing to part with it, but it would be wise if we hid the relic in an even more secure place or perhaps destroyed it. Bastian is getting too close."

"How well acquainted are you with this relic guardian?" Nathaniel asked.

She smiled darkly. "He won't be pleased to see me."

"Old enemies?" I asked.

"Old lovers."

"Oh." I shut my mouth after that.

"Do you need help convincing him to hand it over?" Will asked.

"Yes," Ava said. "If the Preliator is with me, then he will have to forfeit the relic."

I was not keen on going anywhere alone with Ava. I still wasn't entirely convinced of her loyalties. "Do you mean we're going tonight?"

She shook her head. "It's too risky to go after dark. We'll wait until the sun rises tomorrow and the demonic aren't active."

"I have school, though," I said. "Which, unfortunately, takes precedence over me hanging out with you shiesty reapers."

She shrugged. "That's fine, then. I understand. Zane must recognize Will as the Preliator's Guardian and accept that Will would be acting on your behalf."

"Ava's right," Will said. "I'm as good as having Ellie there. He won't be able to refuse me."

I didn't like the idea of Will going with Ava any more than I wanted to go with her. I looked pleadingly at Nathaniel, who offered a small, sympathetic smile back. I wanted to beg Will not to go with her, but I didn't want to be a brat. He could take care of himself, and I trusted him. It was *her* I didn't trust.

"I have to leave," I said abruptly, and stomped back toward the house. "Thank you for everything, Nathaniel."

"Ellie," called Will's voice behind me.

I ignored him and kept going, but he caught up to me as I climbed the deck stairs. He looked up at me from the bottom step and touched my sleeve.

"Ellie," he said again, turning me around to face him. I looked down at him and chewed on my bottom lip.

"What?" I asked a little too sharply.

"I know what's wrong."

"Good job, Sherlock." What was *wrong* with me? I closed my eyes and took a deep breath.

"If you tell me not to go, then I won't," he said. "She can take Nathaniel."

"No," I said. "I'm sorry. It's important that you go in my place. I'm just being . . . I don't know. Just ignore me." I continued to climb the stairs, but he took my arm a little more firmly and pulled me back.

His gaze was gentle and I melted inside. "I'm not going to ignore you."

"I didn't mean it literally," I said, unable to repress the smile that grew with my words. Even with those pleading puppy-dog eyes, he was the most gorgeous thing I'd ever seen.

"I know," he said, his hand softening around my arm,

his thumb stroking gently, comfortingly. "But I meant what I said. I don't want to upset you."

"I'm not upset," I lied. "I know how childish I'm acting over the whole thing, but I can't help it."

He smiled, taking my breath away. "It's the same reason I disliked Landon when I first met him."

I almost laughed. "He's not that bad."

"I thought there might be something between you two," he confessed. "Because he wanted you."

My smile faded. "And Ava doesn't want you?"

"No, I'm very sure she doesn't."

I took a nervous breath and my lips trembled. "That's impossible."

He didn't say anything, but he didn't look away either. My pulse pounded heavier and heavier with each passing moment, and I ached from the tension. If Ava and Nathaniel hadn't been staring at us from across the lawn, then . . . I don't know what I would have done. But standing there without moving, looking at him as he touched me, was killing me.

"Good-bye, Will," I said, and backed farther up the stairs.

"Good-bye."

He didn't break eye contact with me until I turned at the top of the stairs and let myself into the house.

I stopped channel surfing when I found one of MTV's trashy reality shows, and frankly, it just made me feel more hostile than I already was. I sat on the floor of Kate's room with my back up against her bed. She lay on her stomach above me, running her fingers through my hair and braiding and twisting random locks. The feeling was soothing and almost enough to make me forget about Ava's intrusion and the stupid show I was watching on TV.

"I love your hair," Kate said as she wound a thick piece of it into a doughnut on top of my head. "Do you remember when we were little and I used to call you Ariel from *The Little Mermaid*?"

"Yeah." I changed the channel. Now it was some show on convicts in prison. Mild improvement, but surprisingly less violent than the girls fighting over some jerk on the last channel.

"And then all you wanted for months was a purple bra, even though we were too young for even training bras. You drove your mom crazy, so she bought you one anyway."

"That purple training bra was amazing." I grimaced at the TV as an inmate described the crime that had landed him in a maximum security prison.

Kate sighed as she yanked on another chunk of my hair. "And now push-up bras are amazing. It's incredible how the world turns."

I winced at the pain. "I'll trade my hair for your boobs."

"Never mind," Kate said. "I don't want your hair that bad."

"I thought I'd just throw it out there."

"I love you."

"I know."

"Why are you so crotchety tonight?" She tugged even harder on my hair, and my head tilted back to look up at her.

"Because you're pulling my hair, schizoid."

"But it's so pretty. What are you watching on my TV? I didn't approve this."

"I have no clue, but I think that guy killed three other inmates. He's kind of hot in a homicidal sociopath kind of way." I changed the channel again.

"Ew. You *would* like that. Wait—does this mean Will's tats are legit prison ink? Is there something you need to tell me?"

I let out a very loud, obnoxious snort as I tried to keep myself from laughing hysterically. "No, trust me. And I don't have a thing for guys in prison. Stop reading into everything like a shrink."

Kate smoothed my hair back out as straight as it would go. "So are you going to answer me? You're only getting more crotchety."

"I'm only crotchety for the same reason you're crotchety," I confessed.

She made a noise under her breath. "So does it have something to do with Will? You didn't have sex with him, did you?"

I almost choked on my tongue. "*No*, no. He still hasn't even kissed me since . . . So, he has this really old friend, and she's gorgeous, and she keeps popping up."

"Ew, old as in cougar old?"

Well, that was relative. What was a few decades to a reaper? "No, they've just been friends for a long time."

"*Ruh-roh*. Did they date?"

I sighed. "He swears they never did, but she's freaking gorgeous and there's no reason why every guy on the planet wouldn't want to be with her. I trust Will, but I can't help feeling so awful about it."

"Sounds like you're jealous."

"I know I am, Dr. Phil. Please don't tell me I'm paying you by the hour."

"Shut up. That just means you still love him and you don't want to see him with anyone else. Totally reasonable."

"I hate to admit it, but she's actually kind of cool," I said, thinking of our last fight against the nycterids. "I didn't like her at first, but I respect her."

"You still don't trust her, though."

"No. And she and Will are hanging out tomorrow."

She got a little rougher with my hair in surprise. "Whoa, what?"

"It's a school project thing," I assured her. "But I still feel all . . . yuck."

"*I* would tail them," she blurted.

"What do you mean?"

"Find out where they're going," she said. "This chick obviously wants to move in on him. Don't you want to know if there's something going on between them? You can see for yourself."

That was an idea. A potentially bad one, but she was right. If I had the chance to spy on Will and Ava alone together, then I could see once and for all if they liked each other. There was just one little problem. "But I have school."

Kate leaned over me and winked. "Leave it to me, lover."

10

WHEN I GOT TO SCHOOL IN THE MORNING, I LOOKED
for Kate's red BMW like she had instructed. She was sitting
inside since it was about negative four thousand degrees out,
so I hopped into her passenger seat.

"What time are they doing their thing today?" she asked,
pulling her cell out of her purse.

"Ten."

Kate scrolled through her phone book until she found the
number she wanted. On the second ring, whoever was on the
other line picked up. "Yes, this is Diane Monroe," she said,
mimicking my mom's voice almost flawlessly. "Elisabeth
Monroe's mother. Yes. She has a doctor's appointment at ten
this morning. If you'll have her excused at nine thirty . . .
Yes, she'll be returning to class afterward. That's perfect.

Thank you so much. Buh-bye." She dropped her phone back into her purse. "It's done."

"You are going to get me suspended," I said as nerves wound their way into my gut.

"Only if you're stupid and get yourself caught."

"This isn't going to work."

"It will if you stop acting like such a boob. If you freak out and look suspicious, then they'll *get* suspicious. This is a covert op. Try not to look like you're up to something, and no one will think that you are."

I had such a bad, bad feeling about this.

The note excusing me from class came halfway through first period. That meant I got to stare at it for about an hour while my nerves got the better of me and I lost confidence in my ability to pull this off. I'd never cut class before. My heart pounded like a jackhammer as I dropped off my backpack at my locker and headed for the office with just my purse and coat. The secretary was pleasant to me and I signed out, barely able to breathe the whole time.

I followed the directions I'd printed to an older apartment complex on a street off Orchard Lake Road. The parking lot was quiet and the property was heavily wooded. I sat for a few minutes with my car running to stay warm, wondering if Will and Ava had beaten me here. I hadn't realized I was so tense until my phone buzzed and I jumped with fright. I pulled it out to see that Kate had sent me a text message.

Hows it going, 007?

I took a long, bored breath and texted back.

Nothing yet.

Want me 2 bring u a cappuccino?

That sounded so good.

We arent both skipping school.

U know u want 1.

Movement out my window caught my attention. Appearing from the Grim, Will and Ava dropped gracefully from the sky with their wings wide before feathers and all melted back into their shoulders.

Thats them. text u later.

I turned off my car and pulled my coat tighter around me as I climbed out. It was hard to meet the look of disappointment in Will's cool green gaze. Every time I did, stabs of ice hit my stomach. I had everything planned until what I'd say when Will got there.

"Ellie," he said gently. "What are you doing?"

"I should be doing this with you," I said. "We're a team. I'm already out of school, so take me with you."

Then he smiled, much to my shock and relief. "All right. To be honest, I'm glad you're here. I didn't want to do a mission without you."

"I'm ready for this."

His smile widened. "Then let's go."

"Keep your energy suppressed," Ava said. "Zane has been the guardian of this relic for a long time, and he will sense us coming. We don't want him to think he's under attack and retaliate against us. He likes to cause damage and ask questions later—and he can cause a *lot* of damage."

"But won't he recognize you?" I asked, confused as to why he'd start a fight if he knew Ava.

She grinned. "Like I said, I'm not his favorite person. I haven't been for decades."

"Just stay calm," Will said to me. "We're not expecting a fight. Just be on guard."

His words made me relax some, but I couldn't help feeling like something was already very wrong. We climbed the stairs to the third floor and found apartment 310. The door was ajar and the wood was splintered as if it'd been forced open. The ill feeling in my gut spun and festered. I knew we were too late.

Ava didn't waste any time; she pushed the door open carefully. She summoned the long, vicious talons through her fingertips and crept into the living room. Will followed, calling his sword, and entered on the other side of her, his back close to the wall.

It looked as if a tornado had blown through the apartment. Couches were shredded, their stuffing blanketing the living room like snow. End tables were overturned and one was shattered. Something had smashed the television, and paper, shards of glass and plastic, and a potted plant were strewn everywhere. I looked at Ava, whose face was hard and pale as she examined the room.

Then a rancid and overripe odor filled my nose and I clamped my hand over my mouth, almost gagging. Something was very clearly rotting. "Oh, God," I groaned. "What is that?" It couldn't be the relic guardian. Reapers didn't rot when they died. They either burned up in angelfire or demonfire, or they turned to stone. Was it human?

Will stepped by me, following the scent into the kitchen, where he stopped in the doorway, his expression turning grave. At his feet was a river of dried blood that had flowed from the kitchen into the dining room.

"What is it?" I asked, my voice trembling.

"Don't come in here," he responded firmly. "Stay back, Ellie."

Ava turned toward him, her gaze darkening. "Is it a body?"

My heart plummeted when he nodded. "Human. She may have heard the commotion and come to check on the place. The face is too badly damaged and her rib cage has been torn open. She was definitely fed on by reapers. There are no large bites, so she must have been killed by demonic vir."

"How long has she been there?" I asked, bile swarming in my throat. Images of brutal reaper kills I'd seen before flashed in my head, and I was very okay with taking Will's advice to stay put. I had vision of my own half-eaten body lying at the feet of the mysterious vir that Cadan had warned me about. I could be next.

Will didn't look up. "Days."

Ava's jaw tightened and she stomped toward the back rooms. She kicked open a closed door, took one look, and moved to the second bedroom. Will and I followed right behind her, and in the mess of the bedroom, I could see congealed blood splattered across the walls and carpet.

And the pile of gray stones in the far corner. We'd found Zane.

Ava stepped up to the rubble hesitantly and knelt down, her movements slow and quiet. She picked up the largest piece of stone and cradled it in her hands. Biting down on her lip, she brushed her thumb across stone lips and a square jaw, all that remained of his face. Her shoulders slumped, and she drew a long breath before tucking the piece into the inside of her jacket. She was still and silent for several moments until she rose and stared at Will.

"I'm sure the relic is gone," she said. "But I know where he kept it in every location he stayed in. I'll check anyway."

Will nodded and she passed us both, heading for the kitchen. She pulled open the drawer beneath the stove and slipped her hand inside, feeling left and right across the ceiling of the drawer. With a cry of rage she ripped her hand back out and punched the front of the stove, her fist tearing right through the steel with an agonizing metallic groan. She straightened and ignored the blood running down her arm and pooling at her feet. "It's not here. They took it. They killed him and took it."

"I'm so sorry, Ava," I said, watching her carefully.

Her eyes snapped to mine. "Do not weep for me or for the relic guardian. He did his duty. The only thing of value that we lost today was the relic."

My heart broke for her and for Zane. I didn't understand why the angelic reapers valued their lives so little. All life was too precious to just throw away.

A flash of power behind us made Will and me spin around. A blond-haired girl—no, a vir reaper—had appeared in the doorway. I willed my swords into my hands and lit them up just as her large eyes, dark and glossy as obsidian, fell to them, widening in surprise.

"You," she breathed, gaping at my swords.

Before I could attack, Ava blurred past me and grabbed the girl by the throat and crushed her back into the wall across the hallway. To my shock, the girl knocked Ava's arm away, freeing herself, and threw a punch. Ava ducked and kicked high, striking the side of the girl's head. The girl hit the ground, blond hair flying, and rolled right back up to her feet.

"Wait!" she cried, but Ava kept coming. Ava jumped up, kicked into the wall, and propelled herself higher, wheeling through the air to strike the girl again, but the girl leaned back and avoided the blow. "Stop!"

Ava landed and launched herself at the girl again with her foot-long talons springing free.

"Ava, wait!" Will shouted, darting past me to the battling reapers. He grabbed Ava's shoulder and wrenched her back, throwing her into the wall and putting himself between the two. He called his sword into his free hand and poised it at the unknown reaper in warning. Ava struggled against his grip, blind with rage.

"Identify yourself," he ordered the girl, who flinched at his voice. "Or I let this one go. She seems to like you."

The girl straightened up, smoothing out her disheveled hair and touching her jaw, momentarily squeezing her eyes shut with pain. "I'm Sabina," she said. "I work with Zane. However, judging by the damage here, I assume he's dead. Is that true?"

He ignored her question. "You're angelic?"

"Of course I am."

"Ellie," Will said, meeting my eyes and then looking pointedly at Sabina.

I knew what he wanted me to do: test her the way I'd tested him the day we met, so many lifetimes ago. The unknown reaper's black eyes, eyes that reminded me of Ragnuk's demonic glare, were fixed on my swords again. Eyes that made me doubt her angelic heritage.

She looked back up to my face. "I know who you are, though I never thought I'd ever see you myself. You're *real*."

"Sure am," I said, a little embarrassed by her invasive

staring. Occasionally I met a reaper like her, one who had heard about me for hundreds of years but had never come across any of my incarnations. To most reapers, I was like Bigfoot, just a ridiculous story with a few questionable pieces of evidence left behind. I stepped up carefully to Sabina, who held out her arm, opening her palm. I raised my sword.

"Do what you must, Preliator," she said.

I cut her hand, angelfire covering her skin. I lowered my sword, and she held up her palm so we could see the wound healing to perfection. Sabina was an angelic vir, just as she claimed.

Ava shook herself away from Will's grip and their gazes clashed, her anger with him deadly clear. He'd done the right thing and she knew it, and I guessed that made her even more furious. She rolled against the wall and examined her arm, which ran with blood.

"I'm sorry," Sabina said to Ava. "I didn't kill him. He was my friend. I'm sorry, if he was yours too."

Without a word, Ava was gone, storming from the apartment and slamming the door shut behind her.

I started to follow her, but Will put a hand on my shoulder to stop me. "Wait," he said gently. "Give her a moment."

He was right. I began to believe that Ava and Zane had been much more than just lovers—and for a long time too, if she knew where he preferred to stash the relic he protected.

"Your name is . . . Ellie?" Sabina asked, studying me in the curious, shameless way that many reapers had. After all, it was kind of a human thing for children to be taught not to stare.

I nodded.

She looked at Will. "And you're the Preliator's Guardian. It is incredible to meet you both. Were you here for the Constantina necklace?"

"The what?" I asked, confused.

"The relic," Sabina explained. "The Constantina necklace that Zane was sworn to protect. If he's dead, then they probably found it. They wouldn't leave unless they had it."

A shiver went through me. "By 'they,' you mean Bastian's vir."

Her jaw set. "Bastian has been searching for the necklace for some time."

"Why are you here now?" I asked, still a little suspicious of this stranger.

"Zane hasn't returned my phone calls for a few days," she said, her voice falling. "I came to check on him and found you. Is he in there still?"

She must have been referring to his stone remains. "Yeah," I said. "But the relic was gone from under the stove."

She blinked at me, confusion filling her gaze. "What? The stove?"

"That's where Ava said he kept it," I elaborated.

Sabina blinked again, her confusion now mixed with surprise. "I never knew where he hid the relic. He never told me."

And with that, I knew the truth between Ava and Zane, and suddenly I felt even worse for her than I had seconds ago. There was nothing more sad than losing the one you loved.

"Zane is gone," Sabina said. "I need a new mission. Do you have need of me, Preliator?"

"Um . . ." I was a little taken back. I thought of Ava and Marcus, who made up our little army. Even they might not be enough.

"I'm a good fighter and I'm strong," she urged.

I watched her carefully. "Is that what you did for Zane? Fought alongside him?"

"When he needed me," she said. "That's why I came today. He'd never gone this long without contact. I'll give you my number and you can call me anytime. It would be an honor to fight for you."

These reapers and their missions. I took out my phone and saved Sabina's number.

"Let's go," Will said, and touched my arm.

I followed him out to my car, where Ava sat on the hood,

staring into the woods beyond the parking lot. Will stopped, but I kept going and stood next to her. She didn't look at me or acknowledge my presence, but her blue-violet eyes were red and raw. The space between us was fragile in the chill air, the uncertainty like tiny cracks spreading through thin glass.

"Ava," I said. "I *am* sorry. Don't think his death doesn't matter. I know he mattered to you. I'm sick of you reapers and your feelings of worthlessness. The relic is gone, but it's not as important as anyone's life. We'll get the necklace back, I promise you."

To my shock, she smiled sadly, gazing through the trees. "He mattered to me, but the only thing that mattered to him was that stupid necklace."

I studied her face. She took a deep breath and seemed to grow smaller, more vulnerable. A single tear fell from her eye. She wiped at it angrily, as if it were an ugly blemish she wanted no one else to see.

"He loved me," she said. "I know he did. But his duty to protect the relic was more important to him. So I left him to his duty. I knew he'd die because of it one day, but I wanted to live my life. He was so angry when I left. That surprised me—how furious he was with me. He was so willing to hate me, but so hesitant to love me."

Tucking her hair behind her ears and folding her arms across her chest, she looked at me finally, offering me a kind, hopeful smile. She looked so human in that moment. "At least he put up a hell of a fight, huh?"

I smiled weakly back. "Yeah."

"I just want to know why no one else heard," she said, and suddenly she was all business again. She straightened herself and looked to Will. "What do you think?"

He shrugged. "Think about Nathaniel's aspect. If the attacking reaper was strong enough, he could wipe the minds of any humans close enough to have overheard. Either they never noticed or they remember nothing of the incident. Human minds are easily tampered with. Nathaniel would have had no trouble covering this up."

"Right," Ava grumbled bitterly. "Well, Bastian has quite the assortment of thugs. I'm sure he's got a vir for every occasion."

The idea of Nathaniel, or another vir, being capable of manipulating the human mind disturbed me. It seemed like the ultimate violation of a person. The mind was supposed to be a safe, sacred place, and for it to be torn open and completely vulnerable was a terrifying idea. I had no clue how to protect myself against such an attack and prayed that I'd never have to.

Suddenly, I couldn't bear to be in the parking lot, so close to that place of death. "I've got to go back to school," I said briskly. "I can only get away with playing hooky for so long."

"All right," Will said. "But let's go back to Nathaniel's and eat first. You should have a rest before going back."

That sounded like a wonderful idea. As soon as the thought of food entered my mind, my stomach clenched and growled. I blushed when I saw Will grin.

He gestured toward my car. "Let's get out of here."

We rode back to Nathaniel's house. Ava took off, and Will made lunch for the two of us. When I glanced at my cell, I saw a text from Kate but didn't answer it. Instead I checked the time.

"I've got to run," I said, stuffing the phone into my back pocket and taking my dishes to the sink to scrub them clean and stick them in the dishwasher.

Will watched me silently from his seat at the table before he rose to follow me out into the living room toward the front door. He caught up to me and pulled lightly on my fingertips, slowing me to a stop. I turned to him and smiled, studying his gaze when he didn't say anything.

"What's up?" I asked, allowing him to pull more of my hand into his own and rub my palm with his thumb. He sucked in his upper lip, and I knew then that he was nervous. My smile faded.

"I have to tell you something," he said. "Because it's not right that I keep this from you any longer. I don't want to keep anything from you."

"Okay . . ."

"Do you remember when we said no more secrets?" he asked as he stared at the ground, his voice faint and small.

I swallowed hard and something tightened in my chest. "Yeah." The word was almost nothing.

"It's been eating away at me," he said. "Devouring me from the inside out."

I shook my head, studying his dull green eyes in confusion. "What are you talking about?"

"I thought everything was over." His voice was cracking, and he took a long, deep breath to steady it, but the effort was useless. "I believed that I'd failed for the last time, that you were gone forever, because of what I'd failed to do for you."

Fear tightened around my throat as I tried to figure out what he was trying to tell me.

"I loved you," he continued, looking up to meet my gaze at last. "And I was broken for so long. For forty years, I waited and waited and searched for you. I hadn't seen Nathaniel in over a decade, and I was so alone. Marcus and Ava came around a few times, and after being alone for *so long*, I stopped thinking or feeling. I *hated* myself for losing you."

I felt an urge to reach for him, but I was afraid to. "I don't understand. What are you trying to tell me?"

"Ava and I grew close," he said, looking away from me. "We . . ."

"So it's true, then. You slept with Ava?"

"Yes." The word was barely audible, barely anything more than a small exhale of air through those lips I'd kissed and loved.

"I don't even know what to say." I swallowed hard.

"You don't have to say anything, Ellie."

My fingers were numb. I tightened them into balls and stretched them back out to regain sensation, but as I did, the rest of my body began to lose feeling everywhere. "So she's not demonic or a spy or anything. The only reason she hates me is because you slept together. All this time, you told me there was nothing between you two, and there was."

He started to reach for my hands. "She's only my friend. She is nothing compared to the way I feel about you."

"You don't have *sex* with people who are *only friends*!"

"Ellie." He sighed my name in that way of his that could calm me during any storm but this one.

"You told me it wasn't what I thought! You *lied* to me!"

"I didn't lie to you," he said tiredly. "I never dated her. We were never anything more."

"Well, you wanted *something* from her!" As soon as I said it, I was sickened by myself. I didn't even know what I was saying anymore.

His expression darkened and his brow furrowed as anger boiled to the surface. "I didn't *want* anything from her! It was a mistake!"

Tears were streaming down both sides of my face now, pooling in the corners of my mouth. I didn't know how I'd gotten so upset so quickly. "So you broke it off with her? Just like you did with me?"

"I thought you were *gone*!" he repeated, his voice

breaking. When he spoke again, his voice was lower, but he had little more control. "I was *dead* inside. I believed I'd lost you, the only thing that made my life worth something! You are all I knew, Ellie, and I'd died along with you. I never loved her, never loved anyone but you in all these centuries. You were gone and I gave up. When I found you again, barely a year afterward . . . I can't describe to you what it felt like to see you again after believing with every last thread of my soul that you were gone forever. Seeing your smile brought me back to life and killed me again at the same time. I felt like I had to tell you, after all these centuries, how much you meant to me, how much I have always loved you, in case I lost you again and you never came back. In case I never got to say it to you at all."

I was sobbing now, and at some point I had sat down on the sofa and hadn't even realized it. I buried my face in my hands, tugging at my hair, desperate to rip the images of Will and Ava kissing, touching, out of my head forever. He sat tentatively next to me, but he didn't reach to comfort me, didn't murmur into my hair the way he often did when I was upset. He did nothing. When I pulled my hands away from my face and looked at him, he was watching me, his eyes dull and dark. It wasn't like we were together then, or even now, and it wasn't like he cheated on me. I didn't have a claim to him, but I felt like I did, and knowing all that didn't make it hurt any less. I couldn't be mad at him or hate him, because I didn't have a right to.

I stopped crying, wiped at my face with my hands, and climbed shakily to my feet. I faced him, looking down at him where he sat. He took my hand, his gaze lingering on it soberly, and I allowed him to pull me close. His touch was warm, unsteady, and gentle as he ran his fingers across my palm and wrist and then wrapped both his arms around my body. His palms opened on my lower back, and he tugged me toward him gently as he sat there, and he rested his face against my belly. He gave a small squeeze and kissed me there, his lips pressing to the sweater I wore. It took me a few moments to regain my composure and the strength to pick my hands up to touch his face, lift his chin, and smooth my fingers over his rough cheeks, his lips—and then he smiled beneath my fingertips, and my heart broke.

"I need you," he said, and turned his face to kiss my palm.

Something collapsed in my chest and my lips trembled. "I need you, too." I ran my fingers through the silk of his hair.

"Nothing has ever meant more to me than you," he whispered. "You are all I know."

"Don't say that," I said, shaking my head. "It's not true."

"I have never lied to you."

I had to leave before I started crying again. I pulled away from him, and his hands slipped from around my waist and fell. "I've got to get back to school before lunch hour is over."

"I know," he said.

Without saying good-bye, I left Nathaniel's house and drove back to school. The rest of the day went by in a blurred daze, and I made a point of avoiding meeting Kate, only texting her back to tell her that I had learned nothing at all.

11

I WROTE TWO PAPERS FOR SCHOOL THAT WEEK, AND by Thursday I needed some down time and to get out of my house. Will and I were still a little shaky after our fight-slash-discussion about his history with Ava. No one I knew would bother me at the library, and it sounded like the perfect escape. Snow began to fall, lightly enough that it would be safe to drive in the dark if I went slowly, but tomorrow I'd have to shovel the driveway for sure. Three hours before closing was the perfect amount of time for me to find a good book and curl up in one of the giant sofa chairs on the second floor.

After some searching through the stacks, I selected a book I'd first found on my mom's shelf when I was in middle school. I remembered being sucked in by the romance, so I grabbed it off the shelf and padded up the creaky stairs to the second-floor lounge, where it was quieter. I settled into a squishy chair next to an end table and lamp and lost myself in the novel. I didn't even notice the reaper in the room quietly suppressing his energy until he dipped his head over my shoulder and cast his shadow over the pages.

I jerked out of my seat to face him and dropped the book, startled by the sensation of the reaper's energy crawling on my skin like feather-light spider legs. "Cadan!" I cried out in a hushed voice.

He wore a gentle smile edged with amusement. The warm light in the library made the gold color of his hair even richer. "That book must be pretty good. You didn't even notice me until I was right next to you."

"What do you want?" For some reason, I wasn't afraid of him—though I really, *really* should have been. I couldn't explain the feeling. He never made me feel threatened.

"To see you."

I blinked. *"Why?"*

He didn't seem bothered by my suspicion. "Why not?"

Was he serious? "Cadan, we're enemies."

"Who decided that?" he asked, sounding genuinely curious. He stepped around my chair to sit in the one across from me. "If we were enemies, then I would have tried to kill you already."

"So far you haven't."

"But if you truly thought we were enemies, then wouldn't you have tried to kill *me* by now? You hunt the demonic almost every night, so it's not like you wait around to be attacked. You could have come after me, but you haven't, though I can't say I'm not disappointed." He touched my hair the way he had the night we first met. I watched his fingers treat the lock as if it were delicate. The tips of his fingers brushed my neck and trailed across my collarbone, sending my heart pounding.

I wasn't about to show any fear by backing away from him. "Don't make me get violent."

"Oh, baby," he whispered, his voice husky and his smile darkening. "Please do."

"You're into that sort of thing, are you?"

"I'm into *you*."

"This is extremely awkward," I said, unsure of how to react to his blatant flirting.

"I disagree." He let my hair fall, but he didn't step away. "I very much like this."

"It's barely even nighttime," I noted. "Shouldn't you nocturnal types be sleeping at this hour?"

"What can I say? I'm an early riser."

I was tired of being toyed with. "Why did you find me, Cadan? Besides to try to shower me with your charm. Last time I saw you, you came with a warning."

His smile faded again. "I'm sorry to say that I have another. Bastian has a relic, the Constantina necklace."

I frowned, thinking of Ava's anguish over Zane's death. "Tell something I don't know."

"So you located the relic's guardian," he deduced.

"What was left of him, yes."

His mouth tightened. "I suspected that he must have been killed in order to take the relic from him. The guardians never surrender."

"Who did it?"

"Vir," he said. "Their names are Merodach and Kelaeno. They are the ones helping Bastian find what he needs. And once they do that, they'll be coming for you."

"If Orek fails, you mean."

His gaze burned into mine. "Yes, I'm sorry. The situation is only going to get worse for you."

I studied his face, my head spinning to come up with the answer of his true allegiance. He knew so much about Bastian's plans, so they had to be close, but he was willing to risk everything to help me. "Why the espionage, Cadan?"

"I've already told you."

"The risk is too great," I insisted. "There must be something more. What's in it for you? Are you going to betray me?"

That smile came to life again. "Even if I said no, would you believe me?"

"I don't know. I don't even know if it's Bastian you're spying on or if it's me."

"Why can't you believe that I want you to stop him?" he asked earnestly.

I narrowed my gaze. "Why don't you do it yourself?"

He didn't answer me at first, and a strange look came over his face as his shoulders stiffened. His eyes broke away from mine and searched around us before returning. "It's complicated."

"No more complicated than our own arrangement."

His brow flickered with amusement, the uncertainty washing away in an instant. "Arrangement? And on what terms is this *arrangement*?"

I ignored that. "Is it because you aren't strong enough to kill him, or because you don't want to?"

His gaze moved slowly over my mouth and back up to my eyes. "Both."

"You're still loyal to him," I said. "And now to me, for some reason."

"I suppose you're right."

"You'll have to choose a side, Cadan."

He grinned and gave a single soft huff of a laugh, though his eyes looked sad. "That is also true."

I wasn't sure what to make of him. He was gorgeous and very mysterious, and I was indisputably drawn to him. Those things all made him dangerous, even if I believed he wouldn't raise a hand to me. Simply being his friend was dangerous to us both. I picked my book off the floor and set it on the end table before I sank back into the soft chair. "What is this necklace supposed to do, anyway?"

He sat down in the chair opposite mine and dragged it

closer. He leaned forward and spoke softly. "It was crafted by the Grigori Cardinal Lord of the East, Aldebaran. He tricked Constantina, the eldest daughter of the Roman emperor Constantine, into taking it."

"I remember her," I said, frowning as the memories flooded back to me. Constantina had been the driving force behind some of the earliest witch hunts, seventeen hundred years ago, executing innocent people and then taking everything valuable they owned for herself. The Grigori weren't exactly like the Fallen imprisoned in Hell, and they were bound to earth to help humans in penance. That meant they were not entirely evil, but they were also not entirely good. Aldebaran knew of Constantina's evil, and her underlings gave her the necklace cursed with angelic magic. Ever the greedy tyrant, she took it without hesitation, and within a month she was dead.

"If Bastian needs angelic magic," Cadan explained, "he'd want it straight from a Grigori Lord. The Lords hold the secrets of all angelic magic and medicine. The power of the Constantina necklace came from Aldebaran, and in its purest form."

"Were you around when the relic was created?" I asked.

"No, I'm not that old," he said. "I was born during the Fourth Crusade."

I gave a nervous laugh. "Oh, not that old. Only about eight centuries."

"My father is over a thousand years old," he mused.

"Only the most powerful of my kind live to be ancient."

I wondered exactly how strong Cadan was. "Is your father still alive?"

He hesitated in answering. "He is."

"Have you ever met a Grigori?"

"I have."

When it didn't appear that he'd elaborate, I asked him, "And?"

"She hates me."

"Really? That's so surprising," I asked, my sarcasm obvious.

"I tried to kill her." The statement was crisp and matter-of-fact.

"Well, then you can't blame her."

He smiled widely and I smiled back. "I suppose you're right."

"I hope there's a good story to go along with that," I said.

"Don't you humans have a Valentine's Day ritual coming?" he asked. "I believe I understand how it works. Two of you pair up in the name of love. That would make for a good story. Especially if I were involved."

I glowered. "Don't change the subject."

"You seem so sore. No date?"

"I don't need one."

He tilted his head at me with a silly, adorable smile. "I'll be your valentine."

I laughed out loud. "Yeah, right. That'll go over well."

"It doesn't sound like you're against the idea. Do you think your Guardian would be jealous?"

I did my best to give him a serious look as I fought back laughter. "Cadan, you are not going to be my date. And you're avoiding all of my questions."

He frowned. "The answers aren't so exciting, believe me."

I recalled Ava's story about the relic guardian. "So, this Grigori who hates you. You aren't old lovers, are you?"

"No." He laughed. "No, no. She had something I wanted, and she wouldn't give it to me. It's a story for another time."

I folded my arms over my chest. "If you won't talk about the Grigori, then I won't talk about Valentine's Day."

That sly smile crept back into his sculpted lips. "I meant it when I said I'd be your date. I love parties. We first met at a party. Don't you find it oddly romantic?"

I narrowed my eyes. "Odd, yes. Romantic, no."

He frowned. "That hurts. Really."

"I'm sure you'll survive."

"Speaking of romance," he started, "are you going to tell me about this book you were so engrossed in that you barely even noticed me?"

I gave him a sidelong glance. "You really want to know?"

"I'd like to understand what captivates you," he said. "So that I may aspire to do the same."

"Would you like a little wine to go with all that cheese?" I asked.

"Would you like me better if I were gloomy and morose?" He grinned, his eyes teasing.

"I wouldn't like you much at all if you were either of those."

He leaned back and lazily put his elbows up on the back of his chair. "Then what is the appeal of your Guardian? He is quite definitely gloomy and morose."

I'd let Cadan have one point. "Don't you think morose is a little severe?"

"You must agree that he is rather moody and glum."

"He's not glum."

His grin widened. "So you admit that he's gloomy and moody."

"I never said that."

"But you don't deny it."

I exhaled in annoyance. "You're obnoxious."

"But at least I'm not morose."

"Will isn't *morose*."

"Tell me about the book you're reading."

I blinked in surprise. Was he serious? He sat beaming with self-satisfaction. Playing games with my head was apparently hilarious. He was insufferable.

"Please?"

I stared at him. He was serious. "Okay then."

I didn't even realize what time it was until the librarian came into the room and told us they were closing. I was shocked that I'd had such a good time and that I was sorry it was over.

"And this is where I leave you," he said, standing.

I followed, watching him carefully. "It was nice talking to you."

He took my hand and kissed my knuckles, his lips and breath warm. "It's always a pleasure."

He stepped aside and held out his arm to allow me first through the door. He followed me out of the library, and I stopped at the bottom of the steps. The night air was very cold, and snow fell generously. I turned toward Cadan and looked up at him. He wasn't quite as tall as Will, but he was built strong, and he was beautiful.

"Really, Cadan," I said. "Thank you. I've had a pretty bad week, but you made me feel better."

"Then I can die happy," he replied dramatically.

I rolled my eyes. "Cut it out. I'm being serious. I enjoyed talking to you."

He smiled warmly. "I hope we can do it again soon."

"Are you going to tell me that story?" I teased. "About the Grigori?"

His smile widened. "Maybe. Good night, Ellie."

"Good night." I smiled at him before walking away.

I was conflicted. I felt like Cadan was my friend and definitely not my enemy. He was demonic by birth, but there was nothing about him that radiated evil. Will was so sure that demonic reapers only wanted the destruction of the world and my death above all, but Cadan didn't want to kill me. He'd had a thousand opportunities so far.

Or was I just an incredible fool?

A shadow passed over my head, and I looked up, startled.

A reaper appeared out of the Grim, ash-gray wings spread wide through the falling snow. White-blond hair billowed and settled as the reaper landed. Cold, pale eyes locked on mine.

Ivar. Her body moved so fast that the heavy cloth of the black cloak she wore lifted in the air behind her. The gray furred hood fell off her head as she lunged for me, clawed hand outstretched. I knocked her arm aside, stopping her fingers from clenching around my throat. I scrambled back as she recovered her balance and beat her wings to take another leap for me. Her cloak and dress swelled midflight.

She vanished.

Something invisible struck me viciously in the chest, sending me flying across the empty parking lot. I landed and skidded nearly twenty feet on the slick pavement before I stopped myself and jumped to my feet. I threw off my coat and followed Ivar into the Grim before she could strike me again. Her form materialized, and I whirled out of the way as her talons slashed at my face. She blurred by me, and I took the moment to breathe.

"You crazy psycho!" I shouted at her back. Will was miles away from me. By this time, he would have sensed my distress and be on his way, but until he arrived I'd have to fight Ivar alone.

She spun to face me. Her eyes were bright and wild, her expression twisted with rage. I willed my swords into my hands as she began to circle me. Angelfire erupted and lit up the rage on her face. She held out both arms and long blades appeared.

"He's *mine*," she snarled, raising the hair on the back of my neck. She leaped into the air, high over my head, blades diving down at my body. I braced on my heel and summoned my power.

Another sword swung up and clanged against Ivar's swords between us. She hissed and reeled back, landing a few feet away.

Cadan.

I gaped at him as he stepped between Ivar and me. His own wings—feathers again, the silver-gray flashing gold in the streetlights—stretched out from his back, and he pointed his sword at Ivar. Snowflakes stuck to our hair and clothes.

"You raise your blade to me?" Ivar snarled, her voice shaking with surprise and hurt.

"Ivar," he bellowed. "What are you doing?"

Her lips pulled back, exposing needlelike fangs. Her blades gleamed as she raised them menacingly. "What are *you* doing? To *me*?"

Cadan glared impatiently, the annoyance plain in his face. "I haven't done anything to you."

"Haven't you?" Her voice cracked with desperation.

Suddenly I understood, and it was all very disturbing. This was not a love triangle I wanted to be caught up in. Perhaps love wasn't the right word—it was more like a psycho-demonic-reaper-obsession triangle.

"You've lost your mind, Ivar," he said, folding and lowering his wings. He may have meant the gesture to make him appear less aggressive, but he looked no less frightening.

She laughed high and smoothly. "And you? Spending quality time with the Preliator? Our eternal enemy? You've lost *your* mind, Cadan."

"None of you would unders—"

"If Bastian only knew."

"He doesn't have to know."

"You shame him!" she screeched. "And me! I love you, Cadan!"

His jaw tightened and he swallowed.

"Okay," I said slowly. "This is clearly none of my business, so I'll just go." I started to back away, but Ivar jumped into the air and landed right behind me. I threw my swords up, ready to defend myself.

"I refuse to watch you with her," Ivar said, stepping toward me, her eyes on me. "She's an archangel, Cadan. You know how wrong this is! You know that you belong to me!"

His gaze darkened, and his opal eyes blazed with fire of every color, the light bright in the darkness. "I belong to no one."

"Tell me you love me," she begged. "Say it, and I won't harm her this night."

I looked at Cadan, who'd stepped up to my side. Ivar's expression was wiped clean of the disgust and rage. She waited and I held my breath so that the only thing I heard was my heart pounding in my chest. She was about to kill me.

"Cadan, I really think you should say it," I suggested.

"Not now, Ellie." His voice was cold. For the first time since I'd met him, it was clear he was in no mood to joke.

Ivar's lip curled. "What will it be?"

He remained silent.

"Then so be it," she said.

Her wings spread and flapped, sending her body rocketing toward me, swords flying. I ducked under one blade and Cadan's sword stopped her other. I slashed a sword across her face, and she stumbled back with a grunt but stayed standing, cheek bleeding. She righted herself and blasted her power into Cadan's chest, blowing him away from us. She charged, snarling in rage, and cracked her elbow into my cheek. I hit the ground hard. Dazed, I barely saw Ivar drive her blade down at my face—but Cadan, appearing between us in a flash, shoved his sword into her chest. She doubled over, her hair brushing my face, and her arms hung limp at her sides. Blood dribbled from her lips and poured down Cadan's sword. The seconds dragged on as she lost her strength to keep her swords and they slipped back into nothingness. I scrambled away and climbed to my feet.

Cadan stood and tugged his sword from her body. Things cracked inside, and she cried out in agony, falling onto her knees. Her body suddenly lurched upright, but she lost her balance and staggered back, nearly collapsing again. Her hand clutched the wound in her chest as blood seeped from it. She lifted her head heavily and stared at Cadan. The look in her eyes broke my heart, despite my hatred for her.

"Why?" she sputtered.

Cadan's expression remained cruelly resolute as he stepped up to her and raised his sword again, the blade glossy and wet with Ivar's blood.

Her eyes were glued to his. "You're going to kill me?"

"I'm sorry," he said. "But I can't let you go back to Bastian knowing what you know. I can't let any of this happen."

He swung, lightning fast, sweeping the blade through her neck cleanly. Her head slipped free, hit the ground, and rolled away, her pale hair streaked with red. Her body hardened to stone, and as she collapsed, it shattered into a thousand pieces.

I shut my eyes for just a moment, feeling Ivar's pain echoing through my heart. When I opened them again, I saw that Cadan hadn't moved except to let his arms hang heavily. He stared at Ivar's remains and said nothing.

I stepped closer to him, reaching out a hand to touch him, but he jerked away from me. "Cadan—?"

He turned his face only slightly in my direction, but it

was enough for me to see the shattering pain across his face. With that look, I wondered if he might have loved Ivar once or if something had happened between them.

"Don't, Ellie," he said. His voice wasn't cold or cruel, just full of hurt.

I studied his face carefully, perplexed by what had just happened. "Are you okay?"

His fiery eyes were dull, and he didn't look away from me. Snowflakes clung to his hair. "No."

His wings spread and he leaped into the air, disappearing from sight as he melted into the Grim.

And then it was just me and Ivar's crumbled remains. I didn't move, didn't speak, just sat there on the cold pavement as the snow settled on me. The cold was beginning to affect me, but I couldn't bring myself to move to reach my coat.

"Ellie?"

I blinked at the sound of my name. My first thought was that Cadan had come back, but then I saw Will running toward me.

"Ellie," he called again as he reached me and dropped to his knees. He inspected me as usual, but I didn't even have a scratch on me. Thanks to Cadan. Fuzz balls swarmed in my head again as the reality hit me.

"What happened?" Will asked. "Are you hurt?"

I shook my head. "He killed her."

"Who?" he asked, brushing my hair out of my face. "Who killed who?" He noticed my shivering and grabbed my coat and wrapped it around my shoulders. It didn't help at all.

"Cadan," I said robotically, still staring at the stone pile in front of me. "He killed Ivar."

Will paused, maybe to absorb the absurd truth I'd just given him. "Are you serious?"

"Yes. She was going to tell Bastian that Cadan has been talking to me and then she attacked me. He stopped her from doing both. He killed her to protect me."

"Ivar's dead," Will said in disbelief. "And Cadan tracked you down again? Ellie, you can't—"

"It's not like that," I interjected. "He's helped me! The necklace Zane was protecting, it was made by Aldebaran, the Lord of the East, and it's cursed with some seriously strong mojo. It's the real deal, and Cadan warned me that the same demonic vir who took Zane out will be coming for me next. Their names are Merodach and Kelaeno, and they've got almost everything they need for Bastian. Cadan killed Ivar to protect the information he told me, so don't just dismiss this."

Will's jaw tightened. "All right. We'll look into this with Nathaniel, but please don't see Cadan alone again. *Please.*"

"It's not like I'm going looking for him," I grumbled. "Cadan really wants to help us. He's risking his life to do so."

Another long silence. I couldn't blame him. I wouldn't have believed me, either. At least there was one less of Bastian's lackeys to worry about. A demonic reaper asked to be my valentine and then killed his crazy ex-girlfriend to save my life. Tomorrow I was starting up antipsychotic meds.

"Let's get you home before your fingers freeze off," Will suggested. He stood and took my hand, then helped me to my feet, and we walked to my car in silence.

12

"WHAT ARE YOU DOING AGAIN?" WILL ASKED IN A bored voice, on the other side of my closet door. "A Valentine's Day party?"

I rolled my eyes as I shimmied the red strapless sheath dress up and over my hips. The difficulty in accomplishing this made me wish I'd started putting it on over my head. "It is not a Valentine's Day party. That would be lame."

He laughed. "It's the same thing."

"No, it's not," I grumbled. "This is a Hearts Afire party. Totally different."

"How is it different? Valentine's Day is in a few days."

"It's a *Hearts Afire* party." The seam along the side of the dress was ruched and allowed a little movement, and the pencil shape gave me more of an hourglass figure than I had in normal clothes. I leaned against the closet shelves to keep my balance as I slipped on a pair of black heels.

All I needed now was someone to zip up my dress in the back. I examined myself vainly from every angle in the floor-length mirror hooked onto the back of my closet door. It used to be on the other side of my door, but the more Will hung out over here while I was getting ready, the more I had needed to switch it so I could change in private. I had to make sure I looked good *before* leaving the closet. "Why do you care anyway?"

"You go to these parties a lot."

"Do not. This is my first party in practically a month."

"Didn't Kate have a party two weeks ago?"

I glowered. "That was in *January*. It's February now. What are you going to do when I'm at college and go to parties three nights a week? You're going to go crazy."

"I hope you can fit patrolling in between all these future parties."

"I live like five different lives. I'm the goddess of multitasking. You know this."

I opened the closet door and stepped out. Heat flushed through me when Will's eyes went wide and he gaped at me from my desk chair.

I strode across the room toward him, my hand pinning the front of my dress to my chest. "I need your help."

"What?" His eyebrows lifted almost imperceptibly, but there was no way I could have missed that look.

I chomped on the inside of my cheek to keep from

grinning like an idiot and turned my back to him. "Zip me?"

"Uh, yeah."

The heat of his gaze on my back was scorching as he stood up. His fingers brushed my bare skin as he zipped up the remaining inches of my open dress.

"You look . . . beautiful," he said softly, the breath of his words on my neck.

I inhaled deeply and swallowed hard as I imagined him drawing the zipper in the opposite direction and his lips touching the place his breath had warmed. Things fluttered in my chest, and I shivered. "Thank you."

He didn't step away and I didn't move for the longest, most excruciating moment. At last I turned to my dresser to touch up my makeup in the mirror. I glanced at him from the corner of my eye and grinned, my confidence returning.

"You've got a little drool," I teased, tapping the corner of my mouth. "Right here."

His cheeks actually grew rosy and he gave a nervous laugh as he sat back down on the chair. "You're funny. Really."

I looked back into the mirror and applied another coat of mascara. My heart pounded as I tried to be fearless. "Not as funny as your face right now."

"How can you walk in those heels?" he asked, changing the subject.

"You have entirely too little faith in me." I turned around to look at his outfit. I grimaced. "Is that what you're wearing? Really?"

He frowned and looked down at his jeans and long-sleeved tee. "What's wrong with it?"

I tilted my head to examine him. "You look normal. You don't look afire at all. At least your shirt is black. Dress code said red or black only. Anything else will get you thrown out, just warning you."

"Ellie," he said, sucking in his top lip, "I know you love these parties and I don't mind going with you. I *prefer* being with you. But I hate it when you make me dress up for them. That's just not me."

I stepped toward him and ran my hand through his hair, something that I knew calmed him—and me. He closed his eyes, and butterflies danced through my belly. "I'm sorry. I just really like to torture you."

He opened his green eyes to meet mine, but he didn't respond. This was the first time I'd really looked into his face since the night he told me he'd slept with Ava. I tried so hard not to think about her, and about Will's hands on her the way I wanted them on me, but the longer my gaze lingered on his, the more the vise around my heart tightened. I felt my lip quiver once and I tightened my jaw immediately, but it was too late. He caught the break in my expression and a look of worry passed across his face.

"Are you ready?" I asked, wheeling away from him before I let a tear come.

He let out a tired breath. "Yeah."

Josie Newport's parents had an obscene amount of money, and their house was gorgeous. Since they were always out of town and the housekeepers let her do just about whatever she wanted, her parties were amazing. Josie and I had been close when we were little because our moms were friends, but as the years went by, Josie's mom became more interested in pricey vacations and making sure her husband's wandering eye didn't turn into wandering hands and other wandering whatnots. Josie was a sweetheart, though, and my friends and I got invited to her parties.

I strolled up the plowed drive in my four-inch heels with Will trailing behind me. The line of parked cars stretched all the way down the drive to the gatehouse by the main road. Before I even entered the mansion, I could hear the music thumping. I glanced back at Will, who met my gaze after he finished surveying the snow-covered lawn. I gave him a reassuring smile.

I raised my hand to knock, but the butler opened the door at just that moment. The walls of Josie's grand foyer were draped with textured red cloth, and bright red light streamed up from the floor. We followed the red drapes through a vast corridor where they were blown by a wind machine. They looked gorgeous clouding in the wind with the red floor lights dancing against the cloth.

The corridor opened up to the banquet hall—which was a lot more like a ballroom—and I smiled wide when I saw practically the entire senior class dancing, all wearing red or black as required. More drapes hung from a chandelier in the center of the room and extended to the walls. White lights hung from the ceiling like stars, and the DJ booth at the front of the long room glittered with white and red lights.

Knowing Will wouldn't dance with me, I looked around at the many faces in hopes that I'd spot Kate. I told Will that I'd be right back and pushed my way through the sea of red and black but didn't find her anywhere. Doubling back, I looked for Will and scowled. He already had some girl on him, running her mouth, and he looked entirely bored.

When I walked up to them, the girl gave me a dirty look. I just rolled my eyes and grabbed Will's arm before dragging him off, despite her protest.

"I can't take you anywhere, can I?" I grumbled.

"I was waiting for you to come back," he replied. "I didn't move."

I sighed. "I'm still looking for Kate, so try not to get picked up while I'm gone, all right?"

He gave me a puzzled look. How anyone could be that clueless was beyond me. "She's right there," he said, looking over my shoulder.

I followed his gaze. Sure enough, Kate stomped toward us like a supermodel on the catwalk, wearing a bubble cocktail dress made of gleaming white satin.

"The invitation said black or red only," I said, raising an eyebrow. "What happened to the dress you tried on?"

"I don't like to blend in," she said dismissively. She gave me a wide smile. "Your dress looks gorgeous on you. Doesn't she look gorgeous, Will?" She stared at him expectantly.

"Always," he said.

Kate grinned with approval. She looked around and waved at someone across the room. Marcus. He sauntered over to us wearing a deep-red tuxedo. He wrapped an arm around Kate's waist and kissed her on the cheek, lighting a spark of uneasiness in my gut.

"Will, Ellie." He greeted us with a smile and met my gaze. "You're looking lovely."

"Thanks," I said. "I like your suit. You look like the fanciest tomato I've ever seen in my life."

He laughed. "How sweet of you. I really do like your dress. Red is a good color on you."

A river of ice rushed through my veins. Bastian had said the same thing to me when I'd met him, but instead of wearing a red dress that night, I had been drenched with blood.

Marcus gave me a strange look. "You okay, Ell?"

I brushed it off. "I'm fine. I'll be right back." I needed a cool drink. The refreshments buffet was along the adjacent wall, near some plush chairs and loveseats set in the darkest corner of the room. I walked over and filled a cup with punch and sipped quickly, relishing the cool, sugary syrup running down my throat.

"Did I say something wrong?" asked Marcus as he stopped by my side.

I waved a hand at him. "When you said red was a good color on me, it reminded me . . . it's just something that Bastian said to me. Got a little freaked out for a second. I'm all right."

"I'm sorry," he said gently. "I didn't mean to bring up a bad memory." He held out a hand. "Dance with me."

I stared at his hand and then his face. "Really?"

"Oh, yes," he said. "I am a superb dancer. Now, I want to see a smile on your face."

He led me out to the dance floor and immediately spun and twirled me around like a professional. We dipped and whirled through the crowd, laughing and having a great time. I wished that Marcus was someone else, but I was happy having fun with him. When the song ended, I gave him a big hug and he returned it tightly.

"That's much better," he said, laughing. "You're beautiful when you smile."

Suddenly Kate shoved her way through the swarm of dancing people and grabbed my arm. "Save me."

"Why?" I sputtered as she yanked me off the dance floor and dragged me into a quiet parlor down the hall.

"Josie," she said. "Apparently there was a reason why she said everyone had to wear red or black. *She*'s wearing white."

I grimaced. Of course Josie would want to be the one person standing out. "She's pissed, huh?"

"I didn't think she had it in her to get angry, but she gave me a look like straight-up murder."

"Should we flee?"

"No," she said. "Let's just chill in here for a bit. Let her find something sparkly to distract her."

"Wise move," I noted.

Kate's face brightened and she grinned. "Doesn't Marcus look hot tonight?"

"Smokin'."

"I think I'm falling for him, Ell."

I forced a smile. "Really? Are you sure that's a good idea?"

Her grin faded. "What's that supposed to mean?"

"He's just . . . ," I started, trying to dig out the right words. "He's not a normal guy."

"I know!" she chirped. "And that's what makes him so amazing. He's drop-dead gorgeous, so smart, he dresses *so* nice, and his *eyes*. Have you *seen* his eyes? They're like gem-stones. They don't even look *real*. And sometimes I swear they get brighter. Kind of like how Will's eyes get, you know? Not that I was checking him out . . . all the time . . ."

I gave her a fake glare. "Yeah, well . . . ," I trailed off nervously. Marcus and Will were reapers. Their eyes were pretty much out of this world, just like the rest of them.

She smiled to herself. "And he's sweet to me, Ell. No

games, no immature high school boy nonsense. He is everything I want."

"Could it be too good to be true?"

She frowned. "What is the matter with you? Do you think I'm just a piece of ass on his to-do list? I'm sensing a lot of hate here."

"No, no, not hate," I said. "He's just . . . he's dangerous, Kate."

She laughed. "Oh, seriously? What, is he in fight club or something? Oh wait. We're not supposed to talk about that."

"I *am* serious, Kate," I said firmly. "Look, just be careful."

"Why do you want me to stay away from him so badly?" she asked, folding her arms over her chest. "Do *you* like him?"

"No! You know that's not true. You know how I feel about Will."

"I'm sorry, but I just don't understand."

The truth was, I couldn't explain it to her. Maybe it was because immortal reapers descended from Fallen angels didn't make good boyfriends because they had centuries' worth of serious baggage. Maybe it was because they didn't know how to function in the real world and didn't understand human beings. Or maybe I was just talking about Will.

"Will told me," I said hesitantly. "He wouldn't really explain. He just said that Marcus has been in some trouble before."

Kate rolled her eyes and huffed. "You don't believe that story Marcus told about getting his scar in a knife fight, do you? Unless you tell me that he's killed somebody, I'm going to keep seeing him."

I thought better of responding to that. Chances were pretty good that Marcus had killed someone—*many* someones—since he hunted demonic reapers with Ava.

Ugh. Ava. I still hadn't told Kate about what I'd learned. "Do you remember that girl Will was hanging out with who you convinced me to follow a couple weeks ago? Which, by the way, was a terrible idea."

She grimaced. "Yeah, his 'old friend.'"

"Well, my suspicions were right," I admitted.

Her eyes bulged. "No! He cheated on you?"

I shook my head firmly. "He never cheated on me. We weren't together. But he and this girl, Ava . . . they've slept together."

"I'm sorry, Ell. They aren't *still*, are they?"

"No," I said. "It was a long time ago."

"Ell." Kate sighed. "I hate to break it to you, sweetheart, but you're very naïve. People who are 'just friends' have sex all the time. Friends with benefits—ever heard of it?"

The sick feeling was beginning to swirl through my belly again. "Well, he said he had never wanted even *that* with her, that he was going through a horrible time and it was a mistake." I wasn't going to tell her that *I* was the reason behind his dark period.

Her expression became more sympathetic. "Mistakes definitely happen. You can't hold it against him."

"It just makes things so awkward," I said. "I can't be mad at either of them, obviously. I'm just . . . jealous of her, I guess."

She nodded and her expression softened. "I understand. Nobody wants to be around their boyfriend's ex, especially if she's gorgeous."

"Will isn't my boyfriend," I corrected her. He never *had* been in reality, but describing him as my boyfriend to people in the real world helped explain his constant presence in my life. "Which makes it even harder for me to be jealous."

"Same diff," she said. "Whether he's your boyfriend now or last month or whenever, it still hurts. I'm sorry you have to deal with her."

I shrugged. "Yeah. She hangs out with Will and Marcus all the time."

Her eyes darkened. "She'd better not touch Marcus."

I laughed in an attempt to ease the tension in my body. "She doesn't. They work together. Kind of."

Kate sat up and grunted. "Well, girl better keep her claws off both our boys. Marcus and I are going back to his place after the party. And no, I'm not going to sleep with him, so get that out of your head. I've only known him for a few weeks."

Maybe Kate would be fine. Marcus was dangerous, but I didn't think he was a danger to her specifically. I loved Kate like a sister, but I had to trust her judgment. And if Will didn't seem concerned either, then things might just turn out okay. I still wanted to talk to Marcus one more time and get his story straight.

As if he'd heard me say his name in my head or, more likely, he'd heard us talking about him the entire time, Marcus entered the room from the hall with a *very* cocky grin on his face. He'd definitely heard us talking about him.

"Am I interrupting anything?" he asked.

"Talking about you, of course," Kate said.

He laughed. "I figured. Come join the party. Ellie, your Will looks very exhausted from fighting off girls all night. Might you want to rescue him?"

I rolled my eyes. "All he does is scowl and ignore them. The whole thing is hilarious. I have no idea why they keep harassing him."

"Because he's hot and has tattoos," Kate offered, looking at me like I was an idiot. "Why *wouldn't* their hands be all over him? Speaking of, why aren't *your* hands all over him?" She took my hand. "Ready?"

"Yup. Onward."

We headed back out to the dance hall when one of my favorite songs began to play. I spotted Will just where I'd left him, standing there patiently and looking a little bored.

"Are you better?" he asked, placing his hand over mine.

"Yes, much."

He rewarded me with a smile.

"Will you dance with me tonight?"

The smile faded and he hesitated before answering. "Ellie—"

"Forget it," I said, and stomped away from him. He called my name, but I didn't turn back.

Marcus appeared in front of me with a pitying look. "You should have worn a different dress."

I folded my arms over my chest. "I thought you liked it."

"Oh, *very* much, but you're killing your Guardian over there," Marcus said with a nod in Will's direction.

I rolled my eyes and tried not to blush. "Well, he's killing me too." But the last thing I wanted to do was talk to Marcus about my problems with Will. "Can I talk to you about Kate, actually?"

He frowned. "You may."

"You understand what a bad idea it is, right?"

"I understand your concern," he said. "But if it's worth anything to you, I do care about her. She means something to me."

"Why?" I asked. "You're two hundred years old. How many girls have you met, slept with, fallen in love with? How is Kate the one to tame you?"

He laughed. "You have it all wrong. Kate is special. She's a beautiful creature, tough to keep up with, and always gives you everything she's got. But you have to understand. I am immortal. Nothing holds an immortal's attention for very long, save for one exception. You and your Will."

"Will is my Guardian," I snapped back. "It's different."

He huffed and grinned. "Sure it is."

"My situation with Will is not an excuse for you to get innocent human girls to fall in love with you and get into your bed."

"Believe me," he said. "I don't intend to hurt Kate. It's quite the opposite, actually."

"But you intend to leave her when you get bored."

"You completely underestimate her."

"How so?" I asked defiantly.

"Do you really think she'll be heartbroken over me? She's not that kind of girl. She would move on from me in no time."

I narrowed my gaze. "Maybe you're right, but she's starting to fall for you, Marcus. You know how wrong this is."

"How is it any different from you and Will?"

"We aren't together."

"Come on, Ellie," he said. "Don't be ridiculous. You're both mad about each other—have been for as long as I've known either of you, and longer still."

"We *can't* be together," I clarified. "For a million reasons, including the same reason you and Kate will never work out."

The amusement washed away from his expression. "At least you'll always return when you die."

I stared at him. "Then you should at least know better than to end up hurting *yourself*, let alone Kate. It's a little masochistic, don't you think?"

He leaned toward me, anger tracing his brow. "And have you thought of the effects on Will? As each of your lifetimes passes, he's still steady as stone for you. Yes, perhaps I will mourn Kate, but I will only ever mourn her once."

He spun away from me, his anger washing away any trace of his charisma and smoothness. I turned away from the crowd to face the wall, and an awful sob escaped me. I rushed for the bathroom as the music and roar of the party came crashing down on my head.

Just as I got to the door, I felt a warm, strong hand on my bare arm.

"Ellie."

I turned to face Will. His crystalline green gaze was compassionate and worried. "I'm fine," I said sharply.

"No, you're not." He always knew.

I pulled away. "Don't you care about yourself?"

He blinked in confusion. "What?"

"Never mind," I said, putting my back to him, and I kept going.

"Ellie," he called after me, following me. "You're confusing me. I don't know what you're talking about. Did I do something wrong?"

I turned toward him and leaned against the wall beside the bathroom door. "Why do you do this to yourself? Torture yourself by staying as my Guardian?"

He leaned over me until I was drowning in him. "Ellie—"

"I know why you won't be with me," I said, straightening

myself against the wall. "It's not just that you're afraid of Michael. It's because the only way we can stay together is for me to die over and over again."

Will closed his eyes and tightened his mouth without a response, but I knew what he was thinking. Rules he could break. Michael he could fight. He was most afraid that if he let down the wall he built up between us, then it would hurt too much to give in and love me as much as he ached to. If he did, I would still die regardless, and he would finally break.

I took a step back from him, and he let me go without protest. I didn't look away from him until I was inside the bathroom. The door shut behind me and I locked it. My back hit the wall, and I slid to the floor and cried. I heard his fist pound once on the wall in anger, just outside the room. I didn't want to end the night crying on the bathroom floor. It was so hard for me to see him every day and want him so badly, but yet again I had forgotten about how much it hurt him to feel the same way. It was so painful for us to be apart, but I didn't know if either of us was strong enough to be together.

13

ON THE WAY HOME, WILL AND I SAID NOTHING TO each other, and I was glad for it. I parked in my driveway and shut the car off. Neither of us moved to get out, and my muscles just wouldn't listen to my brain. I felt naked, silly, and ridiculous in this tiny dress and painful high heels, with all my makeup washed off my face. I pulled my hair out of its updo and shook it loose to cover my shoulders. It was barely midnight, but I felt like I'd been awake for days.

I opened my mouth to stay something to Will and turned to him, but he'd vanished from the car. Disappointment made me unwilling to move, but I forced the car door open and climbed out. As I went inside, I got a text from Kate. My battery was almost dead, but I read the text quickly.

Love u

I smiled weakly at it before dropping my phone back into

my bag. I heard the TV on in the living room, so I doubled back, opting to go through the kitchen to avoid my parents, but I was too late.

"Ellie Bean?" called my mom's voice. "Home already?"

I let out a long breath and went into the living room to face her. Thankfully, my dad was nowhere in sight. She was sitting on the couch with just the quiet glow of the television on her form and a mug of hot tea in her hand.

"Hey, Mom," I said.

"What's wrong, sweetie?" she asked, holding her arms out as a cue for me to come sit with her.

I plopped beside her, and she set down her mug to wrap me in her arms and hold me close. I sank deep into her, finding peace in the warmth and softness of her robe and pajamas. A couple of leftover Christmas candles were lit on the mantel above the fireplace, and their rich scents flooded the room.

"The night ended not so great," I said with a sigh, and laid my head down in her lap.

She stroked my hair gently, the way she used to when I was a little girl. "I'm sorry, Ell. You look so pretty in your dress."

"Thanks."

She paused. "Was Will there?"

"Yeah."

"Was he rude to you?"

"No," I said. "No, not at all. Things are just . . . complicated between us."

"Want to talk about it?"

"Not tonight. What are you watching?" I looked at the TV screen for the first time and watched thousands of shimmering silver fish move in unison in front of the camera. Their perfection was beautiful, the symmetry of their movement almost hypnotic. I stared at the screen from my horizontal position, listening to a soft piano play as the fish danced their ballet lit by the sunlight filtering through the blue water. My mother's hands brushed my cheek and my hair, gentle like feathers, and I felt like a little girl again, comforted by her touch.

"I love you, Mom," I said softly.

"Love you, too, baby."

I fell quiet again and gazed up at the TV as a diver floated into the wall of silver scales and fins. I let myself drift into senselessness, trying to forget how heartsick I was, to forget how to feel anything at all. The swarm of fish pushed away from the faceless diver and began to spiral around his body like spinning stars.

Will was sitting on my bed when I got to my room. He'd discarded his long-sleeved shirt and had on just his jeans and T-shirt. He looked up as I entered, and our eyes met for a moment. I sat down to his right side on the bed and reached up a hand to smooth out his disheveled hair, and my eyes fell to the silver chain around his neck. The chain slipped between my fingers, and I drew the crucifix out the collar of his shirt. My fingers brushed the silver against his chest, the fondness of my memories of it pressing down on my heart, and my gaze moved to his tattoos. My hand slid across his skin to trace the delicate swirls of ink down his neck and arm. The muscle beneath his skin rippled at my touch, and he watched me in silence. My finger followed each intricate line of ink, and as the memory came, the sadness in my heart sank into my stomach. I realized now that this was the old angelic language I'd forgotten long ago, and it was my true name tattooed down his arm. I brushed my fingertips across the script, and he trembled and took a deep breath.

"It's my name," I said softly. "I remember now. The language in your tattoo that gives you my protection, it's my sigil. It binds you to me, makes you mine. It's my name."

His gaze followed my fingers and rose to meet my eyes. "Gabriel," he said, his lips brushing my ear.

I fought back a tear as he said my true name and kissed my bare shoulder. I pressed into him and squeezed my eyes shut. He pulled me close, wrapping his arms around me, and kissed my hair.

"I'm sorry," he breathed. "You're right. I fear Michael, but I fear losing you so much more. I don't want him to take you away from me, but if I don't keep my distance, I *will* lose you."

And then he drew away suddenly and left me cold. When I opened my eyes, he was halfway across my room, heading toward the window.

"Will," I said.

He turned back to face me, but before he could speak, his cell rang. He gave me an apologetic glance as he took his phone out to answer.

"Ava?"

I felt like I was falling.

His expression became hard and worried. "Are you okay? Where are you? How many of them? No, no. We're coming." He shoved his phone back into his pocket. "Ellie, we have to go. Orek ambushed Ava, and he's fighting her in the mortal world. She can't contain him by herself."

I jumped up and grabbed a pair of jeans and a sweater. I was exhausted and I didn't want to leave my warm house, but I had a duty to carry out. And Ava needed help. "Meet me in my car."

He vanished. I pulled on the warmer clothes and then crept silently from my room through the Grim and down the stairs to the back door. I darted around the house on the concrete sidewalk and down the long driveway to my car. Will waited in the driver's seat, and I jumped in the passenger side.

"Where are they?"

"Downtown."

"Oh, God."

* * *

Will sensed Ava and Orek at the precise moment that I did. He parked my car in a safe place, and we tried to gauge their positions. I focused harder on the reaper energy, and my eyes widened with shock as I realized that they were fighting somewhere above us.

"The rooftops!" I cried, and sprinted into an alley.

We climbed a fire escape and spotted Orek's massive body plainly visible several rooftops away. I didn't see Ava. I took off like a shot, both my Khopesh swords in hand, alight with angelfire, leaping from rooftop to rooftop, praying the busy street below wouldn't take notice.

Orek was atop one of the tallest buildings on the block, six stories above the street. When we got close, I saw that he had Ava pinned beneath one of his powerful hind legs.

"Ava!" I cried.

Orek swung his giant dragonlike head and long neck to look at me with his pale, unseeing eyes. His nostrils flared and his jaw dropped to hiss at me. "Preliator! About damned time. I've grown bored with this one. She doesn't scream."

He stepped off Ava and stomped toward me. The front of Ava's body was soaked red, and she wasn't moving. She had to be alive, since her body hadn't become stone in death, but she was very badly hurt.

Orek's wings spread wide and menacing, and for a moment he looked twice his normal size. "I was hoping you could make it tonight."

"Ellie," Will said in a low voice. "I'm going to distract Orek. Make sure Ava is okay. Get her out of the way so she can heal without further damage."

"He's after *me*," I said back. "I'm the one he'll follow. Let me distract him."

Will called his sword, the silver shimmering in the city lights. "Not a chance."

He charged forward, his blade sweeping, and the nycterid reaper reared up like a dragon. They collided; Will's sword cut through flesh as the reaper's jaws snapped at his body. The giant reaper moved fast, limbs striking and stomping, wings and tail lashing, keeping Will's blade from striking a deadly blow. Orek's teeth gnashed lightning fast, nearly taking a chunk out of Will with each strike. I darted toward where Ava lay as Will and Orek fought above and all around me. I pulled her to the opposite edge of the roof, clear from Orek's thrashing tail and stomping feet.

Her stomach had been slashed open. Her skin was ashen, and blood soaked her clothing and flecked her face. Her eyes drooped and her teeth clenched in pain.

"Ava?" I called to her, brushing her wild hair out of her face. "Ava! Stay awake. It's Ellie. Can you hear me?"

Her lips moved, and she sputtered something unintelligible. She looked up at me, clutching the wound in her abdomen. "I'm . . . I'm not . . ."

"That's good," I said. "Keep talking. Keep your eyes open."

I checked on Will, who had various cuts on his body, and whose shirt was torn and bloodied. Orek had Will's sword sticking out of his shoulder.

"I'm not . . . ," Ava tried again.

"You'll be fine!" I said, applying pressure to her wound.

She squeezed her eyes shut, knocked my hand away, and scowled. "I'm not . . . going to *die* . . . you moron."

I blinked at her and then gave a nervous laugh. I pulled at her shirt and saw that her wound was closing. When her breathing started to return to normal, I wished that I'd brought something for her to eat in order to speed up the healing process. Will always got better faster when he ate, and after every battle, he ate a *lot*.

Ava sat up and picked at her torn-open shirt. "Damn it," she growled. Then her eyes shot wide. "Look out!"

I spun and ducked as Orek's jaws came gnashing down. Ava and I leaped apart, and his snout smashed into the roof-top between us. We scrambled to our feet and got out of the massive reaper's way. Orek lifted his skeletal head slowly, growling, bleeding rage and blood, chunks of concrete falling out from between his teeth. As the reaper recovered, I looked around desperately for Will, but I couldn't see him. Orek rammed into my body, slamming me to the ground, and I screamed as the dagger-sized claw on Orek's wing drove through my shoulder and deep into the concrete beneath me.

Orek's neck snaked back and forth with a dark hunger as he surveyed my wound. "You murdered my Eki. Now I am going to take your head off with my teeth."

I grimaced through my pain and lit my sword. I swung with all my might, and the blade hacked through Orek's wing. He released me and screeched. The force of his claw releasing my body sent me sliding across the roof. He wavered on his hind legs, his balance thwarted by the catastrophic damage to his wing. The angelfire burned through the leathery membranes and hard bones so violently that the reaper shuddered and whined in agony. He staggered back and lashed suddenly with his teeth, clamped down on his wing, and ripped the damaged half from his body. The torn chunk of his wing shimmered and erupted completely into flames as the angelfire destroyed it.

I clutched the bleeding wound on my shoulder, grinding my teeth as the muscles and veins repaired themselves.

Orek charged at me and I held my sword, ready to defend myself. Will appeared out of nowhere to my left and pounded his fist into Orek's head. The nycterid's jaws snapped and crunched air, questing for soft flesh. His tail swung, nailing Will in the chest and sending him rocketing through the air—and over the side of the roof.

"Will!" I shrieked, and threw myself to the rooftop edge.

He plummeted toward the ground, and his white wings sprang free and beat powerfully, righting his body in midair. He hit the middle of the street on one knee, wings spread their full sixteen feet, his sword in hand. Cars swerved to miss him, spiraling into one another, grinding metal against metal as horns honked and tires screeched. A cacophony of screams erupted around him as people scattered in every direction. Those who didn't run stood in shock, staring at the winged boy who had just fallen from the sky.

Will rose and looked desperately up at me. Darkness crashed over on me like a great wave, and I ducked. Orek leaped over my head and sailed off the roof toward the street as I gaped in horror. The nycterid landed with an earth-shattering *thud* right in front of a large U-Haul truck. The driver slammed on the brakes and swerved, nearly tipping the truck over, but the massive reaper hurled his shoulder and wing into the side of the vehicle. It flipped into mid-air and smashed, sliding, into the ground on its side with a violent roar of metal against pavement. Pedestrians bolted in panic, shrieking, slamming into one another in complete pandemonium.

I froze, confused and unsure of how to handle the chaos erupting on the street below. I'd never fought in front of humans. Orek, jaws snapping and tail swinging, descended on Will as he held his sword ready. Ava was next to me suddenly, one foot on the ledge, looking over.

"What do we do?" I asked, my voice shaking and loud above the commotion.

"We can't help him now," she said, her voice eerily calm. "We can't make this any worse than it's already become."

"What do you mean we can't help him?" I cried. "We have to get down there!"

She looked at me, her face hardened. "Will knows he has to lead Orek away from the humans. The mortals have seen too much already. But the chaos is fortunate—they won't understand what they've witnessed."

I stared at her, shaking with fear and rage. What kind of planet did these reapers live on, where chaos was fortunate? *"Orek will kill him!"*

She grabbed hold of my shoulders. "No, he won't. Will knows what he's doing."

I looked back down at my Guardian, battling the reaper for his life in the middle of the busy street. My heart pounded so hard, I thought it might burst from my chest. I tightened the grip on both my swords. I couldn't stand there and watch him die.

I leaped over the edge of the roof as Ava reached out to me and yelled at me to stop. The wind rushed against my body so wildly that I heard nothing but thunderous screams. Orek looked up as I rocketed toward him, and he jumped into the air, beating what was left of his wings awkwardly as he flew higher. His jaws opened wide, and I stared down deep into his gaping throat. I swung my sword as he snapped. The blade sliced cleanly through his neck, and his head went spiraling through the air. I fell through reaper flames and ashes toward the street below as his body exploded into angelfire all around me. I shut my eyes as embers hit my face, searing my skin, and I prepared to hit the ground. Something thudded into me faster than I thought it would've taken for me to reach the street. Arms wrapped around me, and I was suddenly soaring higher and higher. I opened my eyes to Will's determined face. Clutching me in his arms, he flew us both up and over the city streets and rooftops.

We descended in a quiet patch of woods, where Will set me down shakily. I started to collapse on my feet, but he caught me and held me so I wouldn't fall.

"You are out of your mind," he said, his hands and gaze moving all over me, inspecting for injuries. They lingered over every cut on my neck and arms, over the reaper ash caking my skin. "Why would you do something like that?"

I trembled still, trying to forget the images of the reaper fireball bursting all around me and the ground hurtling faster and faster toward my face. Every time I closed my eyes, I saw myself falling through fire. "I was worried about you."

He laughed and kissed my forehead. "Don't ever worry about me. You could have been killed."

I forced a smile. "That wasn't my first thought, I'll admit."

He stared at me, his green eyes bright in the darkness, his breath clouding in the air between us. "You are amazing."

My cheeks flushed red, mostly because of the way he was looking at me, making me want to believe him. His gaze flickered back and forth before he stepped away.

"I've got to check on Ava," he said, "and make sure she gets out of there. Don't move. I'll be right back." His wings beat once, and he rose into the air and into the Grim. Then he was gone, and I was alone in the cold.

I didn't know where he'd taken me, but it looked like a park or maybe one of the few patches of undeveloped or overgrown land in the area. The snow was above my ankles here, and the trees were tall and dark. I could hear the wail of sirens back toward where we had just battled, and I felt a twinge of fear. People—mortals—had seen everything. They'd seen Will's wings, seen him fall. They'd seen a dinosaurid monster flip a truck over and then burst into flames in midair. I prayed no one had seen my face or taken a photo or video.

"Quite the show," said an achingly deep voice behind me.

I spun, lighting my swords up with angelfire. Two vir reapers, a male and a female, stood twenty feet away from me, their forms half hidden in the darkness between the snowy trees. What startled me, though, was that I couldn't feel either of them. Even when reapers suppressed their powers, I could still sense them a little, but these two were just dark. Like two black holes sucking in my emotions and what was left of my strength. Like zero energy.

"I am impressed," the male added as he moved toward me, his voice rough and gravelly, echoing through my gut. Twisted bull's horns stuck out of his bald head, and his body was massive and brawny, but he didn't look like his size would slow him down. His skin was dark, and his accent was thick and unfamiliar. And his eyes—frigid and the color of moonlight on snow—drilled into mine. "You must be the Preliator. How small you are. I could break you in half."

"Who are you?" I asked, studying them both. My first thought went back to Cadan's warning about the vir reapers who would come for me if the nycterids failed. I guessed these two were old—very, *very* old—and so skilled that they could suppress their powers enough that I didn't have a clue what they were really capable of. I made a silent cry to Will to return soon. If I had to fight them both at once, it wouldn't be pretty.

"I am Merodach," he said. "This is Kelaeno."

My fears had just come true. The female, Kelaeno, looked at me with holly-red eyes and a sharp-fanged grin. With long, tangled, dark hair, she was more disturbing than frightening. I stared at her face, perplexed by her skin moving as if something stirred beneath it. Her features contorted just enough to be noticeable, as if the bones changed under her skin. Every other second, her face shifted from an animal's to looking like a woman's and back again. I couldn't tear my eyes away.

"Ellie!" Will landed beside me in the snow, his white wings outstretched, and Ava wasn't with him. He stepped forward and thrust out his sword, poising it at the newcomers. He was still out of breath from the battle, and I hoped that the new reapers weren't here to fight.

Merodach surveyed Will's show of aggression curiously. "The Hammer of Gabriel," he said with a dark smile. "In the flesh." Wings, leathery and black as night, spread from his back like a cobra spreading its hood.

At that moment, I felt a quick flash of smoky black power from Merodach, strong enough that I lost my balance as it rushed past my body. The warning was clear and imminent: He was powerful and more than willing to kill.

"What do you want?" Will asked, not flinching from the demonic vir's display of power.

"We have a warning for the Preliator," Merodach boomed.

Kelaeno stepped forward, pointing a taloned hand at me, her eyes still on mine. Her face continued to change, like its form was unstable, and dusty gray-brown wings appeared out of her back and spread high and wide. Shadows like daggers cast over her face from around the splayed feathers, making me blink hard as I wondered if I was seeing what was truly in front of me. The skin on her face sank and grew taut over the bones as they stretched, elongating until her appearance was utterly inhuman, and then her face returned to normal. She began to speak, her lips having difficulty forming the words as her face transformed back and forth.

"You, the mortal Gabriel, the gift for the demon queen," Kelaeno rasped, her talons curling and unfurling as she stepped toward me, so close I could almost taste her rancid breath. "Your strength in heart and hand will fall to a reaper's bane before your eyes."

Nausea wormed its way up my throat as my body froze. Her golden eyes flashed and her lips curled into a sinister sneer as she gauged my reaction. She tilted her head and licked her lips before she continued.

"Mark me well, for you will lose everything you love most dear before you finally lose your soul."

As her words began to eat their way through my stomach, Will's sword swept between Kelaeno and me. She reeled back with a screech. His foot rammed into her chest, and his ribs cracked sickeningly as she lashed her talons out at his skin. Her power exploded, the spiraling orb of blackness swallowing all the light around us. The blast knocked Will into me, and I darted to the side as he crashed to the ground. I dropped to my knees beside him.

"Kelaeno!" A familiar, terrible voice shattered my senses as it rang out above the chaos.

I froze, ice tearing through my veins, and I looked back up. Will dragged himself to his feet, and I followed him.

Kelaeno's wrist was trapped by another hand—Bastian's. His black hair gleamed like obsidian, and his cerulean eyes blazed neon as he and Kelaeno bared their teeth at each other. Kelaeno snapped her jaws in his face and laughed.

"You will not harm the Guardian," Bastian growled, low and guttural.

Kelaeno sneered mockingly at him and yanked herself free. Bastian blinked and straightened in surprise, as if he hadn't expected her strength—as if she'd been hiding it from him.

"You only want the girl," she snarled back. "I want the Guardian's guts between my teeth."

I shivered and held on to Will's arm as he stepped in

front of me, shielding me. The weight of the immense energy belonging to three reapers thousands of years old pressed on every inch of my skin, sinking through to my brain, making me dizzy as if the altitude had changed suddenly. We couldn't defeat all three of them—especially now, after the fierce battle against Orek.

Bastian took a step closer to Kelaeno, his height overwhelming her slight, bony stature. "I will deal with him *myself*. This is about the Preliator. *He* is not your concern."

She opened her mouth and raised her talons, but Merodach's voice cut through the air like a blade. "Enough. We must go."

Kelaeno craned her neck upward toward the reddening horizon. "The sun," she crooned. Her wings beat once, and she jumped into the air and disappeared into the Grim.

Bastian turned to Merodach, raising a hand to him. "Do not disrupt me again. I haven't time to make sure you are doing your task to my satisfaction."

Merodach didn't appear frightened by Bastian's threat, only annoyed by it.

With a slow smile, Bastian looked at me, his eyes brightening with what looked like admiration. "We meet again, Gabriel."

Will's form flashed between us, his sword gleaming as he roared with fury and swung the blade over his head toward Bastian. The demonic reaper waved a hand, and his power slammed into Will, blowing him back with an immense gust of energy that kicked up a raging blizzard of snow off the ground. Will flipped himself midair and landed crouched. He shot forward again, but Bastian caught his wrist as he swung his sword, and Bastian's other hand tightened around his throat. Will growled and wrenched his body, but he couldn't break free. Bastian squeezed harder, choking Will and forcing him to his knees in the snow. Will's sword toppled out of his slackening grip.

"I am not here to kill you, William," Bastian said, the blue of his eyes almost blinding as his power grew. "But I will if you get in my way."

I ran forward to help Will, summoning what was left of my strength and calling the white hot light into my palms. I grabbed Bastian's arm with both hands and felt the sizzle of his skin beneath his sleeve as the fabric was eaten by flames. He roared and released Will, reeling away from me and clutching his burned arm close to his chest. Will staggered to his feet, gasping for breath, and I pulled him into my arms, smoothing my warm hands over his reddened throat.

"Are you okay?" I asked him. He nodded and glared sidelong at Bastian, who had retreated to where Merodach stood silently.

"That's an interesting trick, Gabriel," Bastian snarled. "Giving me a taste of your glory?"

I stared at him, puzzled. "Glory?"

"That little fireworks show you just did on my arm?" he rasped, baring his teeth. "I know archangel glory when it burns me to the bone. It seems you're waking up, Gabriel. Perhaps that long sleep of yours was exactly what you needed."

"How did you know who I was?" I demanded. "When we met, you said you already knew."

"Because I've spoken to old friends of yours," he replied. The breaking dawn was bearing down on him, and his skin began to smoke. He arched his neck uncomfortably in the growing sunlight. "Those who are ancient enough to know the truth. Voices seep through the bars of Hell, my dear. But never fear. When I take your life again, I'll take your soul, too. When it's time, my hounds will come for you, Gabriel."

With a flash of smoky black power and a growl of painful fury, Bastian vanished into the Grim. Merodach wasn't in the same hurry. The hot orange glow of sunrise spread across his body until he was smoldering like cinders from the tips of the horns on his head to the toes of his heavy boots. He looked every part a demon straight out of Hell.

"I'll be seeing you soon, Preliator," he said before he spread his wings and followed Kelaeno and Bastian into the Grim, slipping away, leaving nothing but smoke and the repulsive odor of sulfur behind him.

I breathed a sigh of relief when the heavy demonic energy disappeared. Will's warm hands fell on my arms, and he pulled me close, his body a wall of warmth against my shivering form.

"Let's get out of here," he said, his voice feather soft. "I doubled back without Ava when I sensed the vir."

"Thank you," I said. "We need to get to Nathaniel's and figure out what the hell just happened, everything we can about Kelaeno and Merodach, and why Bastian wants them to leave you alone."

He pushed my hair behind my ears. "Are you sure you aren't too tired? You need to sleep."

"I'm exhausted, but this is important." Too much had happened tonight for me to sleep.

Footsteps in the snow behind me made me jump. Ava had landed at last, bloodied but healed. She appeared tired and unnerved, and I assumed she sensed our run-in with the demonic vir.

"What happened?" she asked hurriedly. "Is everything okay?"

Will and I looked at each other. I let out a long breath. "We're about to head to Nathaniel's," I said. "We'll explain on the way."

14

AN HOUR LATER, I WAS FALLING ASLEEP ON WILL'S
shoulder as he thumbed through one of Nathaniel's old books
that smelled like my nana's basement. Ava and Nathaniel
were huddled together over another book on the other side of
the room, discussing the traits of the demonic vir. Nathaniel
thought their names sounded familiar, but he didn't know
who they were. I had one eye open to peer over at the book in
Will's hands, but I was barely hanging on to consciousness.
A seriously rough fight with a reaper the size of a Mack truck
takes a lot out of a girl.

"I found Merodach," Ava said, her finger pointing at a
page, the paper browned with age. "And we have a bit of bad
news."

"Bad news?" Will repeated.

"All kinds of it," she said glumly. "He's older than our

earliest records of the Preliator. This book holds the translation of a tablet older than the sarcophagus containing the
Enshi. Merodach may have served this Enshi before it was
imprisoned. He's one of the first-generation original demonic
reapers, a direct offspring of Lilith and Sammael."

That woke me up a bit. "Doesn't that mean he has to be
thousands of years old? Are you sure?"

Nathaniel nodded. "That's what it says."

Sometimes I forgot that reapers could keep on living
if nothing happened to kill them. Cadan had said he was
over eight hundred years old and his father was over a thousand. Will was six hundred. Nathaniel was about a century
older. It made me wonder about Bastian. How old was he?
The way Merodach and Kelaeno seemed completely un-
affected by Bastian's commands made me question if they
were even stronger than he was. It seemed like every day the
odds against me were more and more staggering.

"I hate this job," I said exasperatedly. "I'm quitting and
going to work at McDonald's."

All three angelic reapers stared at me in confusion and
surprise. Will even had a little horror in his expression.

I rolled my eyes. "Or maybe I should work somewhere
that can sell each of you a sense of humor. I'll even give you
my employee discount. Especially *you*." I looked pointedly
at Nathaniel.

He blinked back. "I have a great sense of humor!"

"No, you don't," I mumbled. "So, Merodach. He's solitary,

despite being somehow connected with the Enshi. I'm confused that he's allied with Kelaeno and Bastian. But I'm not surprised that Bastian is gathering the strongest he can in order to free the Enshi. He needs a powerful, impenetrable front to his army. If Merodach has joined him, then he must believe Bastian can pull it off. He wouldn't waste his time or take anyone's orders otherwise."

Will furrowed his brow. "I just don't see a reaper that ancient and powerful taking orders from Bastian."

"Unless Bastian has grown in strength," Ava said. "You know what Bastian can do, Will."

He didn't look at her, but his body visibly tensed. "Either way, Merodach and this Kelaeno are acting under Bastian's orders. They aren't doing it because they enjoy it. You saw the look Merodach gave Bastian."

I could tell the subject of Bastian's capabilities was hard for him. "Kelaeno said something very cryptic and strange to me," I added. "Something about my heart and hand, I don't know."

Nathaniel's gaze turned serious. "What exactly did she say?"

"'Your strength in heart and hand will fall to a reaper's bane.' And then, 'You will lose everything you love before finally you lose your soul.' It was awful."

He paused to think. "She meant Will. Your strength in heart and hand. It's your Guardian, your right hand."

I looked at Will, who stared at the ground. Ava wasn't

taking her eyes off him either. "What did she mean when she said he will fall?" I asked. "What is the reaper's bane?"

"It could mean a lot of things," Nathaniel said. "Anything that can harm a reaper, I suppose. It's a pretty serious threat."

I stared at him firmly. "She means he's going to die."

"Nathaniel," Ava said. "The female vir's name was Kelaeno. Doesn't that sound familiar?"

"Yes," he confirmed. "Aeneas and the Harpies. That's just Greek myth, though."

Both Ava's gaze and her voice became dark. "What if she is real?"

Will remained silent, and his expression hardened.

"What are you talking about?" I asked. "What about Greek myth?"

Nathaniel cleared his throat. "Kelaeno was a Harpy who cursed Aeneas, the leader of the Dardanian Trojans who fought in the battle of Troy. She told him that he would go so hungry that he'd eat his tables by the end of his journey, which came true, according to the story."

"So this threat was more like a prophecy," I said. The words weighed on my heart. The thought of losing Will and my friends and family was too much. I couldn't let anyone get hurt. No one should have to die for me.

"This could very well be the same Kelaeno of Greek mythology," Nathaniel said, rubbing the bridge of his nose tiredly. "People have misidentified reapers since the beginning of time and come up with their own explanations for what they've experienced. Lupines were mistaken for werewolves all the time. People saw vir reapers and believed they were demons and witches, sometimes so fervently that they'd turn on their neighbors in hysteria, burn their friends and families at the stake. It's very likely that the Greeks invented the Harpy myth to explain some of the more avian vir reapers they may have encountered."

That made sense. Kelaeno had been so birdlike that it was disturbing. The way her face seemed to have difficulty retaining a form haunted me. "She said something else, too. She called me 'the gift for the demon queen.' That sounds familiar—"

I shut up midsentence when I saw Nathaniel's face. He stared at me in shock and fear, so startling that my pulse began to pound. "What is it?" I asked shakily.

Nathaniel leaned forward and spoke slowly. "Are you positive that is exactly what Kelaeno said?"

"Yeah," I said. "What's wrong? What was she talking about?"

"Lilith," Will said. "The Fallen Queen of Hell and mother of all demonic reapers."

The blood drained from my face. "Oh. Is that all?" I forced a tiny laugh.

"So Bastian is after Lilith too," Ava thought to herself out loud. "He is really serious about this second war."

"Could they really be trying to summon Lilith?" Will asked.

Ava shook her head. "More than that. If Bastian wants the Preliator and Lilith, then the spell will be more powerful than a summoning ritual. The Preliator is an archangel bound in human form. Her blood would be . . . so *immense* in power. They must want to restore Lilith's corporeal form. They want her in this world, and not just for a visit."

"The ritual would most certainly be contained within the grimoire," Nathaniel suggested. "I believe I have a near-complete copy in my collection that I wrote myself before the original grimoire went missing centuries ago."

The word was familiar and stirred memories within me. "I remember what that is. A book written by a Grigori, right? The Fallen angels bound to Earth instead of Hell?"

Nathaniel nodded. "The book is the most ancient and complete collection of angelic spells and rituals."

"Bastian would definitely need it in order to free Lilith," Will said darkly. "Only Grigori magic would have the kind of power needed to give corporeal form to any angel or one of the Fallen. Otherwise, they can only roam as phantoms in the mortal world."

"What would happen then?" I asked, beginning to panic. "If Lilith is released, in her true form? How could I stop something like that?"

Nathaniel let out a long whistling breath. "I don't think

you, or any of us, can. You as Gabriel, however, could. Lilith was never an archangel. Her power could never match the strength of your own true form."

The solution seemed simple. "Then how can I become Gabriel?"

"If there's a way, only an angel, like a Grigori or archangel, would know," he said. "But you already have a form. I don't know if it's possible for you to become an archangel out of a human body. That kind of transformation would almost certainly destroy you. Just looking upon an angel's glory can burn a human's eyes from their sockets. If your human body somehow transformed into an archangel, even by magic, I would imagine your own glory would incinerate you."

"But it doesn't," I said. When Nathaniel gave me a puzzled look, I continued. "The power I've used to burn—Bastian called it my glory. It didn't hurt me at all, so if he's right then perhaps my human body could survive my full-on archangel glory."

Will shook his head. "Perhaps isn't good enough. Bastian could be wrong."

"Or he's right."

Silence fell on the room. I knew the others, like me, had minds swimming with thoughts and possibilities. What if I were able to become who I really was? What would it be like? What would *I* be like? I wondered if I would be different, like the me of my memories, stonelike and resolute. Those visions of myself scared me, but I could only imagine the archangel side of me. When the archangel Michael came to me on that boat out in the middle of nowhere, he was eerily calm, beautifully serene, but danger leaked from him, thick and blinding like fog. The angels had no emotions, or at most very little. I wondered then: If I remembered my true self, if I became the archangel Gabriel, would I be a heartless creature who only cared about fulfilling a mission, no matter the loss? Would I no longer be in love with Will?

Would I feel anything at all?

Nathaniel stood, wrenching me from my thoughts. "I can check my copy of the original grimoire. Will, would you help me look for it?"

"Of course." He rose to follow Nathaniel but paused and looked down at me, his gaze gentle. "Don't be afraid. We'll fight through this."

I forced a smile and ached for him to offer a comforting touch. And then he touched my cheek, and warmth spread to my toes. He drew away and vanished out the door of Nathaniel's office.

I sat back heavily in my chair. The room was silent for a moment, and I realized that I was alone with Ava. Then I noticed she was staring at me. She studied my face as if I were an amoeba beneath a microscope. The awkward seconds passed, and finally I opened my mouth with words I hadn't really thought about.

"What does the chain tattoo around your neck mean?"
I asked.

Ava hesitated for an agonizing second before she
answered in a quiet voice, "It means I was property."

I blinked. Well, that was not the response I'd expected.
"What?"

"When I was young," she began, "a demonic reaper disguised as a powerful duke kept me as a pet. He bound my
power through the magic in the ink he used to tattoo chains
around my neck. He raped me almost every night for twenty
years. Sometimes he would get bored with me and I wouldn't
see him or anyone else for a week, and I would starve almost
to death."

Bile rose in my throat. "Oh, my God." I thought about
that, unable to comprehend the constant horror she endured
through years of slavery and sexual assault. "How did you
escape?"

Only then did she look away from me. "Will. He'd heard
about this duke keeping angelic reapers as slaves. He fought
his way into the castle and killed the demonic vir so that I
was free. The magical link was severed and my power was
unbound, but this tattoo will always remain for the world to
see." She paused and looked back to me. The corners of her
lips pulled into a small smile. "It doesn't matter, because I'm
free. I owe Will everything."

I didn't respond, but the events of her rescue played out
in my head like a horror movie.

"You see why I value him so much."

I did. How could she not have cared for him after he saved her from that horrible place?

"You know, don't you?" she asked, tilting her head to gaze at me, her dark hair curtaining her shoulders. Her voice was gentle, as though she were speaking to a wounded animal. "He told you. I suspected he would."

I opened my mouth to respond, but nothing came out. I had no idea what to say to her. Talking about this with her made what I knew feel a thousand times more real. I didn't want to think about Will with Ava, or with how many other girls there'd been. I didn't want to think about anyone loving him but me.

"I'm not in love with him," she said as if reading my mind. Before I could respond, she continued. "At least not anymore. He never loved me. Not once. You can tell when someone loves you or doesn't, and I always knew with him. You were an impossible obstacle."

I stared at her, unsure of how to respond. The clock above Nathaniel's desk ticked, driving a stake through the silence between us with each passing second.

"When I met you," she said, "I resented you, but I never hated you. I'm sorry if I haven't been very kind. I just didn't understand how he could be so dedicated to you for that long. He's only able to spend a little while with you before you die again, and then he's lonely for years. I hated seeing him like that, especially this last time when you were gone for so long and wouldn't come back. You will never truly understand what he went through. I was angry at you for causing him so much pain, because he saved my life, *gave* me a life, and I was in love with him then."

My heart kicked in my chest. She was so cruelly blunt. "Ava, I—"

"I was jealous too," she continued, smiling gently at me. "I wanted Will to love me, but his broken heart has always belonged to you, even after he believed he'd lost you forever. He gave up everything for you, and Zane wouldn't give up anything for me."

"That's not totally right," I urged. "Will is my Guardian, the same as Zane was that relic's guardian. So much of everything they do is part of their duty. They have to give up everything when they become a guardian. Zane was no exception, and neither is Will."

She smiled ever so slightly, and the blue-violet of her eyes intensified as her emotions stirred to the surface. "Zane was kind to me, and I've always been drawn to people who take care of me. Zane and I were together a very, very long time ago, and he never loved me the way I wanted to be loved." Her smile grew wider, and the warmth spread to her cold winter eyes. "And that's also why I was jealous of you, because I see you fight against the demonic like no one else can, see you fight for Will, and I understand that he does all of this for *you*. I've never seen anyone look at anyone the way he looks at you."

Will's face appeared in my head, looking at me the way I loved him to, and a flutter of heat shot through me. I couldn't think of him lonely and broken, especially because of me.

"I don't love him anymore, but I still respect him," she said. "Most of the time you come off as a silly young girl to me, but when everything most important to you is at stake, you transform into this fearless thing of wonder, like a true avenging archangel. After watching what you did last night, I respect *you*, Gabriel."

I studied her carefully, waiting for her gaze to falter, but it stayed true. "Everyone keeps calling me that, but it's not me."

"Why do you deny who you truly are?" she asked. "You *are* Gabriel."

"I'm human," I said sadly, my hands tightening on my knees, desperate to keep myself from becoming too emotional in front of Ava. "In this world, I'm human, not some flawless archangel. That's something I can't even wrap my head around. I'm reckless and passionate and imperfect. I die. I'm born human, I live human, and I die human. My body isn't as strong as yours, but my power comes from inside me and I'm as strong as I need to be. But don't call me Gabriel, because that's not who I am, not right now. I'm just Ellie."

She was silent and her expression remained still as stone, but slightly curious. Then she softened, her lips relaxing from the tight line she'd drawn them into, and the color of her eyes dimmed to normal. "All right," she said at last. "Ellie."

Will and Nathaniel returned, and relief washed over me. Nathaniel tossed a book onto the desk and plopped down heavily.

"I've got nothing," he said dismally. "The book I was looking for is gone from my collection, and I don't know where it is. I have another book of angelic magic, but this volume has nothing on what's contained within the grimoire. The author probably doesn't know any more than we do about Enochian spells."

Will frowned apologetically at me. "It doesn't mention a spell to give an angel or one of the Fallen corporeal form, so we still don't know if it's even possible."

"We need to find this grimoire," I said. "Or at least the copy." Inside, I tried not to be angry for not remembering any of the spells myself. Gabriel would know what to do. *Ellie*, on the other hand . . .

"Ava," Will said, "can you and Sabina look into this? You keep in contact with more relic guardians than I'm able to. Someone has to have heard something."

"The reaper we met at Zane's?" Her mouth twitched into a brief grimace before all emotion washed from her expression. "Why not Marcus?"

"I don't trust Marcus with something like this," Will admitted. "He's a great fighter and I'd feel confident that he's got my back, but on a mission for something like this, he would get . . . distracted."

Ava's lips tightened. "All right. Sabina would be a wise choice for a partner."

I pulled out my phone to check the time, but it was dead. I'd completely forgotten to charge it when I got home from the party. I searched the walls in the office for a clock and spotted it behind me. It was almost ten. My eyes bulged. I would be able to conceal myself within the Grim, but hiding my car in broad daylight would prove impossible. "I really have to go. I have to sleep and somehow get back into my house without my parents noticing."

Will laid a hand on my arm. "I'll walk you out."

I smiled to the others as I rose from my chair. "See you later. Thank you, Ava."

She gave me a shallow nod of solidarity.

Will followed close behind me as we left the library and headed out to my car. The sun was bright, but there was a bitter chill in the air. The snow last night had left a light dusting on the parking lot pavement. I dug my keys out of my bag, and they slipped right through my fingers and hit the ground. I groaned as I reached for them, but Will had already swept low and picked them up for me.

"Are you too tired to drive?" he asked gently, watching me carefully as I unlocked my car and opened the door.

"I'm fine," I said. "Really. It's not a far drive and it's Sunday, so there won't be too much traffic."

He studied my face for a few moments and lifted a hand to stroke my cheek. "I meant it when I said you were amazing last night."

"Thanks. So were you."

His eyes fell to my lips briefly. Then he stepped back and pulled the car door open wider. "Get some rest."

I sat down, threw my bag in the passenger seat, and slid my seat belt over me. I looked up at him. "You too. I mean it."

He grinned. "I'm invincible."

I rolled my eyes. "That kind of thinking gets you killed."

He gave a soft laugh. "Have a good day, Ellie."

When I drove away, I was smiling.

I sneaked back into the house and crept up the stairs to my room, shocked not to have run into my parents. I set my things down on my bed and let out a sigh. It was in that moment that I heard shuffling, and then footsteps darting up the stairs. Before I could even think, the door burst open and my mom appeared, her expression wild and her hands covering her mouth in surprise.

Oh, no.

"Richard!" she called out breathlessly. "She's back!"

My heart stopped and my throat squeezed so tightly I couldn't breathe. "Mom, I—"

She ran to me, pulling me into her arms and hugging me. When she let go, she took hold of both my shoulders and stared into my face. "Ellie! Where have you been? I came up to check on you after you went to bed and you were gone. You didn't come back all night! You have no idea how worried your father and—"

"You worthless little bitch," my father hissed as he stomped into my room and right toward me.

My mom and I stared at him in shock. I couldn't believe what had just come out of his mouth.

"Richard!" Mom's voice shook me back to the real world.

"Dad, I can explain—"

"Obviously you know where she's been, Diane," he said. "It's time you opened your eyes to this."

For a moment, I thought he really knew where I'd been. But that wasn't possible. "What are you talking about?"

He moved fast. His hand was suddenly around my jaw, and he jerked my head side to side. "I'm shocked there are no hickeys."

I wanted to throw up. I jerked away from him, rubbing my face where he'd held me so viciously, staring at him in disgust. "What is wrong with you?"

"That is out of line, Richard!" my mom growled, and put herself between us. She pushed his chest, forcing him to take a step back.

"Where else would she have been *all night*?" he shouted, inches from her face. "Obviously she was with that boy!"

While that wasn't exactly untrue, I wasn't with a boy for the reasons he was accusing me of.

My mom looked at me. "Is that true? Were you with Will? I thought you were done with that boy."

That boy. It was so wrong, so demeaning, the taste of the words like the shock of rancid milk on my tongue. If she only knew, if either of them only knew what *that boy* had done for me last night, a thousand nights before. I was so tired of lying. So tired of keeping all these secrets. They were killing me. I took a deep breath. "Yes, I was with Will."

My mom's mouth tightened, but her gaze was sympathetic. Behind her, my dad was laughing.

"You little *slut*!"

Before I could react, my mom wheeled around and open-palm slapped him so hard his head snapped to the side. He wasn't laughing anymore.

"How *dare* you?" she screeched. "Never, ever, ever do you talk to your child that way. *Ever!*"

I knew I needed to say something, but I couldn't speak. First I needed to inhale, but I still couldn't breathe. I needed to defend myself, to stand up to my father, but I was afraid of him because he was my father. At last I found my voice.

"Get out," I rasped. "Get the hell out of my room and out of my life. I don't ever want to see you again."

He turned to me, his face a toxic mixture of rage and amusement. "Oh? And how are you going to pull that off? This is my house!"

"Then I'll leave." My voice was steady, but cracking at its

edges. "I can't take this. I'm done with you."

He got right up in my face. I could feel the heat radiating off him, and it was nauseating. "You're done with *me*?"

I was too physically and emotionally exhausted to go any longer. My lip curled with disgust at him. "Get out of my face before I knock the teeth from your gums."

Something flickered dark in his eyes. He lunged for me, hands outstretched, moving faster than I thought he was capable of. I whirled out of his reach in shock, but I felt his fingers rake my throat, and my mother's screams deafened me. I watched him pass me and my mom dart between us, beating her fists on his chest, screaming at him.

"What is wrong with you?" she shrieked, pounding his chest until he was backing toward my bedroom door. "Get out! *Out!*"

My lungs felt empty as my breaths became quicker and shallower, filling my head with cotton and making me ill. He'd just *attacked* me. I watched my mom force him from my room and slam the door in his face. She let out another furious scream before clutching her robe and fighting to steady her shaking body. I was dizzy—dizzy and bewildered by what had just happened.

Mom turned back to me, her face red and raw, her shoulders rigid with panic. "Are you all right?"

I stared at the door behind her. "No."

"I'm going to leave him, baby," she whispered. "Today I'm going to tell him I want a divorce."

My heart shattered and rejoiced in the same moment. "Oh, Mom. I'm so sorry."

She shook her head. "No. I needed to do it years ago. This was the last straw. I'm going to tell him to start packing and get out by the end of the month. He has to go."

I swallowed hard. "I'm proud of you."

"He's nothing like the man I married," she said. "So there's no reason to be married to him if he's going to hurt you. It's one thing for him to treat me like that, but not my daughter."

I stared at her, barely holding myself together, heartbeats away from falling apart. "I have to ground you, Ellie," Mom said, still shaking. "You sneaked out of the house and you were gone all night. Rules aside, it's just not safe. Don't you understand how dangerous that is, or what could have happened?"

I nodded. I did understand her concern. Lots of girls disappeared every day, were hurt in car accidents, kidnapped by evil people. But I wasn't just a girl—I had responsibilities that forced me to, at the very least, bend these rules and sometimes ignore my own instincts for self-preservation. I could confess to my mother about being out with Will all night, but I couldn't confess to leaping off the top of a building to my near death.

"Last night there was a disturbance downtown," she said shakily, and ice stabbed my spine. "When I saw it on the news this morning and you weren't here, God, I've never been more terrified in my life. People are saying it was a hoax; some are saying it was a terrorist attack. Some witnesses got photos and video on cell phones, but the images are bright and confusing. I don't even know what to believe. Some of the things the witnesses are saying they saw . . . it's just impossible. It's been all over the national news stations all morning."

I swallowed hard, my pulse hammering against my brain. "I'm sure it wasn't what they're saying."

"The point is, Ellie," my mom continued, "taking off in the middle of the night was not the best decision you've made. This is the second time you've run off with him—the second time that I know of, at least. First you're not dating him, then you are, then you aren't, then you are again. You'll be off to college in the fall, and I won't be able to give you any rules then. But judging by your actions and behavior since your senior year began, I don't know if you're ready for that kind of freedom, or if I can even trust you to make the right decisions. I love you. You're my daughter, and I'm terrified for you."

I fought the sob in my throat and said the most honest thing I'd felt since I turned seventeen. "I'm sorry, Mom. I just don't know what I'm doing. I don't know where I'm going or who I am anymore."

She scooped me into a tight, warm hug. "I know, baby. Everyone goes through this at your age. You have to discover who you are and who are the right people to keep in your life."

"That's just it," I said, and the tears broke free, sliding down my cheeks and pooling in the corners of my mouth. "I've learned who I am, but I don't believe it. It's too much for me to handle. I can't take the responsibility. It's ruining me."

"Oh, baby," my mom cooed, stroking my hair. "I know it's scary to grow up, but we all have to."

Not me. I never get to. I pulled away from my mom and forced myself to look at her. "Thanks, Mom."

She looked like she was in agony. "It's my job."

"I'm just going to stay in my room today, okay?" I asked. "I need to be alone."

"Are things getting serious with Will?"

I almost laughed. The sound I made instead was cold and bitter. "Depends on how you look at it."

"You know that if it gets that *kind* of serious," she said tentatively, "you can come to me. You can talk to me about anything."

I forced a smile, wishing that was true. For a moment, I wanted to tell her everything. About what really happened last night, about who Will really was, who I really was. She'd throw me into a psych ward without a doubt, but at least I wouldn't have to lie anymore. "Okay."

"Come down for lunch, okay? You won't be grounded from eating."

"Okay." I wiped at my face, watching her leave and close the door behind her. Suddenly I felt the weight of having not slept for twenty-four hours and was desperate to crash.

I could sense him before he'd even appeared out of the Grim, his achingly familiar scent and presence washing over me like waterfall. A hand came from nowhere and took my wrist, but I didn't fight him. He pulled me into him, his hands now gentle on my face and neck as he examined me for injury, his fingers moving along my jaw to lift my chin. His crystalline green eyes hardened at the sight of the fading red marks on my throat.

"I'm going to kill him," Will snarled, biting back a rage that consumed him like fire. I'd never seen him more furious, but still he touched me as if my skin were made of glass. His control over that combination of emotions was frightening.

"No," I said clearly and coldly. "He's still my father. If I want him dead, I'll do it myself."

"I don't care. No one touches you like that."

"He's human."

"He's a monster."

If I had permitted it, he would've, without a doubt, gone after my dad. "You can't protect me from everything," I said gently.

"Yes, I can." His shoulders eased as he took a long, tired breath. He brushed away my tears with his thumbs, and I closed my eyes at his touch, soaking in the kindness and pushing out the abuse I had just endured. I savored it. I closed the last few inches between our bodies until we touched, and I slid my hands up his back to hold him even tighter. I buried my face in his chest as his cheek touched my hair. He lifted my face and leaned over to kiss my temple, lips brushing my skin, and then he kissed my cheek. I pulled him closer, waiting for his lips to touch mine, but he stopped and his hands fell to my waist.

"I can't do this," he said faintly, his breath soft on my cheek.

I closed my eyes as a new tear rolled down my cheek and he slid out of my hands. When I opened my eyes again, he was halfway across my room.

"If I let this get too far," he said, "I won't be able to protect you, because Michael will execute me."

"It's already gone too far," I said tiredly.

His shoulders sagged and his head hung as his gaze fell away. He'd retreated back into himself once again, drawing closed the shutters that revealed his emotions.

"Is it true, what you told your mother?" he asked.

"You heard?" I wasn't angry or surprised. It was a question I already knew the answer to.

He bit his upper lip, and my heart sank. He looked at me as though he'd been destroyed inside and was slowly caving in on himself. "Do you really think this is ruining you?"

I ran my fingers through my hair roughly and shrugged, throwing out my hands. "I feel so broken inside. I can't keep fighting like this and trying to live a life at the same time."

"Then I'm right," he said, his voice cracking, his eyes barely able to look into mine. "About you and me—I've only made it harder for you. It's my fault. We can't do this. We've changed."

A spark of anger ignited in my throat. "The only thing that changed was you kissing me. We've always felt this way about each other. That never changed."

"And it only proves what a mistake it was to do that."

Another tear came down my face. "What was a mistake? Do you regret kissing me, or being in love with me, or both?"

He hesitated for the longest moment of my life. "They're both mistakes, but I don't regret them."

"You're an idiot if that's what you think," I said, my anger flaring. "How we feel about each other makes us stronger. It makes us fight harder for each other. You're standing there and telling me you can't let Michael kill you because you don't trust anyone else to be my Guardian. Will, you're the best not just because you're the strongest. You protect me like no one else can because you love me. Fighting it weakens us. We're tearing ourselves apart!"

He took a deep, quivering breath. "We can't argue about this now. Your parents could come back."

I could see in his eyes that he knew I was right, and still he was denying it. "Then go. I don't want you here," I lied.

His hands rolled into fists. "Fine," he said sharply, trying to hide the anger in his voice. "I'll go, but I want you to know that if he does touch you again, I *will* kill him, because I know you won't do it."

Then he vanished, and an icy breeze billowed the drapes over my open window. I squeezed my eyes shut and let myself cry.

15

I DIDN'T SEE MY DAD FOR DAYS, BUT I DIDN'T CARE if I ever saw him again. Mom had told him her decision, and he was supposed to be gone soon anyway. Already I could sense her growing relief at the prospect of him leaving, but every moment he was home, she was stiff with fear. I couldn't stand seeing my mom so afraid. I knew my dad was physically powerless against me, the Preliator, but the pain he inflicted on my heart was crippling. I was more than ready to move on from him.

On Wednesday after school, I sat at the kitchen table with my English lit book out while I worked on a paper. During my grounding, I tried to focus my time on schoolwork so at least some good would come out of all this.

"Hey, Ell," Mom called as she sauntered into the kitchen

with a knowing grin on her face. "You got something in the mail today."

I raised an eyebrow at her. "Why are you smiling like that?" I set down my notebook and got up. My mom had something white and narrow in her hand, and when I got close, I saw that it was an envelope.

"You sure you want to see it?" she said with a laugh. "It's from Michigan Sta—"

"Give it," I ordered, and snatched at it.

She yanked it out of my reach and high over her head. My mom, even when she was wearing flip-flops, towered over my petite height. "I thought you didn't want it, Ell."

"Not cool," I grumbled as I hopped up to grab the letter. "You cheat!"

She laughed. "Oh, you're no fun."

She dropped her arm, and I grabbed it out of her hand. "My kind of fun just doesn't include making fun of vertically challenged people."

The letter in my hand was thick and addressed to me from Michigan State University. I let out a long breath, then tore open the top. I fumbled with the papers inside, surprised at the butterflies filling up my belly. This was my future, after all—if I even had a future.

I stared at the top page in shock. "Oh, my God."

"What?" Mom peeked over my shoulder.

"I got in." My voice was barely audible, but my shock

spun into excitement. "I got in!"

My mom scooped me into a hug and squeezed me as tightly as she could, crying out unintelligible things as she kissed my cheek and hair. "I'm so happy for you!" she cried as legit tears ran down her cheeks. Was she really that surprised that I got into college? "We should do something special and fun for dinner. How about pancakes? This is a good pancakes day."

I beamed up at her. "Thanks, Mom. I'm dying for pancakes." I said cheerfully. "I'm so excited. Hey, do you think I could get a little time off and run around the mall this weekend with Kate and stretch my legs?"

"Sure," she replied. "You've been doing so well lately, and I think it would do you some good."

I'd gotten into college and I was going to get a relaxing day at the mall. I'd never looked so forward to anything before.

The next Saturday, Kate and I wandered around the mall, dipping in and out of stores just to look. I didn't have any money to buy anything, but the stale mall air and the absence of Will made the brief freedom so much sweeter.

"I can't wait for fall," Kate said as she munched on her french fries across the table from me in the food court. "We'll be roomies and go to class and party . . . it will be amazing!"

I laughed. "Will you be saving time for Marcus, too?"

She flashed me a sly grin. "I might. If I keep him around long enough."

"Dumping him already?" I took a sip of my Orange Julius.

"We aren't official," she said. "Just . . . hanging out. He's a lot of fun, but my options are open."

"Probably a good idea," I said vaguely. I hoped she would move on quickly so I wouldn't have to worry about her getting mixed up in the world of reapers by dating one.

"Kate!" called an unfamiliar voice.

I turned my head and saw two *really* cute guys approaching. They looked older than us—and I was very sure they weren't in high school.

"What's up, ladies?" The first boy flipped his longish, grungy hair out of his eyes and grinned.

Kate flashed him a languorous smile. "Hey, Jay. Back in town for the weekend?"

He slid up to her, rested a hand on the back of her chair, and kissed her on the cheek. "Only to see you, babe."

"Yeah, right." She laughed and nudged his chest.

He laughed. "We're just here for the afternoon. How have you been?"

"Peachy." She grinned.

The second boy was even cuter and had short, spiky hair. His gaze fell on me, and he gave me a very obvious examination that almost made me blush. "Who's your friend?" he asked with a smile.

"That's Ellie," Kate said with an edge to her voice. "She's my best, which means she's very cool."

"I'm Brian," he said. "Nice to meet you."

I turned on the charm. "Likewise." I took another sip and smiled. He was really cute. *Really* cute.

"Jay and Brian go to State," Kate explained. "How's sophomore year treating you boys?"

Jay shrugged. "It's good."

"Four-day weekends aren't bad," Brian said. "Four hours of classes a day Monday through Thursday, and then the fun begins. What are you girls doing tonight?"

Kate's brow flickered. "I'm not doing anything—yet. What've you got planned?"

"We're having a party at our house," Jay said. "The one we're renting this year. You two should come along."

"Ellie?" Kate bumped her knee into mine. "You game?"

It was tempting. I wouldn't drag Will along or even *let* him come if he wanted to. I had to get out and get away from him, and I didn't need him to protect me. If I could take a centuries-old reaper, then I could take a bunch of drunk college boys.

"I'm in," I said.

Kate let out a squeal of approval. "That's my girl. I'll give you a call, okay, Jay?"

"You'd better." He winked at her.

Brian grinned at me. "See you again?"

"Yeah." I smiled right back at him.

* * *

I knocked on my mom's office door and entered. She was hard at work on a new design for a website, peering down her nose at the monitor through her computer glasses.

"Hey, baby." She greeted me with a warm glance as I sat down in the chair across from her desk. "How was the mall?"

"Good," I replied. "I forgot to give you something earlier." There were family photos organized neatly around her computer, but today I noticed the photos including my dad were gone. One more step to freedom from him, I supposed. I brushed the thought away and set a stack of stapled papers on the desk in front of my mom.

"What's this?" she asked, examining the stack. Her eyes went wide.

"An eighty-seven percent," I said, "on this week's lit paper."

She smiled. "I'll have to stick this one next to the ninety-two on the fridge."

"You really don't have to put my good grades on the fridge anymore," I assured her. "Honestly, I'd be happy with just a gold star and a dollar for every A."

She laughed. "Is that all it takes for you to get good grades?"

"Plus a lot of studying and no-nonsense brain power."

Mom sat back in her chair, her smile growing. "I'm proud

of the difference in you the last two weeks. Your grades have improved already, and you seem more focused. Should I just keep you grounded all the time?"

I huffed. "No, that's okay, really. I did want to ask you, though . . . can I take a break from my grounding?"

Her smile became suspicious. "Didn't you get a break today while you and Kate were at the mall?"

I nodded slowly and took a deep breath to prepare my lie. "I did . . . and it was great. Kate and I were thinking of doing a girls' thing tonight. Just us, at her house. Can I sleep over there? Please?"

"Is Will going to be there?" she asked.

"No," I said. "He won't be around, I promise."

"He hasn't been around much in the last few days," she noted. "Did something happen again?"

I shrugged. "I realized I need to spend less time with him if I want to concentrate on school."

"I just don't want you to make another poor decision," she said gently.

"It won't happen again."

She smiled. "I know. You're a smart girl, Ellie. You're just trying to figure your life out."

That was all too true. "Tell me about it."

She loosed a long, low breath. "Well, I suppose I should say no and be firm about this month of grounding, but one night over at Kate's might be good for you. You've been doing really well in school, so yes. You can stay at Kate's tonight.

On Monday, your grounding can resume."

I brightened, not even bothering to hide my smile. "Really?"

"Really," Mom said. "One night out, then it's all business again. You leaving now?"

I shot to my feet. "Yeah. Thanks, Mom. You're amazing."

She shrugged. "I know. Love you."

"Love you too. See you tomorrow!" I called as I buzzed from her office and leaped up the stairs to my room to pack an overnight bag. But when I walked through my door, I stopped at the sight of Will sitting on my bed.

He looked up at me. "We should go patrolling tonight."

I sighed and dug my duffel bag out from under the bed, tossed it beside him, and yanked it open. "We've gone every night this week. Can I get just one day off?" I pulled open my dresser drawer and pulled out a couple pairs of underwear and knee-high socks and threw them into the bag. Ever the gentleman, he looked away from my undergarments.

"Why do I get the feeling you aren't just staying the night over at Kate's?" he asked, finally looking back at me.

"Do you have a problem with it?" I asked. I tried to keep my voice cool.

"No," he replied. "But if you're going somewhere at night, I should be by your side. I'm your Guar—"

"Yeah, yeah," I grumbled. "You're my Guardian. Don't you want a night off from bodyguard duty?"

He looked entirely perplexed by my question. "It's not a

job, Ellie. I can't take a night off."

"Well, I don't really want you to come with me."

His lips parted and his eyes widened, the pain on his face making it so hard to tell him this. "But I have to," he said.

"No, you don't," I said firmly. "And I don't want you to. I'm going up to State to a party with Kate." I turned from him and went into my closet to pick out an outfit for tonight.

"What am I supposed to do?"

"I don't know. Hang out with Nathaniel. Go kill stuff."

"Ellie, I'm serious."

I left the closet with an armful of clothes and almost stopped when I saw the lost look on his face. I clenched my teeth together and walked over to the bed and stuffed my duffel bag until it was full. "I'm serious, too," I said. "Can't I have one night? I need to feel like myself again."

He took my arm, stopping me. My eyes followed his hand up to his face. His skin was warm against mine, almost electric. "But I know you. This *is* you. This has *always* been you."

I took my arm back and looked away from him. "Maybe that's not me anymore."

He hesitated, and the silence was aching. "You being around other people is dangerous. For *them*. You saw what happened with the fight against Orek."

"I'm not going to be a hermit."

"You're a target," he said. "That makes your friends and

family targets as well. I don't want them to get hurt either."

"What are you saying? I can't just abandon them."

"You may have to."

Our gazes locked. I drew in a long breath as anger churned deep within me. "I can't do that. Being around them makes me feel human. If I lose them, I'll lose myself and be alone."

His shoulders slumped. "You'll have *me*."

"*You* aren't all I need, Will. I need my family and friends, too."

"A long time ago," he began, "you understood how treacherous it was to drag ordinary humans into this world. You kept them away to protect them."

"That's not me anymore," I told him coldly. "That me has died a thousand times before."

"It *is* you. I understand that you love these people and you need them in your life, and I know *you* understand how dangerous your world is for *them*."

"This wasn't my world before you came along!"

"I have known you for five hundred years," he said, touching my cheek and threading his fingers through my hair. "I know you better than anyone, and I know once you truly remember yourself, once you wake up, you'll understand."

"I do understand what you're saying," I said, and pulled away from him. "But I can't give up my life and the people I love."

"Even if you endanger them?"

"I'll protect them," I said defiantly.

"Ellie, please don't be foolish . . ."

I held up a hand. "Not today. Please. I need to spend less time with you."

He blinked, taken aback. "But I'm your Guardian."

"You're not my shadow." My voice was sharper than I'd intended. "Or my babysitter. Lately I've realized that I need to get out of my old routine and into a new one. I need a break."

His lips parted as he stared at me in disbelief, his green eyes wide. "We don't have time for a break. Just *days* ago, a nycterid reaper picked a fight with us above a busy street full of humans. It's been all over the news. There are video clips of this all over the internet. The world is on the brink of either changing or ending."

"This is what I need right now," I said quietly. "I need to think. I know I'm supposed to be this fearless warrior who kicks ass and never bothers with names, but I don't feel like it. Trust me when I say I need this."

"This is a terrible idea."

I threw my duffel bag over my shoulder and picked my purse up off my dresser before turning to him one last time. "Maybe it is, maybe it isn't. I don't want you to follow me tonight. I don't need you there. If you come, I will be really angry."

"Please don't do this. Don't go without me."

"Good-bye, Will," I said. "I'll see you tomorrow. We'll patrol then, okay?"

His mouth tightened into a line before he got up and his form vanished into the Grim. After he was gone, I stood there for a moment, second-guessing myself. But I had already made up my mind. I left my house, climbed into my car, and drove to Kate's without him.

16

I'D BEEN TO STATE BEFORE, BUT NEVER ON A Saturday night. The end-of-February weather was miraculously above freezing, and that only encouraged thousands of college students to swarm the streets.

When we got inside Jay's house, it was so hot that the air was foggy and thick with perspiration and the smell of living bodies and cigarettes. Music pounded my head in heavy, hypnotic beats so hard I could barely open my eyes. The atmosphere alone was intoxicating and disorienting. Kate hooked her fingers with mine and led me through the packed living room. We squeezed through people slick with sweat and spilled beer.

A hand touched my waist, and I blinked twice to focus through the haze. Brian dipped his face so close to mine that our cheeks brushed together and he still had to shout for me to hear him. "I'm glad you came! Are you having a good time?"

I laughed. "Yes! This is insane!"

He drew away and laughed. "You have no idea. Let me get you girls some drinks."

Kate and I followed him into the kitchen, where a keg sat in a kiddie swimming pool covered with cute smiling fish. I laughed out loud when I saw it. Brian filled a couple of cups and handed them to us.

"Have a good time, ladies," he said. The kitchen wasn't much quieter than the living room, but at least we didn't have to yell in order to hear each other. "Beer pong is in the basement, so feel free to roam. I'll go find Jay downstairs and let him know you're here."

"He's playing beer pong?" Kate asked.

"Yeah. Want to join?"

"Hell yes," she said with a grin.

He brightened. "Well then. You're in luck, because I've got next on the table. Right this way."

He led us out of the kitchen and toward an open door in the hallway. We descended the narrow, creaky stairs into the musty basement. A table was set up in the center of the room, with a small crowd of people around it. Everyone was at least a head taller than me, except for a pixielike girl with a waist as narrow as one of my thighs. Her bleached blond hair had black streaks underneath, and she wore a tiny stud in her nose. I wondered if she was pretty under all that makeup.

I saw Jay partnered on the other end of the long table with a very tall, lanky guy with a Mohawk and a shirt that said HAMMERED. Mohawk Guy had a white Ping-Pong ball in one hand and a joint in the other. Jay and Mohawk Guy had three plastic cups, each filled with a little bit of beer, in front of them, and the team they faced had two left. Mohawk Guy sank the ball into a cup and roared with victory. He spun to the side, and Jay took the second ball out of a water cup. He tossed the ball, and it swirled around the cup before hitting the beer. He swore at the top of his lungs and threw a fist in the air in the angriest happy cheer I'd ever seen. The crowd surrounding them cheered and hollered.

Mohawk Guy bobbed and shook his head with the beat of the music upstairs and did a little skip before slapping Jay gently in the chest. "I'd love to play again, but I promised Maggie I'd smoke her down."

Jay nodded. "That's cool. I'll meet you up there in a bit."

Mohawk Guy laid a hand on the tiny blond-and-black-haired girl's back, and they disappeared upstairs.

"Sweet," Brian said. "I've got next." He turned to me and took up a lock of my hair with his hand to examine it curiously. The gesture was so Will-like that it startled me. "Be my partner, gorgeous?"

"Uh, yeah," I said.

Jay playfully tugged on Kate's shirt. "You game?"

She grinned. "Always."

He laughed. "Be right back." He waggled two empty

cups in his hands, which I took to mean he was going to refill for the game. Brian grabbed a couple of our cups to do the same.

Kate slunk up to my side and shimmied her hip against mine. "So what do you think of Brian? He's so cute, isn't he?"

"Yeah, he is." The guilty feeling in my gut kept me from elaborating. Brian was really cute, but he wasn't who I wanted to be flirting with.

"Ell, get over him."

I blinked at her in surprise.

"I don't need to read your mind. Your face is always so black and white. Tonight isn't about anything serious. Just have fun. Brian has gorgeous lips. I'll bet he's an amazing kisser." She squeezed my hip, and I bounced away from her with a squeal.

"Who says I'm going to let him kiss me?" I teased.

"I do," she said firmly. "Because I think you need to kiss someone else. Just a harmless, fun little kiss. Nothing serious."

"Hmm." I wasn't sure if I was ready or even willing to kiss another boy. Not yet. I didn't really know Brian, and while I knew one kiss wasn't that big a deal, I just didn't *want* to kiss anyone else.

The boys returned and arranged the game. They had filled up the cups with beer, and Brian tossed the balls to the other side of the table and turned to me.

"Okay, do you know how to play?" he asked.

"Get the ball in the cups, right?"

"Basically. It takes some technique, but that comes with practice." He nodded to Jay and Kate. "They'll go first because Jay won last round."

Jay tossed his ball. It bounced off the rim of a cup. Kate's ball ricocheted off the table without even touching a cup. Brian put both balls into the water cup to rinse off the linty floor nasties. He tossed one ball, and it dropped into the first cup.

I cheered and stuck out my tongue at Kate as I picked up the second ball. I straightened my arm and aimed. Brian stepped close to me and slid his hand slowly down my arm. His touch, coupled with the coolness of the basement air, sent a shiver through me. His other hand wrapped around my waist as he touched my wrist and guided my arm back.

"Line it up," he said softly into my ear. He was extremely distracting.

I released. The ball tapped the rim of a cup in the back row before falling into the beer. I jumped and threw my hands up as I cheered and Brian scooped me into a hug.

Somehow, Brian and I miraculously won the game. That first cup was the only one I made the whole game, but that didn't take away from the fun I had.

Brian linked his fingers through mine. "Wanna dance?"

"Yes!" I smiled hugely and followed him upstairs.

I was much more at ease with the thundering music after

having a few beers, and Brian was a *really* good dancer. I swayed my hips and he followed me, running his hands down my arms and around my waist. I turned my back into him and his lips brushed against the bend of my neck as we danced, making me feel even hotter in the sultry heat of the house as the party raged all around us. To my frustration, I was reminded of every time I'd asked Will to dance with me. I didn't want to think about him while I was having such a great time with Brian, but I couldn't help it.

I spun my body around to face Brian so that it was his face that I saw, instead of Will's that I imagined. My eyes locked with Brian's, and I noticed for the first time their gorgeous brown color. Like pure, delicious milk chocolate. My world whirled around me as I danced through that alcohol haze. Brian wrapped a hand around my cheek and slid it to cradle the back of my head, his fingers twining through my hair. He lowered his face, and instinctively I withdrew before his lips touched mine. He looked puzzled a moment, but then he gave an apologetic smile and seemed okay that I'd pulled away from his kiss. Kate had told me to kiss someone else, but I still didn't think I could. Will's face was in my mind again, and I couldn't drive it away. Brian didn't try to kiss me again as his hands fell to my hips. We danced until I forgot that there were a hundred other people in that living room, and I completely lost track of time.

I stumbled and laughed when he caught me with an arm around my waist. "Want to take a break?" he asked.

When I righted myself and still felt like I was spinning a hundred miles an hour, I nodded and pressed a hand to my forehead. He took my hand and led me from the room and toward the stairs. As I took that first step, I hesitated, trying to figure out where he was taking me. No way. I was not going into his room. "Where are we going?"

"Don't worry. Kate and Jay and some other people are up here chilling. If we don't find them, then we'll come right back. Okay?"

I chewed on my lip before nodding and following him upstairs. He checked one empty room before moving on to the next. We found a room full of people and went inside. Jay and Kate were sitting on a raggedy couch together, and Mohawk Guy and his girl sat on a lumpy futon next to the couch. Brian sat on the bed, and I sat shakily down next to him.

"There you two are!" Kate exclaimed with a wide joyful grin on her face.

"This is my room," Brian said. "That's Rob and Maggie." He gestured at Mohawk Guy and his girl.

Maggie gave me a smug smile, and Rob acknowledged me with a nod.

"Hey," I greeted them nervously.

Rob winked at me as he packed a bowl with weed. His eyes were already blazing red. "Want to smoke, gorgeous?"

Maggie shot him a ferocious glare, which he ignored. He puffed his chest and blew out a thick cloud of smoke before hacking painfully. He passed it to Maggie, who also took a hit. Brian's turn came next, and then he passed it to me. I held the bowl and lighter in my hands and stared at them. The weed smelled like something had died on Bigfoot's ass and then had gasoline poured all over it.

I frowned at it and passed it on. "No, thanks."

Brian fixed us more drinks, mixing from multiple bottles. Before I knew it, he was passing us shots and cups of liquid that, after a while, didn't taste anything at all like alcohol. The TV was suddenly on. We were watching one of my favorite late-night vulgar cartoons. The next moment, we were watching something else. What time was it? I was leaning against Brian. His hands were around my stomach, fingers toying with the hem of my shirt. My boots were off and across the room. How did they get there? Kate and Jay were making out on the couch. Brian's nose nuzzled my hair, and it just annoyed me. The new show on TV was really funny. Like *really* funny. I didn't even know what was going on, but it was *amazing*. Then Rob and Maggie were gone. It was just me and Brian sitting on his bed. Suddenly Kate and Jay were gone, too. When did they leave?

"Where did everyone go?" I asked, turning around to look at Brian. Turning made my mind swim, and I let my head sag heavily to the side.

"Just downstairs," he said. "They'll be right back."

I moved away from him, but he stopped me. His hand rubbed my side and swept down my waist, tugging me closer to him. My head felt immensely heavy and his shoulder was there, so I laid my cheek on it. For some reason, the cotton of his shirt felt extra cool compared to the air of the stuffy room, and I played with the soft collar. The cotton felt amazing to the touch. I tried to avoid looking up at him.

"How old are you again?" he asked, his hand now grasping around my bare thigh. I felt very self-conscious in that skirt suddenly.

"Seventeen." I looked around for Will, but the room spun like a tornado and my eyes bulged as nausea flooded over me. I pushed myself away from Brian as I remembered that Will was nowhere near, because I had told him I was going to this party without him. I had a sudden strange feeling, like a hole had been ripped inside me.

I was lying on my back, but I had no idea how that had happened. I couldn't remember. The bed was incredibly soft and cool, and my body felt like it was burning up. Brian's body on top of me didn't help at all.

He kissed my neck and nibbled on my earlobe, but it only annoyed me. I felt no little warm shock in my nerves like the ones Will gave me with the slightest touch.

"You're really hot," Brian breathed into my ear. Beer smell blasted my cheek.

I grimaced and turned my face away. "Thanks."

He leaned over me, pushing his chest into me as he sucked on my neck sloppily. His mouth moved and his lips shoved against mine. I jerked my face away and pushed at him, but he was so heavy. Whatever he was doing was kind of gross, like a dog slobbering all over me.

"Don't do that," I said with a grunt. "Brian, no."

He pushed me deeper into the bed. I shoved my hand into his shoulder, but I didn't have the strength to do much. The effort made me so tired, and I relaxed. His hands covered both of my breasts, and I lashed out in fear and shock.

"Okay, Brian," I said, almost suffocating beneath his weight. "That's enough. I said no. Get off me!"

One hand squeezed my hip and played with the bottom of my skirt, his fingers treading dangerously north. I squeezed my knees together and brushed at his hand to move it away, but he pushed his thigh between both of mine, parting them, and his hand kept going. A burning hot finger hooked around the elastic of my underwear.

"Brian, *stop*!" I shoved my hands at his uselessly as tears budded in my eyes. This was getting bad. So, so bad. If my head hadn't been spinning so much, I could have stopped this, but it was impossible to summon my powers.

When his mouth pressed against mine again, my body locked up and I twisted my face around. My power surged weakly, and he startled at the zap against his skin, but his confused pause only lasted an instant before his hand grabbed my chin and forced my head straight and he kissed me harder. I couldn't focus enough to shove him away. Panic was sapping my strength.

I heard two loud, consecutive bangs, and then Brian flew off me. Confused, I opened one eye. Will had plucked Brian up by the back of his shirt. I blinked hard, certain I'd only imagined what I saw. Will tossed him—gently, by reaper standards—across the room, and he slammed into the far wall. The drywall caved, and Brian's body tore off a couple posters and knocked empty bottles off a shelf above him onto the ground. He hit the carpet and swore at the top of his lungs as he staggered to his feet.

"You son of a—" Brian swung at Will, and Will shoved a hand into the human boy's chest, swatting him like a fly, and he crashed to the wall again. As Brian picked himself up off the floor, they stared at each other for way too long, and even though I could see only the back of Will's head, I imagined he was trying to kill Brian with his eyes since he couldn't do it with his hands. The anger in Brian's face was replaced by fear, and he scuttled out of the room. No one gave a look that could kill like my centuries-old Guardian. Will definitely had the intimidation face down pat.

For a moment, I was filled with so much relief that I wanted to throw myself into Will's arms, but then I remembered I was supposed to be mad at him and I frowned up at the ceiling. I lay on the bed, furious with Will for following me out here when I had told him not to. If things had gotten really out of hand, I could have kicked the crap out of that guy. I didn't need or want Will to save me.

"Ellie? Are you okay?" Will whispered, leaning over me, his voice feather soft, his hands politely smoothing my clothes back into place. His presence was all over me, so incredibly close, and I inhaled his scent. I wanted to grab onto him, but I couldn't give in.

I threw a hand over my face to block out the harsh light from above. "Go away, Will."

"Nope" was all he said as he wrapped an arm under my back and the other under my knees. He lifted me up and carried me through the house.

"Put me down," I growled, and tried to wriggle free.

"Nope."

"I'm going to bite you if you don't put me down."

"Go ahead."

All right then. I turned my head into his chest and chomped down on air and a little bit of cloth. "You suck."

"I know."

I glanced at the gaping hole where the doorknob had smashed through the wall. On the other side of the door frame, the wood had shattered where the door had been busted open.

"What are you doing?" asked a voice. "Where are you taking her?"

I peeked to see that Jay had stopped us. He looked pissed.

"Who are you? You can't just take her out of here, man."

Will stared him down the way he had with Brian. "She's mine."

I snarled and ground my knuckles into his chest, but it had no effect. "I am *not* yours, you caveman!"

Will ignored me. "And she's in high school."

Oh, great. Just tell everyone about the drunk high school skank at the college party, getting carried out.

Jay didn't protest anymore, and Will stormed past him and outside. He opened a car door and set me down on the cloth seat. I recognized the interior of Lauren's car.

Will touched my face gently, and his eyes found mine. His expression was a strange mixture of anger and concern. "Where's Kate?" he asked firmly. "I'm getting her out, too."

I waved a hand, motioning back to the house, and I pressed both my hands to my forehead. The car spun around me and I pushed my face into the seat to try and make the world stop, but it didn't work. When I looked, Will was gone.

I heard voices outside the car, and I sat up a little to see out the window. Kate was arguing with Will, but I couldn't understand what she said.

"But I *can't*," Will growled, just loud enough for me to hear. "It's a lot more complicated than you could ever imagine. You have no right to judge me, Kate."

Her face twisted in anger. She said something else and went back into the house. Will opened my door and leaned over me to buckle me in.

"What did she say to you?" I demanded.

"Nothing important."

"Well, it was enough to make both of you angry." I was

so tired, but I struggled to stay awake. He couldn't take me back to my own house. I was supposed to be with Kate at her house, flipping through *Cosmo*, not wasted and with a boy. And especially not with Will.

"Yeah," said a third voice. "It was this random right here." It took me a second to recognize Brian's voice.

Will's eyes flashed and he drew away, his face twisting into a snarl.

Not good.

"Wait, Will!" I clamored, reaching for him uselessly. "Just forget about them. They don't matter. Please don't do this!"

As he disappeared around the back of the car, I struggled with my seat belt until it sprang free, and I climbed out of my seat. My legs wobbled, but I pressed my body against the car and found enough balance to drag myself around.

"Ellie, get back in the car." The anger in Will's voice shocked me. It made me stop in my tracks and stare after him.

Brian stomped up to Will, flanked by Jay and Rob. "He sucker punched me back in the house. Kicked my door right off the damn hinges, too. You're going to pay for that, asshole."

"You have no idea how glad I am that you want to fight me," Will said to the guys starting to circle him. I could see his power simmering the air around him like a hot sun on black pavement, but the humans couldn't see anything at all. They couldn't see what they were really trying to pick a fight with.

Brian stepped forward. "I'm going to mess you up, man."

He swung, but Will stepped aside with ease and Brian staggered past him. Will's blurred movement was too fast for the drunken boy. Each punch clumsily passed Will's head, and as Brian stumbled around swinging, Will tapped his back, and he hit the snow-covered ground hard. Brian rolled around, swearing at the top of his lungs. A crowd of people piled out the front door to watch the fight.

"All right, Will!" I yelled. "You've established that you can kick their asses. Let's just go!" My head hurt, and I fell back against the hood of the car.

He looked back at me for only a fraction of a second as I fell, and Brian shot to his feet and lunged at Will. He caught Will off guard, and his fist barreled into Will's jaw, snapping his head to the side. Brian swung again, but Will caught the motion, wrapping his entire hand around Brian's fist with ease. He squeezed and Brian moaned in agony, his knees buckling until Will was practically holding him up by his fist.

"I want to break your neck for what you did to her," he snarled with so much malice that his words sent tremors of fear through even me. "You're lucky you're human. Otherwise there wouldn't be enough of you left for fertilizer after I finished tearing you apart."

"What are you?" Brian sputtered, his eyes wide with fear.

Will said nothing and smashed his elbow across Brian's

face. Brian went limp instantly, and Will tossed the boy to the ground. Blood trickled from Brian's mouth and dotted the snow around him, but he was alive. Just very, very knocked out. Perhaps minus one tooth. Or two, or three.

Jay and Rob launched themselves at Will on either side, but Will's power slammed into Jay and threw him across the lawn. Will kicked into Rob's chest and sent him flying in the other direction.

"Will, stop!" I cried. "I *order* you to stop."

He halted and straightened, staring at the boys as they rolled around on the ground and groaned.

"Think about what you're doing," I pleaded, amazed that my words had stopped him. "You'll kill them!"

He turned to me, the brightness in his eyes fading as he realized that I was right. He blinked, looking around him at the crowd of shocked and terrified people, and an overwhelming look of shame filled his face.

Kate pushed her way through the crowd gathered on the front porch. Her hand covered her mouth when she saw the fight. "What the—?"

Another girl appeared right behind Kate, cell phone up to her ear. "I'm calling the cops!"

Will was close to me in a heartbeat and threw me over his shoulder like a sack of potatoes.

"You son of a bitch!" I yelled, and beat my fist into his back. "Don't carry me like this!" I kicked and struggled, but he only held me tighter. In seconds, I realized that flailing was doing me no good. I gave up and sagged, making my body dead weight.

"Jackass," I growled as he set me back into the passenger seat and helped buckle my seatbelt.

"Stop calling me names."

"I can't believe you're doing this to me."

He stomped around the car, back to the driver's seat, and started the engine.

"You don't own me."

"You're right," he said. "I don't. But it's my job to protect you, and that's what I'm doing right now. It's not safe for you here."

I made an ugly noise and stared out my window at the world rushing past me. It made me a thousand times dizzier, but I didn't care. I was too tired to keep my eyes open any longer. If I just closed them for a moment, then I'd feel so much better. Just for a moment . . .

17

I MUST HAVE FALLEN ASLEEP IN THE CAR BECAUSE I was abruptly aware that it had stopped and Will was climbing out. A moment later, he had my door open and was lifting me into his arms. He carried me into the house and up a flight of stairs. I tensed and swiveled my head around as he pushed open the door to a room. I took a deep breath and realized instantly that the room smelled like Will. The rich scent made me giddy, and I buried my face in his chest so he wouldn't see my involuntary smile.

When Will put me down on the bed and pulled away, I sat up dizzily. I felt better after sleeping on the drive home, but I was still drunk. I watched Will return with a tank top and cotton shorts. He laid them down beside me and purposely avoided my gaze. The thick tension between us practically fogged my vision.

"These are Lauren's," he said. "She doesn't mind you borrowing them tonight. There's an extra toothbrush in the bathroom if you want it."

"I'll thank her in the morning." I tilted my head to see his eyes better. "Is this your room?"

He nodded and started to turn away.

Will's room. Will's bed. My nerve endings lit on fire.

"Will," I said, touching his arm. Muscle clenched beneath my fingertips.

He turned back to me, still averting his eyes. Anger spiked through me.

"Look at me," I said. It felt strangely intimate being in his bed. Things I shouldn't have wondered swelled inside me, like all the things we could do right here where I was sitting. His scent filled my head, making me feel even more intoxicated.

My anger washed away the second his gaze lifted to mine. My heart felt heavy when I saw how dull the color of his eyes was. I pulled my legs underneath me and stood up on my knees. I toyed with the hem of my skirt and watched his gaze on my fingers and bare skin. His jaw tightened when I edged closer to him. My hand trailed up his arm and shoulder to wrap around the back of his neck. He swallowed and watched my other hand slide up his chest, moving over the ridges of his muscles. My fingers touched his lips, and my other hand pulled his face down closer to mine.

"Kiss me," I whispered slowly, a desperate plea, and I

stroked my thumb across his bottom lip. My heart pounded, and I wanted him so badly it felt like I'd jump out of my skin.

His mouth parted, and his gaze fell to my lips before flickering back up. His hands slid around my hips, and he pulled me against him. "No," he said, but his body betrayed his pledge.

"I order you to kiss me," I said into his lips. My fingers dipped into his waistband and began to unbuckle his belt and jeans. He took a deep breath and his hands tightened on my hips, but he didn't stop me.

He turned his face into my neck and let out a long, frustrated groan, burning my skin with his breath and sending shivers through me. He nuzzled my hair, drinking in my scent as my fingernails ran softly down the back of his neck. "You can't do that to me," he said huskily, his lips brushing my skin.

I slipped my hands under his shirt, and I smoothed them over his solid abdomen. "Then kiss me because you want to."

He lifted his head and brought his face so close to mine that I could feel the heat radiating off him. His breathing was ragged when his mouth finally met mine, the kiss deep and full of something far more carnal than any kiss before it. He kissed me as fiercely as he fought in battle, with as much determination and calculation as he had when he killed, and I melted into his body. No one had ever kissed me like that before, no one *could* ever kiss me like he did. I inhaled the scent of his kiss as I tasted it. He hadn't kissed me in so very long that I was hungry for it, starving for his lips. I wound my hands around his shoulders and nipped his bottom lip gently. He squeezed me into his chest more tightly and let out a low rumble from his throat.

I pulled him over me until his body pushed mine deeper into his bed. My fingers wound through his hair as his hands explored every inch of me. His kisses moved south, and his lips found my stomach. I arched my back, and his arm slid around my waist, pulling me into him, and a soft whimper escaped me. I tugged at his shirt and yanked it over his head before sliding my hands across his bare chest and shoulders, slipping a hand over the tattoos on his arm and digging my nails into solid muscle. His mouth returned to mine, deep and exploring, and he kissed my neck, grazing my skin gently with his teeth. I kissed his shoulder as I finished unbuttoning his jeans and started to slip his belt off from around his waist.

Then his lips at my neck stopped abruptly. Before I could register what had happened, he reeled back until he was no longer touching me. I sat up in a wave of disappointment that beat at my heart and soul.

"Will—"

He backed away from the bed and my mouth clamped shut. "I . . . No. I can't do this."

"What's wrong?" I straightened my shirt, feeling the sudden sting of embarrassment.

"You're drunk," he said, his voice back to normal. He began to button his jeans and put his belt back on, his hands visibly shaking.

I crept to the edge of the bed. "I'm fine."

"You're not you right now," he said firmly, and backed away from me. "You don't know what you're doing."

I slid off the bed and eased toward him. My entire body trembled, and I was still dizzy with desire and alcohol. When I got to him, I smoothed my hands up his bare chest, my fingers lingering over the tattoos on his right arm before threading through his hair. "Yes, I do. And so do you."

He grabbed my wrists and pulled my hands away. "No, you don't. And it's not right that I do."

I searched his eyes for any brightness, any sign of passion left in him. "Don't you want me?"

He deflated against me, exhaling. He dipped his head and kissed my shoulder before brushing his mouth along my jaw, his hands around my wrists tightening just slightly. "You have no idea how much I want you," he whispered against my skin.

I edged closer to him, pushing my body into his heat. "Then you can have me."

"Ellie . . ."

"Don't you love me?"

He softened and kissed my wrist, his breath and lips warm. His mouth and nose nuzzled the delicate skin there and something inside my chest collapsed with a rush. "I do love you. More than anything. And that's exactly why I'm walking away."

He kissed my cheek and as he let go of my wrists, I shoved him away in anger. He blinked at me in surprise, confusion filling his eyes. I backed away from him unsteadily, nearly falling over before catching my balance.

"What's wrong with me?" I spat, narrowing my eyes. "It's not just tonight that you won't kiss me or touch me or anything. It's not just because I'm drunk. Why do you keep doing this?"

He shook his head tiredly. "Nothing's wrong with you. I have to go."

"Don't," I pleaded, reaching for his arms. "Stay with me, Will. *Stay*, please. We don't have to do anything. I just want you here with me."

He squeezed his eyes shut and drew in a long, shaky breath, the muscle in his jaw quivering. "I have to disobey you now. You'll thank me in the morning." He lowered his head to kiss my lips as chastely as in our very first kiss so long ago.

He pulled away and disappeared from the room. After a few minutes of humiliating solitude, I changed into Lauren's pajamas. When I burrowed deep into the mattress and tugged the sheets up to my chin tightly, Will's scent was all over the bed. I imagined him reading a book or playing his guitar in this spot on a quiet afternoon. It turned out that falling asleep in his bed was much easier than I thought it would be.

The next morning, I woke with a pounding headache. The sun pouring in through the window lit the mocha-painted walls of Will's bedroom with a golden glow. It was bare and very clean. The most color came from a large bookcase, and a plush black leather sofa chair sat in a corner. On the wall opposite the bed were three guitars propped up on stands. I recognized all three of them. The room still smelled like him and brought back the memory and shame of last night, when Will had brought me in here. The shirt I had torn off him was still lying on the floor as a brutal reminder. I felt sick to my stomach, not because I was that hung over, but because I was embarrassed and furious with myself for the way I had behaved. I wasn't the kind of girl who threw herself at a boy. I'd made a lot of mistakes last night.

I slid out from underneath the blankets, running my hand along the soft mattress, touching the hem of the pillowcase. Being in his bed felt powerfully intimate, and beneath the smell of last night's party, I caught his scent on my skin. His smell was all over me. I closed my eyes and took a deep breath before dragging myself out of his bed. I moved through his bedroom, touching everything, picking up small things off the dresser. I examined a sprig of dried flowers that looked like jasmine. I loved the scent, especially when mixed with vanilla. I set it down carefully and lifted a decorative hair comb beside it. The piece looked more than a century old and was glossy and delicate. The comb part of it was black and iridescent like an oil slick, and a carved bird of all different shades of purple, gold, and red rose out of what looked like flower petals . . . or flames.

I returned the hair comb to the dresser and stood there, contemplating what to do next. Not wanting to lose the wonderful feeling of Will's scent all over me, I settled on going into the bathroom to wash my face and brush my teeth with the extra toothbrush he had offered. I could feel my mascara crusting around my eyes, and my hair was a tangled mess. Running a brush through my hair was a battle, but soon I felt refreshed with a clean face.

I dug my cell out of the pocket of my skirt. I had three texts from Kate asking where I was and if I was all right. I texted her back that I was alive and with Will and that I'd call her later. What I didn't say, but wanted to, was that I was never sneaking out to a college party with her again—until I was in college, at least. Too much had happened last night that didn't need to happen. She'd left me on my own with a guy I didn't know. The thought of it made me flush briefly with anger. When I saw her next, there would be some words exchanged. I also prayed she'd had the sense enough to grab my purse and jacket from that house when she left.

I didn't have a change of clothes, so I stayed in Lauren's pajamas. They were lightweight and I was a little chilly, but the cold felt good for my hangover. My stomach growled, so I crept out of Will's room. As soon as I opened the door, I caught the thick, delicious scent of eggs and bacon. Nathaniel often made dinner for us when we were over, and even though this was my first time staying the night here, I wasn't surprised that he'd cook breakfast. I forced a smile on my face and straightened out my tank as I stepped downstairs and followed the smells into the kitchen. My gut dropped when I saw it was Will at the stove cooking instead of Nathaniel. My fake smile disappeared. No need for *that* anymore.

He looked up at me as I walked in. And then he looked away. I opened my mouth to speak, but he beat me to it. "How are you feeling?" He prodded at the eggs frying in the pan in front of him.

I gave him a smart smirk and crossed my arms over my chest. "Peachy. How are your knuckles?"

He set his fist down on the counter without dropping the spatula. The eggs smelled like they were burning. "They attacked me first."

"You could have just gotten in the car and driven away."

The look he gave me was serious. "I could have, but I didn't. I made a choice, regardless if it was wrong or right. I wanted to do a lot more than I did."

"You're burning those eggs."

He took a deep breath. "Ellie."

"If you're going to make me breakfast, then don't burn it."

He took the pan away from the heat and scraped out the

eggs with the spatula and placed them on a plate. I caught the faintest glimmer of a smile. "Who says I made these for you?"

I sat down at the bar. "Me."

He filled a glass with orange juice for me and presented it with the plateful of eggs and bacon as if it were a peace offering. "My knuckles are fine."

I took the plate and glass. "That's a shame."

His brow flickered, and he leaned his back against the counter on the other side of the room. Even from this far away, I could see the familiar flash in his eyes. I could've seen it a mile away in the dead of night.

"There was a comb in your room," I said. "On top of your dresser. With a bird on it."

"It's yours. The bird is a phoenix . . . rising from its ashes."

"Has it always been mine, like my necklace?" I asked.

He shook his head. "No. I bought the comb for you over a hundred years ago, from a . . ."

But I didn't hear the rest of what he said. My mind slipped away, drifting into the memories of that day.

The market in Shanghai was packed with people roaming from makeshift tent to makeshift tent, bartering loudly, shopkeepers darting after thieves. The street was a blaze of color, sights, and sounds. Heady scents of oils and spices pulled my attention in every direction. I wanted to see everything there was.

"Dragon," a man called in Chinese.

Will turned his head, and I followed his gaze to a small elderly man behind a table covered with jewelry and figurines carved from ivory and jade. He was smiling, watching us both as we walked through the market. I took Will's hand and led him to the tent, eager to see what the man offered.

"Dragon," the man said again, and nodded to Will, his smile widening. He reached over his beautiful wares and lifted a comb with an intricately carved mythological firebird adorning it. He set it in his palm and held out his hand to me. "Fenghuang. Phoenix."

My eyes captured the comb, roving over the infinite detail and incredible colors. I took it from the man and brushed my fingers over the bird's wings.

"We'll take it," Will said. He pulled a couple coins from his pocket and gave them to the man, who gave a small bow and thanked Will several times.

I drew a little breath when Will turned to me, tucked my hair back on one side, and slid the comb in. "Thank you," I told him, watching his face, mesmerized by the happiness in his eyes and the one corner of his lips that pulled into a smile.

"Beautiful," he said, and his thumb brushed my cheek.

My eyes fluttered and I was back in the present, looking up into Will's face once again. "I remember it," I said. "Were you going to give it back to me? Now that I'm here . . . again. Alive."

His jaw set and he swallowed. "Yes. Eventually. I wanted

to give it back to you when you remembered it. You can have it now if you'd like."

"Thank you," I said, wishing now that it was in my hands so I could touch it. Instead I touched the winged pendant around my neck, watching Will's face as he watched my hand.

"Why do you have jasmine, too, of all things?" I asked curiously, recalling how carefully dried the petals were, how strongly the scent had remained. "Did you know that it's my favorite flower?"

"It reminds me of you," he said in a quiet voice, his gaze still lowered. "You've always smelled like jasmine."

Of course he would know I loved jasmine. He knew *everything* about me. I dug through my memories that shifted in and out of focus, and couldn't remember myself ever choosing a different perfume or scented lotion. I always chose jasmine. For hundreds of years, I had been choosing jasmine.

Overwhelmed with emotion, I felt my eyes burning, and I poked at my plate. "Where's Nathaniel?"

"Out with Lauren."

I took a bite of the eggs to please him. They weren't as burned as I'd thought. He'd made me breakfast despite what had happened last night, and I wasn't sure I had it in me to tell him thank you. Eating the breakfast meant more to him than stupid words. He knew I appreciated it.

"You shouldn't have done what you did last night," I said.

He watched me carefully. "I don't regret anything."

"You shouldn't have interfered. I had everything under control." It was a lie and he knew it. While he had every right to laugh in my face, he didn't.

"That's not what it looked like. That guy was going to take advantage of you. I know you better than anyone. If you were in the right state of mind, you'd never have let him touch you like that."

I took another bite, because I didn't quite know what to say. He was right. Brian was a creep. I didn't know if he was capable of something as awful as rape, but I was also pretty sure I would have been able to stop him if things were about to get that far.

"I don't regret pulling him off you," Will continued, his voice firm, "and I hate that you think I should. I will never regret anything that I have to do in order to protect you."

"Still, you shouldn't have beaten them up. You against a hundred of them still wouldn't be a fair fight. You could have killed them all. You scared me, Will. I thought you were about to snap." I knew he had a temper, and underneath all of that control, there was a darker, volatile nature. This was Will, the one person I knew better than my own self, but I didn't know if there was anything he wouldn't do to protect me.

"I was angry and I know it was wrong, but that guy deserved far worse than what I did to him. If I upset you, then I apologize for that, but I am not sorry for striking any of them."

"You shouldn't have followed us to that party, either. You had no right."

"Ellie, you're being *hunted*," he said. "And I am your Guardian. I kept my distance, but I had to go, just in case. What if you'd been attacked? What if a demonic reaper like Merodach had shown up and killed you or someone else? You shouldn't have put yourself and Kate at risk, let alone everyone else in that house."

I sighed and pushed my plate away, unable to keep eating. "Do we have to talk about this again?"

"I just don't think you're considering the safety of others, let alone yourself."

I ground my teeth and rapped my nails against the counter. "Look. I'd just nearly died fighting Orek, and my own father even tried to hurt me. I've been going through a lot. I feel like I'm going crazy. Getting out and doing something new felt like a good idea."

"I should have been at your side," he said earnestly. "Wherever you go, I should be with you. You are my responsibility, and I can't protect you if you're away from me."

"I can't stand being around you when you treat me as if I'm just your responsibility. Like I'm a *stranger*. I'm the last person who should be a stranger to you."

He frowned, dropping his head and looking up at me through his lashes. "Then what do I need to do?"

I bit down on the inside of my cheek as my chest tightened and I tried not to cry. "If I knew that, I would have ordered you to do it already."

He smiled that beautiful smile of his, and I almost let out

a sob. I wanted him to tuck my hair behind my ear like he did, hold me in his arms that way he did, kiss me like he did last night—*anything* but sit frozen like a statue inches from me. I loved him so much it hurt. He was so close to me, yet impossible to reach.

"It was hard for me to stand outside and wait," he said, his voice breaking more and more. "I knew what he wanted—what he *tried*—to do. I waited and waited for you to wake up and pummel that guy, because I know you could've. I was so angry, and my fists were rolled so tight my hands were bleeding. I tried not to interfere, I really did, but then it was clear that you couldn't get out of there on your own. I couldn't wait anymore."

I was biting hard on the inside of my cheek, imagining him trying to hold himself back and let me handle the situation on my own. I had been in way over my head and too drunk to save myself or even know what was going on.

He continued, looking away from me. "Before things got really bad, I was jealous. When he touched you . . . I wanted to kill him."

"But if I'm not with you, then one day I'll be in a relationship with someone else," I said. "You won't really have a right to be jealous."

"Won't I?"

"Well, we're not together, so I can do whatever I want. Is that what Kate was yelling at you about? Because you were acting like we're together when we weren't?"

He stepped around the bar and sat on the stool beside me. "Do you think I want it this way?"

"Then do something about it, Will!" I shouted. "I don't want to wait on you forever. I don't *have* forever like you do. You can't waltz in on me when I'm with a guy and throw me over your shoulder like a caveman. That's not fair."

"He was going to *rape* you!" His temper erupted and he slammed his fist down on the counter, making me jump.

I recoiled, the unbearable truth of his words stinging, and the next moment, my eyes began to burn. The memory of Brian's hands all over me, the stink of beer on his breath suffocating me—an ill feeling flooded through me, and I swallowed hard. I'd come so close, so treacherously close. This wasn't a joke. This wasn't about Will overstepping his bounds or me refusing to admit I'd put myself in danger. I wasn't invincible. And though I was the Preliator, I was still just a girl. I spent so much time fighting supernatural monsters that I didn't realize ordinary people could hurt me too. The reality of what could have happened clawed at me, and I covered my mouth with my hand and let out a sob. Will touched my arms gently, but I stood and stepped away from him. I could still feel Brian groping me sickeningly, my skin crawling with the memory.

I wiped at my face, choking on the taste of salt in my tears. "It still . . . it's not fair. What if next time I'm with a boy I like?"

"I won't be able to bear it."

"What will it be, Will?" I asked, my voice rising as I fought my tears. "Are you going to storm in and claim me then, too?"

His jaw and lips hardened. His fist, resting on the counter, tightened until his knuckles turned white, as if the war that waged within him grew more violent and he was trapped in silence. His brow darkened and he shook his head, his eyes flashing bright, glued to mine.

"I've already claimed you," he said, and grabbed my hand. He stood and yanked me into him, and his mouth crushed against mine as his other arm wrapped around my waist. His touch erased the memory of Brian's burning hot hands on my body, and I let Will's presence surround me. I threw my arms up and around his shoulders and stood on my tiptoes just to get a little closer to him.

Then my heart twisted and broke. I shoved him away. "No!"

"Ellie—"

"You're driving me insane!" I cried. "I can't take this push and pull anymore. You kiss me and then you won't kiss me and then you do. It's not fair! It's got to be one or the other, Will!"

His body locked up again, and he stared at me. After a long, agonizing minute, he spoke. "What do you want from me? Anything. It's yours."

My lips quivered, holding back a sob. "Do you even have to ask?"

He didn't respond and we returned to that face-off state.

"Will," I said breathlessly. "I just want *you*. Five hundred years you waited to tell me you loved me, and as soon as you do, you tell me you can't because Michael will take you from me. Why is loving me so wrong? I don't care what my brother said to you, and neither should you. Why do you care so much about being perfect? How could you think that you and I are so wrong?" I stepped toward him and ran my hand down the solid muscle of his arm and hooked my fingers around his. "You know how right this is, how right we are. I don't care what I am in some other life. I *was* an archangel. I *was* Gabriel. I *am* Ellie now, Will. This body is human. I *feel* human. I don't want you to treat me like I'm untouchable, because I'm not. I want you to touch me. I want to be yours."

He closed his eyes and his forehead touched mine. "I'm so sorry for everything. I never wanted to hurt you or make you doubt me. I need you to trust me. I need *you*. And I love you. I want you. You know I do. I'll never stop doing any of those things until the day I die for you."

I closed my eyes and took a painful breath at those words. It was a possibility that I had for so long refused to acknowledge, the possibility that he would die defending me, just as every one of my past Guardians had. I felt their losses greatly in my heart, but the idea of losing Will hit me to my soul. I opened my eyes once again to meet his beautiful emerald gaze.

"You told me yesterday in my room that this is me, who I've always been, but I don't feel that way," I said. "Is it me that you love, or is it Gabriel?"

He looked so sad in that instant. "I love this beautiful thing inside of you that makes you human. Your soul, your fragility, your human passion. None of that is Gabriel. It's all *you*, Ellie."

My lips quivered. "If I wasn't human, would you still love me?"

He gave me the smallest smile. "I'd still love you forever."

"You know I'm yours," I whispered, and kissed him softly. He let me step into him without resistance.

"And I'm yours," he said. "I always have been and always will be."

I bit my lip. "I know."

He kissed me then, his lips moving with mine as if they were made for each other. His fingers wound through my hair, and he deepened the kiss further with each passing heartbeat. The sadness receded away from me, and I let myself drown in him instead. Intensity crackled between us and heat rushed through me, longing and desperate. His hands traveled lower, spilling over my shoulders and tightening around my hips. An ache flashed low in my body and a whimper escaped me, a sound that triggered something deep in him as well.

He lifted me off the floor and onto the counter, shoving the plates away and knocking over the glass of orange juice. When he pushed my knees apart, hands running up my thighs and sending a strike of lightning desire up my spine, he crushed his body against mine and I forgot about the mess entirely. His mouth and tongue were hot against my neck, and I buried my hands in his hair as his arms wrapped around me and his fingertips raked down my back. One of his hands found the point of my hip, and his teeth nicked the bend of my neck. I dug my nails into his shoulder and my head fell back, something wild in me craving him. I grabbed a fistful of his shirt, and ached to tear it off him, to do anything to break down the thin, aggravating barrier of cloth between our skin. I fumbled with the buttons, gasping for breath when his mouth wasn't on mine, and I pushed his open shirt over his shoulders, my eyes capturing his muscled chest and the tattoos spreading up his arm and the side of his neck.

"I've wanted you for so long," he murmured against my throat between kisses. "Every time I look at you I feel like I'm about to explode, no matter how still I try to stay around you. Inside I'm like a hurricane. Everything you do . . . you drive me crazy." His mouth returned to mine hungrily. "The way you play with the little curls in the ends of your hair." He kissed me again, his hands squeezing my sides. "The way you wring the hem of your shirt with your fingers and make that little face when you're deep in thought." Another kiss and a small, secret smile. His thumbs glided under my shirt, just an inch, and the contact made me gasp and dig my nails into the back of his neck. "Where you touch me it feels like I'm on fire." Again, he kissed me, long and deep and leisurely.

His hands slipped completely under my shirt, but stayed respectfully around my waist. The sensation of his hot skin on mine numbed my thoughts until my body began to take control, as if it knew exactly what to do. I touched his arms, applying enough pressure to let him know I wanted his hands to keep going. But he was hesitant, careful, and my own feelings were mixed. The more aware I became, the more I questioned what my body wanted. I wanted him, every inch of me did, but I wasn't sure if I was ready to go that far yet. A silent war raged between my mind and my body as he kissed me. I pulled back, and the rigidness in his shoulders collapsed, his hands sliding down my sides and resting around my thighs.

I stared into his face, studying every bit of him that I'd known so well for so long. His lips, that perfect full Cupid's bow. His dark brow, where so much of his intensity came from. His eyes, that gleaming, radioactive green. He wasn't smiling now, but I remembered the little line that grew beside his right eye whenever he did. I brushed the hair off his forehead—it was a wild mess from my hands anyway—and ran my palm across the two-day-old roughness on his jaw. I rarely saw him perfectly shaved, but I liked it that way.

Loved it. Loved *him*. He didn't always make the right decisions, but it always turned out okay. Every imperfection he had was perfect. He was perfect to me.

"Ellie," he sighed, his chest rising and falling with the word. When he said my name, even when he teased me, it was the most wonderful sound in the world. I closed my eyes as he said my name again, this time his lips brushing against my cheek as he spoke. "Ellie, I love you. You weren't supposed to forget that I did. I told you not to."

I shook my head. "I never forgot."

If he didn't love me, he wouldn't have stopped what I'd started last night. If he didn't, he wouldn't be so patient with me right now. If he didn't, he wouldn't fight so hard for me. If he didn't, he wouldn't risk his soul for me.

I touched his cheek and lifted his chin so that our eyes met firmly, so that he understood what I said next to be the absolute truth. "I love you, Will."

He closed his eyes and set his hands down on the counter on either side of me. I wrapped a hand around his cheek and thumbed his jaw gently. He leaned into my hand and kissed my palm.

I heard the garage door rise and my heart sank, but Will didn't move like I thought he would. He leaned forward and rested his forehead against my shoulder, breathing softly. My hands hung around the back of his neck, trembling. A minute later, Nathaniel and Lauren walked in, awkwardly unbuttoning their coats and storing them away in the closet.

Lauren gave Will and me a knowing, apologetic look and tightened her mouth. Heat flushed in my cheeks, but I was grateful and felt braver when Will didn't step away from me. He never showed me affection in front of anyone, so his simple nearness would be the best I'd get.

"Sorry," Lauren said. "We interrupted, didn't we?"

I tucked my hair behind my ear, physically aware of how swollen and numb my lips were from kissing him. "No. You're fine. I was just leaving." I started to slide off the counter, and Will took my hands to help me. After a moment, he took a reluctant step back as if it pained him to do so, and he buttoned his shirt slowly. I grabbed a dish towel and started to mop up the mess of orange juice.

"Stay awhile, Ell," she offered with a smile. "I never get to see you."

The offer was tempting since I really, *really* didn't want to go home and face my mom's wrath just then. I looked up at Will, hoping he would agree and then it would be settled.

He touched my arm. "You should stay."

My gaze fell to his hand on my skin. "All right."

"Good," Lauren said as she walked toward me and took my hand. She pulled me away from Will, who let his hand fall, and I suddenly felt cold. Lauren led me through the kitchen, and I glanced at Nathaniel. He didn't look happy. Just before Lauren took me into the living room, I glanced over my shoulder. Nathaniel and Will were now locked in a staring match. Will shoved his hands into his pockets, and

Nathaniel beckoned with a sideways nod of his head for Will to follow him out into the garage. When they disappeared, I felt a terrible hitch in my gut and wondered if whatever had just ignited between Will and me was already dead.

18

THE TV VOLUME WAS SET LOW, AND I DIDN'T KNOW
what show we were watching or even what channel it was
on. I only stared blankly at the screen. My eyes drifted out
of focus and I was hypnotized by the flashes of light and
color, the dull roar of voices and music filling my head with
white noise. My name was mixed in there somehow, and it
took me a moment to realize Lauren was trying to get my
attention.

"Ell," she said. "Earth to Ellie. You there?"

I took a deep breath. "Yeah. I'm here."

"Are you all right?"

"Yeah, I'm fine," I replied, but I wasn't sure if it was a lie
or not. "Where were you guys this morning?"

Her smile faded. "Nathaniel and I met my parents for

Sunday brunch. We do it every week."

I looked at her, happy to turn away from the TV. "Is he your boyfriend then?"

Her gaze fell away. "Yes. For four years now."

"Wow," I said, my eyes widening. "Does your family know what he is?"

"No. Not yet, at least."

I would never be able to tell my parents about Will's true nature either. "Do they know what *you* are?"

"My mom does," she said. "Her grandmother was a psychic also, so she knows all about reapers but can't see into the Grim like us. I'll have to tell my family the truth about Nathaniel someday. They'll eventually notice that he doesn't age. My family hates all reapers, even the angelic. Honestly, I can't blame my mother for hating them. If I had to watch my child go through what I did when I was young, I'd hate them all too."

Since she didn't elaborate, I wouldn't ask. I didn't like talking about the horrors I saw either. "You must love him."

"I do, so I understand everything, Ellie."

"Do you think you two will have kids someday?" I asked.

She shook her head. "Humans and reapers can't have children together. Something in the genetics, I believe."

"That's sad," I murmured, thinking of more than just Nathaniel and Lauren.

"It's all right," she said. "Who knows what will happen in the future, anyway?" She gave me a small, reassuring smile. "Nathaniel isn't going to kill him, if that's what you're worried about."

My doubt sat heavily in my stomach. "He looked furious."

"Not so much angry," she assured me. "He's worried about what both of you have been going through. He knows Will has been in love with you for a very long time. He understands, so don't think that he doesn't." She took my hand and squeezed it. "I understand, too. I'm here if you need me."

The sound of angry shouts made us both jump. We stared at each other.

"You don't think I know that?" Will's voice hammered through the walls.

Lauren's hand tightened around mine. The shouts died down, the rest of the argument audible from this distance, and Lauren and I sat in silence for a few minutes as she held my hand securely.

"Everything will be okay," she said, and released my hand. "Will needs to talk to Nathaniel. He's been very troubled lately. He needs help, and Nathaniel has been there for him forever."

I nodded. "They're practically brothers."

She paused thoughtfully. "Nathaniel's taken care of Will. It's always been the hardest when he doesn't have you around to give him focus. But Will was so young when his mother died, and Nathaniel has been his only family. Nathaniel is always here when you can't be, and he offers Will guidance, which is what he needs most right now. He needs to be told that it'll all be okay."

I knew what it was like to need to be told that. Even now I forgot that Will needed someone to help keep him standing sometimes, too. "It will be. Everything will be okay."

Lauren smiled at me. "It will."

Sometime later, the door to the garage opened and I heard the boys' footsteps on the hardwood floor. Nathaniel walked into the living room with an even expression and sat down on the loveseat opposite the couch Lauren and I sat on. Will appeared at the edge of the carpet and the wood floor, and his cool green eyes met mine gently. The look he gave me was one I knew well—and feared. He wanted to talk.

I stood and followed him through the house to the stair-case, each of my steps wobbly and weak, my heart fearing the worst. Will led me into his room and shut the door behind us.

"What's wrong?" I asked, my voice childlike and quiet.

He smiled, and relief washed over me. "Nothing. Nathaniel and I had a good conversation."

"That's good." I couldn't keep the suspicious edge from my voice, as if I expected everything to come crashing down any second.

"I want to try it," he said. "Us. I want to give us a try."

My mouth parted in surprise. "You do?"

"You were right. You've been right all along. I've been a coward running from this. I don't want to run anymore. I've tried so hard not to feel what I feel for you, because it's dangerous." He squeezed his eyes shut painfully. "You'll die again, we both know it's true, and Nathaniel helped me realize that I'm more afraid of the pain of losing you than of what Michael could do to me for loving you. I am devoted to *you*, not to Michael, and I am bound to obey *you*, not him. I've tried not to love you, but I've failed. It's easier to love you than to pretend I don't."

"Then be with me," I pleaded.

A small smile curved in his lips. "On one condition."

I grinned back. "What's that?"

He stepped forward and wrapped his arms around the small of my back, tugging me to his chest. I threw my arms around his shoulders, sliding my nails up and down his neck gently. "Stay with me. And with Nathaniel and Lauren. All day. Be happy today."

"That's it?"

He bent down and kissed me richly. "Each time I look at you, I want to see a smile on your beautiful face."

"Will you be looking at me a lot?"

"I'm always stealing glances," he confessed. "You rarely notice."

"Ugh, just don't look at me before I've showered."

"You're always beautiful. Especially when you smile, so today will be dedicated to making that happen. We will do anything you want to do. We'll make it up as we go."

"Can we make root beer floats?" I asked.

He laughed. "Sounds great."

"Can we make Nathaniel and Lauren dinner tonight? I want to thank them for being so good to us."

"Awesome idea. I'm a terrible cook, though."

"The eggs were only a little burned," I teased and kissed his lips, feeling a low ache at the memory of this morning. "Can we build a snowman today?"

"Definitely."

"Play video games?"

"As you wish."

Just as Will promised, I was happy all day. I didn't realize how late it was until I glanced out the window. The sun was setting and the sky was turning violet. I'd stalled going home long enough. When I'd finally show up back home, my mom would ground me for life this time. Begrudgingly, I passed my video game controller over to Nathaniel, just as someone on the other team shot my player dead.

Will looked up at me. "We can play something else, if you'd like."

"It's not that," I assured him. "I've got to get home."

"All right then." He set down his controller and stood.

I smiled and waved to Nathaniel. "See you later."

"Have a good night, Ell." He respawned my player and continued the game.

Lauren rose and gave me a tight hug. "Drive safely. See you soon. I mean it."

"Of course." I waved good-bye and jogged upstairs to

grab my clothes from last night. When I came back down, Will was waiting for me at the bottom of the steps. I stopped when I reached the third-to-last step, which made me just above being level with his eyes, so that I looked down into his face.

"Got everything?" His expression as he looked up at me was gentle and warm.

"Yep," I said. "I think I'm going to go home by myself. I was supposed to be home in the morning, so my mom is going to be really mad about my being so late. Can you drive me to Kate's so I can get my car?"

"If you need me," he said, "I'll be there within minutes."

I smiled and ran my fingers through the front of his hair so that it stuck straight up. "I know I can count on you."

He smiled back. "You can always count on me."

I leaned down, one hand on the railing, and I kissed him gently. He tugged on the belt loop of my jeans and pulled me another step down so that I was eye level with him. He grinned, and I laughed and kissed him harder.

"Are you sure you don't want me to come with you?" he asked against my lips in a way that almost made me reconsider.

I drew back and touched his face, smiling. "I'm tired and I'm about to walk into World War Mom. Let's go for a run tomorrow instead of patrolling, okay? I could use a good run."

"Okay." He kissed me sweetly. "Let's get Lauren's car again."

He drove me to Kate's house, and as we sat in her driveway for a minute, it was hard to say good-bye to him again.

"Thanks for the ride," I said, and opened the door. "I'll see you soon."

Kate's mom answered the door, and I went up to Kate's room, where she was watching TV. She sprang to her feet when she saw me.

"Where the hell have you *been*?" she shouted, and yanked me into a tight hug.

"With Will," I confessed. "He took me back to his place last night."

"And?" She didn't even hesitate.

"And . . . I don't know. I'm glad he showed up and took me home."

"We were having such a great time." She seemed disappointed.

I laughed nervously. "Uh, yeah. Up until Brian started taking my clothes off."

That made her pause. "Are you serious? Will didn't say anything about that when he took you."

I wouldn't have expected him to. He was more of kick-ass-now-explain-self-later kind of guy. "Well, I'm glad he showed up. I was so gone I didn't even know what planet I was on."

"I'm going to freaking *gut* Brian. *And* Jay."

"I can't believe you left me alone with him," I said, struggling to keep my voice even. "You have no idea—"

"God, Ell," she said, her voice cracking. "I'm so sorry. I wasn't even thinking when we left the room. It's all my fault."

I exhaled. "We've got to look out for each other when we go to things like this."

"I know . . ."

"Were you okay after I left?" I asked. "Why didn't you come with us?"

"I was mad, I guess. Will pissed me off, and I wasn't ready to leave. I don't even remember crashing. At least Will beat the crap out of Brian and those guys out on the lawn. After you left, it was all anyone could talk about."

I gave her an unintelligible grumble in response to that.

"Are you okay, Ell? Really?"

I let out a long breath and sat on the edge of her bed. "I think so. I think everything is going to be okay." I gave her a vague recap of how Will drove me an hour and a half back to his house, how I had thrown myself at him and he'd told me no, what had happened at breakfast, and then what he told me about wanting to give us a try. Telling that part to Kate didn't make it feel any more real, but I got the familiar spins in my stomach when I thought about how fiercely Will had kissed me only hours ago. Remembering all he'd said to me made me dizzy, and I chewed on my lip to bring myself back down to earth.

"You two were made for each other," Kate said.

He was a piece of me and when he wasn't around, I never felt whole. "What did you say to him as we were leaving? I saw you yell at him from the porch."

"Oh. Well, I had no idea what Brian had tried to do, and if I had I probably would haven't yelled so much at Will. I feel bad about some of it now. I was just pissed at him for storming in there acting like your boyfriend, so I told him it wasn't fair to you."

It was impossible for me to explain the depth of my relationship with Will to Kate. "Thanks, girl. I've got to get home. Do you have my stuff?"

"Of course," she said in a gentle voice, and handed me my purse and duffel bag. "Call me if you need to talk. I'm sorry I left you alone with that jerk. It'll never happen again, I swear. I've got your back, girl."

"I know. It's okay. We all made bad decisions last night."

"Love you."

"Love you too." We said good-bye and I went outside to my car.

When I got home, the garage was open, so I went through the door leading into the kitchen. I shut the door quietly behind me and heard the shuffle of footsteps on the stone tiles of the foyer. I slowly made my way through the kitchen, fearing the consequences of coming home so late.

"Mom?" I called. "I'm home."

I rounded the staircase and saw my mom and dad together. Their bodies were so close I wondered if they were hugging—and *why* they were hugging, since they despised each other. When I saw my mom, I froze solid in my tracks. Ice flowed through my veins and the blood washed from my face as something kicked in my stomach, and my heart launched into hyperspeed. Blood caked her swollen and bruised face, her hair a rat's nest. My dad held a tight fistful of hair, and his other hand was clamped around her throat. He wrenched her around to look at me, his face twisted with violence and a look so savage it took me a moment to recognize him. My mom's eyes were wide and wild with terror and pain.

"Dad?" I choked, my eyes shifting from his to my mom's and back. "What are you doing?"

"Your daddy's been dead a long time, sweetheart." He jerked my mother to get a better grip on her. His lips curled into a smile too sinister to be human, and then he began to change. His fingernails grew into talons that dug into my mom's tender skin until more blood popped and she squirmed. Four pairs of fangs slid from his smile, and spikes tore through the back of his shirt, casting monstrous shadows across the floor in the porch light pouring in from behind him. "I should know. I tore out his rib cage myself."

"Who are you?" I breathed, the words struggling to escape as if claws were around my own throat. Will's words echoed in my mind: *If you come across a vir, you may not know what he is until it's too late. They'll shape-shift to take the form of a human in order to infiltrate.*

"That's not very important. But it's been fun. Good times, kid. Sorry for calling you a slut." He looked up at the ceiling thoughtfully. "Actually, no. I meant that."

I couldn't breathe, couldn't speak. I could only stare at the reaper, at the terror and disorientation on my mother's face. I couldn't move.

"What? How? Why?" he gasped in a mocking tone. "Speechless, are we, *Ellie*?"

The way he said my name felt so invasive. The demonic only called me the Preliator. But this one knew me. Lived with me. With my mother.

He took his hand off my mother's throat and pulled the collar of his shirt down to reveal a strange tattoo over his heart, a circle with an Enochian symbol within it. "This is what you're wondering. The magic is old, so ancient, that only Bastian could have learned of it. It lets me walk in the sun without harm. You know, all those little complications that would have given me away. The spell was difficult, but he pulled it off. You never knew a thing, did you? I was good, so good."

He jerked my mother's head back and met her wild, frightened eyes. "By the way, I didn't get that tattoo at your cousin's bachelor party. I didn't even go to that. You're a moron, Diane."

She whimpered and turned her face away from his. He looked back at me and grinned a mouthful of fangs.

"Anyway, Bastian sends his affection," the reaper crooned in a malicious voice, his face no longer anything like my father's, but belonging to an entirely different creature. "And he told me to leave a little something for you. Let's say it's a belated seventeenth birthday gift."

He snapped my mother's neck. She hit the floor with a dry, cold thud. Dead.

My pulse flooded my ears, drowning out the reaper's next words. I stared at my mother—her body—at his feet. Fire crackled from my fingers and toes, devouring my body to my core, burning away like the wick of a stick of dynamite. The edges of my eyes spun and filled with white, and my power throbbed. Visions came to me, the missing pieces belonging to thousands of years of memories, as Gabriel's presence and power overwhelmed me. The darkness churned and exploded, taking me with it. I was gone, and all that was left of me was rage.

I launched myself at the reaper, pushing off the floor with my toes, my power detonating behind me, demolishing the wall and shattering the tile floor. The reaper was too slow for me. I swung my elbow across my chest and pounded the bone into his skull. He crumpled to his knees. I kicked the back of his head and his palms hit the floor. He tried to rise, but my power erupted into his face, sending him flying across the foyer and crashing into the staircase. Wood splintered and exploded, the cloud of dust almost blinding. The reaper staggered to his feet, stumbling down the steps. I stepped up to him, the torrent of rage swallowing me and releasing everything I'd been afraid of inside of me. I didn't care what sort of damage I caused. I *wanted* to damage. My hair whipped around my face in the tempest that the white light of my power and the darkness within me had created. He took a swing at me, but my senses were spinning so fast that I sidestepped his blow and smashed my fist into his face. His jaw made a sickening tearing sound and whirled loose, flinging free and out of sight. I threw my power into his body, knocking the wind from his chest and the feet out from under him. His back hit the floor and I leaped on top of him. I beat his face and shredded his skin with my nails. When his body turned to stone, I still tore at him, dragging my nails across rock until they were bloodied and broken. Dust soaked thickly into the blood splattered across my face and clothes, filling my lungs until I was choking on it.

Hands grabbed me and looped around my waist and tried to pull me back. I shrieked and thrashed, fighting off the hands and clawing the air wildly to get back to the reaper's remains. A horrible, snarling animal noise tore from my throat—a sound that couldn't possibly have been my own voice.

"Ellie!" the owner of the hands shouted uselessly. "Ellie, *stop*!" The voice was warped and distant, as if I were underwater and he was shouting at me from somewhere above the surface.

The fury cloaked my vision like a whiteout. I swung a wild fist and connected with soft tissue. My attacker grunted and his grip loosened, allowing me to break free and get back to pounding at the pile of stone near my mother's corpse.

His hands found me again. He grabbed my shoulders

roughly and jerked me around with an angry, exhausted groan. I clawed at his face and arms, drawing blood. Another intruder knelt beside my mother and touched her neck. I screeched and launched myself at him to protect her body, but the first set of hands grabbed me again, yanking me back. I hit the cold, broken-up floor, flailing my limbs and power into my attacker's body. He swore and pushed through the blows, battered and bloody.

"Ellie, please stop fighting me!" His hands gripped my wrists and pinned me to the floor. "It's me! It's *me*, Ellie. *Stop!*"

I thrashed against him and let out a bloodcurdling scream until my ears rang.

"Her eyes!" he roared, turning back to the other intruder. "They're solid white. It's happened again. Nathaniel! I need you *now*! Put her out before she kills us both!"

I shrieked, and my power erupted again. An explosion of white light filled the house, blinding me and rocketing into my attacker's body. He flew off me and crashed through the far wall as the light swallowed us all and slammed into the walls around us. The house shook and groaned. He crumpled to the ground and I was on my feet in a blur. A form appeared beside me. I only saw a flash of copper eyes.

"*Sleep.*"

And I slipped into oblivion.

PART TWO

The Mortal Archangel

19

I WOKE UP SCREAMING.

I sat straight up and threw out my arms in rage. Someone shoved my chest and slammed me back into the bed. He pinned me down, but he couldn't hold me forever. I broke free and struck him in the face, ripping his lip open. I flew off the bed and made a dash for the door as he screamed my name and grabbed at me, his fingers only tagging my clothes. I was too fast and too wild. Then he screamed someone else's name, and another attacker appeared in the room. Two pairs of arms took strong hold of me and dragged me across the room.

That word slithered through my brain again: *"Sleep."*

My body went slack against their grip, and I fell into dark memories of lives past and blood spilled upon ancient ground.

Before me lay a valley littered with the dead. Snow settled on the bodies as I walked among them, blood staining the ground black, the stench of carrion flooding my senses. Torn and soiled red cloth lay draped over dull metal and frostbitten skin. The Romans should never have come here to Britain. The massacre was devastating, and the reapers had already descended to feed. Every single man fallen in battle was already burning in Hell. My Guardian and I were too late.

The bitter wind blew my tangled hair around my face streaked with war paint, biting through the wool robes I wore, given to me by a family living in the nearby village that the Romans had attempted to sack. The invaders were most unsuccessful.

A flash of light in the sky made me duck and shield my eyes. When the light dimmed, I looked toward the sky. An angel descended, his golden armor shining, wings spread wide. His face was ethereally beautiful—and vaguely familiar.

"Sister," he said, his voice musical and elegant.

I stared at him in confusion. "Who are you?"

"Don't you know me?" His blue eyes studied me curiously and with pity.

"I do know you," I said, digging deep through my memories. There was something there, far older than my human memories clouding the surface. "Michael. It's you."

He nodded. "Yes, Gabriel, my sister. You're slowly

forgetting who you are. You're becoming more and more human. I hardly recognize you. With all that paint smeared across your face, you look like an animal."

I lifted my chin in defiance. "It marks me as a warrior."

"It marks you as human."

I swallowed and my gaze faltered. I wasn't human. I was . . . something else. I was like Michael, an archangel. But I was losing myself. I remembered now that the more times I lived and died, the more like my human vessel I became and the more I left my archangel origins behind.

"Why are you so far north?" Michael asked, his armored boots settling on the frozen ground. He stepped closer to me, the summer warmth of his glory melting the light snow around us.

I was determined not to let his nearness frighten me. "The reapers follow the armies hoping for blood, and every last inch of this island is drenched in it. I've come for the reapers harvesting the souls of the fallen soldiers."

To my surprise, the archangel smiled. "That was a wise tactic. You will need these skills in the future. Many centuries from now, Lucifer's most powerful servants will be unleashed, and they will attempt to free the ever-expanding armies of Hell. You must stop them."

"Who are these servants?" I asked. The wind grew stronger, howling in my ears, making it harder to hear anything else.

My vision blurred as the snow fell more heavily, whipping

in the air and obscuring Michael's bright form.

"You know them," Michael said, but I could barely make out his words. "They are . . ."

But the wind was too loud, the snow too thick. I couldn't hear anything. All I heard was a dull roar; I felt the stinging bite of winter, and then someone else's voice tore me from my memories.

"Wake up, Ellie, and relax," a voice whispered in my head. It was so gentle and soothing that I took a long, deep breath and melted into the bed. I had every reason to relax. I would be happy if I relaxed. *"You're safe. Relax."* As soon as I obeyed, warmth spread through me and pushed away the dark. I settled deeper into the rumpled blankets, not smiling, but not angry. Just content.

"Ellie?" The second voice, a voice I knew and ached for, I heard with my ears and not my mind. I opened my eyes and looked up into Will's face. He leaned over me, his warm hand brushing my hair back, his eyes so bright I had to squint when I looked into them. His face was pale and raw as if he was frightened and tired. I wanted to speak to him, tell him that we were safe, but my lips wouldn't work.

"You're going to break your necklace if you keep lashing out," he said gently.

I didn't look away from Will. I wanted to reach up and touch him, but my arms felt like they were filled with sandbags and sewn together with thread. He leaned over me, and his hands fumbled at something around my neck and then lifted an object off my skin. It was so bright, so blinding white that I couldn't even make out its shape. I slit my eyes against the brightness, but it seemed that I was the only one who was affected. Will set the blazing object down behind him and brought his hand back to stroke my face.

"Are her eyes back?" Nathaniel asked from somewhere near me.

"She's back," Will said.

A shadow fell over my face, but my gaze was still locked on my Guardian. I couldn't look away even if I wanted to.

"Not for long," Nathaniel murmured. "I don't know how long I can hold her mind. She's pounding at the wall with everything she's got. I've never seen her this bad. Those other times, all I had to do was put her to sleep and she was back to normal when she woke up. But this . . ."

Will smoothed a hand over my hair, brushing it away from my face. "She's still in there. She'll come back."

"We can't let her lose it again," Nathaniel said. "She can kill us, Will. You know this. You saw what she did to that demonic vir, and she almost killed you back at the house. I know you love her, but you have to remember that we must protect ourselves as well as her. Lauren is downstairs, terrified. We must be prepared to do *anything*—"

"I've told you what I'm willing and not willing to do," Will said through gritted teeth.

"Sometimes there is no choice."

"I can't . . ." he breathed, trailing off. "She's just a—"

"She's just a what?" Nathaniel asked, cutting him off. "Just a girl? She's *not* just a girl, Will. She's an *archangel*. In *human form*. Every emotion she feels risks overloading, and then she loses herself to it. Gabriel knows and understands that if she becomes dangerous—"

"She's not Gabriel!" Will roared, but his booming voice didn't make me even flinch. I was too perplexed by the lines of fury on his face, the rigidness of his muscles, to really be listening to his words. I ached to hold and soothe him, but I still couldn't move. Then he deflated, and his voice became low and faint. "She's not Gabriel. She's just . . . Ellie."

When he said my name, I melted deeper into the bed as if his voice were a lullaby. Nathaniel was silent and Will relaxed after a few moments, his eyes returning to mine. His hand touched my face again, thumb brushing along my jaw. My eyes fluttered shut for a moment.

"We've got to go back and clean it up," Nathaniel said. "We've got some time before anyone notices the damage in the house or the humans missing."

"How?" Will snapped. "We can't leave her alone. What if she wakes up while we're not here? While Lauren's here? We can't leave her alone until she's lucid."

"That could take days. You stay with her and I'll clean up."

He shook his head, and I weakly shook my own, in a daze, to mimic him. "No. I won't be able to stop her if she breaks free. You can put her under, I can't, and I refuse to strike her. I will *never* hit her, Nathaniel, and I will *never* kill her to stop her from killing me. Not even when she loses control. You can't ask me to do that. I can't do it. I won't do it. I'd give my own life before I'd ever take hers for any reason."

A long moment passed, and I was still hypnotized by Will's jeweled eyes. I wanted to touch him so badly, to feel him, and finally my hand twitched, fingers reaching up. His gaze fell to my hand and he swallowed hard. I was confused. There was fear in his beautiful eyes now. Why would he be afraid of me?

"She's coming out of it," Nathaniel said. "I'll stay. You go clean up the scene. There is a book in my office, second shelf from the bottom. I believe page six hundred four will tell you what spell you'll need to use. Get rid of any of the reaper blood. That includes ours. Leave only her mother's. The scene has to look like a typical homicide. Do you understand?"

Will glared. "Yes," he hissed. "I get it. Just keep her asleep until I return. We can try again later to bring her back. Don't try it on your own. She will kill you."

"Don't worry about me. Now go."

Will paused before he looked back down at me. The backs of his fingers brushed my temple gently, and he leaned over me, the mattress shifting beneath us. He kissed my cheek, letting his lips linger. "I love you," he whispered as he touched his forehead to mine. "Please don't hate me when you come back to me. I'm doing the best I can."

Then he was gone.

My eyes snapped open. I turned my head to look around, but the beating of my pulse on the inside of my skull made me squeeze my eyes shut in pain. The pressure was so strong that I groaned and pressed my palms to my forehead.

"Ellie," called a voice.

I opened my eyes to see Nathaniel crossing the room. He knelt by the bed. Will's bed. I was in Will's room, but Will wasn't there.

"How are you feeling?"

I was puzzled by the worried look he gave me. He also looked exhausted. "Hey, Nathaniel. I feel terrible, like I'm hung over. Was I drinking?"

He shook his head, and that worry spun into sadness. "No. I'm glad to see you're awake."

I frowned up at him. "Yeah, I guess. I'm fine. My head just *hurts*. What am I doing here? I thought I left to go home."

"Ellie . . ." His gaze drifted away.

Then I saw the blood and dust caked across my clothes and skin as if I'd bathed in it. Seeing it, I remembered why I was there, and my veins filled with ice. Images flashed through my head, each stabbing like cold metal as it hit me. My past human incarnations, feathered wings splashed with blood, winds blowing the dust of ancient cities over barren landscapes, silver blades clashing with silver blades and ripping flesh. My mother. My father. The thing that killed her killed them both. Will tried to stop me and I hurt him. He tried to pull me away from my mother's body, and I'd nearly killed him.

"No," I breathed.

"Ellie." Nathaniel's voice was calm and cool.

I shook my head, weakly at first, then furiously. "No. *No!*" More images flashed in my mind, but I couldn't handle them all at once. They were tearing my brain apart. I sat up, scrambling off the bed, and my feet touched the carpet. Nathaniel moved with me, keeping himself between me and the door.

"Ellie, relax." His voice was in my head, warm and comforting, but no. No!

"My mother!" I shrieked. "Oh, my God. *Oh, my God!*" My entire body shook and I covered my mouth with my hands. I dry-heaved agonizingly.

"Ellie, please!" Nathaniel cried. *"Sleep, sleep!"*

I ignored the voice in my head, his mind tricks. "Where's Will?" I cried, knocking Nathaniel's hands away when he reached for me. "Where is he? *Where's Will?*"

"Stop! Ellie, stop *now!*" He was shouting now, giving up on controlling my mind. I was too strong for him in every way.

I shoved my hands into his chest with a burst of power, and his back hit the far wall. Bones cracked and he moaned in pain, but I didn't watch him hit the ground. Making a dash for the bedroom door, I slid on the carpet and into the hallway wall. I screamed Will's name as I ran down the hall, knocking over an end table and a vase and smacking into the balcony railing overlooking the living room. I screamed wordlessly as I flung myself down the stairs, slipping again at the bottom. Pushing through the pain shooting up my legs, I dragged myself to my feet and scrambled for the kitchen.

The front door burst open and I felt the warm rush of Will's presence. "Ellie!"

I doubled back and flung around the corner toward the foyer. He was there in the open front door, his white wings spread wide as if he'd just landed, his chest heaving, out of breath. I threw myself into his arms, the only place I felt safe, the only thing I had left, and we sank to the floor as I sobbed and wailed. He whispered something to me, stroking my hair and holding me close, but I couldn't hear him. I screamed for my mother, screamed for my family over and over until my throat and lungs burned and became useless.

I pulled away from him and struggled to my feet, wiping at my face, my legs trembling as I backed away. My tears streaked through someone else's blood on my face. "I have to go back," I sobbed. "I have to take care of her."

"It's done," Will said, standing and reaching for me, his own hand and voice shaking. His wings lifted and spread as much as they could in the house. "Come to me. *Please*, Ellie. Come to me."

"I have to take care of her!" I was so hysterical that I wasn't sure if any of my words were even comprehensible. He grabbed my arm as I twisted away from him. I pounded my fist on his arm and he cried out but kept his grip firm. "Let me go! Let me go to her!"

He yanked me around and threw me back onto the floor as I screamed and flailed against him. He leaped over me, straddling me, pinning both my arms over my head, and the shadow of his wings blanketed us both in darkness. His power shoved me deeper into the floor, so strongly I could barely move, the countless rivulets of inky smoke spreading over me and on the floor around me until I felt like I was falling into shadows, suffocating in them. I screamed and swung my head side to side, yanking my arms down and kicking my legs, but he wouldn't give an inch.

"Let me go!" I shrieked the words over and over until I stopped thrashing. I shuddered and lay still, breathless and voiceless from exhaustion. My lips moved, but nothing came out except for tiny whimpers.

"Ellie." His voice was soft and cracked with pain as he pressed his forehead to mine. "Ellie, please. Stop. *Please, stop.*"

I went limp heavily, sobbing, my lungs and throat shredded. His grip loosened, but even though I stopped struggling against him, he didn't release me.

"Ellie, *please*. Please, stop fighting me. Please, stop."

* * *

I stared out at the desolate desert of snow and ice that covered the lake behind Nathaniel's house. The wind blew cruelly, pitching up clouds of white powder and casting it toward the trees and the porch where I sat. I pulled the blanket wrapping my body tighter and didn't push my hair out of my face as it whipped around my head. I barely noticed the frigid air, since I was already so cold inside.

"Ellie," Lauren said as she slid the porch door open. "You've been out here long enough today. You're going to freeze to death."

I didn't reply. She hesitated for a few seconds before going back in and shutting the door behind her. It wasn't long before the door opened again and I sensed Will. I ground my teeth together to keep myself from shouting at him. He stepped slowly across the porch and knelt in front of me, resting both his hands on the sides of my chair. I glared down at him, and he only gave me a gentle gaze in return.

More memories flooded my head, and I buried my face in my hands, whimpering. "Go away," I snarled hoarsely.

"You need to talk to me."

I dropped my hands. "I'm telling you to go away."

His mouth tightened in frustration for a split second. "Please, Ellie, come inside before you freeze to death."

I snarled and spoke slowly, emphasizing each word so he knew that I was dead serious. "You framed my real father for my mother's murder. If you don't get the hell away from me right now, I'm going to punch your head right off your shoulders. You know better than anyone how capable I am of that."

After a long, painful moment, he stood. Instead of looking up at him, I stared at the snowy porch floorboards.

"I am sorry, Ellie," he said, his voice cold and formal. "But everything I do is to protect you at any cost, even if it means sacrificing your father's reputation. I'm sure he was a good man, but for years the thing you knew as your father wasn't him. It is a tragedy what happened to your family, but you have to understand that we cannot risk exposing our world to the human world. I hope one day you will forgive me."

I looked up to meet his steady gaze. *Our* world. My family was my world. This nightmare I fell into the day I turned seventeen could never change that. I wanted to fly to my feet and hit him and scream at him, but it would do me no good. In truth, I was terrified of letting my emotions go. I'd lost control of my power for the first time in a long time, and from what little I could piece together from my memory, I'd hurt Will and Nathaniel. I'd hurt them badly, and I felt terrible for it. But my regret couldn't make me forgive Will for what he'd done to my father's name.

His gaze narrowed and darkened at me. "Your mother fought like hell for her life, and here you are ready to throw your own away."

He turned and walked back into the house.

I didn't follow him. I pulled out my phone. There were

eleven voice mails. All of them were from Kate, one of my only remaining ties to the human world. It was just me and the darkness now.

My mother's funeral went by in a haze. Fake friends and family I'd forgotten I had all attended, shared their condolences, gave me lifeless hugs. They all looked at me with pity, some with fear. The little girl whose daddy killed her mama and took off. When I stepped up to my mother's coffin, I saw that they'd cleaned her up. No one could tell how the bones in her neck were shattered to dust, see the cracks in her skull or the bruises and gashes beneath all the makeup. They'd even put lipstick on her. When I touched her face, her skin was hard and cold, nothing like the softness and warmth that I had always known. She looked like a doll, frozen and clothed in a dress suit I knew she hated. She never wore it. That was why it looked brand-new. I think Nana had picked it out. How morbid, I thought, to have to pick out the clothes your daughter would be buried in. Perhaps it was even worse for the poor fool who did her hair and put the lipstick on her mouth. They could all be glad, though. No one saw her die but me.

I felt the strange glances from everyone at the funeral who expected me to be crying. That wasn't going to happen. Nana had wanted me to say something about my mother to everyone, but I couldn't do it. I couldn't stand up there and feel all those eyes on me, knowing exactly what was going through their heads. Instead, Nana got up and spoke about how kind and generous my mother was, what a good daughter and mother she had been. Nana said nothing about my father, which was a wise decision. That day the world pretended my father had never existed. No one wanted to think about him, but of course he was on all our minds.

I could feel Will there at the funeral the entire time, hidden within the Grim, but he only let me see him once without me having to follow him into that Hell dimension. I never spoke even a word to him.

I would be moving in with Nana until I left for college in the fall, but I wasn't ready to yet. I needed Kate. I needed to feel like a teenage girl. I needed to get away from reapers.

That night I curled up in Kate's bed with my knees tucked to my chin. I hadn't cried since the night my mother died, and I didn't want to start again. It hurt too much. Kate's mom forced me to eat dinner and even made hot cocoa, but I only took it because she was relentless. Now I felt sick to my stomach, and every time I closed my eyes to try and sleep, I was hit by terrible memories in the darkness of my mind.

Kate inched up behind me and rested her chin on my shoulder. She wrapped her arms around me and squeezed gently. I knew she meant well, so I wouldn't punish her for being kind to me. She, like everyone else, thought my dad had killed my mom. Thanks to Will and Nathaniel.

"They'll find him," Kate whispered.

I said nothing. There was no way I could tell her the truth, and I wasn't even sure I would want to if I could. Why should I bring her into this horrible world? She didn't deserve that kind of punishment. But then again, why did I?

At Nana's house, I was moved into the guest room, a room filled with too much white and nautical blue and maple wood furniture. It had been my mother's room when she was growing up, but her scent and feel had long since faded. Nana had already gone to my house and packed up certain belongings my mom had kept, things that were special to her, and to Nana and me. All of them were still in boxes on one side of my room that I had only stared at since they'd arrived. My clothes were still in the suitcase or in a pile next to them. The hangers in the closet were empty. To unpack and move in here would be to accept that my old life, my old home— everything—was gone forever.

Returning to my house and walking past where everything happened rebroke my heart with every step. Will had cleaned up all evidence of the reaper like he and Nathaniel had discussed. There was no dark stain in the spot where I'd torn apart the reaper, no dried blood on the walls, no claw marks, nothing. It was as if a tornado had blown through my foyer, and no one had ever died. I don't know how Will did it, but I had a feeling that book of Nathaniel's that Will took wasn't a Martha Stewart home-cleaning guide. Magic had to have been involved. The police had questioned me relentlessly about the inconsistency of the damage, but I had no information for them, and they soon gave up.

A soft knock on the door jarred me from my thoughts. Nana appeared, her white hair pulled into a low ponytail, and her eyes—so much like my mother's eyes, and nothing like my own—were gentle behind her reading glasses. "Hey, sweetheart. Come down for dinner."

I forced an apologetic smile. "I'm not hungry."

She peered over her glasses at me and rested a hand on her hip. "That wasn't a request. I want you downstairs in two minutes."

Nana's enormous dark gray cat, Bluebelle, waltzed through the door and rubbed his wide belly against my leg. Animals always seemed to love me, but Bluebelle couldn't decide between purring and stretching his ugly, smushed face into a ferocious hiss. I reached down to pet him, but he clawed at me and tried to bite off my fingers. Bluebelle was an asshole.

"Bluebelle," Nana called. "Come on, you old grouch. Two minutes, Ellie." Then she disappeared. She was like my mother in so many ways that I wasn't, because I wasn't really related to either of them. When I looked into the mirror, I didn't see anything of my mom.

My eyes fell to one of the boxes filled with stuff from my room. I dragged myself off the bed and opened the box to unpack a framed picture of me and my mom and my dad from our last vacation together.

Nana made pasta for dinner that night and promised all the carbs would give me energy for tomorrow, my first day back to school. I wasn't interested in conversation, but she kept pushing.

"Would you like me to drive you to school tomorrow?" she asked. "I know it's a long commute, and I don't mind."

I poked at the leeks and artichokes mixed in with the pasta. "I'll be fine."

She frowned. "Don't be afraid to accept my help. I love you."

"I know, Nana. And I appreciate everything you've done for me, but I want to feel normal. I want to go to school by myself like it's a normal day."

"That's a very grown-up decision," she said. "I'm proud of how well you're handling this."

My smile vanished. I had everyone fooled. I was angry, and everything was my fault. I should have known, should have done something, should have protected my parents. Will had been right, and I'd been in denial the whole time. I was too stubborn to stay away from the people I loved in order to protect them, and I had just stood there and let that monster kill my mother. Everything was my fault.

20

I HAD BEEN EXPECTING THE STARES. THE WHIS-
pers. The coldness. No one at school knew how to handle
this any better than I did. I walked sluggishly through the
hall, keeping my eyes up and ahead—no way would I stare
at the floor like a coward—hugging my books to my chest.
I knew what they all saw when they stared at me, because
I'd had the misfortune of passing by the bathroom mirror
despite my attempts to avoid it. They all saw the dark circles
the concealer couldn't hide under my eyes, that my hair was
dull and flat and had lost most of its shine, that I was thinner
because I hadn't been eating.

In my literature class I stared at the blank page of my
open notebook as my classmates scribbled furiously. I couldn't
concentrate when my mind kept revisiting the explosion of
memories my amnesia no longer blocked. The assignment

was to write a one-page essay on where we saw ourselves five years from now. No doubt everyone wrote down how they would be graduating college, starting careers, maybe getting engaged, and some would already have had a baby or two. Me—I saw myself dead in five years. Maybe five months. Maybe five days.

When the final bell rang, I stopped by Kate's locker to say good-bye.

"Why don't you come over to my place?" she offered with a concerned look. "We could *not*-study for the psych quiz tomorrow."

I sighed and leaned my head against the locker next to hers. "Maybe tomorrow. I'm a little exhausted, and Nana wants me home for dinner."

She smiled cautiously, and I was grateful that she didn't argue with me. "How about we hit up the bowling alley for a couple hours after school tomorrow?"

"That'd be fun," I said. I knew I needed to force myself to get out and do something besides go to school and hang out at Nana's.

"Does that mean you're coming?" she asked with a hopeful lilt to her voice, raising her eyebrows.

"Yeah," I said. "I'll go."

She played with a lock of my hair. "You'll let me know if you're not okay, right?"

I chewed on my bottom lip. "I'm as okay as I can be. Got to move on with my life, you know?"

"Yeah." She studied me with her cool blue eyes.

I hoisted my backpack higher on my shoulder. "See you tomorrow morning?"

She smiled. "Of course. You know I'm here for you. We'll have plenty of time to talk."

A sickness flooded my heart. If only I could tell her everything. I wanted so badly to talk to her, to tell her every-thing, because I *needed* to talk to someone. I needed to talk to Kate. I needed *her*.

I turned my face away and rubbed my eye before she saw the tears that budded. "Yeah. I'll see you tomorrow."

Before she could respond, I was marching briskly down the hall, leaving her at her locker. When I burst through the doors to the student parking lot, I saw the last person I wanted to see in the entire world leaning against the grill of my car. I rubbed away the tears that threatened to give away my feelings as I approached, feeling the curious eyes of other people around the parking lot.

"What are you doing here?" I asked, my voice sharper than I'd intended it to be.

The green of Will's eyes had been placid but troubled, and then they flashed, as if my words had stung him. He looked down briefly. "I wanted to make sure your day went all right. That *you're* all right."

I walked right past him to the driver's side door. "I'm alive, aren't I?"

He followed me. "I don't want to fight."

I realized then that we hadn't spoken for days, which was strange for me. It seemed like I saw him every single day. I was so used to his presence near me, all around me, and even when I was furious with him, I noticed his absence. I missed him. I missed him even now, when he was standing only two feet away from me. But I was still too mad to give in to the effect he had on me.

"Please just hear me out," Will pleaded.

I opened my mouth to interject, but he spoke again quickly.

"I did what I had to do. I know you don't understand that now, and I don't expect you to. Ellie, I'm sorry that I hurt you." He reached out a hand to touch my face, his fingers warm in the bitter cold air. "You know I'd never hurt you on purpose."

I closed my eyes at his touch and swallowed shakily. "Regardless of your intentions," I said slowly, "you still hurt me. And I'm not ready to forgive you yet."

He took my hand and lifted it to his mouth. His lips kissed my palm, and wings fluttered through my insides. He looked down at my hand for just a moment before returning my gaze painfully. "Please, *please* forgive me. I can't bear the way you look at me now."

I pulled away. "Let's talk in the car."

After I sat down and he climbed into the passenger seat, we fell into an awkward silence.

"She was going to divorce him," I confessed. "She was

going to get out, be safe. But we were too late. I was too late to save her."

"Don't blame yourself." His voice was a whisper.

I frowned and swallowed. "It doesn't matter that you and everyone else keep saying that. I'll feel like this no matter what."

"I know," he said. "But it isn't your fault."

If I continued to argue with him, I would only get angry, and I was desperate not to get mad at him anymore. I was tired of fighting with him.

"You understand why I did it, right?" he asked in a small voice.

He didn't elaborate, but I knew what he was talking about. "There had to be something else you could have done," I said.

"There may have been," he admitted. "I don't deny the possibility of it. But Nathaniel and I made a decision. The reaper said he killed your father years ago, and we don't have a body for the police to find. Your father would have been a suspect anyway. This was the most logical and safest solution for you."

I glared at him. "My *real* dad was a good man, Will. He is a victim in this, and now the whole world thinks he's a monster. He was *never* a monster. A monster is what killed *him*, and now my family and I will have to live with this lie for the rest of our lives!"

I took a deep breath to erase the anger from my voice. "I'm

sorry that I hurt you. I never wanted to hurt you or Nathaniel. I didn't know that it was you trying to hold me back."

"You weren't trying to kill me," Will said. "You were defending yourself and your mother."

"Whether I tried to kill you or not, I almost did. I can't let that happen again. I feel like every slightest emotion that I have is about to send me over the edge. Everything is so magnified. I can't handle myself. I'm dangerous, and you know it."

"You *can* handle this."

"I heard you guys talking when Nathaniel had me under. That I'd never gotten that bad before. That my . . . eyes had *changed*. Nathaniel said that I—Gabriel—knew that if I became dangerous—"

"No."

"—that you would have to—"

"Ellie, that's out of the question."

"But I'll come back," I assured him. "You are the only one who is strong enough to defend yourself against me. If I might hurt someone else, someone who isn't as strong as you, then this may be the only answer."

"No," he repeated firmly, his jaw clenching as he shook his head and shifted uncomfortably in his seat. "No. I won't. Not ever."

"You may not have a choice."

"You can't ask me to do that. Ask me anything else, anything but that. I would let you kill me first."

I watched him sadly, unable to think about losing him, no matter how angry I was or how much my heart hurt. Every one of my Guardians before Will had been killed in battle, and now I remembered each one of their deaths like a knife to my heart.

"Something happened to me that night that I didn't tell you about," I said, my voice breaking. "When I lost it, everything came rushing back to me all at once. I remember everything. I've spent five hundred years with you, and I remember them all."

He laid his hand over mine and held it. I forced myself to take back my hand, but the movement was unbearably difficult. Bastian's face flashed across my mind, and then Merodach and Kelaeno invaded behind him. I couldn't face them without Will. I couldn't save the world on my own.

"I'm going out with Kate tomorrow," I said. "Afterward we will go patrolling. But I need to feel happy at least once before I launch into Terminator mode and go after Bastian. I'm going to kill them all."

"I'll never leave your side."

"I need you there. But I need you to be just my Guardian right now. Nothing more."

"Anything for you."

I looked over to where he sat, but he had vanished.

Just after six the next evening, I stared into the bathroom mirror. My phone sat untouched next to my hand on the counter, waiting for me to call Kate. I could pull this off tonight. Nobody would be paying attention to me. No one even cared.

There was a soft knock on the door.

"Come in," I called.

Nana emerged with Bluebelle on her heels. The cat made an ugly meow as he darted through the door. Once in the bathroom, he gave an irritated shake and sauntered around, as if surveying his territory. He started toward me to rub against my leg, but I didn't reach for him. I knew it would have been a better idea—and possibly less painful—to hug a cactus than to touch Bluebelle.

"How are you doing, honey?" Nana asked, her voice gentle and her gaze studying my face. "Since you're likely not putting on that mascara just to go to bed, I'm assuming you're still meeting your friends at the bowling alley."

I pulled my blush compact and powder brush out of my makeup bag, holding the items hesitantly between my fingers. "Yeah. As long as it's okay with you."

Her eyes met mine in the mirror. "I'm glad you're going. You need to get out and be yourself again."

And that was just it. I didn't know who I was anymore. I was Ellie, but I was also Gabriel. How was I supposed to be myself when I was two completely different people in one body? "Everyone keeps telling me that."

"That's because they love you."

Because they love me. "Nana, do you think Papa would

ever have done something bad to protect you? Because he loved you?"

Her gaze in the mirror flashed with curiosity but turned sympathetic in the next moment. "Your grandfather would have done anything for me. And I would have done anything for him."

I looked down at the powder brush still in my hand. Bluebelle rubbed his fat belly up against my leg. "Even if it was something wrong?"

When I looked back up, the suspicion had returned to her eyes. "Is there something you want to talk to me about, Ellie?"

"Not specifically," I lied. I had to force myself not to spill my guts right then and there about everything I knew about my parents' fates.

"I think it depends on the kind of wrong," she said when I didn't elaborate. "If he had to hurt someone else to protect me, then no. I wouldn't want anyone to suffer for me."

I swallowed. "But if he had hurt someone who isn't around anymore to be affected by it, would you have forgiven him?"

"Are we still talking about Papa?"

I didn't respond, but that was as clear a no to Nana as anything.

She sighed. "It sounds like you need to figure out if whatever happened was really so terrible. Some things we have to do because they're necessary, and not because they're anything we want to do. Life is difficult, and sometimes we must make difficult decisions to protect the ones we love."

I stared at my reflection. Deep down, beneath everything in me that wanted to stay furious with Will, I knew my grandmother was right. I turned to my makeup again and began to dust blush over my cheeks. Nana smiled at me in the mirror.

"Thanks," I said, and returned her smile weakly.

"Of course, baby. What time will you be home tonight? Don't forget you have school tomorrow."

"I'll be back before nine."

"Have a good time, then," she said.

"Thanks, Nana."

"And," she started, making a thoughtful pause before continuing, "whatever happened . . . some paths are easier to take, but they may not always be the right ones. Why don't you consider the alternative: What would have happened if this bad thing was never done? Some bad things may be the right things in the end. Maybe you can forgive him then."

She winked at me before leaving the bathroom. I listened to her slow descent down the stairs, considering her words. I picked up my phone to call Kate.

Will emerged from the Grim and stood next to my car as I walked out the front door. He wore a dark green wool pullover that made the green of his eyes appear even more unnatural. I caught myself staring into them for longer than I should have.

"I don't have to come if you don't want me to," he said as we climbed into my car.

"You're my Guardian." I started the engine, and the car rolled down the driveway. "You need to be wherever I am."

He was silent for some time, staring out the windshield. "Do you *want* me to be here?"

"Not really," I replied slowly, forcing the honest answer out of myself. "But I'm trying."

He glanced at me sidelong, tilting his head just slightly. "I don't want you to be unhappy. As soon as you get uncomfortable, let me know. I'll get you out of there."

I stifled a laugh. "It's as if you're expecting a fight at the bowling alley."

"You know what I mean," he said quietly.

I did know what he meant. There would be other kids there who weren't my friends and didn't care if they hurt my feelings by staring at me or talking about me. But I refused to let them bother me. I took a deep breath and mumbled, "Thanks."

He took my barely audible response as a sign that I didn't want to talk anymore. When we arrived at the bowling alley, my nerves were screaming at me, spinning around a thousand miles an hour through my gut, and my hands trembled as I removed the key from the ignition and touched the door handle.

"You're uncomfortable already," Will observed, watching me carefully.

I scowled at him. "I'm fine. I have to do this."

"No, you don't."

I pushed the door open. "Yes, I *do*," I said as I climbed out.

He made an unintelligible grunt as he followed me into the building, but I tried to ignore it. Inside, Kate tackled me and squeezed me quite literally until I was strangling. A stream of inarticulate noises escaped me as she wrung me from side to side.

"Kate—can't breathe."

She released me, and I sucked in all the air that would fit in my lungs. She was grinning ear to ear and practically dancing with excitement. "I'm so happy you came!"

"Oh, my God, calm down," I said. "You saw me like four hours ago."

She shrugged dismissively. "Yeah, but I wasn't sure you'd come out. And you brought Will!" She grabbed his arm and yanked him into a hug. When she pulled away, she gave Will a stern look and shook a finger in his face. "You'd better be good to her."

He offered her a warm smile. "I try."

"Good," Kate said sharply, and turned to me, grabbing my hand. "Let's go have some fun. Everyone is waiting for you."

She pulled me toward the crowd of people surrounding one of the lanes. The rest of my friends were scattered around as Rachel rolled a gutter ball. Her boyfriend, Evan, pulled her into a hug as she pouted, and he planted a smooch on her cheek. I picked a purple bowling ball and tried it out. To my surprise, I didn't do that badly. After I finished my turn, I watched—chomping on the inside of my cheek to stop myself from laughing—as Kate forced Will to try. He held the ball awkwardly as if he'd never done it before.

"Gently!" I called to him as I sat down on a bench. If he rolled the ball with his normal strength, he'd put a hole in the floor and possibly the wall—and possibly through someone's body.

Gutter ball. I wasn't shocked. Bowling wasn't something I'd expect to be within Will's expertise. Mixed martial arts, sword fighting, video games, getting impaled, kissing—all those were things Will was superb at. Bowling? Well . . . everyone had their limits.

"You'll do better next time," Kate assured him with a look of pity.

He shrugged and sat beside me. When he grinned at me, I felt a rush of happiness. The wool of his sweater was warm as his sleeve brushed against mine, and my heart swelled. I appreciated so, so much how hard he was trying. Bowling with my friends. It was so stupid. And still he was here. After everything that had happened.

"Dude," Landon said as he appeared in front of us with his arms crossed over his chest. He stared down at Will incredulously. "You're as bad as Rachel, and believe me, that's a feat."

Will's expression was impassive. "Sorry. I've never been bowling before."

Landon scoffed. "Are you serious? Everyone in America has bowled at least once in their lives."

Will shrugged and his mouth flattened. "Never got around to it, I guess."

"Do you want me to show you how to roll the ball and not look like a freak?"

Will blinked at Landon. He seemed to weigh Landon's offer for a moment before looking at me. I gave him a small smile of reassurance.

"Okay then," Will said. He got up and allowed Landon to teach him how to hold the ball and roll it. After some direction, Will knocked down four pins.

"All right!" Landon shouted, and raised a hand for a high five from Will. Will just stared at him, and I laughed. Then slowly, tentatively, he raised his own hand, and Landon slapped it.

Then Will flinched, the same instant I felt a rush of power and emotion burst into the building like a flood breaking a dam. Ava and Sabina. Their hair was windblown and their cheeks were flushed as if they'd just flown through the Grim. Sabina cradled her arm to her chest. When Ava's blue-violet eyes settled on us, she marched toward a dark corner of the building and waved us over. She and Sabina looked nervous.

"What's wrong?" Will asked, his brow dark and furrowed with concern.

Ava put her hands on her hips, and she paced back and forth. "We crossed paths with Merodach and Kelaeno. Sabina was wounded."

My hand covered my mouth. "Are you all right?"

Sabina gritted her teeth. "I'm healing. My arm was shattered. Kelaeno is so strong and Merodach—it's as if he feels no pain. He just keeps coming."

I noticed slashes in Ava's zipped-up leather jacket—slits that weren't intentional, like the ones on her back that were for her wings. Still-damp blood darkened the fabric beneath her jacket. "Are you okay, Ava?"

She gave me a fleeting, flippant glance. "I'm fine. Just tired."

"What happened exactly?" Will asked with an edge of authority to his voice. He had transformed into all-business Will.

"We were ambushed," Ava explained. "They made it clear they were looking for you, Ellie."

My blood ran cold, and Will's gentle hand on my back did little to reassure me. So Merodach and Kelaeno were collecting *me* next. "Does this mean they've found whatever else they need?"

Sabina exchanged a look with Ava. "I assume so."

I looked at Will, panic pulsing through me. "What do we do?"

He frowned. "I don't want you to worry about it. You don't need any more stress right now."

I almost laughed. "I have two demonic reapers, both thousands of years old, hunting me, at the moment. This is a slightly different situation than Ragnuk trying to kill me. How can I not worry about it?"

He reached for me again. "Ellie—"

Panic shot through me, and I needed to get away from the reapers. I stepped out of his reach and started back to the lane my friends surrounded. "I'm fine. Just . . . leave me alone for a minute."

I heard his fist slam the wall behind me, but I didn't turn around. When I returned to my friends, Chris put a hand on my shoulder, looking past me to Ava and Sabina.

"Who are *they*?" he asked, his brown eyes wide. "Are they Will's friends?"

I eyed him suspiciously. "Yeah. Why?"

"They are *smoking* hot."

Not *again*. What was with my friends and these reapers? "They're lesbians," I lied. "Don't bother."

Chris grinned stupidly. *"Nice."*

I rolled my eyes and looked over my shoulder at the reapers. Will was speaking rapidly to Ava as Sabina stood silently, but judging by the frustration on his face and the sad look in Ava's eyes, I guessed the subject matter was no longer Merodach and Kelaeno, but me.

The demonic reapers were after me now. I'd killed the nycterids employed by Bastian, and now he was sending his worst after me, just like Cadan had said would happen. I had known my family was in danger, but I was too selfish to do anything about it or to miss out on my stupid social life. All I had left now were my friends, and here I was, perfectly aware that I was in danger and that, by being around them, I put *them* in danger.

I looked around me at my friends' smiling, laughing faces as I leaned heavily against the short wall holding all the bowling balls. I didn't even know what I was doing here. Grabbing my purse, I went up to the shoe rental and returned the bowling shoes for my sneakers. As I walked away, I bit back a sob and a pang of nausea in my gut. The nausea became overwhelming, and I hurried to the restroom, determined not to throw up in front of everyone. I burst in and threw myself into a stall and locked the door behind me. Instead of getting sick, I sat down on the seat and buried my face in my hands. I took long, deep breaths, trying not to cry.

I didn't want to hurt any more people I loved. I was a target and anywhere I was could potentially be ground zero for a battle. If only I—

The restroom door opened, and voices and footsteps echoed off the walls. They rustled around and stopped in front of the sinks.

"A nutjob for sure," one girl exclaimed.

A second girl laughed. "How do you know? Have you even talked to her once?"

"Well, her dad killed her mom," the first girl said. "So the crazy has got to be genetic."

I swallowed hard and felt an icy rush as the blood drained from my face. My pulse hammered through my skull.

"Is that seriously what happened?" a third girl asked incredulously.

"Oh, yeah. My uncle is a cop, and they're looking for the dad. He says they've been talking to the FBI. It's that serious."

The second girl loosed a long whistle. "Wow."

"What was her name again? Emily something?"

"Ellie Monroe. She's that girl who got so wasted at her birthday party that she drove her car through her house and almost died or something. But her parents just bought her a brand-new car to replace the one she totaled, because she's so spoiled. If you ask me, she's probably what drove her dad to kill her mom. He probably killed himself, too. Can't blame him."

My stomach heaved over and over, but nothing came up. I wasn't crying yet, but if I stayed there another moment, I'd start screaming. I shot to my feet, disoriented, and fumbled with the lock a moment before giving up and snapping it completely off the door. I burst out of the stall and rushed past the girls. They gasped and cried out, but I didn't look at any of them. There was no more keeping my head held high. I couldn't face them or anyone else.

Outside the restroom, the crowds and music made my head spin. I was a complete mess. I had to get out of there. If Merodach and Kelaeno found me in this state, there was no way I could fight and protect my friends. I would get Will killed.

I had a terrifying thought: The demonic reapers had probably followed Ava and Sabina here. Ava had to be smarter than that, but I couldn't take the risk. I couldn't stay any longer and get anyone else I loved killed, even the strangers or those nasty girls in the restroom. I had to leave.

"Life is difficult, and sometimes we must make difficult decisions to protect the ones we love," Nana had said to me earlier tonight. She was absolutely right. It was time for me to make a difficult decision, whether it was right or wrong. At this moment, it felt like the right decision.

I caught a glimpse of Will out of the corner of my eye. He was doubled over with one hand on the wall to hold himself up, his eyes squeezed tight and mouth open in physical agony—as if someone had slammed him in the chest with a hammer. I stopped in the crowd, staring at him as he struggled to right himself, Ava's hand on his back, her expression full of worry. But he pushed her away and forced himself to stand tall as he searched wildly over the heads of my friends and classmates, looking for me. Then he barreled through the crowd, spinning and turning in every direction, calling my name in a fearful voice. I studied him, perplexed, and the truth of what I'd just witnessed hit me like a truck. He always knew when I was upset or in pain. Our bond, the magic that I'd put into his tattoos binding him to me, our bond that allowed him to know what I was feeling . . . he always knew I was in pain because my pain caused *him* to hurt. The agony I felt at that moment spilled into him, making him feel through pain what I felt emotionally. I did that to him. I caused him pain. I was cancer, a disease on everyone who knew and loved me.

I ducked behind a wall before he saw me, and I took a deep breath, drawing in as much of my energy as possible and pushing it down until he couldn't sense me. By suppressing my power, I could hide it from him and ultimately hide *myself* from him. I couldn't have him following me.

I kept my head low and my hair over my face as I pushed my way through the crowd and ducked out the front door. I got in my car and I was gone.

Alone.

21

I WAS NUMB AS I DROVE BACK TO NANA'S WITH NO
intent to stay. I entered the house as quietly as I could and
went straight to the guest room. With my duffel bag mostly
still packed from the move, I hurriedly shoved a few more
things into it before heading back out to my car. I drove
somewhere I knew no one would find me, to the north side
of town, to a park I'd been to with my parents a few times
when I was little. It would be empty in the middle of winter
and after dark, and I could avoid any contact with anyone,
especially humans. I parked my car in the lot of an empty
grocery store where it would be safe, and I walked beneath
the lightly falling snow and lonely streetlights. A couple
of cars passed me, and that was it for company. I relished
the solitude and didn't care that it was cold. When I got to
the park, I trudged to its center and found a wrought-iron

bench beneath a snow-covered tree and a single lamppost. I plopped down and immediately began to cry.

"This is a surprise," said a voice to my side.

I jerked, startled, and looked up to see Cadan standing next to me. I wiped my face with my sleeve and made a very unladylike sniffle. I peeked at him and saw that he was staring at me with his head tilted curiously. "What do you want?"

"Did you even have a plan when you ran off?" he asked. "Where are you going? Do you even *have* a place to go?"

I snarled and wiped at the fresh tears on my face before they froze solid on my skin. "You don't know what you're talking about."

"It's no mystery that you're very upset," he said quietly as he sat beside me. "And your Guardian's presence is nowhere to be felt. That is not a good sign."

"Well, it's nothing," I snapped, and turned my gaze to the ground. "And you can go away now."

"I don't think so."

"That was an order. I wasn't asking for your opinion."

"That doesn't work on me, love. I'm not your Guardian."

"Thank God for that."

I expected a sharp retort, but he just looked at me. "I didn't come here to fight with you," he said.

"And I didn't come here hoping to see *you*."

He gave me a patient look. He seemed to tell by my

hostility that I wasn't in the mood for his jokes. At least he was smart. "I'm sorry, Ellie. I know what happened."

I turned on him, snarling. "You don't know shit."

He narrowed his eyes, and fire flashed within them. "Don't talk to me like I'm an idiot."

The harshness in his voice surprised me. I didn't expect him to say anything like that. Perhaps I deserved it. My gut twisted in a rage at the thought of the demonic reapers gloating behind my back. "Come to rub it in then?"

"I'm not your enemy, Ellie."

"Aren't you?"

He was silent.

I ground my teeth. Part of me wanted to fight him for the sake of fighting, but it'd do nothing to get me my revenge. "Why are you really here, then, if you already know what's made me so upset? Do you want to tell me how sorry you are, or do you have another present from Bastian?"

He flinched and his gaze faltered. "I had nothing to do with that. I didn't even know about it. If I had known what was going to happen, I would have done something to prevent it. I'm trying to help you."

"You have nothing to do with everything, don't you?" I snapped callously.

"I'm not going to take any of your crap, you know."

I looked over at him, my mouth parting in shock. He had the nerve to talk to me like that?

His eyes were bright and gleaming, honest. "Your guard dog might be okay with getting bossed around and talked down to—"

"I don't talk down to Will."

"Oh?" He put his arms up on the back of the bench. "You sure about that?"

I opened my mouth to retort, but I had nothing to say.

"I'm sorry," Cadan said.

I sighed. I had no right to be upset with him, since he was right, after all. "It's fine. It's all my fault anyway."

"No, it's not. The blame belongs to those who want to destroy this world and everyone in it."

"I've managed to make Will hate me," I grumbled. "I'm sure my grandmother thinks I'm a delinquent. Lauren's petrified of me, and Nathaniel thinks I'm going to snap and kill them all . . . which I probably will."

"Nah," he said. "You're not crazy."

I huffed. "You haven't seen me at my worst."

"I'd still admire you for exactly what you are."

"Don't speak too soon."

He smiled. "We all have our imperfections."

"Most people's imperfections don't involve going berserk and trying to kill the people they love."

He was quiet for a moment. "You have a lot more to deal with than most people. Nobody is like you. No one else is what you are, or has ever been what you are. You're changing, trying to adapt to this world."

"That's not an excuse for me to let my power control me. There's no excuse for me hurting innocent people."

"True, but we have to try and understand you," he said thoughtfully. "You are a being of two worlds, Heaven and Earth. What you're capable of could be limitless. It's not a question of *if* you can control your energy. Your body is human and your power is archangel—the most powerful being ever created. Something conflicts. An archangel was never meant to live as a human girl."

What he said was almost exactly what Michael had told me when I asked him why I lost myself to emotion and to my power. Maybe he and Cadan were right. "There's something wrong with me."

"No," he said softly, reaching forward to slide his fingers along my jaw toward my chin. The gesture was soothing, and in the frigid cold, his hand was surprisingly warm. The cold never affected the reapers. "There's nothing wrong with you. Through your lifetimes, your humanity has grown stronger. Your human passion is taking over your angelic heritage, and I don't think it knows how to handle all that divine power. Once you understand and can balance the two sides of your-self, you will be unstoppable."

I looked away from him. "If Bastian doesn't find a way to destroy my soul first."

"I'm sorry for what he has done to you," Cadan said. "For everything that he's done to you. I'm not sure if I'm strong enough to kill him, but for you, I'd try."

"I wouldn't ask you to."

He let out a long breath. "But I feel responsible. I should've done something sooner," he said earnestly. "I wish I'd known that you aren't some awful thing who only destroys. Maybe this would all be different."

"I don't think Bastian would've listened to you if you had tried to reason with him. He's out to kill me for good. He's pretty dead set on it, actually, if you'll pardon my morbid pun. God, I'm making fun of myself dying. I am so screwed up."

He shook his head. "You don't understand."

"I *do* understand, Ca—"

"He's my father."

I stared at him, unsure of what I thought I'd just heard him say. "What?" was all I managed to articulate.

"Bastian," Cadan said. "He's my father."

"Oh."

He picked up my hand carefully and studied my skin, touching each of my fingers with a gentleness that entranced me. My fingers were feeling less numb from cold by the second. I couldn't look away, though I knew I shouldn't have let him touch me so much. But for some reason, he was comforting.

"I should have said something to you sooner," he said. "I didn't think if you knew that you'd trust me."

I didn't speak for some time and just sat there processing. "He would kill you for helping me?" I asked. "Even though he's your father?"

"Of course."

I looked up to meet his gaze. The fiery opal flecks in his eyes danced and glimmered, like sunlight hitting newly fallen snow. I didn't understand how something so dark and wicked could create something so beautiful and kind. Cadan was by no means harmless, but he was gentle with me. I trusted him.

"I didn't betray you," he said. "I'd never betray you."

"The guys in my life have too many secrets," I said distantly.

He laughed and touched my cheek with the back of his hand. It seemed that he took any opportunity to touch me, and with the awful way I felt, I ached for any source of comfort. "Maybe you are just terribly imperceptive."

"That could be it." I laughed and wiped at a tear beneath my eye. "You boys are always confusing the hell out of me."

Cadan smiled with the warmth of amusement and fondness. "I never thought you'd be like this."

"Like what?"

"I hear stories of you," he said, "of your violence and ruthlessness. But you're just a girl—a very beautiful, vulnerable girl."

Being called beautiful was one thing, but I couldn't afford to be weak. "Thanks, but I'm not vulnerable."

"You are," he insisted softly. "And I think it may be part of the reason why I'm so drawn to you. I am utterly enthralled. You're innocent, so unlike the beast you're said to be. Ellie, you have this softness about you that I could never dream of damaging. It would be like stomping on a flower. What would be the point?"

I almost laughed. "The point? How about the fact that I kill the demonic? Why would you *not* want to destroy me?"

"You've never once tried to kill me." His statement was matter-of-fact, as if he were telling me something as mundane as the weather.

"Why did you save me from Ivar?" I asked. "Why did you kill her when you're supposed to be on the same side?"

He took a deep breath and let it out slowly. "Because she would have gone back to Bastian and told him that I'd been to see you. He's suspicious enough of me already."

"But Ivar was in love with you," I said. "I'm sure she would have stayed quiet if you'd asked her to."

He shook his head. "No. She would've thought nothing of using me to look better in Bastian's eyes. She never felt love for anything, least of all me."

"Because she's demonic?" I asked. "If that's the reason, then I'd like to know why you're so good to me."

He leaned toward me and rested his elbow on the back of the bench. "I'm not wholly what you think I am."

"What does that mean?" I asked, very aware that we were only inches apart.

His smile then was smooth and warm, like white chocolate melting in my hands. He brushed my hair back over my shoulders. The snowflakes landing in my hair were tangling it. "You're putting yourself in a dangerous position, being out here without your Guardian."

"I can take care of myself," I said, noticing how he'd avoided my question.

"You have to admit, that's a lot easier to accomplish when he's with you," he noted, his eyes on the bare skin exposed after he'd brushed my hair back.

"Why would you say that? You hate Will."

"I don't hate him," Cadan mused, rolling the words around on his tongue as if to taste them. "He's in love with you, too."

I froze and stared at him as he continued to look at my neck instead of my face. I didn't think he breathed for that entire time. His body grew more tense the longer my eyes were glued to him, and at last he swallowed hard and looked into my eyes. The look he gave me was an intense mixture of shame and a desire for approval. He knew that I understood what he'd said, but I didn't see regret on his face.

"That's not very smart of you," I said slowly.

His lips curved sensually, and his fingers trailed along my jaw as he looked down at my lips. "I could do worse." And with that, his confidence had returned.

I barely noticed the snowflakes falling around us anymore. "What could be worse than being in love with your enemy?"

"Acting on it."

He was suddenly even closer, though it looked like he

hadn't moved a muscle. His scent and body warmth wrapped around me, and it felt so safe and good here with him on the bench. His mouth couldn't have been six inches from mine, and my heart pounded harder and harder. His opal eyes were so bright that I almost had to look away. It was strange how these reapers' eyes gave away their emotions so clearly.

"That's true," I breathed, and swallowed. I knew what he wanted to do, and I wasn't entirely sure that I didn't want him to do it. "But Cadan . . ."

His hand brushed my cheek and his fingers slid into my hair. His gaze searched every last inch of my face, maybe looking for a sign in my expression that told him to stop. He leaned so close that I tasted his breath on my lips as my own caught in my chest.

"Cadan, I can't—" Will's face flashed in my mind, and the memory of him made my skin burn like acid everywhere that Cadan touched me. I peeled away from Cadan, and he stared at me with broken eyes. He opened his mouth to speak, and it took several tries for the words to come out.

"That was a terrible idea," he said almost breathlessly. "I am so screwed."

"Cadan," I said, having no idea what to say to him. A demonic reaper had just tried to kiss me. I didn't know him that well, but I trusted him. Something about him reminded me of Will, but at the same time, they were nothing like each other. They were both the opposite of what they were supposed to be: Will was darkness and strength and determination, and Cadan was like sunlight. Refreshing and golden. And right now, I needed anything but more darkness in my life.

He gave me such a sad look that I reached up and touched his cheek and his ear and the silk of his hair, just to make sure the strands weren't spun from gold. "I can't have you, can I?" he whispered.

I frowned. "Cadan . . ."

"If you say my name every day until I die," he said with a gentle laugh, "then even the worst ending for me will be a joyful one."

I smiled and kissed him on the cheek. He lowered his head until it rested on my shoulder, and I stroked his hair. Everything about this was so strange, and yet so comforting. But even though I needed some sort of kindness, I had a feeling that he needed it more than I did. I held him, felt his breath on my shoulder beneath my coat, felt his hand lightly on my arm. This is Cadan. The thought ran through my mind a hundred times, and still I couldn't fully comprehend it. Bastian's son.

He sat up and looked into my eyes, his gaze deep and drilling. "I'll do anything for you," he said, his voice husky and earnest. "I'll kill Bastian. I'll even leave you alone if you want me to."

I exhaled. "I don't know what I want."

He smiled. "You and me both."

I studied his face without speaking for several moments. This time with him was exactly what I needed. "Thank you,

Cadan. You saved me tonight."

"Go back to your Guardian," Cadan said, his smile faint and longing.

I didn't want to, but he was right. If I died without ending any of this awful mess, then my parents would have died for nothing. Will's pain would have been for nothing. And I couldn't let him or Nana down.

I got up and stood in front of Cadan, looking down into his face. I ran my hand through his hair, and he closed his eyes just for that moment. "Good-bye, Cadan."

His eyes opened again, that crystalline opal fire bright in the dark. "Good-bye, Ellie."

I walked slowly back to where I'd parked. Now that I was alone again, I wanted to be anything but. What had happened with Cadan churned my thoughts and my heart. He was the perfect comfort at the perfect moment, and I cared for him, but he wasn't Will. And Will was the only one I loved, despite everything.

As soon as his name echoed through my head, his voice echoed in my ears.

"Ellie!"

I turned my head and saw him darting across the snow-covered street toward me. He scooped me tightly into his arms and sent my body into flutters of joy and longing. I felt every contour of his familiar, warm body through his wool pullover. I ran my hands up his back and traced every ridge and plane, memorizing every part of him. There were holes in his sweater where his wings had grown through. I slipped my fingers through, touched his skin, and I squeezed my eyes shut.

"God, I thought you were gone," he said hoarsely. "I thought they'd taken you. I couldn't feel you anywhere. I flew over the city and then I felt you, but it was so small. I thought you were dying. And then I found your car abandoned. Ellie, I thought I'd lost you."

"I'm fine," I said, my voice small. "Really. No wounds, I promise."

He froze suddenly and gave me a strange look. Then the look turned visibly pained. In that moment, I knew he smelled Cadan on me. "Why couldn't I find you?" he asked. "Were you hiding from me?"

The heartbrokenness in his voice made me feel like the worst person alive. "I'm sorry, Will. I just needed to be alone."

He didn't ask about Cadan. He knew, but he stayed silent. He wasn't going to judge me. He never did. He was perfect, and I loved him so much it hurt.

I started to cry again. "I'm so sorry!" I sobbed, barely comprehensible.

He pulled me closer and made a soft noise into my hair. "It's okay. Everything's going to be all right. Please don't cry."

"Why do you wait for me like this?" I begged, my teeth chattering. "All I do is run away from everything, from *you*.

Why are you so patient and just take all of this pain, no questions asked?"

"Ellie . . ." He looked down and picked up my hands, examining them. He frowned and rubbed them with his. "You're frozen. Your hands are like ice." He lifted my hands and pressed them to his lips, closing his eyes and exhaling warm air gently against my fingertips. Everything in me melted.

"I'm screwed up," I said exasperatedly. "And I'm cold."

Without another word, he scooped me up and cradled me in his arms. We walked toward where my car was parked. I clung tightly to his shirt, shivering, and when we arrived, he set me gently on the cold hood of my car. My fingers shook as I dug through my purse for my keys. When I found them, Will took them and unlocked my car.

"I'll drive," he said softly.

I didn't protest, and he scooped me back into his arms and carried me around to the passenger seat. I watched him, almost amused, as he buckled me in as if I were helpless, but I didn't mind. Taking care of me was more than just his duty. He loved me as much as I loved him and we'd been through too much together not to have respect for each other. I'd disrespected him tonight by taking off, disrespected his loyalty and selflessness toward me, and still, even though he should have been furious with me, he wasn't. He'd carried me when I was tired, cradled me to his chest when I was cold, and now he was buckling my seat belt even though I was perfectly capable of doing so myself. He wasn't reminding me of how much I needed him. That wasn't in his nature. Never, ever, in a million years would I find anyone who matched him in any way.

Will took me back to Nathaniel's house instead of Nana's. He opened the passenger door and began to carry me out, but I stopped him.

"I can walk," I said, my teeth chattering as I climbed out of the car and into the bitter cold.

He didn't contradict me, and he reached forward to take my hand and lead me toward the front door. His fingers threaded through mine as if nothing I'd said or done to him in the last several days had ever happened. Lauren appeared in the doorway, her hand over her mouth. She stepped aside so Will could lead me through, and once the heat of the cozy house melted my aching body, she scooped me into a tight hug.

"We were so worried about you," she said into my hair. "I'm so happy Will found you."

She pulled away and I watched Nathaniel step out of the kitchen, drying his hands with a towel. His expression was sympathetic and his small smile was genuine. "Hey, Ell. You hungry?"

I tucked my hair behind both ears and offered a forced smile. "Yeah."

"Good." His grin widened. "I made spaghetti and you're just in time."

Lauren took my coat and hung it in the closet. "He did something different with the sauce, so you have to tell him it's delicious even if it tastes like motor oil and oregano."

I laughed weakly. "Okay."

"Come on," Lauren said, and walked toward Nathaniel and the kitchen. "Let's get some hot food into you."

Everyone was kind to me during dinner, laughed at my pathetic jokes, and life seemed a little normal despite everything that had happened. I helped Lauren with the dishes as Nathaniel and Will cleared the table and put everything away. Once everything was cleaned up, I leaned over to rest my head on Will's shoulder and yawned.

"You doing okay?" he asked as he bent his head to look into my face.

I gave him a little smile. "Just sleepy. It's been a long day."

"I'll take you upstairs."

"Good night, Ellie," said Lauren.

"Good night. Thank you both." I waved to her and Nathaniel, and followed Will out of the kitchen. He grabbed my duffel bag off the floor and carried it upstairs with him. When he led me into his room, I chewed nervously on my lip.

"You can sleep in here," he offered, and dropped my things next to the nightstand.

"You don't have to give up your bed for me." My voice was small and quiet.

He shrugged. "Well, there's a guest room, but it's not made up and I'm not making you wait until you drop unconscious from exhaustion. Besides, you've slept here before."

I blushed fiercely at the memory of sleeping in his bed. As if he noticed my embarrassment, his gaze fell. After several awkward seconds, he started to walk by me.

"I'll let you change and get some sleep."

"Will, wait." I put a hand to his chest. I wanted to tell him that he could stay, that I wanted him to stay, but I couldn't bring myself to do it. "Do you always feel pain when I do?"

His entire body stiffened, and he took his eyes away from mine. "I didn't want you to know that."

My heart slipped into my stomach. "But it's true, isn't it? I saw . . . back at the bowling alley. How have you hidden this from me all this time? Why?"

He looked at me again. "I don't always feel it when you hurt physically. It hits me when you hurt in your heart more than anything."

I battled a sob that climbed my throat. "I can't believe how much pain I've caused you for so long."

"Some things hurt more than what my body feels," he said gently. "I don't care that it hurts. I can take a lot."

Squeezing my eyes shut, I folded myself into him, and he wrapped his arms around me. He kissed my hair, and that terrible sob escaped me finally. "I don't deserve you," I said, burying my face in his chest.

"Don't say that." He pulled away and cupped my face

in his hands. "Get some sleep. I'll see you in the morning. Good night, Ellie."

"Good night."

As he closed the door behind him, I sat down on the edge of the bed. After all the running I'd done, I felt like I was finally ready to stop.

22

THE NEXT MORNING I FOUND I MUST HAVE HAD A thousand missed calls from my friends and Nana. I texted only one thing to Nana: **I'm ok**. Then I shut off my phone. People were looking for me, but I didn't want to be found. Eventually I would have to go back to the rest of the world, but I didn't want that to be anytime soon. I wasn't ready to face real life without my parents in it.

I dragged myself out of Will's bed and ventured into the hall. I heard voices coming from the study, and I crept toward the cracked-open door and peered through. Lauren leaned against the oak desk beneath the big bay window and Nathaniel stood beside her, resting one hand on the desk's edge. Both their expressions were serious, his a little more pained than hers.

"I don't know what you want from me," he said quietly.

There was no harshness in his voice to alert me that they had been arguing. If anything, they both looked very sad.

Lauren stared at him, her face falling heavily. She seemed emotionally exhausted. "I don't know what to ask."

"We won't end that way," he said. "I promise."

She smiled softly. "You can't promise that."

"I love you," he said, and touched her cheek. "That's all that matters."

"You're sweet," she said, and covered his hand with hers. She pulled away. "But that isn't all that matters, and you know it. You've seen what Will has had to go through for centuries. Don't lie to me. I don't want you to feel that pain for me."

His gaze flickered away from hers and back again, but he stayed quiet. His curly mop of copper hair flopped over his forehead.

"Do you really want that for yourself?" she asked. "I don't belong here and you know it."

"I *know*," he said urgently, leaning into her, his hands running through her dark hair and over her slender shoulders, "that you *do* belong here. With me."

She started to smile, but it faded before it could bloom. "Our ending won't be beautiful."

"Not if it's compared to you."

Her smile came through then, matching his own silly one. "Nathaniel, I'm serious. You'll outlive me by a thousand years at least. Are you prepared for that?"

The laughter left his expression. "I don't care."

She frowned and touched his face. "Nathaniel . . ."

"I'll stay by your side until the end," he said. "Yes, I understand what Will endures, and I'll gladly endure it for you."

Her eyes glimmered, but before she could cry, his lips met hers intensely. When he pulled away, he kissed the tip of her nose and she laughed softly through her tears.

With a strange feeling blurring through me, I left Nathaniel and Lauren to their secret world and decided to go for a long walk.

I returned to a very quiet house. A single lamp lit the living room and I found Nathaniel sitting on a sofa reading a book. He looked up at me and smiled.

"Where is everyone?" I asked, sitting down beside him.

"Lauren is grocery shopping," he replied. "I made Will go with her. It's good for him to get out of the house and do something ordinary."

I laughed. "I'm sure he considers it torture. He doesn't like ordinary very much."

Nathaniel shrugged. "He isn't suited for it. Some of us, like Marcus and I, have been able to adapt to a somewhat normal human life. We can get pretty normal jobs, form human friendships, business relationships, and have hobbies. But others, like Will and Ava—even Sabina—they've never felt comfortable in the human world. Either they feel they don't deserve to integrate into mortal society, or they just feel like they don't belong."

I felt bad for a moment about dragging Will to my stupid high school parties—especially bowling—but maybe Nathaniel was right. Maybe it really was good for him to do something other than fight for his life—for both our lives—every single night. "He needs the distraction."

"A moment's peace," Nathaniel said. "It makes a world of difference. That's why you're so important to him."

I shook my head. "But this whole thing, the whole reason why his life is so terrible, it's because of me. If he didn't have to protect me—"

"He'd still be doing the same thing," he said gently. "He'd still be hunting demonic reapers without you, but *with* you, he has a reason to be happy, a reason to want to do this. You forget that he isn't just your Guardian because Michael gave the sword to him. Will wanted this, *still* wants it."

Sometimes I did forget that. He had accepted this duty from Michael all those years ago. He wasn't forced into it.

Nathaniel watched me carefully. "I'm the only one left alive who knew Will before he met you."

I considered his words, realizing that Will must have felt just as alone as I did. The weight of Will and Nathaniel's bond was more than friendship. They were family.

"I don't mean that to seem patronizing," Nathaniel said, a worried look in his copper eyes.

"No, not at all," I said. "You just mean that you knew a different Will."

"Precisely. He was much more wild back then. Reckless at times."

I laughed. "Will? Wild? I'll never believe it."

"He was very fond of girls and got into a lot of trouble. He found himself in situations that weren't . . ." Nathaniel trailed off as he struggled with the right word. "Let's just say, he settled down a lot when he became your Guardian. He takes himself more seriously."

"*Too* seriously sometimes," I added. "How did you meet him?"

"I knew his mother," he explained. "Madeleine was quite celebrated as a hunter of demonic reapers. When Will decided he'd follow in her footsteps, she instructed me to look out for him. I never knew Will's father, though."

"What was Madeleine like?"

"She was a formidable woman, and so much like Will in that she was very devoted to her duty, but she was also kind." He paused and said, "There's something I want you to know, Ellie."

Nerves prickled in my gut, and I was afraid of what he might have to say. "Okay."

He took a deep breath. "You understand the meaning and function of a relic, yes?"

"For the most part, yeah," I said. "They're objects with a magical connection to a creature from Heaven or Hell."

"They can be anything, even something alive," he said. "From a tree in a forest, to even a human being. And they all need a guardian, even demonic relics. Anything can have a connection to Heaven or Hell, but only the most powerful of all things are relics. Like you, Ellie."

My head spun, and I sat more heavily into my seat. "What are you saying?"

"You are a relic, Ellie."

"Me?"

He nodded. "Your human body, Gabriel's vessel. The most holy of all things on Earth is you. Every relic requires a guardian. Will is yours."

"So Will is a relic guardian. *My* Guardian."

"Correct. *The* Guardian, the most important of all angelic guardians."

"But you're not a relic guardian or Guardian of me or anything, right?"

"No," he said gently. "Not officially, but there are a few items that I keep safe. Records of our world, books of great importance. They were passed to me from my father when he was killed."

"Then why are you involved? You don't have to go through any of this."

He smiled gently. "True, but Will is like my younger brother. I'll always take care of him, and I'll always fight by his side. That's what you do for family and for the ones you love. That's why I also want to protect you, Ellie. Not just because you're the Preliator. You're family, too."

That hit home. The kindness of his words sank deep,

tightening around my heart and rendering me unable to breathe. "Thank you, Nathaniel," I said weakly. "You're my family, too, but what I don't really understand is why any of you would accept this responsibility. Why leave everything behind and dedicate your entire lives to protecting something at any cost?"

He took a deep breath. "What's the point of eternal life if one spends it doing nothing? There is none. It's a waste of eternity."

I remembered what Will had said about the night Michael gave him his sword and the responsibility of being my Guardian: *He gave me purpose, some sort of resolution in my immortality, a focus. You gave me purpose.*

"There are four things you need to understand about war, Ellie," Nathaniel began. "One, every action requires careful tactics. Two, never lose hope and fight only for what is right. Three, be brave, but you don't have to be fearless. And four, be willing to sacrifice."

Willing to sacrifice. Was I? How far would I have to go, how much would I have to sacrifice to win this war? What was I willing to sacrifice? Myself, my friends, my family— Will? I wouldn't sacrifice their lives, but could I be willing to give them up in order to save them?

"I'm going to win this war," I said to Nathaniel.

He smiled gently. "I believe you can."

The front door opened and Will and Lauren emerged, their arms draped in grocery bags. Nathaniel and I rose to our feet and helped them bring in the rest of the bags from Lauren's car. I soaked in the early March sunshine and forty-degree temperature. Spring was on its way.

"How was shopping?" I asked Will.

"Horrible." He sighed. "It was a battle to get past all those women for a carton of eggs. They were vicious."

I laughed. "Soccer moms too much for you?"

"Apparently," he replied, giving me a little smile.

"Will can handle the nastiest reapers around, but soccer moms . . ." Lauren said with a grin as we toted the rest of the bags into the kitchen and unloaded groceries.

"I need to work off some of this aggression," Will said. "Nathaniel, are you game?"

Nathaniel frowned. "Letting you beat the crap out of me for a half hour? I'm always game."

Lauren and I sat on the porch bench and draped a quilt over us to watch the boys spar in the backyard. The melting snow added difficulty to their training, making it harder for them to move, and that was why it worked. Will laughed as Nathaniel slipped and splashed in the wet snow and mud.

"Nice move," Will said, and rested his sword over his shoulder, rolling his eyes.

Nathaniel rolled over and clambered to his feet. He snorted through a wide grin and shoved Will's shoulder. "That doesn't count toward points. I slipped."

Will scoffed. "Come on, man. That's pathetic."

"Hey," Nathaniel said with a wave of his finger. "I'm a reader, not a fighter."

"Keep it friendly, boys," Lauren called. "Maybe I should keep score so nobody cheats." She tugged the blanket a little tighter when a cold breeze blew by, and we exchanged smiles and I shook my head.

Nathaniel spun the sword in his hand just to show off as he advanced on Will. Then he vanished, moving so quickly my eyes lost him for a heartbeat, but Will spun around, sweeping his blade up to meet Nathaniel's as the other vir reappeared. Will's sword dwarfed Nathaniel's, but I was surprised at Nathaniel's skill and ease with the thin, sleek blade. He was definitely much more of a bookworm than a fighter, which was a part of his charm, but that didn't mean he didn't know how to kick some ass. He seemed to match each of Will's strikes, at least until Will tired of going easy on him.

The way Will fought was hypnotizing. His graceful ferocity was the most beautiful, calculated thing I'd ever seen. His movements as he dodged Nathaniel's swift strikes were so slight and effortless that it almost appeared to be a dance he knew to his very soul.

The snow made no hindrance to their battle as it flew everywhere in the air, streaks of white following silver blades and sweeping, feather-light footsteps. Nathaniel deflected Will's sword with his own and Will's elbow smashed into Nathaniel's nose, knocking him back. Nathaniel brought his blade up and Will swung his down, silver crashing together, and Nathaniel kicked his boot into Will's chest, forcing him to stagger on his heels.

"That's two points for each," Lauren explained. "They each made successful offensive and defensive maneuvers."

"How does one of them win?" I asked.

"There's no winning," she said. "They just keep adding points. I forgot both their scores ages ago, but the numbers are ridiculous. Nathaniel holds his own against Will, but it's obvious who is the more talented fighter."

"Nathaniel is brilliant, but I almost never see him fight."

She shrugged. "He'd rather be useful to the war in other ways. Will, on the other hand, can't get enough of fighting. It wears him out physically and emotionally, but it's like a drug to him. He can't function without it."

Something heavy settled in my chest. "It's his life."

Out the corner of my eye, I caught Lauren glancing at me. "It's yours too," she said. "But I'm not sure what Will would do with himself if he didn't have a mission for even five minutes. He'd go crazy."

As I watched him spin his sword through the air, I imagined him living a quieter life where he wasn't constantly trying to survive and save me at the same time.

"Don't even think it," Lauren warned sharply. "I know that look on your face. He agreed to this. It's what he wanted. I can't describe to you the difference I see in him since you came back into his life."

I gazed across the lawn again at Will. Our eyes met, and

I knew he could hear my conversation with Lauren. But he never missed a beat and never let Nathaniel gain the upper hand.

"You chose this too," Lauren said. "Don't forget that either."

She was right. As Gabriel, I chose to become human and fight the reapers. It was my mission to see this through, just as protecting me was Will's mission.

Will's sword ripped open Nathaniel's sleeve and blood shone in the sunlight. Nathaniel spun away with a grunt of pain, holding his arm with his other hand. Will withdrew his sword until it vanished completely.

"I'm done," he said, winded.

Nathaniel studied his face. "All right." He said nothing more.

Will headed toward the house tiredly, snow clinging to his clothes and his hair. I rose to help him clean up as he walked inside.

"Don't track that slush into the house," Lauren scolded Nathaniel. When I glanced behind me, I saw her catch his wrist and mouth the word "wait."

In the kitchen, Will pulled off his boots, set them on the rug beside the glass doors to dry, and yanked off his long-sleeved pullover. I took it from him so he could brush off his jeans and smooth out his white T-shirt.

"You did a good job," I offered, breaking the silence between us.

He didn't look up. "So did Nathaniel."

My insides swam as I watched him closely. "I can take care of your wet clothes while you shower."

That time he looked at me. "You don't have to," he said.

"I want to."

He nodded and watched me for a couple seconds before he disappeared into the bathroom upstairs. When Lauren and Nathaniel came into the house finally, I left the kitchen, taking Will's snow-dampened clothes to the laundry room. I stayed in there, thoughts racing through my head. I wanted everything to be right between us. The churning of the washing machine helped to dull the roar in my mind. I went upstairs toward to my room, but I ran into Will in the darkened hallway. He was dressed in sweatpants and a slightly wrinkled white T-shirt, his hair still wet.

I stepped into him, wrapping my arms around his waist and sliding my palms up his back. He held me tentatively in return, but then he relaxed with a long sigh, shoulders slumping, and he buried his face in my hair at the bend of my neck. He smelled and felt so good and I didn't want to pull away, not ever, but I reluctantly loosened my hold.

He smiled gently down at me. "How are you today?" he asked, sliding my hair behind both my ears with his hands.

I closed my eyes at his touch. "Better. I just feel tired all the time."

"I understand," he said. "You've been through a lot in the last couple of weeks."

I didn't have a response, so I just folded my arms to my chest and tucked myself into his body.

He dropped his hands to my shoulders. "Marcus and Ava want to hunt with us tonight."

"Good," I said. "We'll need all the help we can get. I want them all dead."

"We'll get every single one of them," he promised.

"Want me to make you lunch?" I asked, coiling my fingers around the hem of his shirt. "I know you need to eat. I saw you take some hits from Nathaniel."

He winked at me and my stomach flipped. "I let him get me. I was beginning to feel bad for him. He spent half the fight on the ground, anyway."

I rolled my eyes. "You're so kind. He has no idea."

"Not a clue." His heavy gaze fell to my lips and back up to my eyes, making me wonder if he was thinking about kissing me. "Why are you taking care of me?"

The question surprised me a little, and I had to think about a response. In truth, I hadn't realized that was what I was doing. Was I taking care of him, or was I just being nice to him because I was sorry? "Because . . ." I started to say, but I quickly realized I still didn't have an answer for him. "Do you want me to stop?"

"You have no reason to be good to me," he said.

I couldn't help noticing that he'd avoided my question. "I have every reason to be good to you."

"After what I did?"

Perhaps he was right, but I had to try and fix this. I didn't want to be angry with him. He was too important to me for me to hate him. "After what *I* did."

He deflated with a sigh. "Ellie . . ."

"I'm sorry," I said faintly, forcing it out of myself. "For everything. For running away from you. For blaming you."

"It's okay."

"I thought running away would protect you," I admitted. "It it was probably right to leave my friends and family behind, but not you and Nathaniel and the others. I didn't do anything to punish you, please know that. I wouldn't hurt you on purpose."

He nodded. "I would never mean to hurt you either."

I fought back a sob. "We're both pretty messed up."

He smiled. "We're not meant to be perfect, and we never will be." He bent over to kiss my cheek and let his hands fall to his side.

"Are you going to get a few hours of sleep before we hunt tonight?" I asked.

"I should. I need the energy."

"Can I lie down with you when you do?"

He watched me gently, hesitating. "Of course. You should get some rest, too."

"Let me make you lunch first," I offered.

I took his hand and led him down the stairs to the kitchen. We ate with little conversation, and when we finished he helped me clean up. When we got to Will's room,

I rolled up the blinds and let the afternoon sunlight pour in before I climbed into his bed. He watched me quietly, and when I laid my head against the pillow and brought the blankets up to my chin, he climbed in beside me. I curled close to his chest, breathing him in, and he kissed my hair. All the tension melted away from me as we lay in the warm late-winter sunlight and fell asleep.

23

THE NEXT MORNING WAS COLD, SUNLESS, AND misty, and I was tense with frustration after last night's unsuccessful hunt for Bastian and his goons. I went for a run with Will and took a hot shower as soon as we returned. When I came downstairs, I caught a glimpse of something large through the sliding glass doors in the kitchen.

Wings.

My breath caught in my throat, and I opened the door and stepped out onto the porch. After a moment, I recognized that it was the back of a shirtless Nathaniel, but I'd never before seen his wings, which gleamed a coppery sheen in the sunlight. They stretched as wide as they could go before relaxing and folding to his back, but they didn't vanish. His shirt was sitting on the swing bench a few yards away.

I approached him cautiously. "Hey, Nathaniel."

He turned his head to me as I stopped right beside him, and he smiled warmly at me. "Ellie."

I marveled at his wings, at how they seemed two shades at once. When the sun caught his feathers, the color matched his eyes. "What are you up to?"

"Stretching," he replied.

Prying my eyes away from his feathers was difficult. I didn't often see reaper wings up close unless I was in a fight, and on those occasions I couldn't stop to admire the view. Even Will was shy about his wings, and I could count on one hand how many times I'd seen them. "Will ought to do that once in a while," I suggested with a grin. "He probably wouldn't be so grumpy then."

Nathaniel laughed softly, and his wings folded into his back and disappeared. "Perhaps, but I'm afraid he may be a lost cause." He tugged his shirt back over his head. "It's going to rain today."

Sure enough, a dark cloud was rolling in from the west.

He sat down gracefully on the swing and patted the spot next to him. "Come sit with me."

"I'm sad it's so much colder today than yesterday," I said, hugging my arms to my chest against the chill and lowering myself onto the seat.

"Temperature fluctuations are to be expected." He pushed the swing back and forth slowly with his boot on the mushy, slippery ground. "It's been wonderful having you here, Ellie. Reapers love being around you. It goes beyond how close Will and I are with you, how well Marcus knows you. We feel better when you're around."

"Better?" I asked. "Knowing that you're able to protect me?"

"Yes," Nathaniel said. "But it's so much more than that. There is something about you that draws reapers. It must be your divine origins that we can sense. You *feel* warm . . . *good*. It's impossible to describe. We crave your presence. It makes you even more beautiful to some of us. Others resent that you have some sort of control over them. The angelic aren't the only ones who feel like this, but the demonic react to you in a different way. The angelic instinctively want to protect you, while the demonic . . . they crave you like nothing else. They just want to know what you taste like."

Everything he said completely unsettled me. I didn't want anything to be drawn to me the way he described. It made me wonder also if there was more to Will's love for me, if this was what he meant by feeling innately protective. He always seemed to want to touch me and be physically close, like he couldn't help it, and it was a struggle for him to stay away from me. The way Nathaniel described my effect on the demonic made me a little afraid, too. But Cadan's affection was never malicious or felt wrong in any way. He touched me the way Will touched me, though he didn't make me feel the same need in return. But did Cadan only think he was in love with me because of this innate attraction?

Nathaniel stared out onto the lake. "Your past Guardians were said to have been very devoted to you, but none of them ever served you nearly as long as Will has. A few decades. A hundred years. Though I never knew any of your past Guardians, from what I understand, you've never had a bond with any of them the way you do with Will. He's stronger than any angelic reaper I've ever met, and at the same time, he's darker. I don't know why."

That word, "darker," stabbed like a needle in my arm, bolting me awake. "What do you mean by darker?"

Nathaniel paused, lost in thought. "It's something in his energy, something that feels different from others of our kind. I noticed it about him the day I met him, and others feel it too—angelic and demonic alike. He's a legend among us. His power is unmatched by any angelic reaper."

I'd seen Will do things in battle that both terrified and amazed me, things that reminded me of the demonic, but it was impossible for him to be anything other than angelic. My angelfire had proved that on many occasions. But still . . . in my bones, I knew Nathaniel was right. Something about Will was dark—darker than Nathaniel, darker even than Ava.

Nathaniel leaned back into the swing and sighed. "It's all very curious. I wish I fully understood the bond between you."

Nathaniel's words sparked a memory of Will's lips on mine, a memory so vivid that I could feel his heat as if he was touching me that very moment. I closed my eyes, swallowed, and forced myself to say something, anything to draw me from that thought. "Is the bond dangerous?" I asked.

He nodded. "What Will has told you is likely true. You are the mortal archangel, and he is your Guardian. Neither of you is permitted to love the other. You are both bound to your purposes first."

"I can't remember why I chose this," I said in frustration. "Why would I have ever wanted to give up my wings and become human?"

"Ellie," Nathaniel began carefully. "That's what you need to understand. There's no way you, Gabriel, did this by your own will. Angels don't *have* free will."

I stared at him in shock, letting what he'd just said settle heavily on my shoulders and thoughts. "I was forced to become human?"

"Most likely your orders came from God. Angels only obey. It's your nature—how you were designed."

"But I make my own choices every day. I can do whatever I want."

"You're human now. Only in Heaven are you Gabriel, who must obey without question. Here on Earth, you have the soul and free will of a human girl."

"Why are you telling me this?"

His gaze was intense, boring into my own. "Because I want you to know that you have a choice now. You will always have a choice, because you are human."

I shook my head. "But my Guardians—and Will—they all obey me, but they can also choose to *not* obey me." The memory of Will refusing me the night he rescued me from Brian came to mind. He had struggled to say no to me but he did choose to walk away.

"That is because your Guardian is never an angel," Nathaniel replied. "Reapers have free will, which is why they must accept the role of relic guardian. They can't be forced. But this is the beauty of it: In Heaven you are bound to obey without question, and there you are forbidden to feel any emotion, even love for God. You're not in Heaven anymore."

"Are you saying I'm allowed to love anyone, then?" I asked carefully, trying to decipher his cryptic words. "Will?"

He smiled. "Theoretically. But Will, on the other hand, having chosen his duty and the terms, is still forbidden to do anything but protect you. While you may get off on a technicality, he must still obey Michael, and I can't imagine your brother being very pleased with his divine sister and an Earthbound reaper."

"Would Michael really execute Will?" I asked fearfully.

Nathaniel's smile faded. "By law, he would have every right to."

Ice rushed through my veins, nearly paralyzing me. "Then why would you tell Will to love me if you know that?"

"I didn't," he answered. "When he and I had our . . . *discussion* about you two, I told him that Michael would come for him. I also told him that I wanted him—and you—to be happy, and that when it comes to love, rules were made to be broken. I told Will he needed to make a choice, and he chose loving you."

"I won't let Michael kill him," I promised. "I need Will. How can anyone be killed for love?"

Nathaniel gazed thoughtfully out onto the lake. "Acting on love is forbidden with the divine. Angelic reapers are descended from Fallen angels, the Grigori, and because of that they are no better than worms in the eyes of many angels, especially some archangels. After you had forgotten that you were Gabriel, you'd married human men in your past lives and had children. But even I know most angels believe the offspring of the fallen Grigori to be the vilest of vile, no matter that we aren't demonic. We're unnatural to them. Unnatural, but useful."

Every word hit me hard, one after the other. Once I got past the idea that angels would kill Will for touching me, I was struck completely dumb by that last bombshell: I'd had children. A baby. *Babies.* When he said it, I remembered them, but I couldn't remember the faces of the men I had loved before Will.

"Where are they?" I asked blearily. "My children."

"Their descendants still live," Nathaniel said. "You haven't had a child in at least three hundred years. I don't keep track of them as well as I used to, but there is one bloodline in America that I know of."

"Why do you keep track of them?"

"The mortal scions, your children and their descendants, have always possessed some sort of power that manifests in different forms. They are stronger than any psychic, and much of what they can do resembles a bit of your own abilities, though much more diluted and, of course, no angelfire. A handful of angelic reapers have been selected to watch the scions, in case they become dangerous. Anything with great power is potentially dangerous."

As I wondered what it would be like to know them, I was brought back to thoughts of myself loving someone other than Will. He told me he'd always loved me, and that meant that he had loved me even when I loved someone else. It broke my heart. If I had been with other men in my past lives, how could I think it was wrong for Will to have been with other girls?

"Ellie," Nathaniel said suddenly. "Are you all right?"

I realized I'd been staring at the ground, and my hand was clamped tightly on the arm of the sofa. I let go and blinked at Nathaniel. "Yeah. It's just a lot to digest."

He rested a hand on mine reassuringly. "I don't mean to wear you out. You should be resting."

I shook my head. "I have to go after Bastian and make sure he pays for what he did to my parents."

He beamed at me. "I have to run to the library to check up on a few leads. I may have figured out where my copy of the grimoire is. One of your more active scions is quite the collector of divine artifacts. If I can get it back, we can look into restoring you to your archangel form."

"Do you think it's possible?" I asked.

He smiled and stood. "Anything's possible." Then he was gone, leaving me to my thoughts.

The house was quiet and sure enough, it began to rain, just as Nathaniel had predicted. After my conversation with him, I retreated to the study to read. I'd come to love curling up in the window seat of the big bay window in that room.

Later in the afternoon, I was a little lonely, so I set my book down. I would run out of my last change of clothes tomorrow and would have to do laundry, unless I went back to Nana's. But I wasn't quite ready to rejoin the human world yet.

I crept into the kitchen to make myself a turkey sandwich for dinner, wondering where Will was. I hadn't seen him since we had returned from our run, and I decided to look for him. The house was quiet, but then I heard the delicate strings of Will's acoustic guitar. I followed the sound, up the stairs and toward his bedroom. The door was ajar and I pushed it open. He was sitting at the end of his bed, strumming away. He glanced at me as I walked in.

I moved toward the bed and sat down, leaning my back against his as he played flawlessly, and I rested my head against him. My eyes closed, and I listened to the soft, sweet music filling my head. His shoulders and arms moved with perfect rhythm, lulling me. I didn't recognize the song, but it was beautiful and gentle, something that could sing me to sleep in the middle of a battlefield.

"What song is this?" I asked. "I don't know it."

"I wrote it for you."

I leaned deeper against his back and smiled, feeling a rush of warmth. I turned my head and his hair brushed my cheek. "I love it."

I melted away from reality, captured by this delicate song he had created for me. We sat like this for so long, back to back on his bed, every tiny, sinuous movement in him pulling at all my senses. I forgot about everything but him. I let myself forget about my parents, Nana, my friends, the Enshi, Bastian, Merodach and Kelaeno, Cadan . . . none of that mattered in this moment. The only thing that mattered was the song Will played for me.

When the song ended, I climbed off the bed and he looked up at me. The silence closed in on my skull, heavy, like the pressure would feel on my body if I was sinking through deep water.

"Where are you going?" he asked.

I shrugged and gave him a weak smile for reassurance. "I'm just tired. I think I'll go back downstairs and finish the book I was reading."

He nodded and as I left his room, I didn't hear the guitar again. I returned to the study, pushing the door open gently, exhausted all of a sudden. Instead of picking my book back up, I sat on the window seat, pulled my knees to my chest, and gazed out onto the dark lake raging in the rain.

I was cold everywhere and I imagined my mom wrapping her arms around me and pulling me close. In my memory, her hands petted my hair, winding the unruly dark red waves into braided pigtails. I wished I hadn't lied to her so many times or skipped out on hanging with her because I wanted to be with my friends. People always say that when you lose someone you love, you're consumed with regret. Regret for what you did or didn't do, regret for not doing enough. I felt all those things so heavily in my heart that it was hard to move or breathe. I felt ashamed that I couldn't remember the last moment I saw her, or the very last thing she said to me. I remembered the way she smelled, her perfume, but I couldn't quite imagine the precise color of her brown eyes. It was like with every hour that passed without her alive, my memories of her melted away. It was the most terrible thought, that I could forget her. I didn't want to forget her, and I wanted revenge against those who had taken her from me.

I sensed Will near me, and out of the corner of my eye I saw him appear in the doorway. When I looked at him, his shoulders slumped.

"Are you all right?" he asked. "Please talk to me, Ellie."

My mother's face flashed across my memory, and I sniffed harshly, forcing back a sob. I curled my limbs close to my body and leaned against the window. "I miss my mom."

He sucked in his upper lip for a thoughtful moment, and he came over and sat down on the other side of the window. "I know."

The sob broke free, and before I knew what was happening, tears were pouring down my cheeks, and my lips and hands were shaking. I shuddered, choking on air as suffocating despair filled me up like a flood, filling my lungs and windpipe until I was crying so hard that I couldn't breathe. He pulled me close, wrapping me in his arms as my own hung weakly around him. I buried my face in his chest as I cried, and his warm, familiar scent and hands caressing my hair were soothing. He murmured softly to me, but the words didn't matter. I just needed to feel him around me.

I pulled away from him at last, wiping at the wetness on my face with my sleeves. It took me a few moments to meet his eyes. I managed to get my breathing back under control and to stop my chest from heaving. I tucked my arms and legs close to my body again until I was no longer touching Will. He just sat there, unmoving and silent. We watched each other for some time, the stillness between us peaceful. I listened to the rain as it pounded hard against the house.

"I'm worried about you," he said gently. He put his hand around my knee and then leaned forward to kiss it. An obvious request for peace between us. "And about how you're feeling."

"I'm fine. I feel better after crying a little."

He smiled, his lips brushing my knee, but the smile

faded as soon as it began. "No, you're not. I'm worried that you won't get better for a while."

"I'm healing, Will. That takes time." I tapped the backs of my fingers against the freezing-cold window glass, wishing he would do anything but continue our current conversation.

"I know," he said, and sat back. "You smile sometimes, but I don't think you're happy."

I shrugged and stopped tapping. "It's hard to be happy."

"I understand better than most," he said. "I worry you're shutting down on me. We hunt every night, but it feels like you've lost your spark, some of your light. You won't tell me how you really feel, and I just want to help you."

"I'm in a lot of pain," I told him. "I want revenge, and we haven't found Bastian yet. We have no idea what his next move will be, and I'm going crazy."

He took my hand and rubbed it with both of his. "I need you to keep fighting. Don't give up on me, okay?" He touched my hair and got up to leave.

"Will." I called after him and followed him to the door. I wound my fingers around the bottom of his shirt. "I don't mean to worry you. I've been so numb with grief since I lost my parents. You're doing wonderfully, supporting me, and I appreciate that."

"I just don't know what to say to you or how to act."

"You don't have to say anything." I pleaded, "Just be here . . . like you are now."

He sighed and wrapped his arms around me. "I promise I'll always be here for you."

I felt new tears burning my eyes. "You can't promise me that. I've already lost so much. I can't lose you too, Will."

He pulled back, and his thumbs wiped my tears. "It's a promise I plan to keep, and I've never lied to you. I swear to you that I will be your Guardian forever and I'll keep loving you forever."

More tears rolled down my cheeks, and he kissed them away, his lips soft against my skin. I was so heartsick, so certain that if he died for me, I'd never survive that grief.

He tilted my chin up, his green eyes bright in the dimly lit room. "You believe me, don't you?"

I nodded, my lips quivering. "I do."

He kissed me tenderly and I kissed him back more fiercely, our first kiss since the night my mother died. It felt like years ago, decades, like I hadn't taken a breath in far too long.

"Why don't you get some sleep?" he offered, his hands spilling over my shoulders. "Take it easy tonight."

"Are you going to patrol?"

"No," he said. "I think I'll go down by the lake for a while and get some fresh air. Let's go upstairs and get you into bed."

He took my hand and led me up to his room, where I settled into his bed, pulling my limbs close to my body.

"Will you stay with me?" I asked as I pulled the blankets up to my chin.

"I'll be up in a while," he promised. "Try to sleep, okay?"

I watched him leave the room and close the door behind him. Drifting off took forever, and I kept stirring in and out of sleep for what was likely hours. His bed was so warm and soft, but my heart hurt too much for me to settle into a deep sleep.

Suddenly a tremendous roar blasted my eardrums, and the house gave a violent shake. I thrashed in surprise and terror, unsure if I'd dreamed what I'd just experienced. When my senses returned to me, I threw off the blankets and leaped to my feet. I tore open the bedroom door and darted down the stairs into the settling dust. The overhead lights flickered, buzzed, and went out, cloaking the house in darkness, my ears ringing shrilly. I moved toward the front of the house where the sound had come from, stepping slowly and silently.

"Will?" I called. "Nathaniel?"

The foyer—what was left of it—came into view. The front door had been blasted through, the wall around it demolished. The dust billowing in the moonlight now poured across the foyer tile. I slipped into the Grim and gasped when I saw what had caused the damage. A massive form appeared in the light and dust, the silhouette a jagged and crude shape of a man. But he was no man.

"Preliator!" the deep, gravelly voice of Merodach

boomed, shaking my body to the bone. "Come out and play!"

Behind him, another shape appeared: Kelaeno, trailed by five more vir reapers.

They had found me.

24

KELAENO FLEW ACROSS THE DEBRIS AND LANDED inside, her wings smashing through another wall as if the wood and drywall were made of paper. Her hair was a tangled, stringy mess and her facial features were more stable than when I last saw her. With an established form, she was prettier than I thought she'd be, but the violence and insanity in her eyes shattered the image. She looked as if she already had the taste of my blood in her mouth.

"The time has come to fetch you, little huntress," she sneered, creeping toward me with the quick, sharp movements of something more avian than human. "I think I may have a bite on the way back to Bastian. I've never tasted angel flesh before."

I stared into her wicked face. "Too bad your head will be

rolling in the dirt in about five seconds."

"Bold words," Merodach said as he stepped into the foyer, "for a dead girl." His body was so dark that only the edges were outlined in blue moonlight. His horns spiraled toward the ceiling, and the ones on his back stuck out in every direction.

Will raced by me, appearing out of nowhere, sword in hand. Merodach called his own sword—a hilt decorated with finely sculpted, razor-sharp points, and with sleek, vicious blades on either end. Merodach's double sword met Will's above both their heads, and the rush of energy slammed into either side of the hallway, crushing the walls. Merodach spun his sword so fast the blades blurred and nearly took off Will's head, but my Guardian ducked and rolled, sweeping his sword low, and Merodach leaped into the air, landing on Will's other side. Their blades clashed again, and Will struggled to keep up with Merodach's double blades, slashing and swiping at speeds I could barely see. With each clang of metal against metal, their energies flashed, their eyes like beacons in the dark, so bright the blackness was stained and smeared with color as they moved.

The small army of unknown reapers—three males and two females—held still and silent, as if waiting for orders to engage. The male standing out in front was shorter than the rest and was drooling revolting amounts of saliva that squeezed out from between his lips and sharp teeth and rolled down his chin. Instead of hair, this one had a dozen or so short spikes made of clean white bone sticking out of his skull in every direction.

A hand locked around my throat and threw me across the living room. My body smashed into the stone fireplace, collapsing the mantle, and rubble rained down on me as I hit the floor. Kelaeno was above me suddenly, grabbing a fistful of my hair and yanking me to my feet.

"Time to come with us," she hissed.

My sword appeared in my hand and blazed with angelfire as I swung it up at Kelaeno's face. She ducked, but my blade cut across her cheek, drawing blood and sparking. She shrieked and lashed out with her talons, slicing gashes across my chest. My angelfire seared into her face in a flash of light, and her skin scarred over. She shook her head violently, hissing and snarling and gnashing her teeth. Then she lunged for my throat, swiping, slashing, clawing. I kicked her chest and she hit the floor but bounced right back to her feet. Her hand clamped around my throat, and she threw me to the ground, grinding my back into the floor. Her boot stomped on my sword arm, keeping me from striking her as she crouched over me. I clawed at her hand as it tightened around my throat.

"Such a wild thing! You're like an angry kitten." Kelaeno laughed down at me, and her fingers brushed down my cheek. "And you're so pretty. I want your entrails for ribbons in my hair." She slashed her talon across my skin, and I flinched at the sting and the smell of the blood that followed it, despite the cut healing right away. She laughed again and shoved me harder into the floor.

Suddenly a fist collided with her head, and she was thrown off of me and sent tumbling. Will leaped over me and charged at the demonic reaper as she struggled to her feet. He hit her again and she fell. He swung his fist a third time, but her power lashed out and struck him in the chest, and he landed a few yards away on his back with a grunt.

She stood and cursed at the top of her lungs as she spun around to the waiting reapers. "Rikken!" she roared at the drooling reaper. "Disable the Guardian!"

Rikken gave an eager shake of his spiked head like a dog baring his teeth, and he stomped toward Will. Kelaeno stepped in front of me, blocking my view of Will just as I heard him growl in pain. Fear for his life stabbed at every inch of me. We weren't going to make it out of here alive. There were just too many of them.

I screamed in a rage and called my second sword and slashed it across Kelaeno's chest, ripping her wide open. She roared and reared back, spreading her arms wide with clenched fists, thrashing her head from side to side in fury. I shot forward and swept my sword at her gut, but her hand knocked my arm away and she swung her body into me. A claw swiped my face and I hit the ground, blood seeping over my cheek and lips. I spat and wiped my arm across my face, feeling the numbness of my skin healing.

As I climbed to my feet, I saw two reapers racing toward me—a female with glossy black feathers in her hair and another male—with their claws spread open and teeth bared. I collided with them, spinning, ducking, kicking. I brought down my blade in a sweeping arc, splitting the female reaper's body in two through her shoulder and below her left breast. She burst into flames, gone before any of her even hit the ground.

I wheeled to meet the second reaper directly behind me, but something large and glinting burst through his rib cage, cracking bone and tearing flesh. Blood flecked off silver metal as it halted for a brief moment, only inches from my own chest, and then the reaper's body lifted into the air so that I could see it had been Will who had shoved his sword through the reaper's heart. He flipped the reaper high over his head as the body turned to stone midair and shattered into a thousand pieces when it hit the floor.

Across the hall, Rikken clutched his throat and chest, which had been sliced wide open by Will's sword moments ago, spilling red. He coughed and sputtered, but even from this distance I saw that his wound wasn't fatal and was already healing.

A shadow passed behind Will, and I cried out his name. He turned and met Merodach, who charged through the darkness, driving his sword at Will's chest, but Will spun to the side at the last instant. The blade ripped through his shirt and missed his skin entirely. Merodach slashed his double sword left and right and left and right, meeting Will's giant blade each time.

I didn't see Kelaeno appear beside me until she struck me across the temple. I staggered one step before I found my balance, spun, and reeled my elbow into her jaw. Her Harpy-like face snapped to the side. She swiveled her head around to meet my gaze with her holly red eyes, and she called two short, slick swords into her hands. She moved like lightning, one of her swords raised level with her shoulder before she thrust it at my face. I bounced away, but she followed, slashing and striking. Silver clanged against flaming silver, and her gaze locked onto mine as if she had nothing else to see. She drove one sword at my heart and I twisted away, but her other blade was too fast. Metal plunged into my shoulder, and I screamed as it ripped through my body. I stumbled against the wall and collapsed to my knees in agony.

Then Kelaeno jerked her head to the side in a blur, and her shoulder exploded. I saw Nathaniel standing behind her, staring down the barrel of his gun. Kelaeno had moved too fast for Nathaniel to shoot her in the head. He fired again, but she ducked low until her face was frighteningly close to mine. As she turned her head to look, her cheek brushed my nose and I jerked away, horrified. She slid her sword out from my shoulder, lifting my body as she did so. I shrieked in pain before slumping back against the wall.

Then she vanished.

Nathaniel's eyes grew wide and he waited for her to reappear. When her form blurred into view, she was too fast for him to react. Her swords gone, she grabbed the gun from his hands and snapped it in half like a Popsicle stick before she chucked the pieces at the ground.

Will came out of nowhere and wrapped his arm around Kelaeno's throat, digging up against her windpipe and yanking her back. He held on until she shoved her elbow into his gut and managed to wrench herself free. Nathaniel threw out a fist, but she caught it and struck him in the jaw. Will grabbed his sword off the ground and swiped it at the demonic reaper's back.

Kelaeno's ears pricked as she heard Will coming, and she spun around to defend herself, leaping back as his blade slashed across her chest, leaving a deep, bleeding gash and very nearly slicing off her head. She hissed and swung around in pain, clutching her open wound. The flesh wrapped over itself and wove back together, healing perfectly. Kelaeno's red eyes burned like flames with her rage at receiving another wound of that severity in practically the same spot.

I rushed forward to help Will, but two other vir intercepted—the remaining female and the last male besides the wounded Rikken. They slashed and hissed, throwing punches and kicks that I dodged. I buried one blade in the male reaper's heart on my left side, whirled at the female on my right, and cut off her head with my remaining blade. The male was in flames when I spun back to him, and I caught my falling sword as his body turned to ash.

Kelaeno grasped her clawed hand around my arm, and as I swung the blade in my free hand, she grabbed that wrist and squeezed, nails digging into my skin. I screamed and cried out. Blood seeped, and I was forced to drop my sword.

"Time to go," she said sharply, and began dragging me toward the nearest escape route.

Then Will struck her brutally in the side of her head, so hard that she released me and her knees buckled. Will clamped his hand around the back of her neck, wrenched her off me, and threw her through the kitchen wall with all his strength. Wood shattered around her body as wet, icy-cold air rushed inside through the hole. Kelaeno crashed into the deck, destroying the railing, and she disappeared as she hurtled toward the ground with a scream of fury.

Will turned to me, and I exhaled a sigh of relief.

The breath caught in my throat as Kelaeno burst through the air over the deck, her wings spread and beating violently. Time seemed to slow. I stared deep into Will's eyes, my expression widening in horror, as Kelaeno's outstretched claws grappled at his body, snatching him and yanking him back out the hole in the wall and into the rain and darkness.

"Will!" I shrieked, and grabbed my fallen sword and dived through the demolished wall. The deck groaned and

shifted uneasily beneath my weight, but I didn't care as I ran to the edge and peered over the shattered floorboards. Icy rain stung my skin, and I shivered viciously at the wind whipping my hair, clawing at my clothes, and beating my face.

Down on the cold, muddy ground, dashing through the rain, Will and Kelaeno were fighting. Talons ripped Will's arm wide open and he yelled out, tearing away, as Kelaeno landed in a crouched position. She jumped up and swiped again, her claws shredding Will's shirt. Kelaeno ducked as he swung his sword, and she kicked him in the chest, making him grunt and knocking the sword out of his hand. They collided in a fury of swinging, pounding fists.

I heard a tremendous sound behind me, and I whirled. Merodach and Rikken were nowhere to be seen, but Nathaniel was punching through the only remaining wall in the hallway leading from the kitchen to what was left of the front door. The staircase behind him was a demolished and nearly inaccessible pile of rubble. Nathaniel pounded his fists—left, right, left, right—into the wall, exploding wood, drywall, and insulation. I stared at him, distracted by my confusion as to why he would be trying to knock this wall down. For a second, I almost forgot about the missing demonic reapers.

Then Nathaniel stopped, and the hole he'd created revealed a set of various weapons hidden in the wall. He reached his arm into the wall and pulled out a dark metal object: a mace. The weapon looked old and heavy, and the shaft was long and wrapped in leather. The round head of the mace was made of silver, and deadly looking spikes stuck out in every direction, reminding me of Rikken's skull.

Rikken. Where was he? And Merodach?

"Nathaniel?" came a small voice.

We both spun to find Lauren standing just inside the blasted-open front of the house, her long hair billowing in the violent wind. I was suddenly numb, and I glanced at Nathaniel, whose face was frozen with fear.

He shook his head in disbelief, his copper eyes flashing bright and vibrant like brand-new pennies. "No," he breathed. "Lauren, you've got to—"

Before he could finish, Rikken appeared between them, reaching for Lauren, and Nathaniel hurled the mace with a cry of rage. Rikken leaned back, avoiding the blow easily, and as Nathaniel's torso went down with the arc of his swing, Rikken smashed his elbow into the back of Nathaniel's head, sending him to his knees. He recovered quickly and grabbed Rikken's fist as the demonic reaper swung, and Nathaniel swept the mace up and raked the spikes across Rikken's chest as Rikken jerked his head out of the mace's path. Rikken doubled over, clutching his wounds as saliva poured through his teeth and hit the floor, and Nathaniel rose.

Lauren's hands covered her mouth in terror. "Nathaniel!"

He reached for her, dropping the mace to the floor and

grasping her hands with his own. "You've got to go. I can't protect you."

"Come with me. Please don't stay here!" She let her hands fall, but his closed around them and squeezed them tight.

He shook his head and she started to cry. "I have to stay," he murmured. "I'm sorry."

With an awful sound escaping her, she nodded. He rushed into her and kissed her mouth fiercely, taking his hands from hers to firmly hold her shoulders.

"I love you," he said, his copper eyes glowing. "Now run. Get in your car and drive away as fast as you can. Don't stop until you're out of gas. Lauren, *run!*"

She turned and bolted from the house. Nathaniel was trembling as we listened to her car start up and the tires squeal out of the driveway. I rushed forward to help him, but he held out a hand, stopping me.

"No!" he called. "Go help Will. He has both of them on him now. Go!"

I nodded and obeyed, spinning in the hall, and I darted through the hole in the wall Kelaeno's body had made. Outside, I was back in the stinging, icy rain and she was nowhere to be seen. For a second I couldn't see anyone, but I strained my eyes to make out a crumpled shape in the darkness of the lawn. My stomach dropped.

A hand fastened around my throat and another hand forced my head down. The fingers were like steel, squeezing and squeezing, so hard I couldn't breathe. My knees hit the deck, and I dropped my swords to claw at the hand strangling me. Then I was wrenched to my feet. The hand loosened just enough for me to breathe and turn to find that I was caught in Kelaeno's grasp. I twisted, reaching for my swords, but she spun me around, repositioned her hand so that it clamped around the back of my neck. Her other hand locked both of my wrists together. I wrenched my body, desperate to escape, but it was useless. I heard something snap, and I watched my winged necklace fall to the ground, the chain broken. The temperature felt like it dropped another several degrees, and I shivered.

"You have entirely exhausted my patience," Kelaeno hissed, her breath hot and stinking of roadkill against my cheek. I gagged and twisted away from her face. She shoved me forward, pushing me down the swaying deck stairs to the ground. My shoes slipped in the mud, my balance off with my arms tied behind my back. Every time I slipped, Kelaeno dug her nails into my wrists.

The shape ahead of me came into view. It was Will on his knees in the mud, his sword lying too far away. Merodach stood above him with a tight fistful of Will's hair in his hand and one end of his double blade to Will's throat.

Kelaeno jerked me to the ground in front of Will, her grip tightening ruthlessly. "You shouldn't have angered us like this," she snarled. "We were just going to grab you and go, but now you get to watch your Guardian die first. Bastian's orders be damned."

My eyes met Will's as Merodach's blade pressed deeper into his throat, drawing a fine line of blood. I couldn't let my emotion show in front of the demonic reapers—or in front of Will. I had to be as tough as he was, and he was so much closer to death in that moment.

"Rikken was going to give him a slow, agonizing death," Kelaeno said into my ear. "But it seems he is preoccupied with the other angelic reaper. I think letting your Guardian here bleed out in the mud will do nicely. We can spare a few minutes before we depart."

Merodach yanked Will's head back, exposing his throat to the fullest, and began to draw his knife along my Guardian's skin. Before I could scream out in protest, something zinged by my face, whirling, whipping through the air, and slammed right into Merodach's chest, crunching bone. His body jerked at the impact, and he lost his hold on Will. Nathaniel's mace was half buried in the demonic reaper's ribs. Will shoved Merodach, hard enough to throw him even further off balance and force his dark wings to burst forth to catch himself. Will grabbed the shaft of the mace and tugged it out of Merodach's chest with a crack of bone and a sickening wet slap of flesh, and swiped it at Merodach's head, but the demonic reaper threw a hand up and knocked the weapon away.

I glanced behind me and gasped as Nathaniel leaped off the deck and darted toward us. Beneath Kelaeno's vicious grip, I looked everywhere for Rikken, but he was nowhere within eyesight. I could only hope that Nathaniel had killed him.

Will charged suddenly, a blur in the darkness, and he beat Kelaeno off me. I jumped up and looked around for Merodach, finding that in those few seconds I'd taken my eyes off them, Will had incapacitated Merodach. Across the lawn, the demonic reaper was bent over backward at a disturbing, almost ninety-degree angle, struggling against Will's sword nailing him to the ground. His wings beat against the dead grass and muddy patches of snow.

Kelaeno managed to duck away from Will's monstrous attack, her face and clothes soaking wet with blood and rain. She slipped through the mud and grabbed me again before I could react. She swung me around, contorting my arm so violently in the wrong direction that I cried out and stars danced across my vision. She pressed her knee into my back, shoving my chest and face into the mud, pulling on my arm at the same time, threatening to dislodge the bone from its socket. I ground my teeth and whimpered.

"Not another step, Guardian!" Kelaeno cawed shrilly. "I'll rip her arm right off. Merodach, get over here!"

Though I couldn't see much, I assumed Merodach was still staked to the ground by Will's sword. I recognized Will's feet in front of me, unmoving, and I glanced to my right and saw up to Nathaniel's knees.

Above me, Kelaeno loosed an ugly, impatient growl. "Enough of this."

And then she wrenched my arm right out of the socket. I screamed and crumpled, squeezing my eyes shut. Kelaeno dropped me, and all around where I lay, feet darted and splashed through puddles. I pulled my useless limb closer to my body with my good arm. It felt cold, numb, and lifeless. As the seconds dragged on, the pain intensified. I tried to get up, but shock paralyzed me and my body wouldn't work.

"Ellie." A hand lay on my uninjured shoulder. It was Nathaniel.

He touched my face tenderly and helped me turn over onto my back. He touched my dislocated arm, and I shrieked and twisted from him. As gentle as he was, any contact felt like a thousand knives were driving into my skin. My arm hung limp, like dead weight, and I tried to pull it over my lap, but my whole body was so weak that I could barely even raise my good arm.

Nathaniel murmured to me, trying to soothe me, but all I needed was a distraction from the agony. Will and Kelaeno were fighting, clashing like titans from another world. The earth beneath me roiled with their power, and the air sparked with electricity.

"Ellie," Nathaniel repeated determinedly, snapping my attention back to him. I was getting dizzier with shock by the moment. "We have to put your arm back into the socket. You can't heal otherwise."

I closed my eyes tightly and nodded. "Just do it. I've got to keep fighting."

He took a firm hold of my shoulder and my arm just above the elbow. The pain was blinding, and so brief that once it was over, I was almost a little confused. I could feel tendons and muscles healing themselves, and the sensation was sickening but necessary.

I met Nathaniel's stern gaze and took a deep breath. "Thank you."

"You'll be fine in a moment." He nodded once, and we both looked toward the battle.

Will grabbed Kelaeno's arm and rammed his fist into the side of her head. She staggered about and his knee shoved up into her gut, making her grunt and choke. Will's fist swung to hit Kelaeno again, but her hand shot up and deflected his strike before she closed her fingers around his throat. He gasped painfully from the strength of her grip. She stood, glaring at him, and squeezed as tightly as she could. Will's teeth clenched as he held back his pain and dug his fingers into her wrists. Then his gaze darkened and he summoned his power. He blasted everything he had into Kelaeno's face, and she screamed and released him, spinning away and shielding herself from the explosion of winding, smoky black energy. She hit the mud sliding, and Will, now free, darted toward his sword.

His sword that no longer pinned Merodach to the ground. My breath caught as I felt a rush of dark power close to me.

I heard a gargled, anguished cry behind me, and I spun. Nathaniel was doubled over, and Merodach, soaked with his own blood, had his fist buried in Nathaniel's chest. Something glinted in the moonlight and I blinked. Merodach's sword stuck out of Nathaniel's back—stabbed right through his heart.

My entire body went numb as I watched Merodach tug his sword free and Nathaniel hit the muddy ground on his knees. He wavered unsteadily, blood leaking like a river from his chest. He looked up into Merodach's face and then collapsed and rolled onto his back.

For a moment, I couldn't scream for him, couldn't look away. Nathaniel sputtered and trembled. His skin brightened and shimmered, slowly turning to stone.

He was dying.

Merodach stared at me curiously as I scrambled toward Nathaniel and threw myself over him, running my hands along his graying arms to cup his face. He was just fine this morning, stretching his wings and telling me that anything was possible and to love who I wanted to love. He was just fine moments ago, putting my arm back into its socket and telling me I'd be all right. This couldn't be happening. Not to Nathaniel.

"No, no, no," I moaned in a low voice, rocking back and forth, my entire body shaking.

Nathaniel gaped at me, his face full of surprise and pain. His mouth moved, but no sound came out. He started to lift a hand, but his limbs were growing heavier and stiffer as he bled out and his heart chugged to a stop. His iridescent copper eyes widened and froze as his face turned to stone. Raindrops hit his rock skin, leaving dark, damp dots scattered across the white. Each soft metallic copper hair became pale and brittle and colorless, breaking off at the touch of my fingertips. Then he broke apart, piece by piece in my hands. Tears poured down my face as I screamed his name over and over until he was gone.

I lifted my head and searched for Will as I sobbed hysterically. His green eyes stared at Nathaniel's stone remains; the color drained from his face. His eyes brightened quickly, growing so vibrant that they blazed in the darkness. His hand squeezed the handle of his sword so tightly his fist trembled and I could hear the silver groan. With a cry of unrivaled wrath, he launched himself at Merodach at a speed so high it appeared that he skimmed the ground midflight, and then his white wings burst through his shirt, shredding the fabric. He swept his sword low and then swung it high over his head as he soared through the air. His blade slashed at Merodach, and the demonic reaper swung his own up to catch Will's sword with a deafening screech of metal. They collided, and Will's power slammed into Merodach, sinking the ground beneath Merodach's feet into a crater. The dark flash of shadows and smoke of reaper power cloaked them for an instant, and when it cleared, I saw only Will in the bottom of the fissure he'd created. Merodach had leaped out of it, his own dark wings spread wide behind him. He stepped back on his heel and readied his sword. Will's wings beat once and launched him high into the air, and he came down on Merodach, his sword streaking through the air, slashing, striking, cutting flesh, clanging off the other blade. He was consumed with rage, his attacks all power and no control. Merodach was going to kill him.

"Will!" My voice was strangled, and I leaned protectively over what was left of Nathaniel. "Will, stop!"

He couldn't hear me, couldn't hear or see anything. I realized then how terrified he was for me when I let my emotions and power take over.

"Will, you have to stop! You're going to get yourself killed!"

A blast of power sent tremors through the earth, and I grabbed at the ground for balance.

"Will, stop!" I screamed, but my voice was lost in the chaos.

Merodach's elbow smashed right into Will's nose, knocking him back several steps. The demonic reaper spun and kicked Will so hard he nearly hit the ground. Merodach spun again and pierced his sword right through Will's chest, splashing blood across his white wings. Will collapsed onto his knees, and I screamed, scrambling to my feet and taking off at a run toward him. I couldn't lose them both tonight. I couldn't lose Will. *I couldn't lose him.*

Rikken emerged into my vision a few yards away, drenched with blood as if he'd bathed in it. Nathaniel hadn't killed him after all. A shadow stretched directly over me. I looked up.

The last thing I saw was the back of Kelaeno's hand slamming into my face.

25

"LET ME GO! SOMEBODY HELP ME! HELP ME, *please!*"

The voice screamed inside my head and stung my ears. I groggily shook myself awake, my skull hammering with pain, trying to figure out if the voice screaming was my own or not. My body was vertical, this much I could tell. My wrists were cut by the chains binding them over my head, and my healing shoulder throbbed. I slit my eyes open and could tell the light was dim wherever I was. The air was cold and damp, like I was underground—in a cellar.

"You!" the voice said again, hushed but frantic. "Are you alive? You awake?"

Not my own voice. I lifted my head painfully and forced my eyes open. The low light made it easier, but every muscle and joint in my body ached. I was definitely in a cellar with torches flickering firelight off stone walls.

"Hey! Girl!"

The voice was making my head hurt worse. I looked in the direction it came from and found a blond girl about my age standing next to me a few feet away. No, not standing. Chained. Her wrists were chained to the low ceiling, just as mine were. A stab of panic hit straight through my gut as I snapped my head up. I yanked on the chains as hard as I could, my body shaking with fear. They wouldn't budge. Dust clouded above me, but the chains didn't break. I summoned my power and gave a tremendous jerk, but still nothing. Fear turned into shock and confusion. Iron chains shouldn't be able to hold me. I'd brought down an entire warehouse before, just by willing my power. This made no sense. None of this made sense.

But why was I here? How did I get here?

"Are you okay?" the girl asked. "Hey! Are you deaf?"

"No," I snapped, my voice hoarse. "I'm not deaf. I'm thinking. Or *trying* to, at least." I looked around the room, looking for anything familiar, but I'd never been here or seen this girl before.

And then it hit me, the memory rolling in like acid fog.

Nathaniel.

Will.

Nathaniel was dead and Will probably was too.

I couldn't breathe. I gasped for air—rapid, uncontrolled gasps. My lungs wouldn't work. My heart pounded and my vision faded to black as I sagged heavily against my chains. I felt like I was dying. Tears rolled down my cheeks as I wept for my friends. The memory of Nathaniel turning to stone in my arms and Will taking Merodach's blade to his chest was too much. I cried and thrashed and screamed, cursing the demonic reapers and swearing to tear them apart piece by piece.

Then I swallowed hard and forced my tears to cease. I had to be brave. I had to escape and get back to Will if he was still alive. If he was dead, I'd have known. I'd have felt it in my soul. Now I had to get myself out of this, because no one was coming for me.

And my panic wasn't helping the girl I was imprisoned with to stay calm.

"Are you okay?" she asked once I'd stopped crying. Her face was streaked with dirt and bloody scrapes.

I ignored her question. "Where are we?"

She shook her head weakly. "I don't know. A basement, I think."

Useless. "How long have you been down here?"

"A day. Maybe two. I don't know. They've only come down once since I woke up in here."

"They?"

She was quiet for a moment, her pale blue eyes locking on mine. "Monsters."

Reapers. "Do you know why you're here?"

"No. Do you?"

Yes. Maybe. "We have to stay calm."

"I'm scared," she said, shaking. "And I haven't eaten in so long. I don't feel well."

"Hey," I said sharply, just as she was about to cry. "I'm going to figure out how to get out of here." The problem was, I had no idea how to do that. Something was keeping me weak. I wasn't so sure I could bust out of these chains by brute strength alone.

My necklace was gone, and my strength felt like it had gone with it. Kelaeno had broken it, and I felt its loss dearly. I looked around the room more carefully. On the left wall of the cellar, past the girl beside me, was a staircase. When I looked through the darkness to the opposite wall, my heart stopped and some invisible horror tore through my stomach.

The sarcophagus. The stone box stood vertical against the wall so that I stared at its lid as if it were a doorway. On one side of it was a wooden table with a large, weathered old book opened on it, but it was too far away for me to read the text. Beside the book was a rough clay bowl and an ornate, ancient-looking box. A silver dagger lay on the other side of the book.

Nausea and helplessness swept over me. I began to feel terrified for myself and the girl now. My heart pounded so fiercely I worried it'd hammer right through my rib cage. I thought quickly.

"What's your name?" I asked the girl.

"Emma," she said. "What's yours?"

"Ellie, and I'm going to get us out of here. How old are you, Emma?"

"Fifteen."

I glanced at her. The clothes she wore, a junior varsity track hoodie over a T-shirt, were filthy and torn. "What's the last thing you remember before you woke up here?"

She shook her head and sagged heavily on her chains. "I was out jogging. I have a meet on Saturday. What day is it now? What was the last thing you remember doing?"

Watching Will and Nathaniel die. "Sitting there and doing nothing."

She gave me a puzzled look and I let my eyes fall to the floor.

"The sleeping princess awakens," came Kelaeno's voice. "What a ruckus you make down here. Are you trying to wake the dead?"

I snapped my head up to see her descending the staircase. The demonic reaper's laughter echoed off the walls as I thrashed against my chains again.

"Scream all you want. It's music to my ears."

"When I get out of here," I snarled, "there won't be words for what I do to you—you and that bastard Merodach."

"You *know* them?" Emma asked, staring at us both.

A disgusting, sated smile slit across Kelaeno's face. "We killed her boyfriend."

"He's not dead." I pulled against my chains.

She licked her lips and stepped toward me. "So sure,

aren't you? Looked to me like you were out cold when we started tearing him apart. He was such a *screamer*—"

I shrieked and slammed my power in all directions. It pounded into an invisible wall in front of me and shook the ceiling, but the blast was nothing compared to what I had intended. That scared me. What happened? What was wrong with me?

Kelaeno lifted a finger, waggled it back and forth, and *tsk*ed. "Uh-uh." Then she pointed to the floor beneath me.

I squinted to see something—writing of some kind—etched into the stone in white paint. It was faint, but the closer I looked, the more writing I saw. A pentagram surrounded me, and an Enochian prayer was written around the entire diameter of the circle. I knew what this was. I'd seen it before. It was a circle to bind my power—a trap.

The demonic reaper sneered. "No escape for you."

"What are you?" Emma cried, staring at me wide-eyed. "Are you one of *them*? How are you doing that?"

I glared at Kelaeno. "What do you want with us?"

She laughed. "I'm not giving away the ending to the show just yet. We have a surprise for you, an old friend. Perhaps you will recognize her."

Her? Footsteps scraped the staircase and Bastian descended, his handsome, disturbingly familiar face cool and calm, followed by Merodach and a couple of reapers I had never seen before. Hatred rushed through me like a torrential river, coursing and desperate for release. My power hummed, rising off the floor around me like heat waves, and the closer the demonic reapers approached, the harder my power pressed to the Enochian barrier trapping me.

"The Guardian?" Bastian asked, directing his question to either Merodach or Kelaeno.

Kelaeno made an ugly, triumphant noise at him and bared her teeth.

Bastian stopped abruptly and turned on her. "I ordered you to leave him alive. He is valuable to me. Is the rumor I heard about Rikken accompanying you accurate? You dare to defy me?"

Kelaeno hissed and snapped her jaws at Bastian. "I do as I please."

"Kelaeno," Merodach said in a warning tone.

Bastian's cool gaze shifted from Merodach to Kelaeno. When he faced me, he wore a pleasant smile. "Nice to see you again, Preliator."

I snarled, pulling on my chains. "I'll say the same to you when you're dead at my feet."

"So valiant," he noted, his voice rising with amusement. "But you have no way of escaping unless I free you, and that is not something likely to happen."

"Are you afraid of me?" I taunted, careful to keep Merodach and Kelaeno in my peripheral vision.

He gazed at me thoughtfully. "Yes, I suppose I am. I have no doubt that, after your friend and your Guardian are killed, you will try to avenge them. I haven't forgotten about your human parents, either. You may not be strong enough to kill us, but I'm certain you could do a noticeable amount of damage. None of us wants to be the target of an archangel's wrath. Those sorts of things never end well."

Merodach straightened and looked me dead in the eye. "I do not fear her."

"Nor do I," Kelaeno chirped. "I say we turn her loose. I haven't tasted enough blood this night."

Bastian raised a hand to them both. "She is not ours to set free."

Emma yanked on her chains. "What are you people talking about? Please, just let me go! Please!"

"Silence," Bastian ordered the girl. She shivered and shrunk, her eyes pinned to the floor. "As I was saying, Kelaeno, the Preliator does not belong to us."

"She's *mine*," crooned someone unseen through the basement, a low, sensual voice echoing off stone. It made me cold deep inside, sending ice into my soul.

Before my eyes, an outstretched hand shimmered into existence, followed shortly by the outline of a young woman. Her body was faint, ghostly, and long dark hair flowed as she stepped toward me, but her simple white gown faded to nothingness below the knee so that her feet were invisible. Her features were smooth and soft, her large eyes lovely, her smile elegant, refined—and cruel.

I knew her face. The coldness. The darkness. I knew *her*. The Demon Queen.

Lilith.

The phantom Lilith reached for me, gripping my chin. I jerked my face to the side, but I could only move so far from her reach. The binding pentagram around me seemed to have no effect on her. I barely even noticed that Emma had begun screaming beside me before Kelaeno struck her and silenced her in an instant.

Lilith studied my face with curious disgust. "You're not so shiny in this form, Gabriel," she said, her voice hollow and echoing. "I can look upon you without my eyes bleeding. I'd say it's an improvement, but the human stink all over you makes me want to retch."

Just like Michael's, her touch felt prickly and charged, as if a low-level electric fence had brushed against my skin. Not enough to hurt, but certainly enough to get my attention.

She touched my hair, fingers running down the length of it, and to my shock, she picked up a lock with her ghostly hand. I stared at her fearfully, unable to understand how she could touch my body in this form. Was it because I was a relic, like Nathaniel had said? If she could touch me, that meant she could kill me and I couldn't defend myself. I jerked away harder, pulling my hair from between her fingers.

"You're grieving," she noted, as simply as if she were naming the color of my eyes. "And you're afraid. I can't decide whether it's beautiful or disgusting. Can you weep now, Gabriel, in this human body you're wearing?"

I tried to wipe the emotion from my face, but it was

useless. I couldn't pull myself completely together. By denying my grief for Will and Nathaniel, I'd be denying *them*.

Lilith raised her hand, signaling to the demonic reapers
in the room with us. "Leave us. Gabriel and I have much to
discuss before we begin."

As they ascended the staircase without protest, Lilith
smiled at me, sticky and syrupy sweet.

I stared into her eyes. "Why am I here?"

She ignored my question. "How long has it been,
Gabriel?" she asked pleasantly, as if I were an old friend.
"Ten thousand years? Fifteen thousand? In Hell, time
doesn't exist. Nothing changes. It all just burns. Tell me, has
time been kind to me? Did you miss me?"

"Not at all," I snarled. Memories of Lilith destroying vil-
lages, blood and violence from long ago, flashed behind my
eyes as if I'd seen the horror only yesterday.

She frowned. "I have to say that I'm a little pained. We're
practically sisters, you and I. Your Father created me just
as He created you, though I didn't last long in His favor. He
made me to be a man's property and punished me when I
didn't obey. The Morningstar gladly took me in and made me
like the rest of your kind. In order to be free, I had to go to
Hell. There is something very wrong about that."

"Everything is wrong about you."

One corner of her mouth pulled into a smile. "Without
your wings and glory, you look like a child." She licked her
lips and bared her teeth. "I love children."

Another memory struck me, one I was desperate to wall up in the darkest corners of my mind. The other me, the archangel I was in another life, protected children and couldn't bear the idea of the monster before me devouring them, stretching her jaws implausibly wide, swallowing babies whole.

"What do you want with me?" I snarled, narrowing my eyes at her as my head hung low.

"You are the final relic needed to release us," she said.

"Who is us?" I glanced quickly over at the ancient book. It was the grimoire. It had to be.

"The Lord of Souls and me," she replied.

"Who—*what*—is the Enshi?" I demanded, bracing against my chains.

"The Lord of Souls is a Fallen angel of death, Death himself. He is the Morningstar's second and my beloved: Sammael."

Fear raked the inside of my throat. "It can't be. That's impossible."

Lilith moved away from me. "Don't you remember your brother, whom Azrael exiled?"

The memories clawed at my heart and mind, dragging themselves to the surface. Azrael, the archangel of death since the beginning of time, had indeed cast out Sammael, the lesser angel of death. Sammael and the Queen of Hell had become lovers, and Azrael took it upon himself to implement justice, despite my warnings to him. He and Sammael battled fiercely, but Sammael was no match for the arch-angel Azrael. When Sammael was defeated, he fell and joined Lilith at the Morningstar's side, where he became as powerful as an archangel. We felt his loss greatly, but he turned his back on us for the dark power of Hell.

"Didn't you know why Azrael was cast out from the inner circle?" Lilith crooned. "When my children, the ancestors of the modern demonic reapers, continued my legacy on Earth, Azrael took it personally. When he battled Sammael for the second time, they nearly caused the Apocalypse, but Azrael defeated Sammael once more and used ancient magic to imprison him. For punishing Sammael so greatly, God stripped Azrael of his archangel power. He became an out-cast, weakened, but not quite fallen from grace. And I have waited a very, very long time to see my beloved again."

"And when Sammael is released," I began slowly, "you're going to destroy everything, starting with me."

Lilith made a quiet purring sound. "I am sorry, Gabriel, but you have murdered too many of my children. This cannot go unpunished."

"What is it that you want?" I growled. "To destroy the world?"

She laughed richly. "Our job is to make this world more like our home, a little more habitable for our master."

I shook my head in confusion. "Your master? Sammael?"

Her red lips curled into a smile. "No, Gabriel. The Morningstar."

"Morningstar," I spat. "Morningstar—you mean *Lucifer. The* Morningstar."

"Correct." When I didn't respond, she gazed at me curiously, as if she were seeing right through my skin to examine my human soul. "I almost don't want to let Sammael destroy you. Perhaps I should let the Morningstar pick you apart and see how they made you. He'd love to get his claws on you, Gabriel, and I'd personally love to see your insides. But you are too dangerous to be allowed to exist."

I lifted my chin and swallowed. "So you're going to release Sammael now?"

She raised a finger. "Not yet. First you will make me whole."

"And how is that?" I watched her carefully.

"Patience, archangel," she cooed. She closed her eyes and her brow furrowed as if in concentration. A moment later, Bastian returned to the cellar, flanked by Kelaeno and Merodach, leading me to deduce that Lilith had somehow called them with her mind. Perhaps she was linked telepathically with her demonic, monstrous offspring. She lifted a phantom hand and pointed at the items near the sarcophagus. "Prepare the ritual."

Kelaeno skimmed over the open pages in the book as Bastian collected the clay bowl and silver dagger. Merodach, dark and silent, stood by the wall as he observed the activity. Bastian stepped up to me and raised the dagger. With him standing close to me, I could feel the power in the dagger humming. It was a relic bound to one of the Fallen, a demonic relic.

I stared into his toxic blue eyes. "How did you get that?"

"The Blade of Belial," he said evenly. "You don't want to know what I had to do to get this."

"You need my blood now, don't you?"

"Yes," he said. "I'm sorry that this will hurt. Your death tonight will not be quick or painless." He pressed the dagger to my arm.

"Don't even pretend like you're sorry," I snarled. "You've been working toward this for centuries."

"Over a thousand years," he corrected. "And don't make the mistake of believing that you are the only one who has made sacrifices. I've given up everything for this."

I laughed bitterly. "*You* are whining about what *you've* had to give up while you're trying to destroy the world? How's that working out for you?"

He glared at me and sliced the dagger deeply into my skin, cutting ligaments with the flesh. I gasped and buckled at the pain, but the look in his eyes told me my words had stung him just as much as his blade had stung me. He pressed the bowl against my skin and let my blood fill it. I tried not to watch, since seeing my own blood flow made me dizzy and sick to my stomach. My wound healed and ceased to bleed in only a few seconds. Bastian withdrew without a word and moved away from me. Kelaeno lifted the box off the table and opened the lid. Bastian reached in and removed a necklace—a heavy, clear gemstone set into a gold pendant hanging from a metal wire strung with smaller jewels and precious stones. I recognized it instantly. The Constantina necklace, the relic Zane had died for and failed to protect.

Bastian set the necklace carefully into the bowl of my blood, completely submerging it. Kelaeno began to chant something in an ancient language, reading from the book. I listened carefully, digging deep into my memory for the translation, but I couldn't remember the language. I looked to Lilith, who stood still and entranced, her chin tilted up and her eyes closed, as if the words had power over her. Once Kelaeno's chant ended, Lilith opened her eyes and removed the necklace tentatively from the bowl. My blood dripped off the pendant and drenched the front of her white dress as she fastened the necklace around her neck. Then my blood seemed to move in ways gravity shouldn't have allowed: It spread in every direction, red tracing the veins and arteries beneath Lilith's skin and sinking through until it vanished and no blood remained anywhere to be seen.

And then light. I cried out and squeezed my eyes shut, turning my face away from the blinding flash. I could hear screams, hollow and distant as if the sounds played through an old television, screams that echoed untold millennia of torment and despair wrought by the Demon Queen. Unable to cover my ears with my hands, I pressed my cheek into my chained arm, desperate to drown out the horrible cries of terror and agony.

When the light and screams dissipated, I slit my eyes open to see what had happened. I took in a sharp, deep breath at the sight before me.

Lilith was whole. Her body was no longer a phantom's. She was as solid and real as I was. The Constantina necklace had become a glossy black. She stepped close to me, peering into my face. The scent of dirt and buried bones that came from her made me want to gag. She lifted a hand and traced a crescent with the back of her index finger down my cheek and jaw, the smoothness of her nail sending shivers through my spine. Then her nail traced the same line back up my cheek with the sharp tip and cut through my skin. I gritted my teeth at the sting and felt the warmth of a crescent-shaped line of blood welling on my face.

"That is so much better," Lilith sighed, her voice now full. "I'd love to chat more with you, Gabriel, maybe even rip a few of your fingers off, but I am too full of anticipation. Now it is time to wake my beloved, and then we will have fun with you. Don't worry. Your time will come."

The corners of her lips curved into a dark, slight smile before she turned away and moved toward Bastian. She took the dagger from his hand and cut it deep into her own arm, into precisely the same spot as Bastian had cut me. He held the bowl of my blood up and let Lilith's own blood pour into it. Power leaked from the mixture of our blood, creeping across the floor like rolling fog, sending every hair on my body standing on end.

"Blood of angel," Lilith murmured as she exchanged the dagger for the bowl with Bastian. "Blood of demon. Continue the ritual."

Without questioning, Kelaeno began chanting again, a new spell, different from the one that had given Lilith solid form. The Demon Queen stood in front of the sarcophagus and tipped the bowl over a small notch in the center of the lid, letting the blood pour. It followed grooves in the stone— up, down, left, and right, swirling, filling in the Enochian spell imprisoning Sammael.

Dread filled me. Not just simple fear, but the sensation of unreasonable horror overcame me, sucking away any desire to even feign bravery, sapping my energy like a black hole.

The blood filled the Enochian carvings entirely, and something heaved and hissed within the sarcophagus, as if a safe had been unlocked. I couldn't look away.

Lilith's high, smooth voice shot through my skull like a bullet. "Remove the lid."

26

BASTIAN'S EXPRESSION WAS A MIXTURE OF EXCITE-
ment and trepidation as he stood beside Lilith. Kelaeno
and Merodach pulled the heavy stone lid away from the
sarcophagus and set it aside. I wondered whether Bastian
was, for an instant, regretting all that he'd done, if he was
second-guessing his decision to release Sammael. But he did
nothing, frozen, as I was, waiting for the beast to emerge. He
swallowed, his throat moving up and down, his chest heaving, his gaze locked on the sight before him. I realized then
that he was terrified.

"Bastian," I called to him, trying to muffle my voice. He
looked at me curiously and without any amusement on his
face. "You can't do this, Bastian. Please stop them."

He measured me with his gaze, as if considering whether
or not to take me seriously. "This is the only way."

"Why do you want to destroy the world?" I asked, my voice shaking.

He shook his head. "We aren't destroying the world to just destroy it. We're going to rebuild."

"Who says you will be able to control Sammael?" I shot back. "He's too powerful. You don't know what he's really going to do! He's too dangerous to be released, and you know that. You have to stop them!"

"I will not."

"When I get out of here," I snarled, "I'm going to kill you. You're the reason my parents are dead, the reason the world's gone to hell. I will kill you, that I promise."

Through his fear, a smile broke, something dark and cruel, before he looked back to the sarcophagus. Blackness filled the open tomb like a void, like a doorway into nothingness instead of a mere coffin. The air throbbed as if it had a pulse, and then it was sucked into that void and rushed back out again as if a long, relieved breath was taken by some unseen giant within. Something stepped through the blackness and into the torchlight of the cellar with a flash of inky smoke that reminded me of the Grim. The beast was somehow feline in shape, with a long, sleek body, muscles rippling beneath a coat of dark slate fur. Its face was longer than a lion's, more serpentlike, the golden eyes more slit, and it shook a heavy mane of bone spikes much thicker than the quills of a porcupine. It took one look at me and hissed, flashing strong but delicate-looking fangs. Its spiked mane flared, and its long, scaled tail lashed the air like a whip. It stepped stealthily to the side, and a second beast emerged behind it. The creatures were only slightly smaller than lupine reapers, but far more graceful. They were reapers of a rare breed, the leonine, which I hadn't seen in thousands of years. They hissed and snarled and snapped at one another, their bodies fluid and moving like ripples on a black lake.

Something else stirred within the dark void of the sarcophagus, and an armored hand slid through, long, bony fingers curling around the stone edge. The black metal gauntlet attached to the hand gleamed like obsidian glass formed in the fires of Hell. More of the arm appeared, encased in a couter and rerebrace of the same strange metal. And then he emerged, his chest and shoulders covered in more of the gnarled, sharp armor, points and spikes cutting through the air. His eyes were gold—pure and gleaming metallic, the color deeper than pyrite. His hair was long, straight, and silver-white, and around his high, spiraling horns was a crown of bones. I knew through instinct that the small skulls and other bones were human and realized with horror that they were the bones of children.

As Sammael stepped completely free from the sarcophagus, he looked around with a bored expression on his sharp features. His skin was corpse gray, not white or blue, but the gray of decay. Spread from his back were the charred skeletal remains of what were once magnificent wings—the unmistakable wings of the wicked Fallen, fleshless bones burned and blackened from when he fell. They spread wide, the dry joints clicking and grinding.

I felt Gabriel seeping through the cracks in my amnesia, causing my human soul to stir, and then I was myself again—more Gabriel than Ellie. When I had seen Sammael last, he had been beautiful, radiant, his grace bright and true. This monster resembled nothing of my glorious brother.

Lilith stepped toward Sammael, lips parted and eyes widened. "Is it you, my love?" she asked, her voice weak and trembling. "It is truly you?"

He reached a hand to her, his armored fingers touching her cheek with limited affection, but for her it was enough. She closed her eyes to his touch and shivered. Even from here, his skin and armor looked ice cold.

"I've missed you," she breathed.

His expression hardened. "I know."

My human fear was slowly overcome by sadness and pity for the once-beautiful creature before me. Gabriel shuddered at the overwhelming emotion. "Brother," I said faintly. "Was it worth it? To fall for the power you have now?"

His golden eyes rested on my face, studying me curiously for several long seconds. Surprise lifted his brow for an instant, as if he didn't recognize me at first. "Tell *me*, Gabriel, was it worth it to *you*? To abandon your grace for a mortal body?"

"I have not abandoned my grace," I said, lifting my chin

and pulling against my chains. "It's with me now, even with my mortality."

"I sense no grace. You have fallen."

I shook my head. "Not as you have, Sammael."

His lips curved into a quiet smile. "You will be nothing when I'm finished with you. The Morningstar and I will tear Heaven and Earth apart. After I have destroyed the human soul infesting you, Gabriel, this world will burn until blood and ash rain from the sky."

We stared at each other as memories from the First War flooded through us. The fire and blood. Winged, torn bodies falling with the ash, hitting the scorched earth. Metal stained red as brothers and sisters ripped at one another. No words in any mortal language could describe the violence between angels, creatures who felt no emotion, and the fluid ease of killing without remorse, sorrow, or fear. I was there. I remembered. The orders were to destroy the rebels. Nothing I ever did on Earth fighting the demonic reapers could be compared to the horrors I had seen and done defending Heaven against Lucifer, the Morningstar, so very long ago.

"You can't kill them all," I told him. "There are too many angels."

"We have grown strong and our army is vast, but that is only the beginning," he replied, holding his palms out at his sides, black sparks flickering and snapping at his fingertips. "Soon I will have the power to tear every single human soul on Earth from its vessel and send them all to Hell to join the countless souls the reapers have already collected. In my head I see them now. You can't even imagine how many there are. Souls screaming in agony, tormented until all they understand is violence and rage. When we unleash them upon Earth . . ." He drew in a long, satisfied breath. "It will be magnificent. I will turn our Father's creations against Him, and all that He loves will be destroyed. It is the ultimate revenge."

I trembled, considering the weight of his threat. The End of Days everyone had spoken of, this was it. Opening up the gates of Hell and releasing every last tortured soul into the human world. They would tear it apart. And then the Fallen would tear a hole into Heaven.

Sammael spread his arms wide, opening his palms to the sky, the scales in his obsidian armor clicking. "It's time to start over, light the fires, and burn it all, and from the ashes of Heaven and Earth a new era will rise."

Whimpers beside me tore me from the visions in my head, and the heavy sense of Gabriel washed away from me. I was Ellie again. Emma had regained consciousness and stared at Sammael as tears rolled down her cheeks. She paled, and her body shook with tremors of fear. She was moaning something under her breath, the same thing over and over again: the Act of Contrition.

"Our Savior suffered and died for us," the girl chanted. "In His name, my God, have mercy . . ."

"Emma," I called gently to her. "Emma, it's going to be

okay. Don't look at him. I'll get you out of here."

Sammael laughed, smooth and deep. "You lie now, Gabriel? That is a first. It must be the human infection."

I ignored him. "Don't worry, Emma. We'll get out of here. I won't let him hurt you."

Sammael raised a hand and motioned to Merodach and Kelaeno. "It is time for me to feed. My power must be at its full strength."

I braced myself for the reapers to take me, but they walked right past me, right toward Emma as she screamed. They took Emma down from her chains, handling her flailing body with ease, ducking out of the way of her flying fists and kicking legs. I wrenched at my chains, felt the stone give a little, but I was no match for the magic binding my power. I was useless to help Emma and save her from whatever terrible fate the demonic had planned for her.

"Please!" I screamed at the reapers. "Please don't hurt her! She's just a girl! Take me. Take me instead, please!"

Merodach clenched his hand around the back of Emma's neck and thrust her body forward in front of him as if he offered the girl as a gift to Sammael. I quickly realized that that was exactly what he was doing.

"Don't do this!" I screamed. "You can't kill her! Please take my soul! Let the girl go!"

Lilith turned her face to look at me. My blood ran cold. "Be silent. Your time will come."

Emma stopped struggling. She was sobbing now, her

body limp, shoes dragging on the floor as the reaper held her up to Sammael. The Fallen angel of death held out both his hands, but instead of taking the girl, something long materialized out of thin air in the same way my swords did. Through the shimmering air, the thing in his hands came into view: a scythe. The weapon was enormous; the long helve was as big around as my forearm and decorated with bits of bone, hair, and fur, and human and animal teeth. A human skull was mounted at the top of the gigantic curved blade, which was embedded with the desolate eyes of the soulless damned. The eyes all blinked and stared at the whimpering girl before Sammael. Then the scythe—from the tip of the blade to the bottom of the staff—lit up with fire. Flames danced black and blue; obsidian and midnight. Demonfire.

Before I could say or do anything, Sammael slashed the scythe down through Emma's body like butter, and I let out a sickened shriek as Emma began screaming and writhing in earsplitting agony, her eyes rolling into the back of her head. My stomach twisted and I wanted to throw up but couldn't. I could only keep staring. But there was no blood, no wound, as if the blade had gone through her like she was a ghost. And then Sammael lifted the scythe, and something clung between it and Emma's body, something silvery and viscous. I saw Emma slacken, and I thought her pain was over. A spring of hope went through me until I realized what the silvery-blue thing was, clinging desperately to her body. Her soul.

A face formed in the struggling mass caught between Sammael's soul scythe and the girl's body, a face that belonged to Emma. A perfect imprint of her pretty hair and face frozen in terror was cast in the soul's form like ghostly clay, and limp arms and legs grew, but threads reached for Emma's body, trying to free itself from the blade it was caught on. Sammael grabbed Emma's soul around the throat and lifted it, parting his deathly blue lips. With a deep breath, he sucked Emma's soul into his mouth like a vacuum until there was no more silvery shimmer left. I sobbed hysterically, and Emma fell to the floor in a crumpled, dead heap.

I realized suddenly that it was all over. Nathaniel was dead. Will was probably dead. I was chained up in a room filled with demonic reapers and two of the Fallen, and for a moment I gave up. I sagged against my chains, pressing myself against the wall of the Enochian spell binding my power, making me helpless.

Will's words echoed in my head: *"Don't stop fighting."*

I couldn't quit. I couldn't end my ageless existence defeated and surrendered. I had always died fighting, and I would end fighting. If this was it, then I refused to be destroyed while chained to a wall and powerless. I was Gabriel, the Left Hand of God. I was a warrior.

I forced myself to stop crying as Sammael stepped around Emma's body and moved toward me, raising his scythe.

"I am sorry to have to do this, sister," he said. "But every last angel must die, including, and most importantly, those closest to God. I cannot have you stand in the way of the Morningstar."

Something crashed above me, onto the floor above the cellar, and I flinched. I heard shouts and more crashes. I looked up, staring at the stone ceiling, listening to whatever was going on upstairs. Sammael was also looking up, his cold expression stone hard. Someone let out a scream of pain, and then there was another crash.

"You!" Lilith snapped at one of the demonic reaper lackeys. "Go upstairs. See what's going on."

He darted up the stairs and out of my sight. I heard the cellar door open, and someone let out a muffled cry. Something ripped, and a moment later he tumbled back down the stairs in two halves. By the time his body hit the bottom step, his parts were nothing more than a waterfall of tumbling rocks. Footsteps descended, and the person they belonged to gasped for breath as he came into view.

It was Will.

27

WILL'S CLOTHES AND SKIN WERE DRENCHED WITH rain and blood, his shirt torn from injuries healed and ones acquired moments before. I stared at him, so surprised and overcome with joy to see him alive that I couldn't say a thing. I hadn't even cried out to him. But still, his eyes—crystalline green and bright as stars—were locked on mine, and he knew what I felt inside, because that was exactly how he felt, too. That was as much of a reunion as we would get for now.

Then he charged, sword high, and my elation turned into fear for his life once again. There was no way he could fight everyone in here. They would kill him before he got close enough to Sammael to see the gold of his eyes.

"Destroy the Guardian!" Lilith shrieked above the chaos.

Two of the demonic reaper guards attacked him before he reached the bottom step, both swinging blades. Will dispatched them quickly, shoving his blade into the chest of one of them, splitting bone and flesh before tearing it out and taking off the head of the reaper behind him.

Merodach collided with him next, moving out of the way of Will's sword and calling his own into his hand. He sliced, sweeping one end of the double blade low, and it slashed across Will's side, ripping another tear in his shirt. Will paid it no mind and continued his assault.

I watched Kelaeno bound toward them. "Look out!" I cried to him.

Will slammed his foot into Merodach's chest, knocking the demonic reaper into the wall as Kelaeno jumped into the fray and Will cracked the pommel of his sword into her face. Blood sprayed from her nose, and she reeled back, hissing and snarling. Merodach swung his sword just as Will's body was yanked away abruptly by an unseen force. His back slammed into the far wall, shattering stone. Debris and his sword crashed to the floor, but he hung there, suspended in the air, his body grinding into the wall as he groaned in pain. His fists balled at the ends of his outstretched arms and he strained against the force, but it was too much for him. I stared in confusion and horror, and then I saw Sammael's hand reaching for Will and felt the push of his seemingly infinite strength. My horror thickened, making my heart pound harder, as I realized Sammael was using his power to manipulate Will's body, something no reaper or even I could do. Something I didn't know how to defend against.

A second subtle movement of Sammael's clawed hand dragged Will through the air and slammed him into the ground.

Lilith laid a hand on Sammael's arm. "My lord, don't spend what little energy you have. You'll need it all for Gabriel."

Will lashed out as Sammael released him, but Merodach appeared at his side and struck him—*hard*. Will's head snapped to the side and he grunted, falling to one knee. A deep gash struggled to heal on his cheek. Merodach grabbed Will around the throat and raised his fist.

"That's *enough*," Bastian bellowed, and Merodach froze. "Bring him to me."

Merodach held on to Will tighter and shoved him toward where Bastian stood. I thrashed against my chains and screamed obscenities at them, swearing to tear them apart if they harmed Will. His head hung loosely, the sense knocked out of him. A thin trickle of blood grew out the corner of his mouth. I ached to run to him, to hold him and comfort him, to tear away Merodach's harsh hands. I felt like I was falling deep through the earth, falling fast into the underworld.

Kelaeno took hold of one of Will's arms while Merodach took the other and held an iron grip around the back of his neck, forcing him to his knees and his head down. Bastian stepped up to him, crouching down to peer into Will's face.

"William," Bastian murmured almost gently. "I didn't want you to come here."

Will spat blood onto Bastian's shiny black shoes. "Then you shouldn't have taken her."

Bastian's cerulean eyes fell to the splatter of red on his shoes. "You go where she goes, yes? And yet again, here you are at my mercy. I thought you would have learned better."

"Torture me again all you'd like," Will growled. "It won't make any difference."

"I don't want to torture you. Merodach and Kelaeno were under specific orders not to kill you. I am to have that honor. It's my desire to make your death quick and clean."

Will gave a laugh that sounded more like a grunt. "That's sweet of you. Really. I'm touched. Why the change of heart?"

"I learned something about y—" He stopped midsentence when Sammael came toward them, scythe in hand. My heart dropped into my stomach. No . . . no, no. This couldn't be happening. I couldn't watch Sammael take Will's soul like he had Emma's.

"This one," Sammael said, studying Will with a gaze that seemed to see through skin and bone altogether. "He is not human. He is a reaper born of the Grigori. I have no use for his soul."

Bastian stood and faced Sammael. "You were never to take his soul."

Lilith snarled, baring teeth. "The Lord of Souls may take whomever he chooses."

"He is to die at my hands if he refuses me, and no one else's," Bastian said firmly. "He is too dangerous to let live."

"Why the compassion, Bastian?" Will asked in a sarcastic, bitter voice.

Bastian ignored him. "I need to speak with the Guardian for only a minute, my lord," he pleaded to Sammael. "Before we continue with the Preliator."

"I am anxious to devour Gabriel's human soul," Sammael said, tightening his grip on the scythe. "My stomach growls for her."

"One minute," Bastian repeated. "That's all I need."

The tension in Sammael's shoulders eased. "Very well. I have waited a long time for this moment. I can wait a little longer. Patience is something I have come to know dearly."

"Thank you, my lord." Bastian bowed to him and looked again to Will as Sammael stepped away to rejoin Lilith. "I truly wish you had not come here, but since you have, I might as well make you an offer."

Will huffed in amusement, not quite a laugh. "Is that so?"

Bastian remained calm. "Sammael cannot be stopped. You know now there are only two options. One of which is death."

"And the other is to join you?" Will laughed. "You're a fool for even considering I'd say yes."

"Do you choose death, William?"

"Not going to happen," Will said through gritted teeth.

"Then join me."

Will shook his head. "Never! I am angelic and sworn to

protect Gabriel's vessel and all human souls."

"I don't want to kill you," Bastian confessed.

"I will not join you, and I will not let you kill me," Will said, his head held up in defiance. "My mission is not yet over."

Bastian stared at him for a moment, and then he paced slowly left and right, his gaze quietly on Will. The longer the silence dragged on, the whiter the knuckles on Will's balled fists grew. He pulled against Merodach and Kelaeno, but they held him tightly.

"I learned something very peculiar recently," Bastian said. "About you. You are the son of Madeleine."

Will let out a small, exhausted laugh. I could tell from here that all he wanted was to end the talking and start the fighting. "*And?* What does my mother have to do with this? How do you even know who she is?"

"It means that you are my son as well."

I stared at Will, who gaped speechlessly up at Bastian. It couldn't be. Bastian was demonic. If Bastian was Will's father, then Cadan was—

"*You lie!*" Will roared.

For the first time, Bastian's cool expression cracked like ice and real emotion seeped through. He snarled, but he looked more insulted than furious. "I loved your mother!"

Will tore against Merodach's and Kelaeno's grips. "*Liar!* You are *incapable* of love!"

As I tried to decide the possibility of this, I became more

afraid for Will by the moment. A reaper's heritage was determined by his mother's lineage, not his father's. Madeleine had been angelic, and therefore it was a genetic possibility for Will to have a demonic father, as unlikely as it was. The reason why Bastian's face always looked so familiar to me, the reason why I was so instinctively comfortable being near Cadan . . . they were Will's father and brother.

"William . . ." Bastian whispered gently.

"No!" Will cried. "Do not speak to me! You are not my father! She would never *touch* you! *Never!*"

Bastian raised his voice. "She's alive, William."

Will paused, mouth open, and he didn't appear to breathe. "What?"

"Your mother. She's alive."

Will dropped his face heavily, sagging against the reapers holding him, and he shook his head. "Liar," he said faintly, his voice trembling. "Don't do this to me. Don't tell me this."

"I'm not lying," Bastian said, his voice softer now. "She's alive."

"My mother is dead," Will rasped. "I haven't seen her for centuries. If she were alive, she would have come to me, let me know she was alive. She wouldn't let me think I'd lost her."

Bastian's gaze was sympathetic, and his voice was kind. "She's a relic guardian, William, like you. She had to give up everything for her mission, just as you did. She would be proud of you, as I am, of your power. Those of my line are all abnormally powerful, because each of us is very ancient and our blood is among the purest of our race, the closest to the divine source we were bred from. There are not many of us. You should be grateful."

"You're not my father," Will murmured. "You can't be my father. I could never be grateful for anything from you."

"Why do you reject this knowledge?" Bastian pressed. "Do you refuse to believe that Michael would choose a half-demonic angelic reaper to be the Guardian of the mortal Gabriel? Do you fear the idea that there is something more to being either angelic or demonic—that birthright isn't everything?"

"You *tortured* me!" Will shouted, his pain obvious through his broken voice. "You held me for days and beat me until I nearly died, then let me heal and beat me nearly to death again! Over and over and over for *days*! And then you ordered that monster, Ragnuk, to kill *her* and dump her in front of me? How could you do that to me if I'm your son?"

Bastian's gaze was cool and heavy with regret. "I didn't know you were my son then."

Will shook his head, disgusted. "And that makes it okay to torture someone who *isn't* your child? The only reason you're sorry for what you did to me is because you believe I'm your son?"

"I suppose that's true." There was no shame on Bastian's face.

"Then that settles it," Will said, choking. "You couldn't be my father. You say there is no difference between the angelic and demonic, but you're so wrong. I would never have done anything like that to anyone, not even to my enemies— not even to you. I could never be capable of any of the horrors you're guilty of."

"I see now that you're more like your mother," Bastian said. "Madeleine is an astounding creature—your eyes are startlingly just like hers—but make no mistake, you get your strength from me."

"No!" Will roared, and his power detonated, slamming into the floor and walls all around us. The force blasted into Merodach and Kelaeno, who could only release him and shield themselves. It hit like a tidal wave, crashing over me and sucking me under. I gasped for breath, squeezing my eyes shut as I was battered against my bindings.

I opened my eyes to see Will rushing toward me. He slid to a stop at my feet, raised his fist high over his head, and with a terrible cry, he slammed his fist into the stone floor with a rush of power. The stone cracked and heaved before sinking, shattering the pentagram trapping me. In an instant, I felt my own strength, now free, rush through me, rejuvenating me, and I snapped the chains around my arms with ease. Will rose, his green eyes staring into mine, and I was so overcome with emotion that I was shaking. Before I could say anything to him, he held my face with both his hands, and he kissed me for a single, powerful moment before he broke away.

"Ava and Marcus are on their way," he said breathlessly, breaking apart the manacles around my wrists. "I couldn't wait for them, and we can't wait for them now. We've got to get out of here. We'll die if we try to fight them all at once."

"Will!" I gasped as I saw that Merodach had recovered and was now stomping toward us.

Will spun, calling his sword as he brought his arm up high into a fluid arc, connecting his blade with Merodach's. Will roared, and his power exploded again, blasting into Merodach, forcing him to stagger back. Merodach let out a howl of rage, and they clashed in a fury of flying blades. For them, this had grown to more than just enemies battling on either side of a war. This was now personal.

A hand clamped around my throat and hurled me into the wall. I cracked my skull against the stone and I slumped for a heartbeat, just long enough for a fist to whale on my face. The blow sent me spinning back into the wall, and pain shot through my skull and neck. My eyes misted over but then focused on Kelaeno's furious face above me.

"Bring Gabriel to me!" Sammael's voice roared over all the pandemonium, his orders firm and immediately obeyed.

Kelaeno dragged me toward the Fallen as I struggled, clawing and thrashing at her hands. And then she was gone. I whirled, now free, to find that Will had hauled her off me. His fist pounded into her head over and over, her face snapping side to side with each blow. Blood flecked from her lips and her eyes stared at nothing. She gave her head a shake and darted past him toward me. Will spun to follow her. He grabbed Kelaeno's head with his hands around her forehead and chin and gave a swift twist. Her neck made a sickening crack and her body slumped, whitening to stone. As the ancient reaper's knees hit the ground, her body shattered. Will staggered a step back, taking a deep, triumphant breath, and his blazing eyes locked on Merodach as the demonic reaper ambushed me from the side, his sword slicing through the air at me. The first of my blades caught his as I slashed my second up the side of his throat and face, deep enough to grate against bone, but not deep enough to kill. Through the flying sheet of his blood, Merodach screamed in rage and tore away from me as the angelfire burned a bleached white scar into his dark skin. He clutched at his face, howling in agony.

I launched myself to finish him off, but a light flashed—a light so blinding and quick that I was momentarily paralyzed, burying my face in my hands as my eyes burned like they were on fire. I fell to my knees, curling my limbs into myself, the heat and light just too much. The light dimmed only enough for me to squint up at its source, and the sight took my breath away.

An angel hovered above Will and me, his wings spread and luminous, dividing us from our enemies. He was not Michael, nor was he an archangel. He wore long white robes that billowed around his body in unseen wind, cloaking his brown skin. His face was gentle and determined, his russet eyes settling on me. Chained to his waist was a massive, weathered book, and in his hands he held a long, elegant staff with a beautiful, curved, jeweled blade forged to one end. The other side of me—Gabriel—knew him. He was Azrael, the holy angel of death. The Destroyer.

He nodded to me and smiled. "Gabriel," he said, his voice eerily calm and musical. "I can stay only for a few moments, but I will hold them off. This battle is not to your advantage. For now, my sister, you must run." He looked at Will. "Get her far away from here, Guardian."

"Azrael!" Sammael's cry of fury shook my entire body, and I could feel his rage scraping at my skin as his power oozed through the cellar. The leonine reapers shrieked and screeched metallic cries from somewhere unseen.

Without another word, Will took my hand and we darted through the light, Azrael's glory too bright for me to see anything with my human eyes. I had to trust Will would find the stairs and get us both out safely. My foot hit the bottom step, and I hesitated just long enough for Will to lift me, guiding my feet up the staircase. Safely out of the blinding light drowning the cellar, we found ourselves on the first floor of an old house crumbling from battling reapers and decades of neglect.

I heard crashes from somewhere on this level and ducked instinctively. I was shocked to see Ava slash open the throat of another reaper with a short, thin sword and then drive it into his heart.

She wheeled to face us, breathless. "What's going on down there?"

"Are we too late?" called Marcus's voice. I turned to see Marcus kick a reaper in the chest and yank a blade from his heart as his body turned white hard with death.

Will laid a hand on Marcus's shoulder. "Just in time. Let's get the hell out of here."

We slipped into the Grim, hidden from mortal sight, and the four of us ran toward the front door, down the rickety porch, and into the shadows between dilapidated houses. The whole world seemed to have a layer of gloss over it from the misty sleet, the pavement like mirrors beneath our feet. Horns honked in heavy traffic a few streets away, and the tall buildings of the city could be seen in the distance over the tops of the trees. Between two houses, Will stopped and turned to me. Ava and Marcus spread their wings and lifted into the sky.

"We're going to have to fly now," he said. "It's the quickest way to escape, and they won't be able to track us."

I was breathless from running, but I nodded. He touched my hair as he gazed down at me, his shoulders easing with relief.

"God, I thought I'd lost you," he breathed, his eyes darting back and forth between mine. "I thought I'd be too late to save you."

I shook my head. "Will, I—"

Before I could finish what I'd wanted to say, his lips

pressed against mine fiercely, his hands holding my hips and pulling me closer to him. I threw my arms around his neck and let myself fall into him, dropping my guard for just an instant to feel reprieve from the violence I'd endured.

"William," said the dark, familiar voice behind us.

We sprang apart, only to find that Bastian had caught up to us. Will tore away from me with a cry of anger, his sword filling his hand.

Bastian raised his palms, his expression soft. "I'm not here to fight."

"I will not surrender her to you," Will snarled, pointing his blade to Bastian. "I will not yield this night, not ever!"

"I know, my son," Bastian said. "But the part of you that is demonic yearns for this. You are going against your very nature, against your own kind. Deny it all you want, but I will only offer one more time. Join me, and I will spare your life. Hers, though, I cannot. She can undo everything we've worked for."

Will let out a furious, impatient growl. "No! I will not hand her over to die so you can destroy the world!"

"William, you're making a terrible mistake."

"*No!*" Will shouted, raising his blade higher to Bastian's throat, but I could see that he was shaking. "This is no mistake! *You* are the one who is mistaken and misguided. I cannot throw away five centuries like that. I cannot throw away my *life* like that! I will not sentence her and the rest of the world to death for anything!"

A figure in dark clothes landed and folded his silver birch-colored wings behind his back. Cadan's arrival sent a tremor of shock through my entire body. His wings were bat wings again, to enable him to fly better in the drizzly rain. He stared at me first for what felt like a heartbreaking eternity, and then he looked painfully to Bastian.

Bastian snarled at him. "I told you to—"

"I can't," Cadan said, cutting him off with a quiet voice. "I can't let you do this. This has to stop, and if I'm the one to do it, then so be it."

Bastian's face lit up with shock. "You're turning against me? Was it you who killed Ivar?"

"Yes," Cadan replied, lifting his chin defiantly. "You're wrong about this world, about what it has to offer. The humans—"

"The humans are already destroying this world!" Bastian roared. "They are weak, flighty creatures. They don't deserve to rule this world. They don't deserve to spread their plague to Heaven! Not if *we* can't have it."

Cadan shook his head. "Humans are inherently good. You and I—we don't belong here, or anywhere. We weren't meant to be, and the humans, not us, were meant to go to Heaven. You can't destroy seven billion souls just because you envy them!"

Bastian's reaction was volcanic. He vanished and reappeared in Cadan's face, his fist tight around Cadan's throat, and he slammed Cadan's back into the side of a house, shattering the weathered wooden panels. Will threw an arm over me, shielding me. He knew now that Bastian was his father, but neither he nor Cadan knew that they were half-brothers. I opened my mouth, wishing I could say something, but it wasn't my place. Now wasn't the time. It would have only made things worse.

"How *dare* you?" Bastian rasped. "How dare you accuse me of feeling something so *vile*?"

Cadan swallowed hard. "Because that is all that you are: *vile*."

He blasted his power into Bastian—a strength Bastian must never have foreseen, because there was an immense shock on his face as he barreled through the air and hit the wall of a house. He staggered to his feet, gaping at Cadan as his son descended on him.

Cadan stared down at him. "You deserve Heaven even less than that beast you brought back from the bowels of the earth. You only want to destroy everything because you envy the humans their souls and because you're terrified of death. You can't have Heaven, and neither can I. None of us can! You want revenge you were never entitled to. This is not right! Annihilating the human and angel races is *not right*. I can't allow you to continue. My allegiance is no longer to you. I will defend the Preliator at any cost, even if it takes my life, even if it forces me to destroy you."

Bastian shot to his feet and threw a punch, but Cadan

caught it in his fist, forcing Bastian's arm down. "I am stronger now," Cadan said. He kicked Bastian's chest, forcing him back, and he called a long, elegantly curved blade into his hand and pointed it at his father. "And my act of defiance tonight," he snarled, echoing Bastian's words from their confrontation the night we had thrown Sammael's sarcophagus into the sea, "will be my greatest."

"Will," I said faintly, tugging at his shredded shirt. "We should go."

But he only stared, and I realized he was torn between fleeing and protecting the reaper who called himself his father. I tugged harder, and Will took a single step with me as I backed away.

Cadan lifted his sword, poising it at Bastian, one hand on the hilt, his other palm pressed against the blade to steady it. Bastian drew his own sword from nothingness, a heavier, broader blade, one that looked like it could break Cadan's in half. Then they both launched toward each other, moving so fast they disappeared from sight for a second, but came together in a lightning storm of silver blade against silver blade. Cloth ripped and blood sprayed as the demonic reapers battled.

Cadan's power erupted, the inky black explosion slamming into the houses on either side of him, shattering every single window. Shards of glass and chunks of brick and wood rained down on the reapers. Cadan's wings, with their leathery, batlike design, made him appear sinister, reminding me then that despite how sweet he was to me, he was indeed a demonic reaper.

And then Cadan grunted and doubled over as Bastian's sword shoved into his abdomen, spilling blood. I hid my face in Will's chest, clutching his shirt, and he pulled me closer. I couldn't watch Cadan die. I couldn't watch any more of my friends die tonight.

"It's over," Bastian growled as he forced his blade deeper.

Rage and pain bled over Cadan's face as he tried to rise, gasping in agony, his eyes driving into Bastian's. "For *you*." In a flash, Cadan slammed his sword into Bastian's chest— straight through his heart.

Bastian staggered and convulsed as he backed away, clutching at the blade buried in his heart, staring at his son.

Wrapping his hands around the hilt of Bastian's sword sticking out of his gut, Cadan gave it a strong yank, suppressing a cry of pain, and he tossed it to the ground. His wounds healed. Bastian's did not.

Bastian sank to his knees as stone spread from his wound, covering his skin quickly. Cadan took hold of his sword and slipped it from Bastian's chest as his father moaned, folding into himself in agony. I didn't breathe until Bastian was dead.

Cadan snapped his face to our direction, opal fires blazing in both his eyes. "Will, take her and *go!*"

My fingers dug into Will's arm, and it seemed to snap

him back to reality. He turned to me and his white wings burst from his shoulders, tearing even more holes into his shirt. He pulled me close and lifted me up, cradling me to his chest. Then he was silent as he jumped into the air. The ground below grew farther and farther away the higher and faster Will took us, and I stared down at Cadan until he disappeared into the night.

28

WHEN WE RETURNED TO NATHANIEL'S HOUSE, WILL
and I were still numb with shock, battered on the outside and
broken on the inside. So much had happened in only a matter
of hours, so much that neither of us could ever have been prepared to face. We sat in the living room, on separate couches,
staring at the filthy carpet in silence. Marcus and Ava had
left. Our clothes were torn and bloody, and the first floor of
the house was all but completely destroyed. Nathaniel was
dead. The Demon Queen and the Fallen angel of death were
now running rampant in the human world. Bastian claimed
that Will's mother still lived, that she was somewhere out
there in the world as a relic guardian. Will had seen Cadan
kill his father before his eyes and was unsure if he should
have interfered instead of letting Cadan do it. For so long,
Will had believed that he had no family, that all he had was

me. But now everything had changed. And now I held the secret that Cadan was Will's half-brother, a secret that ate at me from the inside out.

Dawn was creeping over the horizon, casting a glow through the broken windows and breaches in the walls. And finally, after what seemed like a thousand years of sitting in complete silence, Will rose to his feet. He moved past where I sat, looking straight ahead, his body rigid from head to toe. I got up to follow him, keeping a tentative distance.

I followed him out to the deck, where he moved to the edge and stared out onto the destroyed lawn. I was freezing from the icy air and the cold ache in my heart. He descended the stairs slowly, heavily, and headed to where Nathaniel had fallen. He paused there and stared down at the ground. I eased close to him with caution, watching him. His arms hung at his sides and his fists rolled into tight balls, the skin stretching white over his knuckles as his wings grew and slipped through the tears in his shirt. They expanded unhurriedly, solemnly, and the light of the dawn cast a golden glow across the pearlescent feathers. At his feet were Nathaniel's remains.

"Will," I whispered, stepping in front of him. "Say something."

The silence between us was like a void sucking at my brain. He stood there, a statue in the dawn light, his face hardened like the stone Nathaniel had become. I reached for him, a little afraid that he might crumble if I touched him.

"I'm so sorry, Will," I breathed.

He stared down at me, the green of his eyes dulled to a barren gray, and his lips tightened as if he wanted to say something but refused. His wings stretched away from me and folded to his back. I slid my hands around his head and through his hair, stood on my tiptoes, and kissed his cheek. He exhaled but stayed so stiff that I thought he'd shatter any moment. I kissed his lips, stifling a cry, and his shoulders sagged as a tear ran down his cheek.

"I'm so sorry," I said, and kissed him again.

My hands slid down his neck and chest and up his back, his feathers brushing my skin. I rested my cheek against his chest. He moved at last, leaning over me and wrapping his arms around me. He buried his face in my hair at the bend of my neck and squeezed me tight.

I pulled away and he looked into my face sadly, his arms lingering around me. "You need to rest," I told him. "Get some sleep."

He shook his head heavily. "I can't. Not now."

"You will once you lie down." I took his hand and led him back into the house. We stepped through the wreckage and went up what was left of the stairs to his room. The second floor was basically untouched and appeared almost as if nothing had happened at all. In Will's bedroom, the morning light began to stream through the blinds, making the room feel a little warmer than it was.

I shut the door behind us and turned to him. I pushed

his shredded shirt up and over his head. His eyes were glued to mine. His skin was pale from exhaustion and lack of food, making the tattoos covering his right arm, shoulder, and neck contrast even more violently. I turned to drop his shirt on the floor behind me, but when I turned back, he wrapped an arm around my waist and opened his mouth against mine, kissing me much differently than I had kissed him minutes ago outside. He pulled me to his bare chest and his kiss was deep and hot, sending a low ache through my body. I put my hands on his arms, and my grip tightened briefly before I reluctantly pushed him back. He broke his kiss and met my eyes in confusion. I swallowed, hoping my actions told him what I didn't want to say with words. That kind of closeness wasn't what either of us needed right now. It was painfully difficult to refuse him then, but it was for the best. This wasn't the right time.

The rejection melted away from his face, and he looked down at me soberly. I pressed a gentle hand to his chest and guided him to the bed. I climbed in, my fingers loosely entwining with his, and he followed me, crawling under the blankets with me. Within moments it was plenty warm, and with the door shut, no icy drafts blew into the room. I could hear the wind picking up outside, whistling by the window, and as Will settled down and I laid my cheek on his chest, his heartbeat became the only thing I could hear. By some miracle, he fell asleep, and I followed him soon after.

* * *

When I woke, Will was gone. I found him sitting on the swing bench overlooking the lake. I had wrapped a blanket around my shoulders and now lifted it at my feet so the ends didn't drag in the cold, wet grass peeking through patches of melted snow. He sat in silence, leaning forward on his elbows, his lips brushing his knuckles. Something was clasped between his hands, and a delicate gold chain slipped through his fingers. He didn't seem to be looking at anything in particular. For a moment, I regretted intruding on him, but he didn't need to be alone. Not right now. Neither of us did.

"Will," I said gently as I approached him. He didn't look up. "Can I sit down?"

His hesitation made something ball up in my throat. "Of course."

I eased into the seat beside him, studying his profile and furrowed brow. I wouldn't ask him if he was okay. Of course he wasn't okay. Nathaniel was dead. I gazed at his hands. "What's that?" I asked, indicating the chain.

He sat back, exhaling, and opened his hands. It was my lost pendant, unharmed except for the broken chain. He held it out to me and I took it.

"You found it." I clutched it tightly to my chest. It warmed almost on contact. "Thank you."

He said nothing.

I put the necklace in my pocket for safekeeping. I'd have to get a new chain soon. "What are you doing out here by yourself?"

His expression softened, and I was able to feel better about intruding on his solitude. "Coming up with a plan."

I sighed. That was the Will I knew, always focused on the future and never the past or present. It was easier for him to focus on something other than Nathaniel's death.

"At least Bastian is out of the way," I offered.

He didn't answer or acknowledge what I'd said. Perhaps now I understood what Will had been feeling all along, the frustration and need to be there for me when he was unwanted. I didn't want to be unwanted now, and neither did he.

"What should our next move be?" I asked.

"We lie low," he said, surprising me. I think I expected him to demand that we eat a feast and march off to war at dusk. "Azrael came in at the right time, but Sammael also underestimated us. He will not risk making another mistake and losing you a second time. He has been dormant for thousands of years and could still need time to recover his strength, just as you do each time you're awakened. Azrael's glory weakened him, so we may have bought some time."

I gaped at him. "Why are we letting him get stronger? We should take him out now while he's weak."

"Because we can't beat him," Will said firmly. "I am just a reaper, and you have a breakable human body. We will never be able to beat him or Lilith. He is one of the Fallen and the Right Hand of Lucifer. There's no way anything besides an archangel could obliterate him. We need Azrael.

We need the Destroyer."

"But Azrael is an outcast," I said, perplexed. "He's not an archangel anymore."

"He's defeated Sammael twice already. He can do it again."

"What if he can't?" I asked. "He couldn't kill Sammael last night, only hold him off. What about Michael?"

He shook his head. "Michael can't engage until there is outright war. It's not his job. That's why Azrael was punished in the first place. Absolute obedience, or you are cast out, killed, or forced to fall."

"Then it's a good thing I'm human," I said. He gave me a puzzled look and I continued, my temper spinning hot. "Nathaniel told me that angels don't have free will in Heaven, that they never make a single choice on their own. Everything they do is an order. I'm human now, with a human soul, and I have the free will to choose. And I choose to stop the war before it happens rather than sitting around like Michael and waiting for someone to tell me to make a move."

Will paused thoughtfully, and his gaze drifted out over the lake. "I won't let you fight Sammael until I know we can defeat him. With him able to destroy your soul, we can't afford to make a mistake. We only have one shot, and we cannot lose."

There was no changing his mind. At this point, not that I wanted Sammael to eat my soul, but I couldn't rely on someone else to save the world—I couldn't trust anyone with that responsibility but myself. "So then how do we summon Azrael and give him solid form so he can help us?"

"We'll have to find the correct relic and spell," he replied. "If they can do it for Lilith, then we can do the same for Azrael."

"Okay, well, how do we know which are the right ones?"

"The spell will be different to give corporeal form to an angel, but that information will still be in the grimoire."

"The book that Sammael has?"

"Yes."

"Well, life just keeps getting easier and easier." I slumped back into the bench and folded my arms over my chest. "If we can't get Azrael to fight Sammael, then we need an archangel."

His lips formed a tight line of frustration. "That'd be you."

I blinked at him. "Come again?"

"Our last resort would be figuring out a way for you to ascend and become Gabriel again," he said.

"In this world?" I asked, unable to hide the incredulity in my voice. "On Earth, in the human world?"

"I don't know if that's possible," he admitted. "But we've got to find a way to make it happen if worse comes to worst. I just don't know if the transformation would destroy you or what would happen to your soul if you were killed as Gabriel. You might not come back as a human again, or even at all."

I frowned. "If me becoming an archangel in this world is

even possible, then we have to figure out how to do it."

"We will," he said gently. "Everything will be okay."

But I wasn't so sure. It would be difficult enough to summon Azrael and get him to fight for us, but on the minuscule chance that I was able to ascend to my archangel form . . . I didn't know what that really meant. In the last few months I'd come to understand who I really was, something far beyond what I was now. I remembered my past lives and uncovered secrets as they came, but I remembered nothing of being Gabriel. I felt small things, recognized Sammael and Lilith, but those were all memories from Earth. I knew my true name, but I didn't know who I truly was. I didn't know what I was like as Gabriel. I didn't know how much I would change.

"I'm terrified of myself, Will," I admitted. The icy wind flowing off the half-frozen lake whipped my hair around my face. "Of becoming Gabriel. The angels don't feel anything. I don't want to lose myself when I become an archangel. I'm afraid that I'll forget you, that I won't love you anymore because I won't be able to."

His jaw tightened and he looked at me sadly. "That doesn't matter. It's not as important as—"

"It's important to *me*," I said, cutting him off. "I've had enough of that self-deprecating crap from you. *You're* important to me. I'm terrified of losing what I feel inside once I become Gabriel."

"We have to be willing to give up things to do what's right, sometimes," he said, eerily mirroring to me what

Nathaniel had said about war. About sacrifice. In order to win this war, I had to be willing to sacrifice who I was. If it came down to becoming someone else and protecting the people I loved and the rest of the world, then I had to do it. I had to be brave, even though I couldn't be fearless.

"If I do this," I said, "if I become Gabriel, I refuse to forget you. I may become an archangel, but I'll still have my human soul."

He let his head drop and ran his hands through his hair. Something more was troubling him so much that for a second I thought I saw him shaking. He chewed on his upper lip and exhaled heavily.

"What Bastian said about you isn't true," I said, touching his cheek. I turned his face to mine as I brushed the backs of my fingers along the line of his jaw. He closed his eyes so tightly that his brow furled and darkened with pain. I heard his teeth grind together.

"Yes, it is."

"No, Will," I pleaded. "How could you even think that?"

"Because I am full of hate and rage." He pulled away from my hand and looked out at the gray lake. "I want you to promise me one thing, for when this all goes down."

I swallowed hard. "What is it?"

"Save Merodach for me," he said, his voice cold and deadly as thin ice. "He's mine."

I shivered at a chill slicing through my veins. "Okay."

"*Si vis pacem, para bellum,*" he said very quietly. His

hands balled into fists and he drew a long, shaky breath.

If you want peace, prepare for war. If we wanted to win and to be safe, we had to be strong and fight this evil that threatened to tear us apart and steal everything we loved.

We sat in silence until he stood up. "I have work to do on the house."

I nodded, pushing back the wildfire of tears building in my eyes. Within minutes, the pounding of nails and ripping up of shattered floorboards filled my head and numbed my thoughts. But I had work to do as well. I had to call Lauren.

I sat on the floor in the kitchen with my cell phone in my hands. I leaned against the cabinet doors, the metal handles digging into my back. I'd dialed and redialed her number a hundred times and still hadn't found the courage to call her. I squeezed my eyes shut and called at last. On the first ring, she answered.

"Ellie." Her voice was broken, hoarse, as if she'd been crying or screaming, or both.

"Lauren," I said, forcing the word from my lips. "I . . . I don't know how to . . ."

"I know."

She hung up, and I let the phone slip from my fingers onto the tile and just sat there with my back against the wall. Sometime later, I heard a car drive up and its door open and shut. I stumbled to my feet and headed toward the front of the house. As soon as I saw Lauren's quietly smiling face and red, puffy eyes, I let out a choking sob and collapsed at her feet as our arms wound around each other.

We sat in the living room with cups of coffee in our hands, both of us cried out for the moment. The last time she was in this house, she was in Nathaniel's arms and he was telling her he loved her. Minutes later, he was dead.

"I never thought I'd outlive him," Lauren said weakly. "That wasn't the way we were supposed to end. I knew the things he and Will did were dangerous and would kill him eventually, but . . ."

She leaned over the end table beside her, resting on her elbow, and buried her face in her hands, her fingers threading through her dark hair, and she started crying again.

My lips trembled as I fought my own tears. "I'm so sorry, Lauren."

She wiped at her face with the sleeves of her sweater and forced a small laugh. "It's okay. I'm really going to miss him and his stupid jokes."

I laughed with her, letting out an ugly, half-sobbing noise. "Yeah. His jokes were so bad."

We laughed and cried for a little while, recalling many of Nathaniel's silly habits and sayings, but also reminiscing about how wise he was. How good he was. How much he took care of us all. How much he'd made this house a home. The lights were on in here, but outside the skies were dark with rain clouds, and it felt like we were in a cave. Rain beat the windows, and Will clunked something heavy around some-where in the house and then hammered it.

When it came time for Lauren to go home, she wandered through the house, surveying the damage, running her fin-gers down the shredded walls, pausing to touch things that had belonged to Nathaniel.

"Anything you want should be yours," I said, following her through the wreckage. Will had cleaned up so much of it already that the floors were mostly cleared.

Lauren nodded absently. "It'd be strange to take any of it, since it was his. Maybe one day I'll be able to. It still doesn't feel like he's gone—it's like he'll come back any day because he'd miss all this old junk of his."

I looked around the house, purposely avoiding her gaze. "And once Will puts the house back together, it'll look like nothing even happened here."

"He's certainly on a roll, isn't he?" She gave a small laugh that faded away sadly. "I should get going."

I pulled her into a tight hug. "Come back soon," I said. "Anytime, please. We'd love to see you."

She smiled. "Of course. Let me know if Will needs any help cleaning up the place."

I shrugged. "I think he's on a mission to do it all by him-self. I'm sorry he didn't come down to see you."

"It's all right," she said, her smile fading to a tight, pained line. Her lips quivered. "He's hurting. It's best to leave him be. He'll come around when he's ready."

"I know." What she said was true, but every second Will spent in his own world made my heart ache a little more. I walked Lauren outside. "I'm trying not to worry about him. I don't want to worry about you either, okay?"

"You don't have to," she said. "I'll be okay. It'll just be hard for a while. We'll all get through this."

"Thank you, Lauren," I said. "Call me soon, okay?"

She smiled. "I will. Check in with your grandmother, okay?" Then she climbed into her car and was gone.

For the next several days, Will and I said very little to each other. He had thrown himself fully into restoring Nathaniel's house. I made sure he ate and slept, but between our brief exchanges of conversation was complete silence, and the loneliness was killing me. My phone was off and no one knew where I was. I didn't know what to tell Nana and my friends about what had happened or where I'd been.

Kelaeno was dead, but that didn't mean her prophecy had died with her. In my heart, I feared that it was coming true, bit by bit. For so long I had believed that the scariest thing in the world would be losing my soul, or Will, but now that I had been faced with nearly losing both in one night, I realized that I was more afraid of losing him.

I told Will once that I didn't want to just survive, I wanted to live. And here I was, the living dead, waiting for the inevitable. I felt like I was giving up already, and I couldn't let myself think that. I had to survive this. I had to live. And locking myself inside this big house to rot was not living. It was existing. I wanted to feel alive again, and in order to do that, I needed my friends and family. I wanted a future. I wanted to get my life back.

29

I TOOK A DEEP BREATH BEFORE I RAISED MY HAND
to knock on the door. Nana flung it open before I could
knock a second time, so quickly, as if she'd been waiting by
the door the entire time.

"Oh, my . . ." my grandmother murmured, touching her
fingers to her mouth in surprise. "Ellie."

"Hey, Nana," I said with a weak smile. "I'm so sorry."

She ushered me in through the door, soaking me with her
radiance and relief at seeing me. "Come in, honey. It's freezing out there. I'll get you some hot tea."

A few minutes later, I sat at the kitchen table with a cup
of tea as Nana fixed me soup at the stove. "You don't have to
do that," I said, watching her sadly. "I'm not hungry, really.
I don't want you to go through the trouble." In truth, I was
starving, but it felt so wrong to just show up back at her house

and have her make me dinner. It made me feel even lower than I already did, and that was saying a lot.

"Yes, I do," she said. "The least I can do after you've been gone for almost two weeks is make you a hot meal."

"But you don't owe me anything," I assured her. "I really don't deserve it."

She removed the pot to let it cool. "After what you've been through, child, you do."

I stared at her in surprise and puzzlement. Why wasn't she yelling at me, scolding me for running off and showing up after weeks of no contact? Why wasn't she furious?

She came to the table and sat down next to me. She took my hand and held it in both of hers. "You've lost your parents and so much more. I was angry when you left, but I've done a lot of thinking, and I realize that much of this could have been avoided if I'd done better for you."

I shook my head. "None of this is your fault. You didn't do anything wrong."

"Yes, I did," she corrected me firmly. "I owe you an explanation. I'm angry with myself for making you go through this alone. I had the power to help you, but I was afraid and partially in denial. I was afraid of getting involved."

I studied her eyes, searching for answers. "What are you talking about?"

She swallowed. "I knew, child. I knew everything. I know who you are."

"Who I—?"

"I know you are the Preliator."

She knew? How? I had never revealed who I was to a soul who wasn't already in my world. "I don't understand," I squeaked, my voice quaking. "How can you know?"

"I am a psychic, Ellie," she said simply. "I have always seen the reapers, but I had no idea that my granddaughter would ever be Gabriel's vessel. I didn't believe Frank when he told me until he showed me an old photograph of the two of you and your Guardian."

"Frank," I repeated, running names through my head. "Frank Meyer? My teacher?"

She nodded. "There aren't many of us, and most of us know one another. I kept in contact with him for many years, and when he told me that *you* were the Preliator, I had a hard time believing him. And then these rumors began flying around about you actually being Gabriel. . . ."

"Why didn't you say anything to me?" I asked, and pulled my hand away from hers, unable to help the bitterness I felt.

"Frank told me it was best not to interfere." She sounded genuinely penitent. "He promised that your Guardian would care for you. But I knew how hard it was for you, and I regret staying out of it all. And now the reapers have killed Frank, and they've killed my daughter and son-in-law. It's my punishment, I suppose."

"I spent all this time lying and hiding things from my family!" I said angrily. "And you knew the whole time. I was completely alone!"

Nana shook her head. "You were never alone. We've all looked out for you. Frank was killed hunting a reaper that had tracked you to your home. He died trying to keep it from telling its master where you lived, where your family lived. Not that it matters now. Bastian always knew where you lived, and he had your father killed so that beast could take his place and spy on you. We know that now. But you aren't alone. Your Guardian protects you. I know about Will. I'm sorry you had to lie to your mother about him. She would have liked him more if she'd known what he truly was to you. You did what you had to do."

I made a disgusted, choking sound. "What I had to do? You have no idea what I've had to do! What I've seen and been through!"

"I do, honey," she said calmly. "I know where you've been. Lauren let me know that you were safe. I knew you were safer with the angelic reapers than here with me. I'm just an old woman. I would only have gotten in your way. Your soup is probably ready." She got up from the table to pour me a bowl of soup and set it on the mat in front of me. "You need to eat."

The steaming soup smelled delicious, but I was afraid that if I took a bite I wouldn't be able to keep it down. I forced a spoonful, and the warmth filled up my whole body. "You said Frank gave you a photograph of us. Do you still have it?"

She turned to her purse on the counter and slipped something out of one of the pockets. She held the weathered photograph out to me, and I took it tentatively from her fingers. The black-and-white picture's edges were torn and wrinkled, and right in the center of the image was me, with my dark hair pulled back into a ponytail. Beside me was Will, with a genuine smile on his face and one hand on the shoulder of a young, lanky man with shaggy hair. I brought the photo closer and squinted to make out his face. The boy's eyes and smile gave him away, and in my mind I pictured him laughing. It was Frank Meyer.

My entire world—everything I knew—spun through my head like a tornado. "I can't believe any of this. I can't . . . get my mind around it."

She smiled and slid an arm around my shoulders. "I know. When I found out, it was impossible for me to believe this little fire-haired girl was the archangel Gabriel. I felt so much for you. Your nightmares, your slipping grades, the sneaking out. I don't know what I would have done if I'd been you. I should have been there for you, but I was terrified of messing up your cycle."

"You wouldn't have messed anything up," I said in a small voice. "I needed my family more than anything, but I understand why you did it." I took a deep breath of relief, feeling the weight melt from my shoulders. In spite of myself, I smiled. "You can't know how good this feels."

Her own smile brightened. "Oh, I do, believe me. I'm so happy that you know who *I* am as well. I want to help you in any way possible. Whatever you need to do, please don't worry about making up a story to do it. I understand this is your duty, who you are. But don't forget, Gabriel, that you have to be Ellie too, or you'll lose yourself."

Lose myself. Something I was terrified of. "I need to go back to school. I need to have a life on top of all this. I need some kind of normalcy."

She nodded. "Good girl. Let's get you back into school, then. But eat your soup first. I don't want to see a speck left in that bowl before you go to bed."

I smiled and picked up the spoon. "Okay, Nana."

The next few months until graduation were going to kick my ass sideways. Nana scored me visits with my principal and counselors, to get me on a track that would catch me up in classes. She explained that after the horrible events I'd gone through, I went to stay with other family—which wasn't entirely untrue—and my school was sympathetic and willing to help. I had a new determination in me to prevent any more demonic things from stealing the rest of my youth.

Managing my time between patrolling for reapers and spending extra hours at school with my teachers was exhausting. The Saturday after my return to school, Kate demanded that I get to her house at eight for a "small thing" and to bring Will. I figured after visiting Kate, Will and I could go kill stuff. I got ready, just pulling on jeans and a sweater over a tank, and waited for him to come over. Tonight we had plans for Nana to meet him, especially since she knew his—and my—true identity. She was very curious about him, as all psychics and angelic reapers tended to be about the both of us. We were like Elvis—minus the drugs and triple the bluesy angst.

When he arrived, I let him in and he followed me through the house to the parlor where Nana sat with a cup of tea and a thick, old leather book. Her eyes instantly rested on him and she smiled. She put her things down and climbed to her feet rather gracefully for her age.

"It's a pleasure to meet Ellie's Guardian," she said, and held out a hand to shake his firmly. She studied him curiously, her gaze lingering on his tattoos.

"You, too," he said politely. "She's told me great things about you."

She smiled. "Forgive my excitement. I've heard about you my entire life—you *and* Ellie, or rather her previous incarnations. It's taken quite a while for me to get used to the knowledge that my beautiful granddaughter is the vessel of Gabriel. But Frank Meyer knew her as soon as he saw her."

Will nodded and his lips tightened. "Frank was a great man and a good friend."

Nana's expression grew serious. "I'm sorry he didn't have a way of contacting you sooner to tell you he'd found her. No one knew where you were. We all know you exist, but so few of us had ever seen you. You had been searching for her for a long time, from what I'd heard."

He swallowed. "Yes."

I watched him carefully, fully aware of what a difficult subject my absence was for him. My grandmother perhaps had an idea, but she didn't understand how much it truly hurt him. "But Will did find me. He always finds me." I squeezed his hand. After a moment, his fingers closed tighter around mine.

She studied his face carefully, her eyes flickering to our enclosed hands. "You love her."

Something closed around my heart as he nodded. "I do," he said.

"Then you'll do anything you can to protect her."

He lifted his chin. "I always have."

She smiled and nodded, her fierce gaze softening in an instant. "I have so many questions to ask you, but I'll save them for another time. You have places to be tonight."

I began to turn to leave the parlor with Will. "I'll see you when I get back."

"See you then," Nana said. "It was wonderful meeting you, Will."

"Have a nice evening," he said in return with a nod.

We headed out to my car and drove away. Of course, I realized that Kate's "small thing" plan was a trick as soon as we entered her basement and all of my friends jumped out of hiding places to surprise me and welcome me back with warm, open arms. I cried as I hugged everyone, so over-whelmed by the love in the room and by how much I had missed them. Why was I ever scared of facing them again? My friends never judged me, never condemned me for aban-doning them.

I passed on the alcohol, letting Kate know that I was going home after this to sleep and to get up early and do more makeup work. Sweetly, she gave me a smile and a kiss on the cheek, fully understanding. Marcus surprised me by show-ing up, the scars on his neck and jaw plainly visible around the collar of his sweater. He and Kate were something like official now, and I was okay with it. Will was good to me; Nathaniel had been good to Lauren. There was no reason why Marcus and Kate couldn't make it work in their own way. The only difference was that Kate didn't know Marcus wasn't human, and I wasn't sure when—or if—he would ever reveal his true nature to her. But that was their business, and I would leave it to them. He was sweet and affectionate with her, and more polite to me than he had reason to be.

With a drink in one hand, he wrapped his other around mine, pulling my fingers to his lips for a gracious kiss. "May I borrow her?" he asked Will.

Will gave me a small smile before narrowing his gaze sidelong at Marcus. "Just bring her back and don't put that mouth of yours anywhere else."

I tried not to laugh when Marcus winked at Will before leading me away into a quiet corner. Although "quiet" was relative, since Kate's basement had Chris's DJ talents making the walls shake. How her parents even slept at night was beyond me.

Marcus leaned against the wall and grinned at me. "Hello, beautiful. How are you?"

I couldn't help but smile back up at him. "All right. Surviving. Living."

"How is your Will?"

My Will. They always called him my Will. I glanced over to where Kate was talking to him, and he actually appeared to be engaged in the conversation. I couldn't hear what they were saying over the music and twenty or so other voices, but at last he seemed comfortable talking to her. I didn't think they'd spoken more than two words to each other since the night up at State, but they seemed okay now. "He's better," I said. "It's been especially hard for him. Losing Nathaniel and all."

"And all . . . ?" His brow flicked curiously.

"How much do you know about what happened that night?" I asked. "Do you know about Bastian?"

Marcus shrugged. "Will told me Cadan finished Bastian off, but that was it. I'm a little surprised, to be honest. I didn't think he was that powerful."

"Will didn't tell you anything else?" I asked, biting my lip.

"No. Why?"

I swallowed hard. "Bastian said that Will is his son."

Marcus blinked in surprise but shook it off. "That can't be true."

"Yeah," I said. "I don't think he was lying, and neither does Will. But we won't ever know for sure. He also said that Will's mother, Madeleine, is alive."

Marcus let out a long breath. "Intense."

"There's more," I said hesitantly, hushing my voice. "Cadan is also Bastian's son."

He gaped at me. "They're *brothers*?"

"Half," I corrected. "Madeleine was—*is*—angelic. Cadan's mother must have been demonic. I haven't used angelfire against him, but I saw the way the sun burned him once. I'm certain Cadan's demonic, like Bastian."

"Does Will know?"

I shook my head. "I'm afraid to tell him. I think it would make him very upset. He *despises* Cadan."

"He'll have to learn eventually," Marcus said. "But for now, you're right. He doesn't need to deal with this too, on top of everything."

I nodded. "Where's Ava tonight?"

He eyed me suspiciously. "Out. This isn't really her scene."

I made an ugly noise. "I think that *I'm* just not her scene."

He gave a slow nod, his mouth forming a tight line. "She didn't tell me that you knew."

"About her and Will?" I asked, my voice a little more snarly than I meant it to be. "Yeah."

He pushed himself off the wall and moved around me so that he stood in my line of sight to Will. "If you want an outside opinion, I say don't stress over it. He felt pretty bad after it happened and told no one. Not even Nathaniel. I only know because Ava told me."

"Did you and Ava ever . . . ?"

He laughed. "No, she's too serious for me. She's absolutely no fun at all, and I have a lot of fun. I have an open mind."

I rolled my eyes. "Then Kate is just your type."

He grinned widely. "She's perfect. I want you to know that I'm a one-woman kind of guy when I have one. You don't have to worry about her."

I stared at him. "I better not."

"May I ask you something, Ellie, my love?"

"Of course, but I'm not your love."

"What's Heaven like?"

I paused. "Why? That's kind of random."

He shrugged. "I've come to the realization recently that I am not invincible. I'm immortal, but there is a very real possibility that I will die in battle. Any of us could die. Nathaniel is gone. Since reapers don't have an afterlife, I'll never get to see what Heaven looks like. You're the only angel I'm cool with, so I thought I'd ask you."

I blinked. "I don't know. I never remember Heaven. Never have."

He frowned. "That's too bad. I guess I will never know."

"Marcus," I said, examining his scars. "How did you get those scars?"

He pulled his collar wider. "Demonfire from the blade of one of the Fallen."

"Who?"

"Belial," he answered. "A long time ago, he was summoned by humans messing with angelic magic they had no business messing with. They wanted him to fight on their side in a war between men. They call it the Second World War. Thankfully the spell was short-lived, and Belial was sent back to Hell before he did too much damage. He killed three of my friends in the process and split me wide open from here"—he pointed to the right side of his rib cage and drew a line with his finger up to his cheek—"to here. His demonfire scarred me, but I survived."

I absorbed his story, imagining the horror of it all.

"It's okay, though," he said with a grin. "The scar makes me look like a badass. Kate loves it."

I laughed. "If you say so."

My smile faded when his did, and he grew very serious suddenly. "Believe Will when he says he doesn't want you to fight Sammael and Lilith until he knows you can beat them. Belial was *Hell* on two legs, Ellie. I wouldn't be here right now if that spell hadn't sucked that monster back to where he came from. Be patient. Grow as strong as you can, be as prepared as you can. Michael and the other angels don't care what happens down here unless Heaven is compromised. If your soul is destroyed, then Earth will be at Lucifer's mercy."

"Do you think I can beat them?"

He studied my face, his sapphire gaze invasive. "You?" he asked. "No. Azrael? Maybe. Gabriel? Definitely."

I nodded. I knew what we had to do: summon Azrael. If he couldn't do it, then I needed to become an archangel, and I needed to stop worrying about what would happen to me once I did.

Will's presence flooded over me, and I looked to see that he had wandered over to where Marcus and I were standing. His smile was pleasant. "Can I have her back yet?"

Marcus slapped Will's shoulder, took a swig of his beer, and started to walk away. "Have your way with her."

My hand rushed to my mouth as heat flushed into my cheeks.

Will dipped his head low to mine. "Ignore him. Are you having a good time?"

I pressed my body into his, just to feel the security his closeness offered me. "Yes. Are you?"

His hands came down on my shoulders and rested around my arms. "I am if you are." His hands touched my waist.

I pushed my palms up his chest and around the back of his neck. I tilted my head back and he leaned forward, his face inches from my own. "Dance with me."

"I can't dance to this music. It's not even music at all."

"You're a big bad demonic reaper hunter and you're too shy to dance with me? That's kind of sad in a huge way."

"I'm sorry," he said.

"I could just order you to dance with me."

He sighed and nuzzled my neck. "Don't make me. I beg you."

Shivers rushed through me. "You're lucky you're so cute. Otherwise I'd definitely make you do it."

He kissed my shoulder. "You're very merciful."

I pulled away to look into his face. "How are you tonight? We can leave if you want to go home."

He shook his head and smiled at me. "It's your party. We're not leaving."

I smiled, happy to see him so willing to be with me in my human world. I hadn't been out with my friends in . . . I didn't even know when the last time was. I needed this, and I was grateful to him. I didn't want to go anywhere without him. I touched my fingertips to his lips. His gaze softened. "You're good to me," I said.

"You're everything to me." He kissed my fingertips. "Let's go back to your party."

He took my hand and I followed him back out into the crowd of my friends, determined not to let the end of the world take this happiness, this single peaceful moment, from us.

30

BEING THE SUBJECT OF MOST GOSSIP IN SCHOOL made me long for open campus during lunch hours. That was always the worst part of my day. It was finally May, but the storm still had not quelled. In the hallways, as students were all rushing to get to their next classes or swarming around lockers talking about the upcoming prom, I went mostly unnoticed. But at lunch, we always sat near the corner, and the entire cafeteria looked only in one very obvious direction: right at me.

"Ellie." Kate's fingers snapped in my face. "Ignore them," she said, loudly enough that the surrounding tables heard her very easily. "They're idiots, and they're just jealous because you're pretty."

I wanted to hide under the table. "I don't think the second part is all that true."

Rachel gave me a sad look. "I think you're pretty."

I smiled weakly at her. "Thanks, Rach."

"It's been over two months," Landon growled. "They ought to just ignore you and concentrate on the downtown hysteria."

I nodded but was thinking otherwise. Landon was referring to my final and very public fight with Orek. The media storm surrounding the incident had only gotten worse since it had happened, and on top of the gossip at school, I lived in fear every day of someone connecting me or Will to the grainy cell phone videos taken that night.

"Speaking of," Chris began, fluttering with excitement. "Did you hear that special effects expert they had on CNN last night ruled out animatronics? He said we don't have the technology to make something that big and that complex. Something about the way it moved. I can't remember exactly what he said."

Landon huffed. "That's because it was aliens, dude."

"It wasn't aliens, man," Evan grumbled and folded his arms across his chest. "It was probably some brand-new 3-D technology, something so good it was like a hologram."

Chris gave them both reproachful looks. "Anyway, they also had a witness on who said he saw a girl jump off the roof into the explosion. You know, the one that made the monster disappear? But she disappeared too, and so did the guy with wings."

My heart pounded like a hammer against my rib cage.

"That's why I'm thinking it wasn't even real," Kate chimed in. "Everything just disappeared afterward. Maybe that expert last night was in on the hoax and was just trying to cover it up."

"I wonder if the people behind it will go to jail," Rachel said, looking out the window.

I swallowed hard. "See, now this is way more exciting gossip for people to concentrate on than me."

"Exactly," Landon said. "You'd think they'd get over what happened to you."

I'd already accepted that I'd have to endure this until, at the very least, graduation. If I wasn't so determined, I'd have begged Nana to homeschool me for the last couple months of school, but I wasn't a wimp and I was determined to be normal. As normal as possible for me, anyway.

Chris laughed. "Not going to happen. I can't believe people were saying you were in rehab while you were gone."

"Why are there so many psychos in this school?" Kate grumbled. Then she suddenly perked up and stared directly at me. "I have to pee."

"Uh, okay," I said, eyeing her. "Thanks for the memo, but I'm not changing your Depends."

She shot to her feet and grabbed my hand. "Come with me, Ellie Bean."

She dragged me away from the table as I looked back at the rest of my friends pleadingly; they didn't even move to save me. They knew better than to get between Kate and

Kate's mission. She shoved through the door to the girls' restroom, let me go, and proceeded to kick open each of the stalls until she came to one that was locked.

"Get out," she ordered as she pounded on the door. "You've got five seconds. The toilet's for pissing, not for loitering."

The girl in the stall made small, frightened noises as she finished her business and flushed. She appeared—she had to be a freshman, the poor thing—her eyes wide and terrified, and she skirted around Kate to get to the sink.

"Did you piss on your hands or something?" Kate barked sharply. "Get out of here! There are Purell dispensers in every hallway. Keep your pee fingers off the faucet."

The girl whimpered as she darted from the restroom, letting the door slam shut behind her.

"Kate, really?" I asked, giving her a disparaging look. "That was mean."

She shrugged. "What? We only have fifteen minutes left of lunch, and we need to talk."

"About . . . ?"

"Are you ever going to tell me what happened?" she asked. "Or where you've been?"

I had strategically avoided this conversation for months because I didn't want to lie to her anymore and I didn't know how to be honest without dragging her into my mess of a life. "I stayed with Will and a friend of ours. That's where I was. It was safe there."

Safe. As soon as I said it, I realized how untrue that really was. Merodach and Kelaeno had found us and killed Nathaniel.

Kate nodded, her gaze gentle and forgiving. "I'm glad you were with him. I was so worried you were alone all that time, but your grandma kept telling me you were all right."

I shrugged. "Sort of. I wasn't exactly civil for a while."

She didn't laugh. "No one can blame you for that. I can't even imagine what you went through. I just wish you'd have let me be there for you."

"I missed you," I told her. "But I just couldn't deal . . . I blamed myself for everything and I was so lost. I felt like my world had ended and kept dragging on like it didn't get the memo."

When Kate pulled me into her arms and squeezed me tight, I lost it. I wrapped my arms around her and cried into her shoulder. I had missed her so much. As she held me, I realized what a mistake it had been to shut her out. She was like my sister, and I'd just lost my parents. I needed an anchor to my humanity, and I'd practically cut the rope and allowed myself to drift away.

"I'm so sorry," I said between sobs against her sweater.

"It's okay," she murmured back. "I'm glad you're going to be all right."

I pulled away, forcing a smile as I wiped at my face and then wiped her shoulder. "I got drool all over your sweater," I said with a small laugh.

She smiled back and shrugged. "I'll just get it dry-cleaned, so it's somebody else's problem."

"You're horrible," I said with a loud sniffle. "I love you."

"Love you too."

I leaned heavily against the counter, folding my arms over my chest, and I stared at the floor. We fell into silence for some time until I spoke at last. "My dad didn't kill my mom," I said. "I know that for sure. Whoever killed her killed them both."

Kate stepped closer to me, her voice hushed. "Ellie, do you know something? If you know something, then you have to go to the police."

"I . . ." I trailed off and shook my head. "I don't know anything that would help the police, but I do know they'll never catch who did it."

"Don't think that," she said. "The cops are good. It's their job to solve crimes."

They'd never solve this one, though. "I know," I said. I couldn't bear arguing with her about it.

"How are you and Will?" she asked, changing the subject. "Are you okay yet?"

I nodded and shrugged at the same time. "Yeah. It's just hard. He . . . lost his best friend not long after my mom died—the friend we had been staying with."

She frowned. "Wow. What are the odds that you both would go through that at the same time?"

I huffed. What were the odds? For normal people, sure, it

was pretty crazy. But not for me or Will. Death surrounded us.

Her phone buzzed and she slipped it out of her purse. Then she grinned. "Marcus just texted me and says he has a surprise. It's probably another cupcake. This boy is going to make me fat."

"It's still really sweet that he surprises you at school," I said longingly. I couldn't help feeling a twinge of jealousy at this, but I knew it wasn't right to feel that way. I was happy for Kate and Marcus, though I didn't approve of Marcus keeping his secrets from her. But then again, it wasn't like he could exactly tell her that he wasn't human. Ugh. That was a conundrum for someone else to solve.

She took my hand. "Come with me to see him before we go back to class?"

I nodded and followed her out of the restroom and toward the front doors of the school. Marcus was standing in front of a sleek black Maserati. Kate squealed and skipped up to him before launching herself into his arms. They kissed briefly, politely, since I was standing there.

"Nice car," I said, eyeing him.

"Thanks," he replied. "I let Ava use it sometimes, so if you see her in it, she didn't steal it. She's not a car person. She doesn't know how to appreciate a fine machine like this."

The suggestive way he said that made me wonder whether he was talking about the car or himself. I chose not to ask.

He turned his back and ducked into his car for a moment before returning with a small white box in his hand. He presented it to Kate. She flashed me a knowing look and then beamed and squealed at him as she tore open the box to find—of course—a cupcake with pink frosting. She danced and threw an arm around his neck and kissed him again.

"I've even got one for you, too, Ellie," he said, untangling himself from Kate, and he took a second small box from inside the car. He handed it to me, and inside was another cupcake.

"Wow, thank you, Marcus." I was kind of surprised that he would have gotten one for me, too, but I wasn't going to argue with him.

"The second one was supposed to be mine," he admitted with a shrug. "But since I don't want to look like a jackass, I'll give it to you. See what a nice guy I am?"

I rolled my eyes at him. "God, Marcus, you're the sweetest guy ever."

He grinned stupidly. "Actually, that's not true. I got it for you to begin with, because you two are attached at the hip and I figured you'd show up together. You're so predictable."

"And you're not?" Kate shot back, shoving his shoulder playfully. "You show up here again with yet another cupcake?"

He scoffed. "I'm not being predictable. It's self-preservation. I know you love these."

"Whatever you say," I grumbled, and marveled at the treat I was aching to devour. My day was about to get a billion times better.

"We've got to run or we'll be tardy," Kate said to him with a pout. "See you soon?"

"Of course." He smiled and kissed her good-bye.

She waved to him, and we headed back inside for our lockers as he drove away. "I think I love him," she said. We walked down the hallway, and she took a bite out of her cupcake.

I raised my eyebrows. "Oh? As of just now?" I took a bite of my own. It was sugar and deliciousness and so good.

"No," she said thoughtfully. "I think I have for a while, but I was just in denial. I've never actually loved a boy before. They're hard to love, you know? At least Marcus doesn't smell. I think that's why I love him. And because of the cupcakes."

"So I guess you're sleeping with him now?"

"For a few weeks," she replied. "He's marvelous, by the way. Thanks for asking."

I frowned, unsurprised. Marcus had two hundred years of practice with that. Then, of course, my thoughts went to Will. . . . "It was a simple yes-or-no question. I didn't need details."

"Oh, I won't go into details while we're at school," she said. "I'll tell you more later. You've missed a lot since you've been gone and then busy catching up in classes."

"I'm sure," I said. "We need to have a heart-to-heart all-nighter."

"What are you doing tonight?" she asked, nudging my

shoulder and frowning as we walked down the hall. "You should come over. Maybe stay the night Friday or Saturday."

"I can't," I said honestly. "I'm sorry. I'll let you know about this weekend, though. Tonight is a me-and-Will thing."

"Can't skip it for me?"

"It's his birthday, actually," I said. "He doesn't know I'm planning anything, but I wanted to do something sweet for him."

Kate nodded. "He needs it. And so do you. Did you get him anything?"

"He wouldn't like a present if I got him one," I said. "The celebration will be enough for him. Probably *too* much."

"He'll love it," she said, grinning. "Even if he doesn't freak out or anything—which of course he won't, because he thinks he's too cool to let anyone know he likes something—he'll still love it. I think it's a great idea."

I smiled, mostly to myself. It would make him happy, and I wanted him to be happy. "Yeah. I'm pretty sure it'll embarrass him, but oh, well. It's funny when he's embarrassed."

"We're really mean to boys."

"They're mean back."

I bought a plain white cake at the grocery store after school, and as soon as I got home, I realized I didn't want tonight to be just Will and me. I wanted all of his friends there, so he knew that he still had them, that he hadn't lost everything but me. I called up Lauren, Marcus, and even Ava and made sure they'd be at my grandmother's house. Lauren, thankfully, volunteered to come over and hang out with me before the party.

I also bought some icing tubes to scribble all over Will's birthday cake, but once I got to decorating, I decided I didn't want to make some boring cake. I wanted to create something that would make him laugh. Lauren sat across from me at the kitchen table as I kinda drew snarling stick reapers with angry eyes and sharp, gaping mouths on their bubble heads and outspread wings, all surrounding a figure in the middle who was supposed to be Will. I stopped in the middle of the icing drawing and frowned disapprovingly. The stick Will didn't look much like real Will, so I dabbed on a pair of green eyes, outlined him a pair of wings, and painted a sword in his hand that wasn't quite as fancy as the real thing. Then I took the red icing tube and splattered the whole cake with it until it was a freaking massacre of frosting stick reapers. I even smeared red on the sword and wrote HAPPY BIRTHDAY WILL across the top in the drippy red icing. Nana glared at me and cleared her throat noticeably as she passed the table, and Lauren looked up at her apologetically. Regular cakes are no fun. This one was awesome.

At seven, Nana left to go play poker with her girl friends. (Or I should say she went to go *destroy* her girl friends at poker. Since she was psychic, it was sort of cheating.) I called Will to come over. Everyone arrived a few minutes before he did and went into the kitchen. It would have been impossible to truly surprise Will, since he'd notice Marcus's and Lauren's cars parked in the driveway—which of course he did—but he came inside very confused. I had on a ridiculous grin as I led him through the house toward the kitchen.

As soon as Will saw the cake, he burst out laughing and shook his head, running a hand through his hair. His cheeks were beginning to buzz with red and my heart lifted. "Ellie, what is this?"

I kissed his cheek. "Happy birthday, old man. I didn't put all the candles on your cake, because it'd end up being a bonfire in my nana's kitchen. And I know you don't like cake, but I like cake and I'm pretty sure Lauren does too."

Marcus raised a hand. "I like cake."

Ava frowned at the sugary mountain of stick-reaper murder. "I do not."

"Well." I huffed and poked Will's chest. "You and Ava can go pout in the corner and be losers together."

He laughed again and pulled me toward him, but I wriggled away, fighting a smile.

"Don't even try it," I warned him. "I slaved over this cake! I waited for probably *five minutes* in line at the grocery store for it, and then you don't even want to know how many hours I spent slaving over the frosting art. And Lauren watched. She knows what's up."

"I sure did," Lauren said. "She squirted all that red frosting on there by herself, if you can believe that."

I waved a dismissive hand at him. "This masterpiece

puts Michelangelo to shame, and you don't even want to eat it." I turned to Lauren. "I should be a professional cake decorator, shouldn't I?"

She nodded firmly, keeping a straight face. "Definitely."

He took my hand and pulled me back to him. "Fine, fine." He laughed. "I'll have a piece. You pick it."

I lifted the knife and a plate. "I'm going to give you a corner piece so all that frosting makes you sick. That's what you get for your initial rejection."

He stepped up close behind me and buried his face in the bend of my neck. I could feel his smile against my skin, and his happiness melted into me. "You're very spiteful to me."

I chose a corner piece that had a decapitated stick-reaper head on it and plopped the piece onto the plate. I turned around and shoved it at him. "It's not spite; it's vengeance. Shut up and eat your cake."

He took the plate and picked up a fork. He took a big bite and smiled at me. "Delicious."

"Duh," I grumbled, and began serving the others. Even Ava accepted a plate with a small sliver of cake and minimal icing. We all sat around the kitchen and laughed and joked, reminiscing about good times we'd had, and about Nathaniel.

Later that evening, after everyone had left, I was cleaning dishes and Will came up behind me. He bent over to kiss my shoulder and said, "Thank you." He moved around to help me by lifting clean dishes and drying them with a towel.

470 🖎

"I didn't embarrass you, did I?" I asked.

"Just a lot."

"Are you happy?"

"Yes," he said, and his eyes fell over every inch of my face. "You made a mess, too."

I stuck my tongue out at him. "It's not that bad. There isn't much to clean up at all."

He grinned. "I meant on your face."

I jumped and wiped at my cheeks. "Are you serious? There's cake on my face?"

His grin widened.

I gasped at him and shoved him while he laughed. "I can't believe you knew it was there all night and didn't say anything to me!"

He shrugged and gave a playful, smug look. "It's not spite; it's vengeance."

"You're such a jerk!"

"No, I'm not," he said. "I'll even help you clean it up." He leaned forward and slowly kissed the smudge of frosting on my cheek, sending a mix of shivers and heat straight to my toes. I wobbled and had to lean against the counter for support.

It was hard for me to gather enough breath in order to speak. "That didn't help at all."

"Forgive me," he whispered very unconvincingly, and kissed my lips without any hurry, as if he had all the time in the world.

"That's not frosting," I scolded him, very aware that his lips still brushed mine.

"Tastes like it." He didn't wait for me to respond before he opened his mouth against mine and pressed himself into me. My hands were still wet from washing dishes, but I couldn't stop myself from putting them all over him. He didn't seem to mind as he tugged me as close as possible to his body and kissed me thoroughly. I made a little noise as I smiled against his kiss and his mouth moved south to my jaw and neck. His hands slid down my sides to my hips as his lips and teeth grazed my throat. His fingers were hot as they slipped just under my shirt, brushing my belly.

"We should go upstairs," he whispered hotly, and his lips found mine again.

Heat flushed through me. "Upstairs?"

"Or we should stay right here." His hands smoothed lower over my hips, and his fingers dipped into my jeans. His teeth nipped my bottom lip as he kissed me.

The spinning through my body made me dizzy, and I was about to faint. "My grandmother will be home soon."

"Or we should go someplace that's not here."

I bounced the idea around inside my head, but it was very difficult to think with him kissing me the way he was. I wanted to say yes to him, to agree to anything that he suggested, but something other than desire made me question what I really wanted. I wasn't afraid of having sex with him—that wasn't what it was. I just . . . it wasn't right yet. It wasn't the right time. I wasn't ready yet.

"I don't . . ." I started, and felt him tense immediately. "No, Will."

He studied my face, his green eyes gentle and not full of anger or annoyance. "Okay."

I could feel the scarlet rushing into my cheeks. "Just for right now."

He gave me a genuine smile and pulled his hands out away from my skin. "Of course." He kissed me sweetly and made a real attempt at cleaning up the frosting on my cheek with his thumb. "How did you even get this on your face? Were you shoving the whole piece into your mouth?"

"No," I grumbled at him, feeling the awkwardness wash away. He made me feel completely at ease. "I think it had a whole reaper body on it, so there was a lot of frosting. Don't judge me."

"I never judge you."

"You're judging me right now," I retorted. "You'd better be nice to me or I'll never make you another root beer float again, which means no more root beer float kisses."

He laughed. "That's a little harsh."

"What was your favorite food before root beer floats were invented?" I asked curiously.

He gave me a weird look and shrugged. "I don't know. Food was terrible before people started putting lots of chemicals and artificial flavors into it to make it taste better. I guess I've always like carrots a lot."

"Carrots?" I blurted out, gaping at him. "Your other favorite food is *carrots*? What is wrong with you?"

"Hey now, you were just getting mad at me for being judgmental. Don't be a hypocrite. Besides, carrots have a very pleasant taste when they aren't sour."

I ignored that remark. *"Please* tell me there is some other food that you like more than *carrots*."

"I suppose I like strawberries a lot, too," he offered.

I rolled my eyes. "I will never understand you."

"I know what *your* favorite food is," he challenged.

"Oh?"

"Cold Stone," he said with a grin. "Cold Stone anything."

My grin matched his, and I slipped my arms around his waist. "You know me too well."

31

BEFORE I EVEN EXITED THE SCHOOL BUILDING ON Monday afternoon, I sensed him. Instead of continuing toward the student parking lot, I veered left and eased toward the tree he stood under, protecting himself from the sunlight. I ignored the stares and whispers of students behind me and smiled carefully at him. Cadan gave me a warm smile in return, his pale gold hair shining even in the shade and blowing gently in the spring breeze. I stopped under the tree with him, lugging my backpack higher over my shoulder.

"Hello," he said, his voice as gentle as his smile.

"Hello," I said back, resisting the urge to reach for him and hold him close. The events from the last time I had seen him replayed over in my head, everything he had said and done. All that he had risked, and how courageous he'd been to stand up to his father. I couldn't tell him how much I had admired him, or how much I cared about him, or how much sadness I felt in my heart for him.

Things were far more awkward than I'd ever wanted them to be between us, but after all that we'd been through together, how could it be any different? We'd seen each other at our most vulnerable, and there was nothing to hide anymore. I cared about him—and I had never cared about a demonic reaper before. He had told me that he was in love with me. This was new for the both of us.

"How are you, Cadan?" I asked, forcing myself to say something, *anything*.

He shrugged. "Could be better. How have you been?"

Even though he held his emotions firmly, the affection in his gaze as he looked at me was obvious and comforting. "Tired," I confessed. "Finding it hard to return to a normal life."

"Your life will never be normal."

I frowned a little. "Not all of it, no. But it's all relative, I guess. I have two lives, but each is its own kind of normal. I just need to learn how not to let the Preliator reaper killer side bleed into the Ellie side. I don't want the Preliator to be all that I am."

"No," he mused. "You're always Ellie, but you're also always the Preliator. The two mix more seamlessly than you think."

"So there really is no escape." I sighed. "I'm stuck with you winged boys forever."

"I'm sorry. I won't bother you anymore after this." He gave me a sad look that made me instantly want to take back what I'd just said.

"No," I said quickly. "I meant that as a joke. I'm glad to see you."

"Right back at you. I didn't just come to see you, though."

My brow lifted. "Oh?"

"I heard something," he said, the gleam in his eyes going out like candle flames. "Before my father . . . died. About something he was very afraid of, something he didn't want you to find. The hallowed glaive. It sounds very important."

"The hallowed glaive?" I repeated, putting the puzzle pieces together in my head. "A glaive is a type of blade, so it may be a weapon of some kind."

He nodded. "Yes. I think it's perhaps one that can destroy Sammael and even Lilith. I think you should look into it."

"It could even be a relic."

"Maybe," he said. "But maybe not. Information on something like this would be in the grimoire, but Sammael still has it, and there's no way I would be able to infiltrate and get it back. They know me as a traitor now."

My lips tightened. "You're right. It would be too dangerous for you to go back."

"For you, as well."

"I know," I said. "But I don't have a choice. We need that book." But as soon as I said it, I remembered there may be another hope. "Then again, Nathaniel said he had a copy of the grimoire. It's missing from his collection, but we've got to find it. This book is our only hope. I can't face Sammael again without a real chance at beating him. We need the big guns for this one."

His face brightened with hope. "Any idea who could have taken it?"

I shook my head, and an invisible force tightened around my heart. "No. Nathaniel is dead. He's the only one who knew anything about that book." I slumped against the tree beside Cadan. He pushed himself off the trunk and faced me, looking down serenely.

"There's always a chance," he said. "I'll help you find it."

That put a smile on my face. I knew he'd keep that promise as well as he could. He'd given up all that he knew because he believed in me. I needed to believe in him, too. "Thank you, Cadan."

"Of course."

I bit on my lip and stared at the ground, battling inwardly with myself. I wanted to tell him what I'd learned about Will, but I wasn't sure if I ought to, especially since Will didn't know yet.

"Whatever you want to say must be important if you're making that little face."

"Oh!" I jumped, embarrassed, and felt heat rushing into my cheeks. "Yeah, it's important."

"Are you going to tell me?" he pressed.

"It's about Bastian," I admitted, unable to hold it in any longer. "Back in that creepy basement, he was talking to Will, asking him to join him, and he said . . . that Will was his son."

Cadan's eyes widened in surprise, and his lips parted. He didn't move or blink for what felt like minutes.

I continued, speaking slowly and carefully. "If what he said is true, then Will is your half-brother. His mother is an angelic reaper. Yours, I assume, is demonic."

At last there was life on his face. He swallowed painfully hard. "Are you sure?"

"That's what Bastian claimed." I didn't tell him that Bastian had also said he had loved Madeleine. That somehow seemed private, even though Bastian had thrown it into Will's face in front of everyone in that room. Cadan also probably didn't want to hear that part. I knew nothing of his mother and how Bastian may have treated her. I didn't get the impression that Bastian had ever been kind to Cadan, so why would he have been kind to his mother?

Cadan stared through me at nothing, his eyes unfocused and dazed. I could see him calculating in his mind, lost in thought.

"Are you okay?" I asked.

He blinked. "I'm just . . . very surprised. No wonder we never liked each other. Innate brotherly rivalry, I suppose, besides loving the same girl. Anyway, Will has every right to hate me."

I frowned. "What did you do?"

"Nothing."

"I don't understand."

"I did nothing," he said again. "Geir and I were the ones who captured Will and took him to Bastian. The night Ragnuk killed you and took you to where Bastian held Will, I was there. And I did nothing. I just let it all happen."

We fell into silence. I could hear the regret in Cadan's voice. He hadn't been able to stand up to those who controlled him until now. I understood that feeling of helplessness better than most. It took an extraordinary amount of courage to stand up to those you fear, whether they were Hellspawn or blood family or both.

"It's rather strange that the first time I saw you," he said, swallowing hard at a pause, "you were dead. I like it better when you're alive."

"That's funny. Me too."

He smiled sideways for an instant. "I'm serious, Ellie."

"But you didn't do nothing the night Bastian took me," I assured him. "You came to save me, didn't you?"

His gaze fell to the grass at our feet. He nodded.

"Bastian was going to fight Will and probably kill him," I continued. "You stopped that. You saved both our lives. You protected us, and you stood up for humanity. That took a lot of courage and good in you. Thank you, Cadan."

He opened his mouth to speak but was hesitant. "I killed my own father to do it."

I chose my words carefully. "Do you believe what you did was wrong?"

His brow furrowed and his eyes darkened as he continued to stare at the ground. "What he wanted was wrong. I just didn't know how else to stop him. But I feel . . ." He looked up at the green canopy of the tree above us. "I feel like it doesn't matter that he's dead. Sammael and Lilith are alive. Merodach is still out there, and there's no telling how many other demonic reapers are in league with them. I felt like it was in vain. Like nothing good came out of it anyway."

I studied his face, the sorrow in his eyes. He was beautiful, even when he was sad. "That's not true," I said gently. "You're free."

His gaze slowly fell to mine and his eyes flashed. He watched me as I had just watched him, and a quiet smile curved his lips. "I suppose you're right."

"What are you going to do?" I asked. "Now that you aren't doing Bastian's bidding?"

He shrugged. "Live, I guess. Help you find that book maybe. Take up knitting. Who knows where the wind will take me?"

I made a serious face and nodded. "Knitting sounds right up your alley."

He grinned and gave a soft laugh. "I hear it's all the rage."

We laughed, and after a few moments, an ache grew in my heart. "Thank you for everything, Cadan."

"Of course." His shoulders sank as if he knew where this was going.

"I can't tell you how much it means to me," I said. "How much *you* mean to me."

"I feel a *but* coming."

I sighed and purposely avoided using that word. "Will is my Guardian. We've been through so much together, and I'm in love with him."

He didn't reply right away, but his gaze fell to my lips for only a heartbeat before returning to my eyes. "I know, and it's okay."

"Are *you* okay, though?"

He gave me a beautiful smile. "I'll never be okay. I'll never stop wanting you, but . . . I can't have you and I've accepted that."

Sadness pulled me down like a churning undertow. "I'm sorry. I mean it. But you know that . . ." I trailed off, afraid of hurting him anymore with what needed to be said.

There was a curious little smile in the corner of his lips, and an icy hand squeezed my heart. "What?"

I took a deep breath and tried again. "You have to know that the only reason you feel like this is because of what I am."

He shook his head, confusion filling his eyes like cold water washing away the opal flames. "What . . . you are?"

"The Preliator," I continued painfully. "Gabriel. Because I'm an archangel. Nathaniel told me that it's instinctive, this attraction, or whatever you want to call it."

His smile vanished and his jaw set, muscles clenching. "Love."

"Yeah," I said, and my lip trembled with the word. "It's an effect that the divine have over all reapers. It's not real. It's an infatuation." That sounded so harsh, but it was true. At least, unlike most demonic reapers', Cadan's attraction was romantic instead of violent.

"And what about Will?" he asked almost defensively. "Is his love for you real?"

I chewed on my lip. "Will and I . . . we have five hundred years of history. We've been through the best and worst things two people can endure together. We've fought *for* this, fought *against* what we feel, for a very long time. Cadan, you and I—we barely know each other."

He looked away from me for only seconds, but it felt like a lifetime. He swallowed hard. "It feels real to me."

"I'm sorry," I said, my heart threatening to crack like glass.

His face softened, and the anger that had just traced his brow melted from his gentle gaze. "I'm glad I still feel what I feel, whatever it means. It feels good. I can't regret that."

I bit on my lip, swallowing back tears, and I quelled the urge to move to him, to curl myself into him and feel his presence all around me. "Cadan . . ."

He touched my cheek. "No matter what you choose, I'll

defend you against anything. I can't be your Guardian, but I'll protect you like one."

"Thank you," I said quietly. "I trust you."

"Even though I'm demonic?"

I grinned back and sniffed, my smile trembling. "Even though you're demonic."

His smile grew. "Even the demonic can be blessed. Who'd have thought?"

I stood up on my toes and kissed his cheek gently, kissing him good-bye. His hands took my hips and pulled me closer to him. He kissed my neck and moved his lips toward my own, wanting more, but I drew back and put my hand to his chest, stopping him. I couldn't give him what he wanted. I couldn't give him more.

"Get a room!" someone shouted behind us, the words followed by a chorus of laughter. Mortified, I covered my face in my hands and didn't turn around.

A sly smile darkened Cadan's expression, and he nodded over to the rude kid. "I like the way he thinks."

I smacked his chest. "Shut up." But I was grinning, happy to see him back to his old self.

His smirk eased effortlessly into a warm smile, and he thumbed my cheek. "I'm going to miss this."

I let out a snort. "What? Me smacking you?"

He laughed. "No," he said softly. "Touching you. Kissing you. I envy my brother."

Sadness filled me heavily, and I felt like a bag of sand

stitched together with string, unable to move without ripping open. "You won't have to miss *me*, though. I want you to be my friend. I don't want to lose you."

He sighed. "I know. And I want to be your friend, too, even though I want more. But I will love just being your friend, Ellie."

"I'm glad," I said. "I need you in my life."

"Ask me for anything, any task, and I'll do it for you," he promised. "Call me anytime, for anything. I wish you well."

I smiled as Will's brother disappeared into the Grim, fading away like smoke from a flame. "Good-bye, Cadan."

32

FOR AN ENTIRE WEEK, I WAS FORCED TO LISTEN TO every single senior girl run her mouth off about prom. It was to be held on Saturday night at a fancy hotel, and by Wednesday, with only three days left, it was all anyone could manage to talk about. I was so sick of hearing about it.

I must have heard the exact colors of Kate's and Rachel's dresses a thousand times. I knew what shoes they were going to wear. I knew what shades of makeup and nail polish they'd get done at the salon. Of course Kate was going with Marcus and Rachel was going with Evan. Of course they'd harassed the guys into matching the colors of their dresses. Prom was going to be perfect.

For them.

I wasn't going. I'd been gone too long, and I was too exhausted from struggling with catching up in school so I could graduate with my friends, too absorbed with things that actually *mattered* to have gone out and looked for dresses. Not that prom didn't matter to me at one time, but I supposed it didn't matter anymore. The plan had always been for Kate and me to pick out dresses together, but she had to get one while I was AWOL, before the selection at the mall was picked clean.

My grumpiness had not gone unnoticed by Will. I had snapped at him a few times that week, though I hadn't meant to. My agitation had caused my temper to be short, and I hated that I kept taking it out on him.

"What's wrong?" he asked as we sat in his living room watching TV after I'd done a load of homework. I had been lying across his lap for a little while, but something he'd said had annoyed me for no reason and I'd grumbled slightly nasty things at him and shoved myself to the other end of the couch like a brat.

"Nothing," I replied sharply.

He let out an aggravated sigh. "It's not nothing. Frankly, you've been on edge for days. I don't even know what I just said a minute ago to make you mad at me."

I laid my head back against the couch. "Sorry. I'm just in a bad mood."

"For days?"

"It's been a bad week, okay?" I tried to keep my voice even, but I doubted my success at doing so.

"Well, tell me about it," he offered. "Maybe I can help."

"You really can't." The snark was back. I wanted to smack myself. He didn't deserve this.

"Let me try."

I took a long, deep breath and let it out slowly, forcing the tension from my body and the snap from my voice. "I'm just tired of hearing about prom from my friends. It's all they talk about, and I wish this week would go by faster so it'd be over with. But of course next week, prom will still be the only thing anyone will talk about, and I can't escape it."

He looked around thoughtfully, his boy brain visibly struggling to solve my predicament. "It's this weekend?"

"Saturday."

"Why don't you just go then?" he offered foolishly. "That way you can talk about it with your friends instead of being left out."

I sighed. "It's a lot more complicated than that."

"I think you're the one making it complicated."

I glared at him from across the couch. "Thanks. You're so helpful."

"I mean it," he said gently. "I don't see why there's any reason you can't go."

"It's too late, Will. I don't have a ticket or a dress or anything. Prom isn't something you can just throw together at the last second. No one can pull that off."

"You have three days left, not one second."

"Don't be a smart-ass."

"Don't be so stubborn."

My glare got darker. "You don't get it."

He let out a small laugh and a shrug. "No, I really don't. I know how much you want to go. You wouldn't want to miss out on this. You've worked so hard to get yourself through your last couple months of high school, so I'm not buying it. You deserve to go."

"Why do you even care?" I asked. "You're centuries old. Prom is a silly high school thing to you."

"I don't think it's silly," he said with a frown. "Especially since it's important to you. Nothing that's important to you is silly to me."

I watched him, the sincerity in his eyes, and I crawled back across the couch toward him and rested my head on his shoulder. He kissed the top of my head. I was being ridiculous toward him, but I honestly couldn't bring myself to go to prom. I didn't want to go alone, even though I'd be with all of my friends, and there was only one person I'd want for my date and he would never agree to it. I wasn't even going to ask him. Marcus might have been going with Kate, but he seemed to enjoy parading around pretending to be a perfect human boyfriend like it was a game to him to see how good he was at it. He was the weirdest person I'd ever met. Will was weird, too, but at least he made sense. Kind of.

"Marcus asked me something strange awhile ago," I said.

"What was that?" he asked into my hair.

"He asked me what Heaven is like," I said. "I have no idea. I don't remember what Heaven is like, but I remember missing being human. I missed *feeling*—feeling *anything*, feeling happiness, sadness . . . I missed touching, being close to others. I missed *you*, Will. I don't really want to go back there. To Heaven. I want to stay here."

He paused for a few moments, as if digesting what I had just said. "I want you to stay here, too."

"But I'll have to go," I said gently. "Eventually."

He didn't respond to that. The voices from the TV show we weren't watching filled the silence between us.

I buried myself deeper into him. "I wish I had more time."

"You have all the time in the world."

I exhaled and disentangled myself from him while climbing to my feet. "I'm going to head out. Thanks for letting me come over to do my homework."

"Of course," he said, and politely stood with me. "I love when you come over. I miss having you here every day."

"Want to go for a run tomorrow?"

"Definitely," he said. "Have a good night. Try not to worry about so much at once. Everything will work out the way it's meant to."

I smiled weakly at him. As I left with my backpack over my shoulder, I repeated what he had said to me in my head. Everything will work out the way it's meant to.

On Saturday evening, I was alone in Nana's house. She was out again (it was pretty bad that her social life was more exciting than mine these days), and my friends were all getting ready for prom. I, on the other hand, was already in sweatpants and a way-too-big T-shirt that I suspected may have actually belonged to Will and finagled its way into my laundry, and I was ready to fall asleep to a movie in my room. I was determined to go to bed early so I wouldn't sit up all night thinking about what everyone else was doing.

Halfway through my movie, I heard a knock at the door. I ignored it for a moment, since I was not climbing out of my ridiculously comfortable bed-and-blanket burrito. There wasn't an iceberg's chance in hell that I'd move.

Another knock.

"Really?" I grumbled aloud to no one.

I gave in and climbed out of my little nest to turn off the TV and force myself downstairs to the front door. When I opened the door, my heart kicked in my chest. Will stood there in the doorway, dressed in a sleek tuxedo, a corsage in a plastic container in one hand and a long garment bag in the other. His tuxedo was perfectly tailored around his broad shoulders and his waist. His hair was neatly combed back, and it looked like he might even have had a haircut. He looked excruciatingly handsome and adorable all dressed up with a terrified look on his face. Parked behind him in the driveway was Marcus's shiny black Maserati.

"Don't be mad" was the first thing he said. He really was terrified, as if the most frightening reaper on the planet was no scarier than a mouse, and yet put him in a tux and it was the Apocalypse.

The noise that came out of me was some kind of freak-ish, embarrassing cross between a laugh and a sob. I could barely breathe and, as a result, could barely speak. "I'm not mad, Will."

"It was my idea," he rambled quickly and nervously. "So don't yell at Kate, but she helped me a lot. She got two tickets for you weeks ago, because she knew you still wanted to go even though you told her you didn't. She helped me to pick out a dress for you the day before yesterday, and she made sure I wore something that fit me. Honestly, she scares me a little. I tried so hard to do this right for you, so please forgive me if I did anything wrong."

My lips and hands were trembling. "You didn't do any-thing wrong."

His eyes were so bright and wide as he fumbled over himself. "Will you go, then? Will you come with me? Please say yes."

Then the tears came. They were hot against my cheeks, making my eyes burn, and I had to cover my mouth as I cried. He gave me a worried look as I fell apart in front of him. I put down my hands and nodded, smiling at him from ear to ear. "Yes. I'll go."

His entire body seemed to relax at once, and he gave me a little smile. "Please don't cry," he said.

I wiped at more tears. "I can't help it."

He lifted the garment bag and held it out to me. "Go put

it on," he said. "I think you'll like it."

I took it from him, feeling the weight of the heavy dress in my arms, and I went up to my room. I hung up the bag on my closet door and unzipped it to pull out the dress inside. I climbed out of my baggy pajamas, pulled the gown over my head, and tugged it over my hips. The zipper was on the side beneath my arm, and I had no trouble with it. The dress fit like a glove. I stepped back and gazed at myself in the floor-length mirror. Kate was a genius. The rich, deep plum fabric gleamed, crisscrossing over the strapless bodice, and beneath an elegant, ruched empire waist, the folds of chiffon fell to the floor. I stood up on my bare tiptoes to see what it would look like in heels and decided that I looked rather silly being barefoot in this extravagant gown. I needed the right heels. I rummaged through the closet and tossed out unwanted shoes until I found a pair of strappy gold sandals, and I slipped them on. With the added inches of height, I nodded in approval.

Will knocked at the door. "Are you ready?"

"Yeah," I answered nervously. "Come in."

The door opened and he stopped dead in his tracks. I fought the urge to fold my arms over myself in embarrassment as he stared at me. He swallowed hard as he came into the room, each of his steps slow and careful. His lips moved soundlessly for a second before he finally made words come out. "You're beautiful."

My cheeks flushed as red and dark as my hair. "Thanks.

I don't have any makeup on and my hair isn't done."

"Doesn't matter."

The flush was only getting worse. I touched my cheeks and they were red-hot. "I don't have a boutonniere or anything for you."

He looked at the ceiling for a brief second as if he didn't know what I was talking about. "Oh, right. Yeah, that's in here." He held out the corsage box. "Sorry, I don't know how any of this goes. Kate said to give this to you and you would know."

I grinned stupidly at him fumbling over himself. He removed the corsage from the container, and instantly I smelled jasmine. The delicate, satiny white flowers dotted a mixture of green leaves and smaller flowers whose colors matched my dress.

"I know how much you love jasmine," he said, his eyes on my wrist as he slipped the corsage over my hand. "I told Kate that's the flower you would want."

I nodded, fighting the tears again. If I was really going through with this, I'd have to clean up my face and put on makeup. I didn't have a whole lot of time to do it all if we weren't going to be late. I took out the boutonniere and started to pin it to Will's tuxedo as he took a deep breath and set his jaw tight. I looked up to meet his eyes.

"Nervous?" I asked with a quick smile before going back to pinning the boutonniere so I wouldn't stab him accidentally. He seemed to get impaled a lot during fights, so I didn't want to be guilty of that too.

"Yeah." He softened and forced himself to relax a little more. "I've never done anything like this before."

"It's not so bad," I promised, finishing and straightening the boutonniere. There were jasmine flowers in it that matched my corsage. "Humans do it every year. I think you're tough enough to survive prom."

"I want to do this, though," he assured me. "For you, because it would make you happy."

I looked back up at him, feeling the sting of more stupid tears. I was such a crybaby. "Thank you."

"I'd do anything for you," he said in a quiet voice. "Gladly."

"I know," I replied.

"Are you about ready? What else has to be done?"

"I have to do my hair," I said, sniffling very unattractively.

"Leave it down, just the way it is. I like it when it's down." He reached into his pocket and pulled out a piece of folded satin. Within was the beautiful phoenix hair comb. I nearly choked on another sob. "Wear this in it."

My hands shook as I accepted the comb and headed to the bathroom down the hall. I studied my hair, deciding what to do with it, and settled on pulling bits of it up and pinning it with the comb. The deep shades of red, purple, and gold swirling through the firebird burned in my dark chocolate red hair, matching my dress perfectly. I adjusted the comb and turned my head side to side, admiring the piece. Then

I washed my face and dug through my makeup bag to make myself look presentable.

I only needed one more thing. I went back into my room to my dresser, feeling Will's eyes on me. I grabbed my winged necklace, and before I could put it on, Will was there, lifting the necklace and latching it around my neck. As soon as the glossy pendant touched my skin, I felt warmer, more contented, braver, as if it had a power of its own.

I turned around to face Will, and he was smiling down at me. "Ready?" he asked as his hands settled on my hips.

"Almost." I threw my arms around his neck and pulled him down to me so that his forehead touched mine. Tears rolled down my cheeks and I cupped his face in my hands. "I love you. I don't think you have any idea how much."

He smiled. "I do." He dipped his head and I tilted mine back to let him kiss me, but he stopped halfway, his mouth inches from mine. His body was stiff against me, his hands unmoving on my hips.

"What's the matter?" I asked, searching his eyes.

"If I kiss you now, I won't be able to stop," he breathed. "We'll miss the party."

I considered suggesting that we just stay here in my room, but he'd gone through so much trouble to make sure I went to my prom. Still, it was feeling more right by the second, more right to just take this silly dress back off and stay in.

I slid my hands from his cheek and down his neck and

chest, not wanting to let him go, and I wound my fingers around his collar. "We should get going." The disappointment in my voice was obvious, and I didn't care.

"Kate said to meet everyone at her house," he said.

"Okay."

"She's having a party there after we get back," he added. "She said you should bring a bag to stay the night. I've already talked to your grandmother about it."

"Or we could go back to your house," I suggested carefully. "After Kate's party."

His eyes searched mine. "Okay. If you want to."

I smiled and tugged on his collar so that his face came closer to mine. "I want to."

He smiled back, his eyes on my lips. "Okay." Then he kissed me lightly, briefly, and pulled away—only just—and hovered there, as if he was contemplating doing it again. When he didn't, I tugged on his collar one more time, closing the last few inches between us, and I kissed him. He hands came up and held my face as he kissed me deeper, and with a groan, he pushed himself away and let me go. "We should get out of here."

I was breathless. "Yeah. Kate's going to be mad if we're late."

"I don't want Kate to be mad at me. I wasn't kidding when I said she scares me."

I laughed and grabbed a bag to shove my overnight stuff

into. When I was ready, I came back to him.

He took my hand and held my wrist to his lips. "Let's go."

I followed him downstairs and out the front door, heading toward a wonderful night.

33

I'D NEVER HUGGED KATE SO HARD IN MY LIFE. SHE was amazing. We both cried so much that we had to go inside and redo our makeup, but that was okay. The boys didn't quite understand why we cried, but that was okay, too. Will and Marcus hung out together in the we-ancient-angelic-reapers-are-too-cool-for-you-but-that-really-just-means-we're-boring club, away from most of us as we goofed around and had pictures taken. It was so nice of Marcus to let Will use his car, but he wasn't above bantering with Will about it every few minutes. Finally we all climbed into the limousine that would take us to the hotel. None of my friends treated me like a freak, or like they needed to walk on eggshells around me. They treated me like Ellie, just plain old me.

The hotel was beautiful and the hall the dance was held in was decorated with silver and midnight-blue silk streamers, balloons, drapes, and tablecloths. Hanging from the ceiling in the same colors were pretty paper lanterns shaped like jagged stars and orblike moons. At the front of the hall were a fondue table, a dance floor, and a DJ setup. My group found our table and sat down. While we waited for our dinners, we talked about the high school years we were leaving behind and the college years ahead of us. Kate and I were going to State together and were determined to be roommates. Landon had a full soccer scholarship there as well, and Chris was going to school an hour west of State. Everything seemed to be falling into place. And then I would glance at Will beside me, who watched me curiously, not as if he found it all funny, but more as if he marveled at me.

After dinner, Kate grabbed my hand and dragged me and Rachel toward the dance floor with everyone else. We joked around and danced like idiots, twirling each other around, not caring if we annoyed the gross couples booty-grinding each other. If they didn't like us, they could leave—which was what we wanted them to do anyway. I looked back to our table, where Will and Marcus still sat like bumps on a log. Their faces were close as they talked, and when I caught Will's eyes, he grinned mischievously at me. I took Kate's arm and pulled her over.

"They're plotting something," I said into her ear.

She narrowed her eyes at them. "They sure are. They are up to no good at all."

After more exchanges of words, they both rose from the

table. Will eased his way toward me, moving around people and obstacles. I looked over at Marcus, who rounded the dance floor and made his way to the DJ. He said something to the guy, who nodded a moment later, and then the music changed. I listened to the new music, which was buried beneath the chorus of groans and F-bombs from everyone else, trying to figure out which song it had changed to, and after a few notes, I realized it was completely different. It was a waltz.

Will held his hand out to me and smiled beautifully. "May I have this dance?"

It took everything in me to keep myself from crying again as I nodded and let him take my hand. He pulled me close, his eyes bright and locked on mine. He stepped back, guiding me toward the slowly clearing floor, and his other hand clasped around mine to take the lead. Then we moved, spinning, stepping into a dance my grandfather had taught me when I was a little girl. I was a little unsure on my feet, but Will moved as if he'd done it every day for a hundred years, with a flawless grace that surprised me, made me lose myself completely in the dance, in his face. He was still smiling at me, and we stepped into perfect rhythm with the beautiful music as it led us both like a summer breeze. I felt myself blushing, and I looked away as he twirled me and paused to kiss my cheek. I laughed and he squeezed my hand. Then I noticed that the floor was completely empty, and my nerves were suddenly on fire. Faces surrounded us, watching us dance, and my body locked up with fright.

"Ellie," he whispered, and I trembled in his arms.

I looked up into his face and I was brought back to him fully, his voice always capturing me without fail. He spun me around again, and I was lost in the music once more. When the song ended, the hall was silent for the longest moment of my life, and his lips found mine. He kissed me sweetly, in front of everyone, one hand on my waist, the other tight around my own. A storm of emotion—joy, sadness, exhaustion—twisted and rushed through me, so much that I couldn't breathe or stand without threatening to fall, and a tear spilled down my cheek as he kissed me. When he pulled away, his eyes were blazing green, practically glowing in the dark ballroom.

"Are you happy?" he asked, his voice gentle and eager.

I nodded and smiled, my entire body rushing with heat and wings. "Yes. I've never been happier in my life." I was laughing and crying then, even as the song changed back to the modern, upbeat music the DJ had been playing all night and everyone else spilled back onto the dance floor with us. As I let myself drown out the voices and faces and music consuming the hall, I never wanted the moment to end. I believed, in that moment, that everything we'd endured for hundreds of years together, that it was all building up to this moment, always predestined, always meant to be. We were kissing again, arms wrapped around each other, pulling away and smiling, his fingers in my hair, my hands on his shoulders, kissing and laughing. I held him tight, memorizing the moment, the feel of him, the curve of his smile, the sound of his voice, and nothing else existed in the entire world but him and me.

Back at Kate's for the after party, I was rejuvenated. We were all much more relaxed, and Will took off his tie and unbuttoned his collar, complaining that it'd been strangling him all night. While the boys untucked their dress shirts, we girls all stayed in our gowns, getting as much use out of them as possible, but by this time we'd all taken off our heels, to give our feet a break.

As the night wore on and I'd had enough of dancing and beer pong, I found Will and eased up to him. I pressed my hands into his chest and slid them south. A playful grin toyed with the corners of his mouth as I bit my lower lip and slipped the tips of my fingers into his waistband. I tugged him closer to me. "I need some air," I said with an edge to my voice. "Do you need some air?"

He nodded. "Yeah, I need some air."

I walked backward, dragging him along by his pants. "Let's go get some air."

Outside, the air was cool but tolerable, and just enough to wake us both up. It was quiet besides our soft laughter, and when we came to a stop, he wrapped a hand around my cheek, smoothing his thumb across my skin.

"Did you have a good time?" he asked.

"Tonight was amazing," I replied with a smile. "Thank you, Will. For everything. You are wonderful."

"I just want you to be happy and safe."

"With you, I am."

He smiled. "Good." He kissed me and I threw my arms around his neck.

"I think," I said as I pulled back to look into his face, "that we should go back to your house soon."

His smile widened. "Yeah?"

I nodded, but the happiness in his expression faded to a frown. He pulled back and his shoulders became rigid. I stared at him and his jaw tightened.

"What's wrong?" I asked, running my fingers up and down his neck soothingly.

He let out an annoyed grunt and squeezed me a little tighter. "Cadan. I'm going to kick his ass. *Again*."

I laughed. "Why?"

"He tried to kiss you."

I rolled my eyes. I knew him well enough to know it was all just hot air. "So? I didn't let him."

"Doesn't matter." His expression and hold on me softened. He kissed my hair and said against it, "You're still mine."

Being sweet wasn't going to make me forget his threat. "I'm so tired of this macho male ridiculousness. If you hit him, I hope he hits you back."

"Me too. Then I'll hit him even harder."

I glared up at him and he grinned at me. "You're ridiculous."

"Well, you're mine," he repeated, softer now, dipping his face to mine. "And kissing you is my job."

"Is it now?"

"Mmm-hmm," he murmured, and kissed me, luxuriously slow.

"So sweet" came a deep, growling voice from the trees.

Will and I sprang apart, startled, and shock waves of terror ripped through my body. Demonic power slithered through the grass toward our feet like a mob of snakes.

It was Merodach. His horned, winged form was cast blue in the moonlight, his dark skin gleaming and sporting the angelfire scar I gave him. Behind him was the spike-headed Rikken, his mouth dribbling thick saliva down his chin.

Will threw a protective arm over me and stepped forward. How had they found me? I didn't want to fight. I wanted the demonic reapers to go away. This night had been too perfect, too incredible—too good to be true. This couldn't be happening. I didn't want to fight tonight. I just wanted to be with Will . . . for one night of peace and happiness. . . . That was all I wanted, and I couldn't have anything I wanted. Hell had to ruin everything.

"The war is nigh, Preliator, and the storm is coming," Merodach boomed, his power pressing on my skin like cold, heavy snow.

"Did you come all the way out here just to tell us the

forecast?" Will snarled, charging right into battle mode, his sweetness and tenderness only a faint memory now. An instant was all it took for him to become prepared to kill.

Merodach snapped his eyes to Will. "I have come to finish what I started. Sammael and Lilith have no use for you, Guardian. They require the vessel of Gabriel only."

"Your boss is dead," I shouted at him. "Bastian is gone, so why are you still trying to capture me?"

"Bastian was naught but a foolish pawn," Merodach said defiantly. "He was never in control. *I* am in control, and I want *you* to suffer. Rikken, make the Guardian bleed."

It all happened so fast, I hadn't even had time to react. Rikken vanished and reappeared directly in front of Will. Will threw a punch, and Rikken ducked and grabbed his left arm. His grasp was firm, and then he sank his teeth into Will's forearm. Will shouted out in pain and protest before ripping his arm back. Rikken grinned, baring teeth as Will's blood dribbled past his lips, mixing with the viscous drool that always seemed to be pouring from his mouth. Will stared in astonishment at the bite in his arm, at the torn tissue and blood seeping from the wound. It didn't look like something he would bleed to death from, but he looked more pissed off and surprised than in pain. He growled a curse and shot forward. His punch slammed into Rikken's face—*through* it—and the demonic reaper's head exploded as if Will's fist were dynamite. Rikken's skull erupted into chunks of rock and his back hit the ground, his stone body shattering on impact. Rikken was gone in a heartbeat.

Will came to a stop and staggered, staring at the ground. I watched him, confused, as he wobbled like he'd just spun in circles and was dizzy. I moved toward him, staring at him. Before I could ask if he was okay, he lifted his head heavily, his lips parted, brow furrowed, and his eyes met mine. The green was dulling quickly, and my heart slammed in my chest. Then Will collapsed.

My mouth opened to scream and my lungs burned as if fire flashed through them, but I heard nothing. My arms flailed in front of him, grabbing hold of him as he hit the ground, and I fell with him. He lay there, his body shuddering and his eyes rolling into the back of his head. My hands touched his cheeks and neck and forehead as I stared frantically into his face. Merodach stood behind me, but I'd forgotten him.

Sound surged through my ears, and I was drowning in my own keening wail as tears rolled down my face and into the corners of my mouth. The brutal taste of salt on my lips shook me awake and back to reality. The blood from Rikken's bite seeping out of Will's arm ran down the front of my dress, staining the plum chiffon black-red.

"Will," I sobbed, my hands shaking. *"Will!"*

His head moved side to side, his mouth opening and shutting, and sweat beaded around his brow. He was in pain. His hands clenched and unclenched at his sides and I picked up the hand of his uninjured arm, locking my fingers through his as he squeezed. He opened his eyes briefly to look up into my face, and my lips went numb when I saw his irises had dulled to a pathetic gray.

"What did that thing do?" I screamed at Merodach. "What did you do to him?"

Behind me, Merodach laughed, his heavy, gravelly voice so loud and deep that it weighed me down and disoriented me. "You should have heeded Kelaeno's warning. She may be dead, but soon your Guardian will join her."

"No!" I screamed it over and over.

"I'll come back for you, Gabriel," Merodach added. "Once your heart is dead from the loss of your Guardian, I'll be back for your soul."

Will groaned, and his grip on my hand slackened and went limp. I touched his cheeks and neck and chest, my gaze lingering fearfully on the vicious wound in his arm. On the thick clear liquid from Rikken's bite mixing with Will's blood.

"I don't know what to do!" I cried. "Please tell me, Will. I don't know how to help you!" I leaned over him and kissed his cheeks and forehead, holding his body close to mine as the ache in my heart crippled me.

He was slipping away, weakening by the moment. This couldn't be happening. I couldn't lose him after everything, after all of this. Merodach stepped away and spread his dark wings wide before vanishing into the Grim, leaving me alone on the cold ground with Will dying in my arms.

I smoothed his hair away from his clammy forehead with my palm, and then he began convulsing. I screamed, but my wails were drowned by the thumping music pouring out of Kate's house. Liquid oozed from the bite in Will's arm, and it grew darker by the moment until it was black mixing with the red of Will's blood. The wound wasn't healing.

"Ellie?" came a frightened voice behind me.

I snapped my head around to see Marcus jogging toward me, his gleaming sapphire eyes locked on Will's shuddering form. My own body was shaking uncontrollably as Marcus knelt on the other side of Will, one hand on his chest and the other on his face.

"What's wrong?" Marcus asked, the fear clear on his face. Of course a reaper would be the only one to hear my screams. "What happened?"

"Rikken bit him!" I wailed. "And he collapsed! I don't know what's wrong! I don't know how to help him!"

If even a single word of what I'd just said was comprehensible, it would've been a miracle. Marcus stared at Will, carefully inspecting the wound in his arm.

"Hold his head still," he directed. When I just sat there, sobbing, he repeated the order more firmly. "Ellie! Hold his head still. He's seizing. If you want him to live, then you've got to pull yourself together. I'll be right back. Can you handle this?"

No. I nodded anyway, choking on a sob. Marcus vanished and I was alone again, breaking apart bit by bit. I couldn't lose Will. I couldn't. For the past few months, I'd tried to force myself into believing that I didn't need him, but it was all a lie. I needed his comfort, but I could only sit there on the ground in my prom dress as the air grew steadily colder and watch him die.

Marcus came back and put his hand on my arm. "Come on. Let's get him into the car." He ripped off the sleeve of his tuxedo and wrapped it around Will's arm like a tourniquet. The wound wouldn't heal. Will's wounds—even the ones a hundred times more severe than this—always healed. He was always fine. He always got better.

Marcus lifted Will's limp form and threw him over his shoulder. We rounded the front of the house and wove our way through a crowd of kids holding plastic cups. Kate's red BMW sat in the driveway, and I opened the back door and Marcus laid Will across the seat. I climbed into the back with him as Marcus jumped into the driver's seat. Will was semiconscious. His head rolled left and right as he groaned in agony. I held his face in my hands and murmured to him. I kissed his cheek, but he didn't respond to me.

"Will," I said firmly, turning his face to mine. "Will!"

He tried to tear his head from my hands as he ground his teeth together.

"Will!" I cried again, but he was unresponsive. "Will, damn it. You've been telling me all this time to keep fighting. Don't you give up on me!"

"We're going back to the house," Marcus said from the

front seat. "Rikken bit him, right?"

"Yes." I met his eyes in the rearview mirror.

"It must be poison of some kind. Venom."

A rush of coldness swept through me, and the blood drained from my face. *"Your strength in heart and hand will fall to a reaper's bane,"* Kelaeno had said. The prophecy. It was all coming true.

He dug his phone out of his pocket and dialed. "Ava. Find Sabina and get to the house as quickly as you can. Will is wounded. I'll explain when you get there. Yes, she's with me. Just get to the house." He hung up.

I swallowed hard. "Will Ava know how to help him?"

"I don't know."

"Will Sabina?"

"I don't know."

Marcus drove fast—inhumanly fast. When we blurred into the driveway of Nathaniel's house, Marcus wasted no time, jumping out of the car to help me get Will out of the backseat. He moaned, and his tuxedo was damp with sweat. Ava and Sabina were waiting on the front porch, their expressions hardened and focused instead of mirroring the fear and grief on my own. I watched them carry Will into the kitchen and lay him on the dining table. I was trembling head to toe.

"What happened?" Ava asked, examining Will's bite wound.

"Merodach," I squeaked. "And Rikken. They ambushed

us. Rikken bit him."

"Rikken?" Sabina repeated. "That was the name of the reaper?"

I nodded, my eyes on Will's shuddering form.

"I know him," she said. "No one has survived a bite from Rikken."

A wail escaped from me and Marcus stomped in front of me, snarling at Sabina. "That is not helping. What's the matter with you?"

Her mouth opened and her eyes widened as if she didn't know what she'd just said. "I—I'm sorry. Rikken's venom takes about a week to kill. We have that long to save the Guardian."

A week. A week left for Will to live. A week of horrific torture and pain. I was starting to hyperventilate.

"I'll be right back," Marcus said, touching my cheek to reassure me. "I have to return Kate's car to her and bring my own back before she gets suspicious and wonders where you and Will are. The less she knows, the better."

I nodded and chewed on my bottom lip as it trembled against another sob building in my throat. Marcus disappeared, and a quiver of despair shot through me. My face was sticky with tears and smeared makeup, but I didn't care that I looked like a train wreck. Sabina and Ava turned back to the table and began removing Will's jacket. He shuddered with every breath, and his eyes were closed tightly with pain. I didn't know if he was conscious.

Ava held out her hand and summoned her sword. She

leaned over Will and touched the blade to his chest.

I was there in a flash, my sword in my hand, the tip pressed into Ava's jugular. She froze in place and looked at me out the corner of her eye. "What are you doing?" I snarled hoarsely through my tears.

"I need to see how badly it has spread," she responded in a calm voice.

For a moment, I felt absurd pointing a sword at Ava's throat while wearing my prom dress. It was ripped and bloodied—completely destroyed. I looked from Ava to Will and back again.

"Ellie?"

I startled, letting my weapon disappear and nodding numbly. She eyed me for a few more seconds before drawing her blade across Will's sleeve, carefully cutting it open to reveal the terrible wound on his arm. She removed the cloth of his shirt until he was naked from the waist up. When I saw his skin, my heart lodged in my throat. Black spiderweblike lines extended up his wounded arm and across his chest, pooling thickly over his heart. The black lines traced every vein and artery beneath his skin, and a powerful memory struck me hard: The day of my seventeenth birthday, in the girls' room, the same spidery lines had covered my face the way they covered Will's body. Had I foreseen the same event that Kelaeno had prophesied? Had the darkness I originally saw in myself really been a warning?

Your strength in heart and hand will fall. . . .

Ava was saying something to Sabina and possibly to me, but I couldn't hear a word. I was shaking, staring at Will as his body trembled and his head thrashed from side to side in agony.

"Ellie. Ellie!"

I was brought back to my senses at Ava's sharp voice barking my name.

"Sabina, get her out of here," Ava growled. "She can't handle this."

"No!" I flailed against Sabina as she turned me around. "Let go of me!" I shoved Sabina in the chest and she lost her balance. Stepping back, I slammed into Marcus's body as he appeared in the doorway. His hands grabbed a firm hold of my shoulders.

"What's going on?" he asked, his voice and expression filled with concern.

I shoved him off me. "Nothing! I'll just go."

Marcus blinked at me and exchanged glances with Ava. "Why? We need you here."

"No, you don't," I snarled back. "I'm going to do something about this. Give me your keys."

"To my car?"

"Yes!" I held out my hand. "Give them to me before I take them from you!"

He dropped the keys into my palm. "I don't know where you're going, but please, for the love of God, don't scratch my car."

I made an ugly noise and stomped past him. I yanked open the door of Marcus's Maserati and threw myself into the seat. I wasn't even sure I remembered how to drive a stick like this. My dad had taught me how, but that was so long ago. My knees curled up to my chest, and I buried my face in my hands. I let myself cry for just a minute, just long enough to clear my thoughts for an instant, just long enough to remember something that Will had said to me months ago, something I already knew.

The Maserati's tires squealed as I peeled out of the driveway. The car had a voice-recognition satellite phone built into it. I instructed the car to dial a number.

After one ring at the other end of the line, a slightly surprised voice answered, "This had better be a booty call."

"Cadan." I was exhausted and irritated, my voice barely able to work. "Where are you?"

"So it *is* a booty call."

"Cadan!" I shouted, half sobbing. I took a deep breath to calm myself. "This is serious. Where are you?"

A hesitation. "My apartment. In Troy."

"What's the address?"

I barged through the door of his apartment and moved through the entry into the living area. He stood in the center of the room, one hand holding a glass of deep gold liquid, the other in his pocket. His fiery opal eyes opened wide as he registered my terrible appearance, my ripped and bloodied dress, my makeup smeared with tears down my cheeks.

A look of horror and sadness overcame him. "Ellie?"

I was sick of everyone saying my name but Will. His voice was the only one I wanted to hear, calm and serene as he always was, not moaning in pain trapped within some internal Hell.

"Are you okay?" His voice was gentle, as if he were speaking to a frightened, cornered animal. He set down his glass. "What can I do?"

I lifted my arm and willed a single Khopesh sword into my hand. Angelfire blazed, lighting up his surprised face, and my power spiraled around me, lifting my tangled hair and the shredded folds of my dress.

He stared at me, fearing what might come from my threat. "You don't ever need to raise your sword to me."

"Will is dying," I said, my voice withering. "Did you speak the truth when you said you know a Grigori?"

He hesitated before he nodded. "Yes."

I swallowed hard, shaking. "You have to take me to the Grigori. I don't care what it takes. I'll do anything. You have to help me save him."